THE BLACK TSAR

JACK BONAFIDE BOOK ONE

JORDAN VEZINA

MOUNTAIN WOLF PRESS

Texarkana, Texas
June 2, 1965

"Sir, where is Vietnam?"

Corbett Bonafide glanced sideways at his son sitting beside him in the Ford truck and then turned his eyes back to the road.

"Why are you asking?" The father asked the son.

Jack Bonafide turned his eyes back to his well-worn copy of B.H. Liddel Hart's The Real War. For any other fifteen-year-old the World War One chronicle may have seemed like odd reading material, but for Jack Bonafide it fit like a glove.

"I heard you were going there."

"Where did you hear that?" Corbett asked, looking back to his son with a scowl on his face.

"Sorry, sir. Heard it through the wall the other night. I wasn't eavesdropping, I promise!"

"Knew I should have made those walls thicker," Corbett said, thinking back to the summer he had spent building the little two-bedroom house with his brother John after the two came back from War Two. "Ain't your fault I suppose. And I know I talk a might loud. So, now you want to know where I'm going? Keeping tabs on me are you?"

"No, sir. Just curious is all."

"It's next to Japan," Corbett said in response to Jack's first question.

The truth was that Corbett was only vaguely aware of where Vietnam was. All he really knew was that he had received a call from headquarters Marine Corps asking if he would be amenable to an assignment attaching him to a MAAG (military assistance advisory group) heading overseas to Vietnam. That was enough for Corbett, so he started packing his seabag and put in for leave with Ranger division.

"Why are you going there?" Jack asked.

Corbett thought on this for a moment.

"Jack, sometimes there are folks that need killing, so this country needs its killers to clock back in and do what needs doin'." Corbett looked at his son again. "That's why I'm going to Vietnam. Don't trouble yourself on it too much, though. I'll come back. I always do."

Jack seemed to accept this answer and surveyed the town of Texarkana as they passed through it on their way home.

"Will I go to Vietnam?" Jack asked.

"Way things are going? I reckon you will."

Corbett slowed the truck down as something caught his eye, some activity between two of the storefronts. He brought the Ford to a full stop and peered down the alleyway.

"What is it?" Jack asked.

"Nothing much," Corbett said as he opened his door and stepped out onto the street. "Just some folks who are a little behind the times."

Jack got out and walked behind his father.

"Here," Corbett said, drawing his Colt Peacemaker and handing it to his son. "Hold on to that."

Jack took the Colt and held it in his right hand, his book grasped in the other. His father had done this before, and it usually meant he was fixing to give a man a beating.

Corbett took a step into the alley and stopped a dozen feet from the two men. One was holding a black man up against a wall by the throat, and the other stood with his fists bared. With their tunnel vision in full effect, neither man had yet seen Corbett Bonafide. This was no easy task.

Corbett stood six foot four and was two hundred and twenty pounds of carved stone. His were eyes that had seen war on two different occasions. In the Pacific during War Two and once more in Korea at the Chosin Reservoir. He'd been a Texas Ranger since the Division would have him, and now those same eyes, perpetually half closed by the Texas sun, were locked on these two men. At the end of the alleyway was a white woman, curled into a ball and sobbing, rocking herself back and forth in the half-light.

"Pardon the interruption," Corbett called out. "But once you're done with your transaction, I'll need you both to walk yourselves down to the Ranger station."

Both men stopped as if frozen in time. They knew who this man was and they knew his history. Like most folks in Texarkana who occasionally found themselves on the wrong side of the law, they also knew what it meant to see the young boy standing behind his Ranger father holding the Colt Peacemaker. Corbett Bonafide was displeased.

The man who had been baring his fists lowered them and turned to Corbett, but the other man did not release his quarry.

"See here, Corbett. You know what this is, right?" He asked, his voice wavering. "You see her, right? They was walking together. Holding hands!"

"I see it," Corbett nodded. "But you're about a year late. In case you hadn't heard, the world has changed.

No more Jim Crow. You don't have to like it, but you damn well better fall in line."

"Time was, your brother would have been in here lending a hand, not siding with the likes of them!" The man snapped.

"And look where that got him," Corbett spat. "Reaping the fucking whirlwind."

Neither man moved.

Corbett took a step forward.

"Goddammit boys, I was just on my way home and was fixing to crack open a Lonestar. You should know that when my mouth is dry, I'm easily aggravated. It's gettin' drier by the minute on account of all this talkin' you're making me do, so don't make me tell you again."

The second man released his victim and stepped back.

"Good," Corbett said, and held out his hand. Jack placed the Colt in it and Corbett slid it back into the holster on his hip. "Now, walk down to the Company B Ranger Station and have yourselves booked in for aggravated assault. That's the best I can do."

"Yes, sir," the men said in unison.

"And I tell you what, if you don't show up there in a timely fashion, I'll track you down and show you what aggravated assault feels like. Just in case you're pondering."

"Yes, sir," the men repeated as they filed out of the alleyway.

Neither man had wanted to give in, but also knew when they were outmatched.

The victim of the assault stepped forward, cleared his throat and touched Corbett Bonafide on the arm.

"Thank you so much, friend. I thought I was—"

"Take your fucking hand off me, boy," Corbett snarled. "I ain't your friend."

The man stepped back, shock registering on his face, but the message was received. Times had changed, but only by degrees.

Corbett slid back into the Ford beside his son and slammed the door shut with a loud metallic report. He tapped the weapon on his hip and started the engine.

"They were breaking the law?" Jack asked.

"That they were."

"It wasn't always that way, right?" Jack asked.

"No, it wasn't."

"You don't like them much, do you?" Jack asked. "The colored folk, I mean."

"Can't say as I like them or don't," Corbett replied. "Just always been that way."

"Should I like them?" Jack asked. "Or not?"

"I can't speak on what you should or shouldn't do, Jack. You gotta find your own way." Corbett seemed to think on this for a moment. "I'll say that a man always lets you know who he is by the end of the first handshake. Is it firm, or weak? Dry or moist? Does he look you in the eye or look at the ground? Maybe that's a start. From that point on you think for yourself and do what's right."

"Is that why you stopped those men? Because it was the right thing to do?"

Corbett nodded.

"Doing the right thing ain't easy Jack, but that's what separates the men from the animals. We do the right thing even when it ain't in our nature."

CHAPTER 1

Desert One
Tabas, Iran
April 24, 1980

F irst Sergeant Jack Bonafide stood on the lone road that lead to the operational site designated Desert One and watched the plume of fire spitting into the night sky on the other side of his position. It was at least several hundred feet high, punching a hole through the darkness.

They had watched Lieutenant Winsell jump onto one of the Yamaha motorbikes with a Ranger and a LAW rocket and take off down the road, and this was clearly the result of whatever they had done.

"Shit. No way is that good," Big Eddie said as he

adjusted his large pack full of explosives and turned back to the road leading in.

"I thought you loved explosions?" Jack asked the big man.

"No, it's not that," Eddie said with a wry smile. "It's just that I left my marshmallows back at Bragg. Now I feel like a first class asshole."

Jack laughed a little. Considering the turn things had taken in the past hour, it was good they were still keeping their sense of humor.

The American Embassy in Tehran, Iran had been taken hostage by a group of Iranian college students five months earlier. These weren't just simple college kids who'd had one too many, they were members of the Muslim Student Followers of the Imam's Line and supporters of the Iranian Revolution. None of that was good for the fifty-two Americans held there.

Special Forces Operational Detachment Delta was tasked with getting the hostages back. A message needed to be sent to the world, and they were going to be the ones to do it. It was an impossible task, but that was the whole point of Delta. That was how Colonel Charlie Beckwith had sold the unit to the Department of Defense, and now those chips were being cashed in.

There were problems during the planning and training, and that was normal. Jack would have been far more concerned if training had gone too smoothly. You wanted bumps in the road so you could practice working out those problems in real time.

This was different. From the time they hit the staging area in Masirah, Oman things began heading south. Even basics such as clean living spaces and working toilets couldn't seem to be handled.

Then they hit Desert One. This would be where they met the RH-53 helicopters that would then ferry them to Desert Two, just fifty-two miles away from Tehran. The CIA agents were already in place in the city and would meet Delta at Desert Two with trucks to ferry them to the city and finally the embassy. They would then assault the compound and deliver the hostages to a nearby soccer stadium where the helicopters would pick them up.

Except it was looking like they wouldn't even make it to Desert Two, much less to Tehran. Not long after they hit the ground at D1 a bus load of Iranians had driven right into their staging area. A bus load of them! They had handled it (such an incident had been planned for) but the support staff were now babysitting a busload of Iranians.

Then, whatever Lieutenant Wade Winsell and his Ranger buddy had just gotten into had sent a flare into the night announcing their location for all to see. True, they were far enough out in the desert it was unlikely to be a problem, but still not ideal.

Now, First Sergeant Jack Bonafide and Master

Sergeant Eddie Wilson were standing watch at the other end of the only road that lead into the staging area they called D1.

Eddie saw headlights in the distance. They were faint, but they were there. He put his binoculars to his eyes and let out a sigh.

"Well, fuck me runnin' and call me Sally."

"What is it?" Jack asked.

"Fucking Iranian Army. Coming in fast. They must have seen Wade's shit show over there."

"How many?" Jack asked.

"Just the one truck."

Jack reached into his patrol pack and retrieved the claymore landmine he had stashed away.

"I'm wearing a backpack with enough explosives in it to launch this place to the fucking moon," Eddie said. "Why are you carrying around a claymore?"

"In case something exactly like this happened," Jack said, staging the mine on the side of the road. "Do you have a claymore?"

"No," Eddie grudgingly replied. He had everything else, but not a claymore.

Jack set the device up in a way that it would blow the incoming vehicle off the side of the road without killing everyone riding in it. While Jack had no compunctions about smoking Iranian military, he did not know for certain who would be in the oncoming vehicle.

Jack signaled for Eddie to join him off the side of the road and took a half kneeling position with the detonator in hand. Two minutes later the vehicle passed them, and Jack hit the trigger. His timing was perfect. A flash of light and then he watched the vehicle go ass over teakettle. He had triggered it to hit the rear of the vehicle, and as a result the small truck was mostly intact.

"Get out! Get out!" Jack shouted in Farsi as he and Eddie moved in on the vehicle with their carbines at the ready. "Surrender!"

Two flashes came from the jeep, and Jack could hear a loud 'snap' as a round passed his head. By pure reflex he and Eddie fired into the cabin until they were satisfied that no one could have survived what they had just done. Jack had been willing to take these men alive if possible, but now all bets were off.

Jack held up an open palm to stop Eddie from following him, and advanced on the vehicle, letting his carbine hang by its sling while he drew his Colt 1911. He could see a hand dangling out of the passenger side window of the truck, but there was no movement. The flames in the sky were still bright enough that he could see inside.

"Shit," Jack said.

"What is it?" Eddie asked.

Jack looked into the cabin and saw two young men,

neither of them over eighteen. One was still gripping the pistol he had shot at Jack with.

"Kids," Jack said. "They're fucking kids."

"Soldiers," Eddie corrected him. "Don't matter what their birth certificate says. They're soldiers, Jack. Remember that. We both saw kids a hell of a lot younger than that running around with AK's in the A Shau Valley."

Jack nodded. He knew Eddie was right, but he also knew he didn't have to like it.

Jack looked down at his watch, then back to the main staging area and to Eddie. They both heard it. It was the sound of the helicopters arriving.

"They're late," Jack said. "Really late."

For the first time, Jack saw Eddie looking truly concerned. He knew that the Master Sergeant wasn't worried about executing the mission. The man would be happy to stroll into Tehran and hop over the embassy wall any day of the week. No, the only thing that would have worried Eddie like this was the mission being aborted.

The radios had also stopped working. At least, Jack's had. He played with the frequency again but wasn't getting anything.

"Fuck this. We're going back in," Jack said, turning back to the staging area and jogging down the road.

In the dim light Jack could see that Colonel Beckwith was on the horn with someone, most likely higher command. Whatever he was talking about, the Colonel was obviously unhappy with the conversation. Finally, the Colonel finished with some shouting and threw the handset into the dirt.

Jack stopped. He had first met Colonel Charlie Beckwith in Vietnam, when the man was just a major trying to get something going to put a dent in the Viet Cong. Jack was a wet behind the ears Ranger who had literally run away from his unit to join what was at the time called "Project Delta". Jack had seen one of the flyers that young Major Beckwith had posted around the different camps.

Get a medal, a body bag or both. Join Project Delta.

Those words triggered something in Jack, and he had been with the Colonel ever since. Something in Jack's gut told him that this would be the end of that journey. This mission ending like this, might also be the end of Delta.

Colonel Beckwith met Jack's eyes and just shook his head.

"It's over?" Jack asked.

"Sorry, Jack. We've hit a tipping point. The helicopters are too late and we're too far off schedule. You know I hate like hell to do this, but we have to pull out and head back to Misery," The Colonel replied, using the nickname they had given the base at Masirah.

Jack thought about that for a moment and then took a chance.

"Send me."

"What?" the Colonel asked, clearly confused.

"Me and three other guys. This is what we trained for in OTC, to insert ourselves into a foreign population and accomplish the mission. It's a hell of a lot more what Delta's about than even the original plan."

"We can't do it Jack."

"The CIA are already in the hide site!" Jack said. "All the other pieces are still in place. We can't get everyone out, but we can sure as shit get the ambassador and a few key personnel!"

"Jack, look, it's not happening."

"I'll go," Eddie said.

"No!" Beckwith snapped.

"I can do it!" Jack said, raising his voice. "I'll take full responsibility!"

"First Sergeant Bonafide, stand down!" Colonel Beckwith shouted.

Jack gritted his teeth.

"Count to five, Jack," Colonel Beckwith said, and within a five count he saw his lead First Sergeant's jaw relax.

"Yes, sir," Jack said.

"It's not up to us anymore. They're already refueling to head back."

Jack could see that Eddie was looking with wide

eyes at something behind where Colonel Beckwith was standing.

"Why the hell is he pulling forward?" Eddie asked in dismay.

Jack turned to see one of the RH-53 helicopters pulling forward into the rear stabilizer of the big EC-130 plane. Jack realized what was happening.

The rotors had created a mini sandstorm, and the air force combat controller directing the hovering helicopter from the ground had walked backward to get clear of the sand blowing in his face. The disoriented pilot saw this and thought his aircraft was drifting backward when he was actually sitting still. He corrected by applying forward stick to hold position, which moved him forward, and he couldn't see the big transport plane right in front of him through the sand.

By the time the pilot realized what was happening it was too late.

Jack felt the heat on his face and then the shock wave as the helicopter collided with the plane.

Headquarters, Special Forces Operational Detachment Delta
Fort Bragg, North Carolina
December 18, 1980

Jack Bonafide pulled his old Ford truck up to the perimeter gate and rolled to a stop at the specific instruction of the gate sentry. These weren't your average rent-a-cops or even military police. Every man who worked site security for Special Forces Operational Detachment Delta was a former special forces Sergeant Major. When Charlie Beckwith had put out the call that he was looking for men like this to pull security for what would become the military's premiere counter-terror unit, he had no shortage of applicants.

Colonel Charlie Beckwith was a respected war fighter and innovator, who had seen the threat coming long before most. Ever since Colonel Beckwith's time with the British SAS he had understood that the United States not having a similar unit exposed a serious deficiency in their readiness.

Establishing Delta as a viable unit within the often politically charged atmosphere of the United States Army had not been without its challenges, just as Colonel Beckwith was not without his detractors. Despite this (after many, many delays) the whole process had been amazingly smooth, particularly considering that most observing from the outside never thought it would get off the ground at all.

Then Iran happened. It hadn't been the end of Delta, but it had been damn close

The whole operation ended with several dead and a helicopter and transport plane both burning in the desert. Despite this catastrophe, Colonel Beckwith did not allow himself to rest, and soon secured First Sergeant Jack Bonafide a position as an observer with a special operations unit operating out of Israel. Jack had heard about this unit and that they had experienced their own disaster during a failed rescue mission into Beirut, Lebanon several months earlier.

Even though this Israeli unit initially failed, they pulled themselves out of it and eventually took down the responsible parties, one of whom was their own operative. It sounded like something out of a movie, too impossible to believe, but once Jack hit Israel, he had seen that it was all too real. Not only that, but he soon found himself conscripted to lead an assault team in this same unit.

That was when he learned about the Black Tsar, and that it was somewhere in the continental United States.

Jack parked his truck in the assigned space and stepped out onto the gravel pathway leading to the old brig that now served as Delta headquarters. The roses always got to him, triggered something in his sinuses. Seeing as he was a senior non-commissioned officer in the unit, he had thought a few times about asking Colonel Beckwith if they could replace all the damn rose bushes with something else, but he never did. For whatever reason, the Delta Commander had planted rose bushes all around the compound.

Inside of the HQ things were quiet and stopping into S3 (Operations) Jack saw that most of the Unit was deployed or out at the long gun range. Maybe that was better. He wouldn't have to answer a bunch of questions or deal with a lot of long and drawn out goodbyes.

Goodbye. That was a strange idea. Jack had been in the Army since he was seventeen, and with Delta from the beginning, and now he would no longer be either of those things. As far as anyone knew he was about to become a civilian again.

That was not the truth. Jack Bonafide was about to become one of the future Assistant Director of the CIA Mike Tresham's Ghost Operatives. The way Jack understood it, these were non-official cover operatives on steroids. Figuratively, if not literally. Mike Tresham had approached Jack about this after the operation in Israel was over, and normally Jack would have told the CIA case officer (politely) to go pound sand. That he would not only leave Delta just when it was up and running but also leave the Army was (to put it flatly) a non-starter.

Then Jack found out about the Black Tsar. It was like something out of a bad spy movie. In nineteen sixty-one the Soviets had built and tested the most powerful bomb in the world's history. It was capable of a nearly sixty megaton yield. Hiroshima was only fifteen megatons. The power of this new bomb alarmed even the Soviets enough that they scrapped plans to produce more and retired what they called the Tsar Bomba project.

What the higher-ups in the Soviet Politburo did not know was that the scientists working on the Tsar Bomba project had produced two devices. They were known respectively as the White Tsar and the Black Tsar. The White Tsar was the sixty-megaton yield device tested over the Mityushikha Bay nuclear testing range. During development the device was rated with a potential one hundred megaton yield, due to the application of a uranium-238 fusion tamper instead of the simple lead tamper that they eventually settled on. The scientists decided that a one hundred megaton blast would produce too much fallout, and the plane dropping the device would not escape the blast.

The White Tsar detonated at eleven thirty-two hours Moscow time on October 30th, 1961. While this great victory over the west was being celebrated, the Black Tsar sat in a darkened warehouse, complete with its uranium-238 fusion damper, enabling it to create a one hundred megaton blast.

On October 31st, 1961 The Black Tsar vanished.

"You should be worried about the Tsar in your own country."

Soviet Agent Anna Willink had spoken those words to Jack just before she bit down on her cyanide capsule in the Tel Aviv airport. Had it not been for that, yes, Jack Bonafide would have politely told the future Assistant Director of the CIA Mike Tresham to go pound sand.

Instead, Jack accepted Mike's offer, and they developed a plan for getting him out of Delta without arousing any suspicions. It had not been hard. Jack just checked in with the unit physician and told him about what had been going on for quite a while at that point.

The tremoring hands, the ringing in his ears and the slurred speech would be enough to get him bounced out of the unit and the Army faster than you can say 'boo'. At first Mike Tresham was concerned about these symptoms, but Jack assured him it was only ever a problem when he was off duty, and it was unlikely there would be much of that in the days ahead.

Standing in the headquarters building, Jack looked down at his hands and sure enough, they were steady as a rock. It seemed that all he had to do was step into the building or pick up a gun and the tremors stopped. Jack Bonafide wasn't sure if that was a good thing or a bad thing. He had a couple other tricks that also worked for calming the symptoms, if needed.

Jack rapped three times on his commanding officer's open door. Inside he could see Charlie Beckwith sitting at his desk engaging in his least favorite pastime, paperwork.

"First Sergeant Bonafide, reporting."

Colonel Beckwith looked up and smiled, but Jack could see that it was strained.

"Jack, have a seat."

Jack Bonafide complied with what was essentially an order. Delta didn't engage in the niceties and traditions beloved by the rest of the Army, and though they were casual enough around HQ there was something different in Charlie's voice.

"I heard from Doc. You're... well it looks like you will be leaving us. Leaving the Army."

Jack paused for a moment, framing what he was about to say. He could see by the look in his CO's eyes that the Colonel was thinking about what his own reaction would be if someone told him he could no longer be in the military. Jack knew that the Colonel was already thinking about taking his own retirement after what had happened in Iran, but had not pulled the trigger yet.

"I put it off as long as I could, sir. After the operation in Israel, it got a lot worse. If my... condition somehow endangered the other men in the unit, I could never live with myself."

"That was a hell of a job you did over there, Jack. A hell of a job. I don't know that anyone else could have pulled it off. We're already using your after-action reports to update the training manuals and we're looking into this Fluid Dynamics company that was supplying the gear." Charlie sat back in his seat and looked the young man over. There had always been a good-natured rivalry between the two, with Jack being a born and bred Texan and Charlie Beckwith being a dyed in the wool Georgia boy. "You know, just because you're leaving the Unit doesn't mean you have to leave the Army. We can find something for you so you can stay on. At least until it's time to retire."

"I'm a gunfighter, sir. If staying on means sitting in a warehouse somewhere checking in boots, I wouldn't want it."

"So, what will you do?"

Jack shrugged.

"Go back to Texarkana. See if I can get on with the Rangers."

"Really?" Charlie asked, familiar with the Bonafide family history. "I thought that was off the table?"

"I figure time has passed since my Uncle did what he did, and I'd like to think we can put that behind us. I'm still in touch with Merle Harwith, the former Company B commander. He seems to think I can get in."

"And the tremors?"

"It's never a problem when I have gun in my hand, sir."

Charlie Beckwith seemed to accept this and standing up he reached across the table and shook Jack's hand.

"I'm sorry to see you go, Jack. Have a good one."

▭

The Good Night Lodge
Fayetteville, North Carolina
December 20, 1980

▭

Jack Bonafide looked around the parking lot of the motel and then into the back of his truck where he had secured his duffel bags. There were four, collectively containing all of his belongings. Some may have found that depressing, the only evidence of his existence being small enough to fill only four duffel bags. For Jack, it meant that his life was clean and efficient, the way it should be.

The parking lot seemed quiet enough, and the bags were locked shut and chained to the eye bolts he'd secured into the bed of the truck. If that wasn't enough to dissuade any would-be thieves, the shotgun mounted in in the rear window should be. Plus, he would only be a dozen feet away in the motel room he was meeting Mike Tresham in.

It had been such a simple thing, far simpler than Jack would have thought it would be. Just like that he was walking away from the only life he had ever really known. Jack thought back to his conversation with Mike Tresham in Israel, about how Jack had not understood why it had to be him. The CIA had endless resources for recruiting operatives and must already have people in the field who knew a hell of a lot more about how to do something like this than Jack Bonafide did.

To be fair, Jack had a strong field craft for espionage work. It was part of every Delta soldier's training when they went through OTC (Operator Training Course) and Jack had found that he took to the work and maybe even had a talent for it.

Now he was standing in the parking lot of the Good Night Lodge getting ready to step into the world of the vaunted Central Intelligence Agency. He only hoped he would be up to the task.

Jack knocked on the door of room eighteen three times, and Mike Tresham opened it, standing with a donut in one hand and a remote control in the other.

"Look," Mike Tresham said, holding up the remote. "No wire. It just shoots a beam or something right to the television. Isn't technology a miracle?"

"I think those have been around for quite a while, Mister Tresham," Jack said cautiously, not sure if this was some strange test. "Like twenty years."

"Well, I've never seen one," Mike said, taking a bite out of his donut and waving Jack in.

Jack closed the door behind him and took a seat in one of the two chairs that were sitting in the middle of the room. Jack noticed there was no bed in the room, which seemed strange.

"Are you ready for this?" Mike asked.

"Yes, Sir," Jack replied.

"Don't bullshit me, Jack. I know that you think this is outside your wheelhouse."

"It's not that," Jack said. "I know I can do what you're asking."

"So, what's the problem?"

"I just find it hard to believe there's no one more qualified."

Mike Tresham looked hard at Jack for a moment.

"I have a knack for reading people, Jack. Yes, we have plenty of operatives in the field, very skilled men and women we could call upon to do this kind of work, but you've got something they don't, something that can't be trained."

"You mind if I ask what that is?" Jack replied.

"I'll let you know when I figure it out. For now, all I can tell you is that I know it when I see it." Mike seemed to think about this for a moment. "There's a quote by a Greek philosopher named Heraclitus. It goes like this: Out of every one hundred men, ten shouldn't even be there, eighty are just targets and nine are the real fighters. One man, one is a warrior, and he will bring the others back."

"I reckon you think that's me?"

"I'm not sure, Jack. I just want you to find a goddam hydrogen bomb that's loose in our country," Mike said. "And the bottom line is that we don't currently have enough actionable intelligence to officially put the CIA or the FBI to work on it. All we have are some dispatches from sources in Moscow and the rantings of a woman who seconds later took her own life. So I need an off-book spook to chase this thing down. That's you."

The working theory on how this weapon had been imported was that it was done a piece at a time, over years, possibly even a decade. Piece by piece. Once the entire device was carried over it would be re-assembled and made operational. What happened after that would be anyone's guess. Mike Tresham doubted that the plan was to detonate and cause mass casualties, but it was very plausible that the Black Tsar would become a gun to America's head if the Soviets ever needed one.

"Where should I start?" Jack asked.

Mike fished a packet out of his briefcase and handed it to Jack.

"Red River Army Depot."

Jack looked up with surprise as he opened the packet and looked inside. There were a few documents, a map of the Texarkana area and what looked like different credentials and a bundle of cash.

"Red River?" Jack asked. It couldn't be a coincidence. The Red River Army Depot was just outside Texarkana.

"Call it a happy accident," Mike said. "You get to go home for Christmas, and we get to mark this one off of our list."

"What list?"

"We've narrowed it down to a handful of entry points where this Black Tsar could have been smuggled in, at least the tamper, which is the main component we need to find. Red River is one. It makes sense. They handle a lot of transport repair including tanks and such, coming from all over the world. From there the shipments would be moved again. If this is the place, there's chatter that the Soviets may also be using it as a pipeline to smuggle something else in, but we don't know what that something is. Highly unlikely it's as big a problem as this weapon."

"I know Red River," Jack said, closing the packet up.

"Good, then this will be easier. You've got DOD credentials in there identifying you as an assistant to the Secretary of Defense."

"No shit?" Jack asked.

"No shit," Mike replied. "You have to be able to move freely, but those credentials will not stand up to close scrutiny. Someone calls around and you're fucked, so don't hang around too long."

"Pardon my asking, Sir, but why not just get the real thing?"

"What part of non-official cover do you not understand, Mister Bonafide?" Mike asked. "I apologize for my bluntness, but if you get burned it can't blow back on us."

"Understood," Jack nodded. Truthfully, he wasn't a big fan of this idea, but he understood why it had to be that way.

"They'll be expecting you Christmas Eve around midnight. All they'll know is that you're passing through from DOD and need to have a quick meeting with the base commander. He will not be happy, for obvious reasons. We also gave strict instructions that it's a fifteen-minute meet and greet, no inspections or bullshit. The place should be like a ghost town."

"So I just ask if I can have a look around?"

"Basically. They're used to it. That base has been a prize pony for a long time, they're accustomed to VIP's dropping in. They'll put you with an escort but that's about it."

"And what am I looking for?"

"Anything that isn't right. We've also got someone in there doing an independent audit of their books. Assuming that the shipments are going to Red River, she's trying to figure out where they go from there, and what exactly they are."

"She?" Jack asked.

Mike shrugged.

"Looks like the women's lib crowd won after all."

Jack laughed. The old CIA agent wasn't much for cracking jokes, but when he did, he made them count.

Jack stepped back out into the cool night and closed the door to room eighteen behind him. He stopped and watched the men that surrounded his truck. None of the three had noticed him. One was leaning in his driver's side window (which meant he must have broken it) while the other two were in the bed.

Finally, the man rummaging through the cab caught sight of him and stood up. He had a cigarette hanging from his mouth and a sick smile on his face.

"This your truck?" the man asked.

"Reckon it is," Jack replied.

"We'll be done in a minute."

Jack shook his head and walked toward the man. Jack was carrying his Colt 1911 in a skeleton holster in his low back, but knew that bringing it into play would only cause trouble. His shotgun still sat in the rack in the rear window, where it was locked up.

Jack guessed that this man was former military. He

had the look about him aside from his facial scruff and was right about Jack's same height and weight. The other two men had stopped what they were doing in the truck's bed, and watched the exchange intently. While the leader may have been ready to fight, these two didn't seem as eager.

"I think you're done now." Jack looked down at where some of his belongings had been thrown from the cab and onto the ground. He saw his copy of Wichita Lineman laying on the pavement, broken in half. His brother Mac had given him the tape before his third deployment to Vietnam, and he'd carried it with him everywhere since then. Something about it got to him in a way that few things did. "Shit. That's my favorite tape."

The man turned and spit on the broken cassette.

"That's cow fucker music."

Jack shook his head again.

"Why did you have to go and do that?"

"You need to walk away, cow fucker."

Jack smiled.

"I don't think so."

While the two men in the back of the truck may not have been as eager as their comrade to get in a fight, they both hopped out and walked up behind him just the same. They weren't nearly as big, and one looked as if he may have already been hit in the head one time too many.

It was a clumsy haymaker, the kind you could see

coming from three counties away. More than mildly pissed about the destruction of his Glen Campbell tape Jack thrust his head forward, slamming it into the nose of his attacker. In the same movement he snatched the cigarette out of the man's mouth as he fell, and took a drag off of it.

"Holy shit!" one of the other men shouted as he looked at his fallen leader.

The tall man was lying on the ground unconscious, his nose broken.

"Gimme your license," Jack said, holding out his hand to the shorter man. The third man stood in silence, understanding that his fun was over for the night.

"What?"

"Gimme your god damn license!"

The man's hands were shaking as he pulled out his wallet, found his license and handed it over to Jack Bonafide.

Jack inspected the cabin of his truck for further damage and retrieved a pen and paper. He scrawled something on the piece of paper and handed it to the man.

"You owe me a Glenn Campbell tape. Wichita Lineman. If that tape ain't in my mailbox in a few days I'm gonna find you. You reading me five by five?"

"Yes, sir," the man replied.

"Wichita fucking lineman. None of that new shit.

I find a copy of Rhinestone Cowboy in my mailbox and I tell you what... you ain't gonna like what happens."

Jack pocketed the man's driver's license.

"Yes, sir."

The Home of Jack Bonafide
Texarkana, Texas
December 24, 1980

The house was quiet. Jack could see that, even from behind the wheel of his truck as he pulled into the gravel driveway. It was quiet in the way that a funeral home is quiet, quiet in a way that a man doesn't want to find his home. Out in front of the house Jack saw a familiar face. A man much older than him was sitting on the porch shucking corn and smoking a cigarette.

Ricky Michaels stood up out of the old wicker rocking chair on the porch and waved to Jack. Ricky was a friend of the Bonafide Family, and had been close with two of Jack's cousins, Roarke and Jack Napier Bonafide. Jack Napier had been killed on Guadalcanal and Roarke was killed years later during a misadventure in the West Texas desert. No one knew for sure what had happened, but that same misadventure had

resulted in the death of Jack's aunt and uncle, John and
Carrie Bonafide.

Ricky was a War Two vet like Jack's father and had
been on Guadalcanal with Jack Napier Bonafide when
the latter was beheaded by a Japanese officer.

The Bonafide and Michaels families had always
been close, so it made sense that Jack had taken up with
Ricky's daughter Angeline, and that they were eventually married. Angeline had always been a loyal woman.

Things had been tough on Angeline ever since Jack
threw in with Delta, and she had not handled the news
of Jack's assignment as an observer in Israel very well.
Particularly considering what had just happened in
Iran, and that he had nearly died. Some things had
been said that both probably wished they could take
back, and Jack had walked out without saying the one
thing that should always be said when a husband or
wife leaves the house, no matter what.

I love you. I'll be back.

Now, Jack was coming home to find Angeline's
father sitting on his front porch with a bottle of Old
Grandad and two glasses.

"Evening, Jack," Ricky called out, dropping the ear
of corn he was working on into a large basin and
pushing it out of the way with his boot.

"Evening, sir."

"You can stop calling me sir, Jack. It don't hang
very well." Ricky scooped the two glasses up off of the

deck with one hand and thumbed the cork out of the bottle with the other. "You game?"

"Reckon I am," Jack said, and took the glass after Ricky had filled it.

Jack leaned back against one of the support posts on the deck and looked into the front window of the simple two-bedroom prairie house as the evening Texas wind blew across his face. He had a hard time remembering another moment so peaceful.

"She doesn't want to see you, Jack," Ricky said, sitting back down in the wicker rocking chair and sipping from his glass. "Can't say as I blame her much."

"I had that coming," Jack acquiesced. "But you know better than anyone that I didn't have a choice."

"Man always has a choice. It's just a matter of whether or not you're willing to make the right one." Ricky paused for a second, looking down at the slats on the deck. "Shit, sorry Jack. You don't deserve that."

"Ain't a matter of deserve," Jack replied. "Folks always get what they've got coming to them, and maybe I had this coming. I could have tried harder, done more. Written more letters."

Ricky stood up out of the chair and looked out to where the sun was beginning to set.

"Maybe, but it ain't my place to say. It'd be one thing if you were some no-account son of a bitch laying hands on her, but you ain't that. You're a good man, Jack Bonafide. Your heart's in the right place.

Just, in this instance, your body wasn't in the right place."

A smile crept across Ricky's face and Jack laughed at that.

"She's staying with us for the time being," Ricky went on. "Look, you come around tomorrow morning for breakfast."

"I thought you said she didn't want to see me?"

"Well, she may not, but I do. And if you don't show up, Charlene isn't going to let me drink a beer with my breakfast, but if you're there it'll be rude not to let you, and then I'll just share yours."

"Then I'll be there," Jack said. "I wouldn't want the Lone Star Beer supply getting too out of control. Speaking of which, you heard anything from Mac?"

"He's bouncing at Dutch's every night starting at ten."

"What do you mean?" Jack asked, his tone changing.

Jack's brother, Mac Bonafide had been a sailor with SEAL Team Two for three years, until he applied for duty with SEAL Team Six. It was only when Mac was subjected to ST6's more rigorous psychological screening that it was discovered he was mildly schizophrenic. He had most likely always harbored the disorder, but it had worsened with time and stress. This meant that Mac was immediately discharged from SEAL Team Two, but what Jack had not known was that his brother was also then completely discharged from the Navy and had arrived back in Texarkana just two weeks prior.

"He's out of the Navy, Jack. Shit, I thought you knew that."

"I knew he popped for some psyche stuff trying to go to a new unit, but I didn't know it was that bad. How's he taking it?"

"That's probably something you should ask the man himself."

Jack nodded his agreement.

Jack turned to the mailbox next to his front steps, opened the small door and reached inside. He pulled out a rectangular package, ripped it open and emptied the contents into his hand. It was a copy of Wichita Lineman. Jack smiled and stuffed the tape into his back pocket.

▭

Dutch's Road House
Victory City, Texas
December 24, 1980

▭

Jack and Mac Bonafide were only a year apart in age, but truthfully, the brothers could not have been more different. Jack stood six feet tall and weighed two hundred pounds and was "just handsome enough to get him into trouble," as Jack's mother had put it. Jack was the more thoughtful of the two, and early on in life had taken his mother's advice that whenever he was angry he should count to five before doing something that he may regret. Jack took that to heart, and while he may not have ever been very good at math, he could count to five just like he was ringing a bell.

Mac on the other hand, took their father's sage advice.

"You hit that son of a bitch before he even knows it's coming, and you hit him so hard his grandchildren will feel it."

Mac was also the bigger of the two, standing six foot four and weighing two forty. This significant size disadvantage did not stop Jack (the older of the two) from giving his brother a licking every now and then, mostly when he deserved it, and sometimes when he didn't. That is just the way of brothers, and these men were no different.

Despite Mac's quick temper, the man had learned that he had to play by the rules as best he could if he didn't want to end up like most of the Bonafide men, who all seemed to die by misadventure. Mac had also felt the shadow of their uncle John Bonafide being cast over him his entire life, and going into the Navy and then the Teams had been his way of trying to atone for a very dark and blood-stained family history.

Dutch's Road House was a Texas institution, and while Dutch himself had long since gone on to his heavenly reward, his two sons now ran the place. It was a fine enough establishment as East Texas bars went, but it did yield a reasonable amount of work for the son of a bitch unlucky enough to be manning the door.

On Christmas Eve, that son of a bitch was Mac Bonafide.

"I.D," Mac said, holding out his hand.

The young man in question showed Mac his Texas driver's license and was waved in.

Reaching back to the stool behind him, Mac grabbed the bottle of Lone Star and took a swig, expertly negotiating his way around the cigarette that was still in his mouth. That was one thing Mac didn't miss about being in the teams; not being able to smoke a goddam cigarette. Sure, you could still smoke all you wanted, but Mac had found that when he smoked, he couldn't run for shit. Well, now at least that problem was solved.

"They having a lot of problems with teenage girls trying to rough up the place?" Jack called out as he crossed the parking lot. "On account of I reckon that's the only sort you could whip if it came down to it."

A broad smile broke out on Mac's face and setting

the bottle back down he reached out and shook his brother's hand.

"Well, I'll be a son of a bitch, it's Captain America himself. What the hell are you doing out here?" Mac looked around conspiratorially. "Hey, you know Angeline's pissed at you, right?"

"Yeah, I know," Jack replied sheepishly. "Ain't nothing I can do about that right now. Ricky was on my porch shucking corn when I showed up at the house. Told me you were down here?"

"Shucking corn? He only does that when he's pissed," Mac said. "And this? Seeing as how I'm not fit for the Navy anymore, got to pay the bills somehow."

"How are you doing?"

Jack looked at his brother for a moment and Mac could read the man like a book.

"Look, I went out for this new unit Marcinko was putting together. You remember the guy? My Team Two leader in Vietnam?"

"Yeah, I know him," Jack replied. Everyone knew about Dick Marcinko, the legendary SEAL who was starting a new counter-terror unit within Naval Special Warfare that sounded a hell of a lot like Delta. At least that was what Jack thought. Either way, Jack Bonafide figured it couldn't hurt to have another high-level unit in the national arsenal.

"Well, I smoked the tryout, left everyone in the dust. Then they started asking me all of these questions, real strange ones." Jack knew about this too. Delta had subjected him to an intense psychological screening intended to expose any problems to the light of day. "I got... I don't know. I got confused and maybe some of my answers didn't sound right. Next thing I know I'm at the naval hospital in Norfolk with a bunch of docs asking me questions and having me take tests."

Jack could see that this troubled his brother. Bonafide men weren't exactly known for showing their emotions, and this was about as much emotion as Jack had ever seen from his little brother.

"I went through the same thing with the Unit," Jack said slowly. "So I get it. A lot of those questions, I had to think real hard about—"

"The answers they wanted to hear," Mac cut him off, meeting his brother's gaze. "Not what you really thought?"

"That's about the size of it," Jack agreed. It was the truth. There had been several times that Jack had to work to figure out what the right answer was. "Doesn't mean something's wrong with you."

Mac reached into his pocket, retrieved a prescription bottle and shook the pills inside.

"These little guys disagree. Diagnosed with mild schizophrenia, whatever the hell that means. Seems like these help with some things, but they make me feel like shit, dull my reflexes. Feel fucking stiff all the time." Mac looked at his brother and his face changed. "I know what you're thinking."

"I didn't say anything," Jack replied.

"We don't know why that son of a bitch did what he did, so I ain't packing it in just yet."

"I'm with you, brother. You know that."

John Bonafide (uncle of Jack and Mac Bonafide) had gone on a notorious killing spree in West Texas in the early nineteen fifties, which ended with the murder of a mother and her child, and a local police officer. Since that event there had been several investigations conducted and even a popular book written on the subject, but none of them ever answered the simple question of *why*? What had caused a decorated Marine and Texas Ranger to go on a rampage that soaked both Texas and the Bonafide family name in blood?

Now, Jack was afraid that he was getting to that *why*. This thing his brother had, was that what sent their uncle down such a dark path? If that was the case, would the pills really help?

Across the parking lot Jack heard some hollering and turned to his left to see a group of five men walking toward them. Judging by their haircuts and general demeanor they were most likely soldiers from the nearby Red River Army Depot looking to blow off a little steam before Christmas.

Jack turned back to his brother.

"Look, we'll talk about this later."

Mac nodded his agreement and then turned to the problem at hand.

"I'm sorry, gentlemen. No military in groups larger than three," Mac called out as he held up both hands.

The group stopped and a shorter man who looked as if he had been born without a neck stepped forward.

"How's that, now?" he asked with a sharp Arkansas accent.

"Club policy. It should have been posted with your S3, so I apologize if it wasn't."

"That's okay," the short man said. "We'll just split up."

"Sorry gents, it doesn't work that way. You're welcome to come back another time, it just can't be tonight."

"Come on Brice, let's go," a taller man leaned in to the shorter one.

"No," Brice shot back. "This ain't right. He's going to let us in, whether he likes it or not."

"Shit," Jack said quietly, and began walking backward away from the situation.

Reaching back to the stool, Mac picked up his beer bottle, took a long swallow, and then stuck it in his front pocket.

"This ain't happening," Mac said calmly. "If you want to take it up with club management, that's your right. But if you think you're getting past me and through that door, you're living in a fairy tale, son."

"I ain't your son, old man," Brice said, stepping nose to chin with Mac Bonafide.

"Old man?" Mac winced. "I'm only twenty-nine goddam years old."

"But you're a busted up twenty-nine, and your sorry ass will still be bouncing at this piece of shit dive bar when you're fifty."

Mac looked hard at the much shorter man, and he saw the shadow out of the corner of his eye. A shadow that looked a hell of a lot like his uncle John Bonafide. Then Mac heard that gravely Texas drawl, the same one that spoke to him when he had wanted to quit during BUDS (Basic Underwater Demolition School) and the same voice that pushed him on while fighting in the A Shau Valley in Vietnam.

If that squirrelly motherfucker talked to me that way, I'd kill him where he stood.

"Well, I ain't you," Mac replied, pulling the bottle back from his pocket and having another drink.

"What?" Brice replied, confused by Mac's nonsensical answer.

"Go to Sporty's down the street," Mac said. "They'll let you in, and no one will have to go to the hospital tonight."

"Let's *go*," the taller man said, more insistently this time as he laid a hand on Brice's shoulder.

It was clear that Brice did not want to let things go, but even he was beginning to understand that this was a contest he would not win. As slowly as they could manage, the five men began to walk away, heading down the street to Sporty's, where they would be served their beer by women in bikini tops and most likely have a better time because of it.

"Since when do you shy away from a fight?" Mac asked, sitting back down on his stool and lighting a new cigarette.

"I figured things were about to get downright biblical, and I can't afford to draw unnecessary attention to myself right now."

"Why's that?" Mac asked, holding out the pack of cigarettes to his brother.

"I left the Unit."

Mac froze. He was the only person alive who knew that Jack was a founding member of Delta Force, and just what that meant. Being the best was all that Jack had ever wanted, and like his brother he also wanted to prove that the Bonafide family weren't just a bunch of maniacs from East Texas.

"Jesus Christ. What the hell happened?" Mac asked.

"Shaky hands," Jack said, holding his hands out. Sure enough, there was a light tremor. Just as Jack had predicted, the only time the tremors came out was when he was off duty.

"Damn brother, I am sorry. Looks like we're both in the same boat."

Not quite, Jack thought to himself.

Jack had briefly considered letting Mac in on what he was doing, but then decided against it. Somehow, Mike Tresham had known that Jack let his brother in on his role in Delta, and it was a reasonable assumption that Mike would also know if Jack told his brother about this.

"It's not too bad. I might have something I can do back in Maryland."

This caught Mack's attention.

"The Agency?" Mac asked.

Jack had momentarily forgotten that despite Mac's lack of formal education, the man was as sharp as a tack. Mac knew about Delta's tight link with the Central Intelligence Agency and had simply put two and two together.

"No, I'm done with that. Might pick up some protection work, bodyguard stuff."

Jack didn't like lying to his brother. In fact, it made him feel like shit. Even worse was that Jack knew Mac Bonafide didn't believe him for a second.

"I've got an idea," Mac said, standing up off of his stool. "Let's race."

Texas High School
Texarkana, Texas

December 24, 1980

Jack and Mac Bonafide walked through the gates of the Texas High School football field and looked up to the rows of empty bleachers. There was enough of a moon out that there was no need for any additional illumination.

Texas High School was one of two high schools in Texarkana (which was really two towns) the other being Arkansas High School. One high school in Texas and the other in Arkansas, with both territories cleanly divided by Stateline Avenue. You've never seen a rivalry as fierce as that between the football teams of these two towns and it had been going on as far back as anyone could remember.

Jack Bonafide had been the quarterback for the Texas Tigers, and when Mac was old enough to attend high school, he joined his brother on the football team as a fullback, because even at fourteen years old Mac Bonafide was built like a fire truck. For the first couple of years Mac accepted his lot living in his older brother's shadow, but at a certain point (as is often the case with brothers close in age) Mac decided that he had to be his own man.

Just before the start of his junior year, Mac Bonafide transferred to Arkansas High School in

Texarkana, Arkansas. At first, he had thought that their father Corbett Bonafide would be angry with him. After all, they were dyed in the wool Texans. Strangely, Corbett seemed to be okay with it.

Jack Bonafide was not nearly as understanding of his brother's decision, and the two stopped speaking after Mac left the house.

At just sixteen years old, Mac Bonafide moved out of the family home, picked up a job working construction and moved into a small one bedroom that could best be described as a shack, but it was a shack on the Arkansas side of the border. Then Mac Bonafide bulldozed his way into the position of quarterback for the Arkansas High School Razorbacks.

When the time came for the first game of the season, you would have thought Judgment Day had come to Texarkana. Police and National Guardsmen lined Stateline Avenue in a show of force to discourage any criminal acts masquerading as "school pride". Privately, the Governor's office was prepared for a full-scale riot if things went in the wrong direction. Part of the problem was that they had no idea just what the wrong direction would be.

That evening Jack and Mac Bonafide met at the fifty-yard line for the coin toss with the referee. The stands had been a cacophony of screams and shouts of both support and condemnation, but now they went quiet. You could hear a pin drop.

Jack reached out to shake his brother's hand. It had been months since they spoke.

Jack shook his brother's hand and smiled.

"Only way you're getting off this field is on a stretcher," Mac Bonafide had said.

"Sounds like your balls dropped," Jack replied. "Good for you."

By any logical and honest account, it was a legendary game within the pantheon of a state known for football. The rest of the two teams might as well have not even been there. It was a war between two brothers, and a war in which neither intended to take prisoners.

It was a game that would leave one brother with a separated shoulder and another with a broken hand, and neither would receive the finish they had hoped for; the final judgment of which Bonafide brother was the alpha.

The game was a tie. After the all-out war that had occurred during their first game of the season, both brothers were sidelined for the rest of the year with their injuries, and to avoid a repeat performance.

<hr />

"What are we racing for?" Mac asked as they stood on the track and he dropped his cigarette.

"Respect," Jack replied. "Like always."

"Shit. I already got that. What else you got?"

"One Lone Star beer," Jack replied.

"Now you're talking."

The two brothers ran this foot race the same way they did everything else, all out and with no quarter. It was one lap, one quarter of a mile, the founding member of Delta Force versus his brother the SEAL, and neither man even considered the possibility that they could lose. It was the unstoppable force colliding with the immovable object.

Mac had all the natural athletic talent, Jack knew that, and this was the way it had always been. When Jack had to stay after practice to keep running drills or get up in the morning an hour early to run a five miler before heading to school, Mac was up late drinking and smoking, hootin' and hollerin'. While it might have seemed like Mac had the better deal in this equation, it also meant that he never developed the type of discipline his brother had, and this was the reason that Jack tended to come out on top.

The brothers ran, harder than they ever had. For Jack, the intensity of the run brought back the memory of running into the woods from Abu Ghraib in Iraq with half of the Republican Guard on his ass. Had that all really happened? Now, back in Texarkana on the Texas High School track it just seemed too incredible to believe.

Jack kept his focus narrowed on the finish line. He

didn't bother looking to see where his brother was, because there was only one place he could be, and that was behind him. Jack could hear the light slapping of Mac's feet on the ground to his right. The man still ran barefoot every chance he got. The running joke in the Army was that country boys like the Bonafide brothers never wore shoes until they showed up at boot camp. For Mac, at least, that had been true. The younger Bonafide brother had even worked construction sites barefoot during the summer months.

Jack could feel his hands getting tight. That was the first clue that he was starting to peter out, and that if he didn't slow himself down, he'd pass out. It had happened before.

Then everything went away. It was quiet. Aside from the beating of his own heart Jack couldn't hear or feel anything. It was like running in some kind of vacuum, maybe like running in space. Nothing could get in and nothing mattered.

Until he crossed the finish line, and Mac Bonafide finished not three steps behind him.

"Son of a bitch!" Mac shouted. He'd had just enough wind to get that out and then immediately vomited on the side of the track.

Jack stumbled to his knees and let out a long, hot breath, trying to slow his breathing down.

"I think... there's something... wrong with us," Jack said, only half-joking.

CHAPTER 2

Red River Army Depot
Texarkana, Texas
December 24, 1980

J ack would have liked to spend more time with his brother, particularly considering every-thing the man was going through. Jack also suspected that there was a lot more swimming beneath the surface, just waiting for the right time to allow its shark's fin to reveal itself.

Unfortunately, he had work to do.

It was half-past eleven, and Jack was right on time to pay the Commanding Officer of Red River Army Depot a very unwanted Christmas Eve visit.

"Such is the burden of command," Jack muttered to

himself as he slowed the Lincoln and finally stopped in front of the gate.

The sound of Glen Campbell singing "If you go away" filtered out through the speakers. Jack reached out and ejected the tape from the deck and slid it into his front pocket.

He had picked the car up from an unlocked garage a few miles down the road. It was waiting there just like Mike Tresham said it would be, with the keys behind the visor. Jack thought that he could get used to this kind of support, but he wasn't about to start relying on it.

All things being equal he would have just taken his truck, but he understood that it wouldn't look quite right for a DOD high muckety-muck to be driving an old truck and dressed like a refugee from a rodeo. That was why Jack had also put on the grey suit he found neatly pressed and laid out in the trunk.

The soldier manning the gate stepped out into the glow of Jack's headlamps and smiled.

"You from DOD?"

"Yes, I am," Jack said, holding out his credentials.

It didn't take a psychic to know who he was. He was almost certainly the only person showing up at the depot on Christmas Eve.

"You okay to get around on your own?" the soldier asked.

Jack was pleased with this. It meant that he probably wouldn't be shackled with an escort and would have more freedom to move.

"Reckon I am," Jack said with a smile. "I've been on a few military bases."

"Great. Pull around the left side of the building, park in the visitor lot and enter through the east door. Use the signs on the wall to find the CO's office. You'll find Colonel Detmeyer waiting for you."

"Thank you, Private," Jack said, taking back his credentials and waiting while the soldier rolled the gate open.

⊏⊐

Mike Tresham had been right, the place was a ghost town. Jack could tell that there were at least a few people in the building, but not even close to what the traffic would normally be like. As he approached the CO's office, Jack Bonafide prepared to go into his whole "reporting for duty" routine and then had a private laugh at that idea. Those days were over.

Instead, Jack knocked twice on the door frame and poked his head into the Commanding Officer's office.

"Colonel Detmeyer?" Jack asked with the best good ol' boy smile he could muster.

The Colonel jumped up from his chair, in the same way that First Sergeant Bonafide would have jumped if a Colonel walked into a room he was in. Again, he could get used to this.

"Mister Bonafide!" the Colonel smiled and thrust out his hand. Normally an officer would salute an elected official, but Colonel Detmeyer wasn't quite sure where Jack fell on that scale. "Pleased to have you here."

Jack shook the Colonel's hand. In this case there had been no need to develop a cover for him. Going under his real name would actually have a benefit to it, due to the Bonafide family's reputation and his own. It was believable that he had joined the Army and over the years worked his way up to become a DOD staff member.

"I was in the Army, Colonel. You don't have to lie to me."

The Colonel laughed.

"Regardless," Detmeyer said. "We'll do our very best to help you out with whatever you need."

"I don't need much," Jack said, and then let out a sigh. "To be honest, I might even want to be here less than you do. I was supposed to have a nice little layover on my way to Camp Pendleton out in California, but when SECDEF remembered that I grew up here, guess what? He was more than happy to arrange me a couple days extra to visit home."

"And he wouldn't mind at all if you dropped in on

Red River and checked that box off for the year?" the Colonel asked, leaning in conspiratorially.

"That's about the size of it," Jack confirmed. "So if you don't mind I'll just make the rounds, make sure no one's on fire and there ain't any Russian spies on the premises, and then leave you to it."

It was there. In the Colonel's left eye. It was probably only a millimeter, but it was there. His eye had twitched.

"Sounds like a plan!"

Jack nodded his agreement and turned to walk out the door, then stopped.

Shit, he thought to himself.

Jack drew his Colt 1911 pistol from his belt, slammed the door shut and raised his weapon.

"What are you doing?" the Colonel shouted.

"Your eye twitched," Jack said quietly. "And keep your voice down."

"What in the hell are you talking about?"

"When I said 'Russian spies' your eye twitched." Jack walked forward, keeping his weapon trained on the Colonel. "What's going on around here? What are you up to?"

If Jack hadn't already known it was possible that the Soviets were trying to smuggle something through Red River he never would have mad such a leap, but he did know, and so he had.

As Colonel Detmeyer looked into Jack Bonafide's eyes he knew that there was no point in lying, no point in trying to buy himself some time. He had met men like this before from the special units, and he knew that Jack Bonafide had already seen through to the bone of him.

"Why did you have to come on Christmas Eve?" the Colonel asked, shaking his head. "Any other fucking night of the year and it wouldn't have mattered. Why tonight?"

"Colonel, right now you have only one mission. Your mission is to not be executed. You accomplish said mission by working with me to the best of your abilities, but I promise you that if you do not, you will be tried and executed as a traitor to this nation."

"Shit," the Colonel spat. "It was just supposed to be a one-time thing."

Jack kept his weapon trained on the Colonel. He waited but nothing came.

"Go on," Jack ordered.

"Back in seventy-one. I was the Executive Officer here and that was when they first approached me."

"Who?"

"Who the fuck do you think?" the Colonel snapped, and then his posture seemed to sag a bit. "Can't say for sure, but almost certainly the Russians. They weren't wearing matching outfits with the hammer and sickle on them or anything, but you can just tell." The Colonel paused for a moment. "Man, let me tell you. These guys are something else. I mean, they're good, you know? You could have one living in your house and you wouldn't know he was a Red."

"What did they have you do?"

"It was supposed to be drugs. We all heard the stories about the bodies of soldiers coming back from Vietnam stuffed full of heroin, and everyone said the same stuff about how they would never do something like that. But when that first duffel bag full of cash shows up in the trunk of your car?" The Colonel let out a long whistle. "Let me tell you, boy, that'll change a lot of minds."

"Get to the damn point!"

"It wasn't drugs," Colonel Detmeyer said. "But I didn't know that until it had already been a few months, and by then I was in too deep."

"What was it?"

The Colonel stared hard at Jack Bonafide.

"Soviets."

"What?" Jack asked, truly shocked for the first time in a long while.

"There's a lot of talk about Soviet sleeper agents getting into the country and setting up shop, but how in the hell do you think they get here? A connecting flight from Moscow? No, this is how. Some bodies are slated for cremation as soon as they get off the plane. Those are the ones they replace. They got some kind of drug they inject them with, slows their heart rate down to almost nothing. Looks like they're dead."

"What does that have to do with what's happening tonight?" Jack asked. "That was nine years ago."

The Colonel parted his lips as if he wanted to say something.

"Spit it out, man!" Jack shouted.

"They asked me to do it again. We have observers in Afghanistan. Three were KIA late last week and the next day I got the call from DOD. They were being sent directly to us." The Colonel looked shaken, perhaps because the gravity of what he had done was finally settling in on him. "Then I found another duffel bag full of money in my trunk with explicit instructions."

"And that's all it takes? To get you to betray your country?"

"And photos of my kids walking into their school." The Colonel paused. "I know it's no excuse, and it doesn't make up for what I did before, but what would you do?"

"I wouldn't have put myself in this position to begin with," Jack said, and reaching to the desk picked up the phone and handed it to the Colonel. "Lock this place down. Now."

"We'll be trapped in here with them!" The Colonel protested.

"Exactly."

Carrie Davidson closed the last set of books in front of her and rubbed her eyes. The recruiters had been right. Working for the CIA was indeed a glamorous life full of adventure and intrigue. The reality was that it may have actually turned out that way had she not been foolish enough to obtain a Master of Professional Accountancy before joining the Central Intelligence Agency.

Carrie had always loved numbers. There was something about the simultaneous simplicity and complexity of them. Perhaps it was a counter-weight to her home life; her unpredictable father at the mercy of Southern Comfort and her mother only sleeping at home when she ran out of other beds to occupy. So Carrie would stay in her room and find refuge in the numbers.

It was only after she finished her training at Camp Peary in Quantico, Virginia that she realized she would not, in fact, be chasing spies in East Germany. No, her destiny was far greater than that. She would instead audit log books in Texarkana, Texas. Hold the applause, please.

It would be one thing if she stumbled upon a vast conspiracy, but instead she was pouring over catalogues of five-ton truck parts, right down to the nut and the bolt. Still, Carrie stayed sharp. She knew as well as anyone that the devil was in the details, and if she relaxed her posture for even a single moment, she might miss something.

Then she found it. Six crates tagged with origin numbers that didn't exist, that had then been routed out to three different military bases. She had only made the connection the day prior, and while it was actionable, it wasn't actionable enough for her to abandon her cover as just another lowly Army Captain and go running back to Langley.

Even if she wouldn't be chasing spies in East Germany, she knew that she was a part of something big, something greater than herself. Now that she had found these anomalies in the books, she knew that Mike Tresham's suspicion that something was happening at Red River was most likely correct, and that the threat was very real.

Ding.

The intercom had just gone off.

"Red River Army Depot is now on lockdown. All personnel shelter in place."

Shelter in place? Carrie thought to herself. That sounded like they were about to be attacked. Who the hell would attack the Red River Army Depot?

She reached down into her purse and retrieved her 1951 Beretta pistol and checked the chamber. It had only taken a few days to realize that security was very lax at Red River, so there was no need to walk around unarmed if she didn't have to.

———

"Move!" Jack said, leading the Colonel into the hall-way. "Am I correct that this is going down tonight, and that the bodies are already here?"

"Yes," Colonel Detmeyer replied, leading Jack down the hallway. "They've timed this shit down to the minute. They must have swapped them out in Afghanistan. That would give them a small enough window to make it work. They just flew into Barksdale and then drove them here."

"You better pray to God they're still in those body bags, son," Jack said as they walked with an increasingly faster pace down the empty hallways.

The Colonel pushed open the doors to the morgue and Jack followed. The room was cold, filled with steel tables set up with the appropriate tools beside them. Jack saw three body bags, but two were empty.

"Jesus," Jack said, lowering his pistol. "You need to get on the line right now and let the Quick Reaction Force know that we have opposition force on site."

The Colonel looked stunned.

"Do it!"

"We— we don't have QRF," the Colonel stuttered. "Where do you think you are, Fort Bragg?"

Then Jack heard it. It was slow and purposeful. The creeping sound of a zipper being pulled down, and with growing concern Jack realized what it was. He turned to see the zipper of the last remaining body bag sliding downward, seemingly of its own accord.

A hand reached out, and a man emerged.

"You've got to be kidding me," Jack said.

The man in the body bag locked eyes with Jack for just a split second and then turned and rolled out of the bag and onto the floor. He was in shorts and a t-shirt but nothing else. Jack noticed that he didn't even have shoes on as he pushed through the rear door of the morgue and into the hallway.

"Shoot him!" the Colonel shouted

"We need him alive!" Jack replied and sprinted through the rear doors into the same hallway.

It was a rookie mistake, and one that Jack would never have made in the Unit. He had just slammed right through the door like some rookie showing up for close quarters battle training on day one, and he was punished with a forearm to his throat. When he saw that this man was just in shorts and a t-shirt he had reflexively downgraded his threat potential, and now he was paying for it. He heard his pistol slide across the floor before he noticed it wasn't in his hand and looked up just in time to block the heel strike that was coming at his face.

Jack spun around on his hip and swept the Russian's leg, knocking the man to the floor beside him. He never fully appreciated the Army's need for everything to be so perfectly clean until that moment. A highly polished floor made it much easier to spin around like that.

The Russian lunged across the floor, attempting to get on top of Jack, but Jack responded by wrapping his legs around the man, putting him into the guard position, just like those two brothers Colonel Beckwith had brought up from Brazil had taught them all to do. For the life of him he couldn't remember their names, but he'd be sure to send a thank you note if he got out of this in one piece.

Whoever this son of a bitch was he was strong, strong enough to stand up with Jack's legs wrapped around him. He picked up the former Delta Force operator and then slammed him back to the floor. That one rattled Jack's brain around in his skull a bit. Jack took advantage of the Russian's instability to unhook one of his legs and spin on the polished linoleum again, this time getting the man's right arm in an armbar lock. There would be no waiting for him to tap out. Jack drove his hips hard against the man's elbow until he heard a sickening 'snap', then rolled out of position and back to his feet.

Shit, Jack thought to himself. *I just broke that son of a bitch's arm and he didn't make so much as a sound.*

What Jack didn't know was that the drug that had been used to slow the heart rate of the Soviet agent and make him appear dead also inhibited pain at the brainstem level and had not completely worn off yet.

Despite the effectiveness of the moves the Brazilian brothers had taught him, Jack decided it was time to go old school and delivered three hard kicks to the Soviet's head as the agent tried to stumble to his feet. The man pivoted and before Jack realized what was happening the Soviet had snatched his lost pistol up off the floor.

The Soviet raised the pistol.

Jack's head whipped to the left and he saw Carrie Davidson running toward him, firing her weapon as she moved. Three loud cracks split the air. One round hit the Soviet agent in the head and two struck him in the chest, killing him.

Jack moved quickly, retrieving his pistol and turning to where Carrie was standing.

"Identify yourself!" Carrie Davidson shouted, keeping her weapon raised. Jack noticed that her hands were shaking.

"DOD! Jack Bonafide," Jack replied as the Colonel emerged from the morgue behind him.

The Colonel turned to Carrie.

"Captain Davidson?" Colonel Detmeyer asked, seeming confused. "Why do you have a weapon?" It was not the standard protocol for admin officers to be carrying firearms in the building. In fact, it was expressly prohibited.

"Saber!" Carrie shouted.

Jack felt his body relax. It was the challenge question Mike Tresham had told him other agents may be using.

"Rattle!" Jack replied. Carrie lowered her pistol.

The Colonel looked down at the dead body.

"What happened to taking him alive?" the Colonel asked.

"He had other ideas," Jack said. "How many ways off this compound driving?"

"Just the front gate."

"Then that's where we're headed," Jack replied, and as he took a step, he felt a crunch in his pocket. He reached down to the pocket he had slid his tape into and could feel that it had been broken in the fight with the Soviet. "Shit."

Jack was the first one out the front door, so he was the first to witness the scene. There were half a dozen dead soldiers strewn about the guardhouse and the gate was open. Jack turned back to the visitor parking lot and saw that one of the cars that had been parked there was missing. It was the one in the Commanding Officer's spot.

"They're gone," Carrie said. "We have to call it in. Put local police and state authorities on alert."

"We do that, and we'll lose them," Jack said. "We need to take them by surprise."

"And how do you intend we do that?"

"East," a weak voice said from the ground, and Jack quickly knelt down beside one of the soldiers. "They went... east on Eighty-Two."

"You hold on," Jack said, feeling the soldier's pulse. "You do not have permission to stand down, do you understand me, soldier?"

"Yes, sir," the soldier replied quietly. Jack wanted to do more, to say more, but he knew time was in short supply.

He stood back up and looked down the road.

How do we take them by surprise?

"What's your license plate number, make and model?" Jack asked as he walked to the guard booth. The Colonel seemed confused and didn't answer right away. "Spit it out, man!"

"Ford Fairlane, Texas plate QCQ117."

"What are you planning?" Carrie asked.

Jack picked up the phone in the guard booth and dialed a number.

"That road runs straight through Victory City. I've got a six foot four surprise for them sitting on a bar stool drinking a Lone Star."

Dutch's Road House
Victory City, Texas

December 25, 1980

━━

Mac Bonafide walked into Dutch's after hearing the bartender Norton call out that someone was on the phone for him. As Mac walked, he knew that the race with Jack was a mistake and that he was going to pay for it the next day. If he was already this sore just an hour later, he didn't want to guess at what he was going to feel like in the morning.

Mac snatched up the phone.

"This is Mac."

"Mac, it's Jack. Listen very carefully. I'm working for the CIA and there are two Soviet agents in a Ford Fairlane, Texas plate number QCQ117 heading straight for you."

Mac laughed out loud.

"Shit, Jack, you didn't wait long after getting out of the Army to start getting into the magic mushrooms, did you?"

"Brother, this is serious."

"You're full of shit," Mac replied, but was slowly beginning to think this was not a joke.

"On our mother's immortal soul. They're coming right at you on Eighty-Two. You have to stop them."

"Jesus, Jack." Mac looked around the room for a moment. "Okay, I'm on it."

Mac slammed the phone down, took another swig from his beer and then stuffed the bottle in his front pocket. Norton knew that tell of his. Whenever Mac stuffed a bottle of beer in his front pocket something was about to happen.

Mac turned and headed for the door.

"Where you headed, Mac?" Norton asked.

"To stop a Russian invasion."

"In Victory City?"

———

A cold wind had picked up outside the bar, and Mac Bonafide stood in the relative silence of the night. State Road Eighty-Two ran through Victory City, and Dutch's Road House sat right on it. He turned west and watched the road. There was nothing.

Jack had always been a bit of a prankster, but that wasn't what this was. Mac knew it. It also wasn't out of the question that Jack would have been recruited by the CIA. Mac was a little hurt that his brother hadn't felt like he could handle that information. They would have to have a conversation about that. As far as Mac was concerned, being brothers was like playing poker; you're all in or you're all out.

Then he saw it. The first faint glow of headlights in the distance. Mac's eyes were good, even better than Jack's (though the older brother would never admit it) so he was able to make out from quite a distance away that the car was indeed a Ford Fairlane.

Mac walked quickly back to the door to the bar and grabbed the stool he had been sitting on by one of its legs.

"Hey!" a voice shouted from his left. "I want to have words with you!"

Mac turned and saw the stocky soldier named Brice from earlier. He had clearly tied one on and it was obvious that his buddies were trying to reign him in.

"Stay back, son!" Mac shouted, and turned to the road.

"I ain't your son, old man!"

Brice was still a safe distance away. If he timed this right, Mac would be able to take care of business without getting hit in the back of the head with a beer bottle.

QCQ117. He saw it. The car was still a couple of hundred feet away, and yes there was some margin for error, but Mac was about 98% sure it was the car he was looking for. If it wasn't, he was about to be in a whole lot of trouble.

As the car roared toward him Mac Bonafide stepped to the side of the road, swung the bar stool back like a baseball bat and hurled it into the windshield of the approaching Ford. The windshield shattered and the car's brakes squealed as it slammed to a stop in the road.

"Holy shit!" one of the drunk soldiers shouted from behind him.

Mac walked into the road. He could see two men in the car, and clearly their bells had been rung good. Mac pulled open the driver's side door and looked at the man sitting behind the wheel.

"Hey there, Ivan," Mac said with a smile. "Welcome to Texas."

Mac slammed his right fist into the side of the driver's head, possibly harder than he had ever hit anyone in his life, and the result showed. The driver was out, possibly never to wake up again.

The passenger was fast. The darker haired man had already unbuckled himself and was out of the car, starting to run for a side street.

Mac slipped his beer bottle out of his pocket, and taking it by the neck threw it as hard as he could, end over end until it broke against the back of the running man's head.

Mac let out a breath. That was the closest he had been to real combat since Vietnam. He realized in that moment how much he missed it. It was the only time that things made sense, that he felt like himself.

Mac turned back to where Brice and his friends were standing.

"Still want to fight?" Mac asked.

"No, sir," Brice said, and led his friends away.

"Didn't think so."

Dutch's Road House
Victory City, Texas
December 25, 1980

Jack had seen the police lights from down the road, but as he got closer, he could make out his brother Mac on his knees in the road with his hands cuffed behind him. Two other men who both looked pretty badly busted up were being treated by a medic. It couldn't have been over ten minutes since this had happened.

"What do we do?" Carrie asked.

"Can't let the police take them," Jack said as he pulled off the road. "We'll have to improvise."

"Do I even want to know what that means?" Carrie asked.

"Probably not," Jack replied.

He stepped out of the car and walked to the scene with both of his hands up. The Sheriff squinted his eyes to better see the man approaching him.

"Is that Jack Bonafide?" Sheriff Alice called out.

"That it is," Jack said with a smile.

"In a suit and everything," Sheriff Gary Alice said.

"Unlike your brother here. I tell you, Jack, we've had some trouble with your darker half over the years, but nothing like this."

"Yeah, about that," Jack said. "I told him to do this."

Sheriff Alice was clearly shocked.

"This some kind of joke?" the Sheriff asked. "Because if it is, it ain't funny."

"No joke," Jack said, fishing out his DOD credentials and showing them to the Sheriff. "These two men are fugitives from justice, and I asked Mac to get in their way. Which he apparently did, in true Bonafide fashion."

Carrie Davidson stood a few feet behind Jack, still in her Army fatigues.

"What are you saying, Jack?"

"I need these men to come with me, and for you to release my brother."

"You know I need a transfer order from the County to release a prisoner, Jack. I can't just hand these men over to you. And as for your brother, he'll get to stand before the judge and make his case, and you're more than welcome to testify on his behalf, but this," the Sheriff looked at the carnage that had befallen Victory City at the hands of just one Bonafide brother, "This cannot stand."

There was no time to keep bargaining with this man. Jack took a step back and drew his weapon. The Sheriff reflexively went for his.

"Do not do it, Sheriff," Jack said. "I will shoot you. I promise you."

The Sheriff froze, as did the deputy behind him. Mac cautiously stood up and walked to where Jack was.

"On your knees. Do it now." Jack waved Carrie over. "Cuff 'em. Medics too."

Carrie made quick work of securing the officers and the medics. Jack kept his eyes trained on the two men sitting in the back of the ambulance. They looked normal. They sure as hell didn't look like Soviet super spies.

"Think about what you're doing," the Sheriff said as Mac Bonafide grabbed the two men from the back of the ambulance and walked them around to the back of Jack's car.

Mac popped the trunk and waved the men into it. They clearly knew the drill, and also understood that they were in no position to try to take these men on. Mac slammed the lid of the trunk closed.

Jack walked to where the Sheriff was kneeling on the pavement with his hands cuffed.

"This isn't personal, Gary. It's business."

"We'll see about that," Sheriff Alice replied.

Jack, Carrie and Mac roared down State Road Eighty-

Two in the Ford Fairlane, with the two Soviet agents secured in the trunk. None of them had said a word over the past few minutes since leaving the Sheriff of Bowie County trussed up like a prize hog in the middle of the road.

"Either of you gonna tell me what I've gotten myself into?" Mac asked.

"No," Jack replied. "And it's better that way. Trust me. You ran some dark ops in Vietnam, you know the drill."

"That I do, but I wasn't running them with you," Mac said, pointing a finger at his brother from the back seat. "How come you didn't tell me you were working for the CIA? And who the hell is she?"

"I'm Carrie," Carrie said, reaching back and shaking Mac's hand.

"Pleased to meet you, ma'am," Mac replied.

"Don't everyone go getting all friendly," Jack said. "We're not going to be together long."

"So, Tresham sent you?" Carrie asked.

"He's not read in," Jack said, tilting his head toward his brother.

"Mike Tresham is about to become the Assistant director of the CIA. That's not classified," Carrie replied.

"He told me you were running the books," Jack said. "Did you find anything?"

"That, actually, is classified," Carrie said. "Even to you."

"Well, this seems like a really great plan!" Mac said with a smile. "I mean, you two are one well-oiled machine. Tell me something, were you planning on stopping these assholes before or after I hurled a bar stool through their windshield?"

"How did you two survive growing up together?" Carrie asked.

"Hell, you haven't even met the rest of the family," Mac said.

Jack slowed the Ford down and pulled a left onto North Peach Street. Mac looked around as Jack made another left onto a long gravel road.

"We going to Ricky's?" Mac asked.

"Who the hell is Ricky?" Carrie asked.

"Angeline's staying there," Jack said. "I need to get right with her before I have to leave."

"Where are we going?" Mac asked.

"You're not going anywhere," Jack replied. "I am."

"Who the hell is Angeline?" Carrie asked.

"Jack's wife," Mac replied.

"Ex-wife," Jack countered.

"Not as far as the law is concerned. Last time I checked you still hadn't signed the papers."

"It's complicated."

"Stop the car!" Carrie shouted.

Jack complied by slamming the brake pedal to the

floor. The Ford Fairlane came to a sudden stop and sat, the engine rumbling in the dark Texas night.

"I don't know what kind of backwoods bullshit this is," Carrie said. "But we are way off of mission tasking. I do have vital information that I need to get passed to Mister Tresham, and you need to help me do it."

"I will," Jack replied. "I just need to square something away first."

"No, you need to get back on point."

"Five minutes," Jack pressed on.

"Are you on drugs right now?" Carrie asked. "I've known you all of an hour. We've already committed multiple felonies together and now you want to take a break to go play house?"

"Five minutes," Jack said again. "Not a minute more."

"You're wasting your time, darling," Mac said. "He's got it stuck in that head of his that he needs to do this. Sooner you let him, sooner we can get back on the road."

Jack and Carrie both turned and looked at Mac.

"I'm becoming concerned that you don't understand you're not coming with us," Carrie said.

Mac smiled.

"We'll see about that." Mac said and then turned to Jack. "Hey, why don't you pop in that Glen Campbell tape I gave you?"

"I don't have it."

"What? You take that thing with you everywhere. Shit, you took it all the way to Iran. Where is it?"

"I don't want to talk about it."

———

The porch light was already on before Jack pulled the Ford Fairlane into Ricky Michaels' driveway. Ricky had heard the car coming a mile away and was already outside his front door with his shotgun at the ready when Jack exited the vehicle.

"Jack?" Ricky called out. "That you?"

"Yes, sir," Jack replied.

"Son, you know what time it is?"

"I do apologize for the late intrusion, but I was hoping I might talk to Angeline."

"What happened to breakfast?"

"Life got in the way," Jack said. "And I'll most likely be leaving town right quick here."

"Do I want to know?" Ricky asked.

"Probably best if you don't."

Ricky looked past Jack to see Carrie and Mac waiting in the car.

"What are you boys up to?"

"Chasing down Soviet spies, saving America. That kind of stuff."

Ricky smiled.

"I wouldn't put it past you Bonafide boys. You're a

bit too much like the rest of your kin for your own good."

Without another word, Ricky walked back into the house and shut the door. Jack was hoping this meant he was getting Angeline, and not just deciding he'd had enough of Jack Bonafide and his antics for one night. A moment later he got his answer.

"What are you doing here?" Angeline asked as she tied her robe shut and walked out onto the porch.

Jack started to walk to her, and she held out her hand.

"Don't."

Jack stopped.

"I just wanted to see you before I go again."

"I thought you were coming to breakfast?" Angeline asked.

"I was," Jack replied. "But something's happened."

Angeline let out a sigh and shook her head.

"Something always comes up with you, Jack," she said. "Seems there are a lot of things in the world more important to you than me."

"That's not how it is."

"Then how is it, Jack?" Angeline asked. "You tell me. Tell me now and maybe there's some hope we can sort this out."

Jack searched for the words, the right ones that would explain his actions over the past year, but there were none. There was no way to make her understand, and he knew it.

"That's what I thought," Angeline said as she walked back to the door. "Sign the papers, Jack. Let me get on with my life. Then maybe you can figure out what the hell you're doing with yours."

━━━

The three were silent as they drove down State Road Eighty-Two, heading for the rally point Jack had been given by Mike Tresham in case things went south, a direction that they had most definitely gone. Jack thought about what Angeline had said and wondered if she was right? For the moment, at least, it seemed like he had a mission, a direction to point himself in. What would happen when that was over? Would it just be on to the next job? Jack Bonafide knew how that story would end. With a stack of ribbons and a handful of ashes. He'd seen a lot of old-timers end that way, and it didn't seem like a good way to go out.

"She seems nice," Carrie finally said, breaking the silence. Mac gave her a quizzical look. "Sorry. It was getting awkward."

"It's fine," Jack said as he drove the car down a side street and parked it in front of an auto parts store. "She wasn't wrong."

A short distance down the street another car flashed its lights twice, and Jack flashed his back.

"That's our contact," Jack said.

"Look, I really do have important information," Carrie said. "I get that this isn't easy for you. We're all doing our best."

Jack nodded and exited the vehicle. A lone man was walking toward them carrying a military style flight bag.

"Saber," Jack said.

"Rattle," the man replied, and held out his hand for Jack to shake. "I assume you're Bonafide?"

"Yes, Sir," Jack replied.

"I'm McMasters. I was expecting the possibility of another agent coming with you. Who's the other man?" McMasters asked, nodding to Mac who was now standing beside the car.

"That's my brother, Mac," Jack said. McMasters raised an eyebrow. "It was unavoidable, and if it wasn't for him, we wouldn't have the two Soviets in the trunk."

"You caught them?" McMasters asked.

"Mac did. Like I said, he pulled our fat out of the fire."

"That's good," McMasters nodded. "We'll be able to use them to get some of our own people back."

"We left a bit of a mess at Red River, and in Victory City," Jack said.

"We already know. We've got a team en route to both locations to do some cleanup."

"I fucked up," Jack said. "I'm sorry."

McMasters cocked his head to the side and raised an eyebrow.

"Fucked up?" he asked. "Do you know how often we actually take these guys alive?" McMasters paused. "Try just about never. You guys did great. Now we need to get them out of the trunk, and I need your wallet."

"My wallet?" Jack asked.

"Texas boy like you, I figure you've got a thick leather wallet. Give it here," McMasters said, holding out his hand.

Jack complied and handed this man his wallet.

"Mac, you got a wallet?" McMasters called out.

"Yes, Sir," Mac replied and pulled out his own wallet. It was much like Jack's but was stamped with the seal of the United States Navy.

McMasters walked to Mac, leaned in and whispered something to him.

"Say what now?" Mac asked.

"You heard me."

"Will do."

Mac turned and popped the trunk. McMasters looked down at the two Soviet agents lying in the back. They didn't look scared. They knew what their mission was, and they also knew that it wasn't over.

McMasters and Mac Bonafide moved fast, shoving the wallets into the mouths of the Soviet agents and holding them in place as the men struggled and gagged. McMasters pulled what looked like a set of custom-made pliers out of his jacket pocket and went to work.

"Jesus Christ," Jack said. "What the hell are you two playing at?"

"Watch and learn," McMasters said as he used the wallet to lever the man's jaw open and get the pliers inside his mouth. After a few seconds and some grunting, the pliers returned to the light holding a bloody tooth. McMasters squinted at it and then threw it away. He looked at the Soviet. "Got it on the first try. You're lucky."

"Suicide pills?" Carrie asked, clearly in awe.

"Almost always in one of the upper back molars," McMasters replied as he went to work on the second man. "The moment they knew all was lost they would have broken them, and we would have been out of luck."

The extraction of the second man's molar was quick, and Jack could tell by the broad smile on McMasters' face that he had also gotten this one on the first attempt.

"Miss, grab my first aid kit out of that bag. I need you to pack these wounds so they don't pass out from blood loss."

Carrie Davidson complied, finding the first aid kit

in the flight bag and moving quickly to pack the holes where the teeth had been, while Mac and McMasters held the men in place. Once this was done, they closed the trunk again.

McMasters let out a breath.

"I have to say, I never expected you two to find all of this. Much less capture two Soviet agents. Looks like I'll have to buy Mike that beer after all."

"Mister Tresham?" Jack asked.

"He has a lot of faith in you, Jack. Well deserved, it would seem." McMasters turned to Carrie. "I assume you have information for me?"

Carrie pulled a set of notebooks out of her fatigue pocket and handed it to him.

"I red flagged shipments departing Red River heading to three different locations. I don't know what they were, but the best guess is more agents or the tamper for the weapon. I don't have the actual locations yet, but if you put a team of analysts on those books, you should be able to figure it out pretty quick. They were all routed through Red River for obvious reason."

"A pliable Colonel," McMasters said as he thumbed through the notebook, nodding his head as he did so. "This is good. Very good. It looks like you three have a lot of work ahead of you."

"Three?" Jack asked.

"Mac, assuming your dance card isn't full at the moment, we can use you. Not forever, but you've proven yourself tonight, and there will almost certainly be more to come."

Mac smiled broadly.

"I got nowhere to be."

"I can tell by the look of you that you're like your brother here. We need men like you to keep the wolves from the door."

"I'll do my best, sir."

"You're going to have to do better than that, Mac. You all will. What about you, miss?" McMasters asked. "You're only supposed to be working on vetting books, but now we're going to ask you to do a lot more than that. You've been pouring over those documents for the past month. You know things about the shipments, where they went and who handled them, and it would take too long to spin these two up on it. Are you ready for this?"

Carrie had to work hard to suppress a smile.

"Yes, sir."

McMasters looked hard at the three standing in front of him.

"There's no one waiting in the wings to step in if you fail, do you understand? Our hope has always been that this Black Tsar was a bluff, a fail-safe in case the Soviets ever needed it. Now we've heard chatter that there's a split within the KGB, and if there is things are about to get really bad. If you fail, the world will change, and it won't be a place any of us will want to leave to our children."

"We won't fail, sir," Jack Bonafide said. "You have my word."

"Good," McMasters replied. "And make sure to change your damn clothes. Jack's dressed like a mortician and you two look like a soldier and a cowboy. You're like the punch-line to a bad joke."

━━

The three stood in the dim light of the auto parts store's overhead lights as McMasters pulled away with the Soviet agents in his trunk. Jack could feel his body relax as the taillights disappeared in the distance.

"Well, that went reasonably well," Carrie said, breaking the silence.

"Depends on who you ask, I guess," Jack replied. "I assume you know where we're going next?"

"First stop is Fort Meade, Maryland. One shipment went there, but according to the manifests it never left."

"I like Maryland," Mac said with a smile. "Pretty girls."

"Fantastic," Carrie said with a sigh.

Jack turned to his left and saw a car heading toward them. His hand hovered over the butt of his pistol.

The vehicle's headlights flashed. They flashed

twice, just like the signal McMasters had given them. Was he back? That was probably a bad sign.

"Any ideas?" Carrie asked.

"Just be cool," Jack replied, moving to his right so he wouldn't be a sitting duck if this visitor wasn't friendly and decided to open up on them.

A man stepped out of the car and walked across the street to where they were standing. He didn't seem like any sort of threat. His gait was too relaxed for that. He was keeping his head on a swivel, but he wasn't nervous.

"Saber!" the man called out.

"Rattle," Jack replied. What in the hell was going on?

"I assume you're Bonafide?"

"Yes," Jack and Mac replied together. Jack shot his brother a dirty look.

"I'm Scarn," the man said, holding out his hand. Jack shook it.

This man was dressed in a dark grey suit, not unlike Jack's.

"I assume you have the Soviets? I picked up on the police band on my way over that you left the scene with them."

"What in the hell is going on?" Jack asked.

Scarn took a step back, and Jack could see that his readiness had just jumped a level.

"I am agent Michael Scarn, tasked with handling

your escape and evasion by Mike Tresham. Why are you confused by that?"

"Shit," Mac muttered.

"Where's McMasters?" Jack asked cautiously.

"Who in the hell is McMasters?"

━━━

Agent Scarn hung up the payphone and tapped it a few times before turning back to Jack, Carrie and Mac.

"Well, I'm not going to pretend that this isn't a world class fuck up. I mean, holy shit!" Scarn practically shouted. "Did you even ask to see his credentials?" Scarn held up a hand to stop them from answering. "Don't bother answering."

Scarn walked back and forth in the street shaking his head before he finally stopped again.

"Tresham wants to give you another shot," Scarn said. "For the record, I disagree. I never liked this whole idea of trying to recycle a used-up commando to do work that should be left to professionals."

Jack felt his blood boiling and stepped forward.

"The same professionals that allowed a Soviet agent to know all of your protocols and our location and identities?"

"It speaks!" Scarn said in mock surprise.

"I didn't ask for this," Jack went on. "If Mister Tresham hadn't called me up I'd be sitting on my porch with a beer right now living off of a nice early retirement."

"You'd be drinking beer on your porch at two in the morning?" Scarn asked.

"Goddam right," Jack said. "But I'm here instead. And whether we keep pursuing this thing ain't up to you. Because I tell you right now, son, if there really is some mother of all bombs loose in this country, I sure as hell ain't leaving it up to you to find it."

Scarn stood his ground, eyes locked with an obviously fired up Jack Bonafide.

"Good. Because we're not even remotely close, and we have exactly zero leads. You're it."

"Shit," Carrie said. "The log book. I gave it to McMasters. He knows where the shipments are now. He'll be heading to those three locations."

"What do you need?" Scarn asked.

"To get to Fort Meade faster than we can drive," Carrie replied.

A Private Airstrip
Texarkana, Texas
December 25, 1980

Despite a rocky introduction, Agent Scarn had come through in securing air transport to Fort Meade as well as a weapons and communication package. It was a short drive to the private airfield just outside of Texarkana, and by the time they arrived everything had been loaded up and was ready to go.

"It's about five hours flight time to Fort Meade," Scarn said as he led Jack, Carrie and Mac to the jet stairway. "We're setting up an attache that you can link up with when you get there."

"No," Jack said. "That McMasters guy knew everything about us. From here on out we're going dark. We'll reach out to you and only you if we need something, but no handlers."

Scarn seemed to consider this for a moment and then nodded. Jack wasn't even supposed to be officially linked up with the CIA to begin with, so in the grand scheme of things this made more sense.

Jack ascended the steps with Carrie and Mac behind him, but Scarn held out a hand and stopped Mac.

"This is as far as you go."

"How's that now?" Mac asked.

"I'm not putting national security in the hands of a schizophrenic who was kicked off the SEAL teams."

"You better count to ten and think again," Mac said, his face becoming stern. "About the next words that come out of your mouth."

Scarn was no push over, that was obvious, but even he knew that Mac Bonafide looked like a hornet's nest a man wouldn't want to go sticking his face in.

"You must understand what I'm saying," Scarn said. "It's not my call, this is just how it is."

"How many skyjackings occur in the United States each year?" Jack asked.

Scarn turned to where Jack was standing on the stairs.

"What the hell are you talking about?"

"Domestic flights, each year. How many are taken over by a man with a gun?"

Scarn looked confused but took the bait.

"None in 1980."

"Well, I'm a man with a gun," Jack said, pushing aside his jacket to reveal the Colt 1911. "And I aim to take this here plane, with or without your permission. So you can either be the visionary who decided to let a decorated Navy SEAL join the mission, or the asshole who lost his plane. Pick one."

"I already hate the two of you," Scarn said, but it was clear he would let Mac go along for the ride.

"Three," Carrie said, raising a hand. "There are three of us. You hate the three of us."

———

Of the three of them, only Jack Bonafide had ever been

on a private jet before. However, it is worth noting that these private jet rides had always been in the context of how on earth Delta would take one of these planes down if it was ever seized by hostile forces. They had collectively drawn the conclusion that it would be a tactical nightmare, bordering on impossible.

A 747 wasn't exactly a walk in the park, but at least it was fairly big. Once you breached the cabin, there was a decent amount of room to move and shoot. Delta's practice runs on the bigger jets had always gone fairly well. Not perfect, but at least everyone didn't die. The few times they had tried to develop a scenario for taking back a Gulfstream III, everyone had died.

Recognizing that (whether he liked it or not) Jack was back in a team lead slot, he did his due diligence, first checking in with the pilots and then the single support crew member. They were on a straight course to Maryland and would be landing at another private airstrip outside of Fort Meade.

Jack walked back into the cabin as they went wheels up. He felt a tap on his shoulder and turned around.

"What's up, brother?" Jack asked.

Mac looked uncomfortable and shifted his stance a bit.

"You know, when it was just taking down a couple of Russkies in Victory City, that was one thing."

"Don't tell me you're getting cold feet."

"No, it's not that. It's just... I'm good in a gunfight, you know that, but I don't know if I'm set up for this cloak and dagger stuff."

Jack looked hard at his brother.

"You'll do fine. I didn't bring you with me for your good looks. If this turns into what I think it will, I'll need someone who's good in a gunfight, and not afraid to throw a bar stool through a windshield."

Mac smiled.

"I tried to think of something more high speed, but that was all I could come up with at that exact time and place."

Jack gave his brother a pat on the shoulder and then walked past him to where Carrie Davidson was sitting in the rear of the cabin. She had swapped out her army fatigues for a flight suit, which wasn't much of an upgrade, but at least she would stick out a little less.

Carrie had been pouring over her back up log books since they sat down on the plane. The copies weren't as detailed as the originals, but she seemed to think she could pull what she needed from them. She did not notice Jack standing over her.

"It's in there?" Jack asked. Carrie looked up with a start. "This Black Tsar? Are you going to be able to find it?"

"Are you going to be able to keep me alive?"

"If you kick off I will have already been dead for quite a bit," Jack replied.

Carrie didn't seem entirely pleased with this answer, but nodded her acceptance.

"I realized something about McMasters," Carrie said.

"What's that?"

"He didn't know my name. He kept calling me 'Miss'. Same thing with Mac. He only knew his name because you told him."

"He fooled us all."

"But I was trained for this. I was trained to go up against people like him, and I never noticed that he didn't use my name." Carrie shook her head. "But he knew who you were. He knew your name."

Jack thought about this.

"So they must have someone inside."

"More likely, multiple someones," Carrie replied. "Do you know the history of this weapon we're tracking?"

"Yes, Ma'am."

"If this thing went off in the United States, it wouldn't just be a matter of destroying a few cities. It would be the end of life as we know it. Society would break down, markets would crash, the power grid would fail." Carrie paused. "That would create a vacuum that could potentially see Soviet tanks rolling on American soil."

"I have to be honest, Carrie. That sounds a little

far-fetched. Even to someone like me, and I've actually gone up against Soviet agents on two occasions."

"Is it really, though? This isn't about peacocking on the world stage, Jack. This is a death match, and one that the Soviets intend to win at all costs. Jesus Christ, they're starving their own people to keep grain exports up!"

Jack thought about this. She wasn't wrong, even if this scenario seemed too fantastic to believe.

"I assume you know about the split within the KGB?" Carrie asked.

"Tresham told me about it," Jack replied.

"If this agent the Israelis sent in doesn't hit his target and this Colonel Sokolov takes control of the KGB, the odds of this weapon being used rise exponentially."

"So find it before that happens."

Carrie looked down at her log books.

"It's like a puzzle," Carrie said. "I have all the pieces, I just have to put them together."

"But we have a starting point."

Carrie nodded.

"Fort Meade," she said.

"Package for you."

Jack turned around to see the crew member he had met when coming on board. The man handed him a small envelope, and as Jack walked back to his seat, he ripped if open. Inside he found a Walkman and a single cassette tape.

Glenn Campbell: Wichita Lineman.

Jack smiled. It was Mike Tresham, it had to be. He sat down in one of the leather seats and slid the tape into the deck. He put on the headphones and hit play. Ever since they had left Victory City, the ringing in his ears started back up again, louder than ever. At least his hands weren't tremoring, but the damn ringing was enough to drive a man insane.

Then it happened, just like it always did. The first notes flowed into his ears from the headphones, and the ringing stopped. Jack didn't understand what it was about that specific album, but it always stopped the ringing. If he had the tremors, it stopped those too.

That was why he always had it with him.

The Circle Eight Motel
Nashville, Tennessee
December 25, 1980

Anatoly Vitka looked down at the CIA issued identification badge he had been carrying and allowed himself a smile. It was a fake, but it was an excellent fake. None of the three Americans had even asked to see it. They had just accepted his word. If this was how poorly the Central Intelligence Agency was training their field operatives, he would have no problem accomplishing his mission.

Amazingly, the female soldier had turned over all of her log books to him! Anatoly had really had to struggle to not smile when she did that. The reason he had been so happy was that he knew something the Americans did not.

The KGB did not know where the Black Tsar was. The weapon had been shipped to the United States over a decade prior, and in so many pieces that detailed logs were needed to track each component to its final destination. After Vladimir Semichastny was removed from his position as Chairman of the KGB and amidst a concurrent power struggle within the Kremlin, those logs were lost. More likely is that some agent within the KGB destroyed them to prevent a horrible weapon from ever being used.

Anatoly Vitka's task was to find those component pieces, see them re-assembled and prepared for use. He had trained three Directorate S agents to assist him and had already lost one at the hands of this Jack Bonafide. That would not do at all. There were other sleeper agents within the United States that he could call upon for assistance, but Anatoly would wait on that as long as possible. It would reflect poorly upon his record if barely a day into his mission he needed to activate support personnel that were meant to be a last resort.

Vladimir and Miron had been handpicked by

Anatoly himself from the respectable pool of Directorate S agents preparing for deployment, and were it not for the wildcard of Mac Bonafide, Anatoly knew that they would have made their escape from Red River without incident.

Anatoly knew that what happened in Victory City was not their fault. He had met Mac Bonafide, and the tall Texan reminded him of Soviet agents he had known in the past. The ones with shark's eyes who would have to be ground to hamburger to be stopped. If that was what Mac Bonafide required, Anatoly Vitka would oblige him.

Anatoly adjusted the lamp on the desk and wet a finger before flipping another page in the logbooks. Then he saw it. He flipped back again to confirm, but yes, it was there.

As if on cue the door unlatched, and Vladimir and Miron walked in, each man holding a bag of groceries. They'd had quite a time finding a grocer open on Christmas Day, but as the Circle Eight was not exactly a Hilton Hotel, their options for finding food were fairly limited. Vladimir could read the look on Anatoly's face.

"You found it," he said with a smile.

Anatoly could see that there was still some blood staining Ilya's teeth. The ruse of pulling their rear molars had been a painful one, but necessary. If the Americans had harbored any doubt as to the legitimacy of the agent McMasters cover, watching him yank out the men's teeth with the supposed suicide pills in them had put those doubts to rest.

Anatoly nodded.

"Where are we going?" Miron asked.

"Maryland," Anatoly said. "A place called Fort Meade."

CHAPTER 3

Port of Baltimore
Baltimore, Maryland
December 25, 1980

M iles Stevens pulled his hood up and cinched it shut as best he could against the driving winds. They had been battering him relentlessly the entire time he walked the line of ships moored at the Port of Baltimore. At least it wouldn't be snowing this close to the ocean, and for that small favor, Miles was grateful.

The truth was, he really had nothing to be complaining about. As a very junior member of Local 333 he hadn't been pulling much in the way of hours lately. There weren't many to go around to begin with, what with so much traffic bypassing them and going into Norfolk. What hours there were to hand out mostly went to the senior longshoremen.

Except on Christmas. Some senior guys still wanted the time and a half that came with working a holiday (turning into double time if you had already worked an overtime shift) but good luck getting that idea past their wives.

For a junior guy like Miles though, it was high times. No wife, no kids, no problem. So, this was how he found himself walking the docks of the Port of Baltimore after midnight on Christmas Day. There were worse fates.

There wasn't much coming into the port that time of night on a holiday, and as a result there weren't many longshoremen working. The place was quiet and Miles was just on standby in case he was needed. This deal just kept getting better and better. Not only was he going to be pulling more hours in a week than he normally would in a month, but he'd barely have to work to do it.

As he came up to the container stacks, Miles ducked in between them to shield himself from the cutting wind. Not that he minded the wind at all, but he had a hell of a time lighting his cigarette in it.

Miles uncinched the hood of his sweatshirt and then reached inside his Carhart jacket to retrieve his cigarette and lighter. The wind was louder than hell as it blew past the container stacks, and Miles thought about putting in his earplugs for a moment, but then it seemed to calm down.

Yes, the wind was definitely dying down. That was a nice little Christmas present for him. He put the cigarette between his lips and was about to light it when he saw movement out of the corner of his eye.

He stopped. As quietly as he could, he put the cigarette away and turned to where he had seen the movement. Then he heard it. He heard voices. Miles turned back the way he had come and wondered if he should grab the Port Authority Police. For all the good that would do. If Frankie Wiles was even awake on duty Miles would have a hell of a time getting him out of the patrol car in this cold.

Either way, it was unlikely the mafia were back there trying to highjack a shipment of radios. More likely was that a bunch of kids were hiding out and smoking pot. Either way, it wouldn't hurt to roust them.

Miles walked further down the stacks. He wasn't a big man, but he wasn't small either. He stood about five foot ten and two hundred pounds, physically strong from years working on the docks, and from his time as an Airborne Ranger in Vietnam. Miles thought about that a lot, about how maybe he should have stayed in the service. He'd be a Staff Sergeant by now, at least. He'd also know what in the hell was ahead of him, instead of being left at the mercy of the union.

Now he heard the voices, talking quietly but not whispering, and he could see shadows moving. Someone was definitely back there, but they weren't speaking English. What in the hell language was that?

Just as Miles rounded the corner, it clicked. He recognized the language from a brief training class he'd had at Fort Benning.

It was Russian. They were speaking Russian.

There were at least a dozen of them. They were all dressed in black, carrying what looked like carbines and pistols as well as other gear.

They froze.

"You've got to be fucking kidding me," Miles gasped.

The man closest to him stepped forward, drawing a knife from its scabbard. He had identified Miles as an easy target. A man who could be overwhelmed by violence of action and subdued with little fuss.

He was wrong.

Miles stepped into the attack and threw a punch to the Russian's throat, then grabbed his wrist and broke it with a sickening snap. In the process he snatched the knife and drove it into the man's face, just below his left eye.

"Stop!" a man with a deep voice said. This man held up both his hands. "My name is Arkady. You do not have to die here."

Miles took a step back and brandished the knife in

an overhand grip. He looked to the pistol and carbine at the dead man's feet. Why in the hell hadn't he grabbed one of them? Would he have time to snatch them now?

He saw that the rest of the men were at the ready behind this Arkady character. There was no way Miles could get to the weapons. They would shoot him before he even got close.

"What is your name?" Arkady asked, taking a step forward.

"Eat shit!" Miles spat.

Arkady smiled. This man was not just some dock worker. He was a warrior.

"You're a soldier?" Arkady asked.

Miles said nothing.

"I see," Arkady continued. "I would do no different. But I am telling you that your death here will change nothing. Just put your weapon down and we can come to an arrangement."

"I don't think so," Miles said coldly, taking a step forward.

"My friend, you cannot kill all of us."

"I can damn sure try," Miles said, and without warning lunged forward.

Arkady didn't move, as he knew that a round from one of the suppressed pistols behind him would find its mark, and it did. The longshoreman collapsed to the ground.

"That was unfortunate," Arkady said.

Two of the men were already moving to relocate the body into the shipping container they had arrived in. Colonel Arkady Radovich squeezed his eyes shut and opened them again. The Soviet Alpha Group commander was tired, but he knew there would be no sleep in his future.

The voyage up from Buenos Aires had not been as restful as he hoped it would be, as a bout of dysentery had taken its toll on both himself and his men. Not that it mattered much, as it would do nothing to change the outcome of their mission.

One man walked out of the container as the others passed him with the body of Miles Stevens. This man had been working the satellite phone and relaying messages to and from command.

"We have a change of plans," Marat said as he approached his commander with the communique. "We have to send a detachment to Texas."

This caused Arkady to raise an eyebrow.

"Texas?" He asked. "That's where this agent they are so concerned about is from."

Marat nodded.

"It would seem his wife is there and may be useful if we need leverage."

"I am feeling," Arkady said. "That our friends in the Kremlin have already decided we may fail."

"Comrade Vitka and his men were unsuccessful," Marat went on, referencing the man who was going by the name McMasters. "Whoever the Central Intelligence Agency has tracking the Black Tsar seems to be rather formidable."

"Hm," Arkady grunted as he took the sheet of paper and read the encoded message. "We will see about that. I know Vitka was deployed by Comrade Makar Galkin."

"It is a strange thing," Marat replied.

"What is that?" Arkady asked.

Marat shrugged.

"To have these two rival factions within our own intelligence network. Now we are going against our own people?"

"Makar Galkin wants a different Soviet State, a more Western one. A kinder one." Comrade Sokolov, our commander, wants to go in the other direction. We must ensure he wins out."

Marat nodded his understanding.

"Who should we send?" Marat asked. "I imagine two men to be enough."

Arkady looked at Marat and held his gaze.

"I see," Marat said.

"Take Nestor with you."

Marat turned to where Nestor was preparing his gear with the other men.

"He will not like it. He is hungry for action."

"I care not what Nestor is hungry for," Arkady said coldly. "Those are your orders."

"Yes, Comrade Colonel."

The Terrace View Motel
Baltimore, Maryland
December 27, 1980

Jack Bonafide stood in the parking lot of the Terrace View Motel and watched the traffic go by on West Lafayette Street. He'd only been in Baltimore for a day, and he already didn't think much of the place. Granted, he was in one of the worst parts of the city, but Jack figured you could tell a lot about a place by dropping in on its worst neighborhood.

When they hit the tarmac outside of Fort Meade Jack had wanted to just charge in like the proverbial light brigade. Truth to tell, he was still sore about the way McMasters (or whoever the hell he really was) had fooled him. No way could Jack let something like that stand.

Carrie Davidson had been the voice of reason, convincing him they needed to set up a base of operations and develop an action plan before moving forward. She considered it to be highly unlikely that the Soviets would make a beeline right for Fort Meade. If they were any kind of skilled tacticians, they would need to set up shop before making a serious move. Considering that they had gone to all the trouble of getting into the country inside of body bags, it was unlikely they would take any unnecessary risks.

The more Jack thought about it, the more he realized it was a good thing to have Carrie along for the ride. Both him and his brother Mac had a bad habit of wading into any mess they found with guns blazing and fists swinging. On more than one occasion that had been a mistake.

Jack pulled his trucker hat a little lower over his eyes and watched the gang bangers down the street selling drugs out of the parking lot of the adjacent motel. Personally, Jack couldn't give two shits if these guys wanted to sling some crack on West Lafayette, but he did care if they started drawing unwanted attention.

"This place sucks," Mac said as he walked across the parking lot and lit a cigarette. "I want to go back to Texas."

"Everyone wants to go back to Texas," Jack replied. "Even folks that have never been there before. They just don't know it yet."

Mac laughed at this and offered his brother a cigarette.

Jack looked at it for a moment and then shook his head. He'd noticed lately that anything other than water, meat and vegetables seemed to make the ringing in his ears worse and bring on the tremors. Especially cigarettes and alcohol. He figured it had something to do with the same mechanism that caused alcohol to make you tipsy.

"What are these shit heads up to?" Mac asked, gesturing to the gang members down the street.

"Things shit heads do," Jack replied. "Just dealing and pimping. None of our business."

"Hm," Mac grunted. "I'll tell you what we don't have in Texas. Fucking drug dealers on every corner."

"Give it five years," Jack replied. "We'll get around to it. Texas ain't special, we're just slower on the uptake."

"Blasphemy," Mac said with a smile. "Anyway, the sooner we can wrap this up the better. I left an open beer on the bar at Dutch's."

"We're trying to track down a hydrogen bomb that could probably evaporate this whole city," Jack said. "Not cook an egg."

Mac stared at the men down the street, and one finally took notice of him. He stopped and stared back.

"Think I could whip him?" Mac asked, indicating his counterpart.

Jack grabbed his brother by the shoulder and spun him around.

"Get your fucking head in the game!" Jack snapped. "Are you seriously about to start a fight with a gang member you've never met? What in the hell is wrong with you?"

At first Mac looked angry, but then his eyes changed, and he seemed hurt.

"Nothing's wrong with me," Mac replied. "Shit, Jack. You know how it is. You know how I am."

"I brought you with us, I fought to bring you with us because I thought you could help. You did help back in Victory City. We wouldn't have gotten this far if it weren't for what you did," Jack said. "But if you're still pulling the same old shit, you need to tell me right now so you can pack your ass back to Texas."

Mac's reflex was to push back, and Jack could see it winding up behind the man's eyes. Then Mac did something Jack had never seen him do before. Mac Bonafide pulled in a deep breath, held it and then let it go. He had thought about the situation instead of just snapping.

"I'm sorry, brother," Mac said and shook his head. "You're right. I guess this has been a problem for a long time. I'm still acting like I'm on the football field in high school, or runnin' and gunnin' in the A Shau valley. It's time to grow up. That's what you're saying, right?"

Jack felt badly for his brother, but not bad about what he'd said. Those words had been a long time coming, and he was probably the only man alive (besides their father) who could deliver them without risking a serious beating.

"You know what I always think about when I get pulled into something like this?" Jack asked. "You know what keeps me going in the right direction, what I think about? I think about cities burning. I think about Soviet tanks rolling across East Texas. I think about a war that would make World War Two look like a fight in a sandbox. I think about all the things folks always say could never happen. You know why they don't happen? Because we hold the fucking line. Men like you and me and the old man."

"I hear you," Mac said.

"So, yeah, it's time to grow up. Because if you want to hold the line you've got to be a grown ass man with big fucking balls."

Jack held his steely gaze for a moment and then burst out laughing.

"You're a son of a bitch," Mac said, taking another draw off of his cigarette, but the message had been received.

"And then some," Jack replied and looked back out to the road. "I've got to go out to Fort Meade to run some recon, see what kind of security protocols we're dealing with so we can find this thing."

"Mind if I ask you something?" Mac asked, and Jack could tell he was a little self-conscious about whatever was on his mind.

"Shoot."

"Look, like you said, I'm good in a gunfight, and I'm not too skinny on tactics neither but..."

"You're not sure what we're doing."

Mac nodded.

"There's a lot of moving parts here, brother. That's why it was important to bring Carrie along. The myth of the super spy who can handle it all himself is just that, a myth. That's why we have a team." Jack thought about how to best phrase it. "Three shipments went out of Red River that were traced back to the Soviets. We don't know if it was the Reds themselves handling this or contract smugglers. Either way, whatever those shipments were, they will probably lead us to wherever this Black Tsar is."

"Got it."

"Hey Mac, nothing's changed. I'm the scalpel and you're the hammer."

Mac smiled at this. He knew that was the way it had always been. In his younger days he had misinterpreted it to mean that folks thought he wasn't very bright, but now he understood that the hammer was necessary, as was the scalpel.

"Can you keep an eye on Carrie?" Jack asked, not wanting his brother to feel like he wasn't being included.

"Sure thing," Mac said and headed back to the hotel room.

Jack looked down the street at where the gang bangers were still hanging out. The man that Mac had been exchanging glances with was still watching him. Jack couldn't put his finger on it but there was something wrong there, something more than the usual tough guy bravado.

Carrie Davidson sat at the small, cheap desk inside of the small, cheap motel room and wrote in her notebook as she continued trying to put the pieces together. She knew that they were out on their own on this one, and she also understood why it had to be that way. All the same, she wouldn't have minded some support from Langley right about then.

She was good with the numbers, no question about that, but she lacked something that it was quickly becoming clear they needed a heavy dose of. She wasn't any good at thinking outside of the box. The thing about numbers is that they need a place to be, and that place is inside the box, all lined up in pretty rows. Numbers on their own, though, they mean little. They just point you in a direction.

Carrie stared at the numbers and then realized she wasn't seeing them anymore. She was just seeing his face, the face of the man she had shot at Red River. There was something in his eyes, something she had seen the moment that the bullets hit him. Those eyes had changed. They became filled with terror. Perhaps because he was then staring into the darkness, and something was staring back at him.

She set her pen down and then looked at her hand.

It was shaking. Carrie took a deep breath and tried to still it. It was shaking that same way when she took aim at the man in the hallway at Red River, and she had said a silent prayer that it wouldn't interfere too much with her aim, because if it did that man would surely turn and gun her down. In that moment she had briefly wondered what it would feel like to die. Would it hurt? Would she bleed out slowly on the floor in agony, or would it be like some people say, like slipping into a warm bath and going to sleep?

Then she had pulled the trigger, and her rounds hit their mark. It wasn't like on the range. It wasn't like anyone said it would be. It also wasn't like she imagined it would be. She didn't feel like she was striking a blow for democracy and whittling away at the red horde. No, it didn't feel like that at all. It felt like she was killing someone's son. Someone's son who had just been born in the wrong place at the wrong time.

Carrie focused her eyes again, pushing the image of the man out of her head. She returned to the numbers. They made sense. They were simple. They stayed in their boxes. They knew their place.

The door opened, and she looked up. Mac entered the room and shut the door behind him.

"Jack's heading out to run recon at Fort Meade."

Carrie nodded. She looked at Mac for a moment and then back to the logbooks.

"What's eatin' you?" Mac asked.

How does he know? Carrie thought to herself.

"I'm fine," Carrie said.

Mac sat down on the edge of the bed.

"None of us know how long this will take," Mac said. "I ain't sayin' we have to write each other love letters and take long walks on the beach together, but it would probably be good if we could talk to each other."

Carrie had another protest chambered, but then relented. She knew he meant well. Even though the two had gotten off to a rocky start, she trusted Mac Bonafide, maybe even in a way that she didn't yet trust his brother.

"You've killed people, right?" Carrie asked.

Mac nodded solemnly.

"Maybe more than I'd care to count."

"Do you ever think about it? About them?"

"I do. I think if a man never thinks about the other men he's killed, maybe something's wrong with him."

"I've been thinking a lot about the man at Red River, the one I shot."

"The one who was going to shoot Jack," Mac clarified.

"Yes. I just... I just keep seeing his eyes. The look in his eyes when I shot him, when he knew he was going to die."

Mac thought about this for a moment.

"You know, this is the part where I'm supposed to say it was you or him. Or that he was the bad guy, and you were the good guy... or girl or whatever. That's all probably true, but it won't make you feel any better. You know how old I was when I killed my first man?"

Carrie shook her head.

"Thirteen." Mac paused for a moment. "I drove my daddy's truck out to Dutch's to pick up my mom from her shift waiting tables. I was already damn near six feet tall by then, and most folks didn't pay much mind to a grown boy driving his father's truck. Wasn't even much law back then. She was already in the parking lot waiting for me, smoking her Virginia Slims. She loved those things."

Carrie laughed.

"My mom too," she said.

Mac smiled.

"When I drove up to meet her, some bar fly was trying to talk to her. Looked like he was just being a pest, so she didn't pay him much mind. Then she saw me pulling up and started to walk away. He grabbed her by the shoulder and when she tried to shake him off, she slipped and fell. Hit her head real hard on a parked car. It was raining," Mac said. "I remember the rain. I don't remember anything else. Next thing I know I was sitting in the truck with my father. I was crying and looking at my hands. They were covered in blood. My daddy pulled a bottle of Old Grandad out of the glove box and made me take a belt.

"I looked at him and I remember him glaring at me.

He told me to stop my crying, because that son of a bitch got what he had coming, and if I didn't give it to him someone else would have."

There was only silence for a moment. Carrie didn't know what to say.

"I don't have many nightmares," Mac said. "In fact, I don't dream at all. When I do, though, I never have nightmares about all the men I killed in Vietnam or in Central America. I think about that man, but I can't see his face. I see everything else, but where his face should be, it's just a black hole. So I guess what I'm trying to say is that there's really no trick to getting past it. Even the bad ones, the ones that really need killing, the ones you feel good about after you put them down, they still stay with you."

Fort George G. Meade, Maryland
December 27, 1980

Jack was not pleased with Agent Scarn being his point of contact for this job. It was nothing personal, Jack just felt the man was overly aggressive with them on the tarmac back in Texarkana. There was only room for one bull at this rodeo, and that bull was Jack Bonafide. Agent Scarn would have to get used to that and understand he wasn't the lead on this mission. He would have to eat as much shit as Jack could shovel, and if he didn't like it, he could go pound sand.

So far, Agent Scarn seemed to get it. When Jack called in to check on new credentials, Agent Scarn had told him that his previously issued DOD cover was still intact, and there was no need to change it up. Jack couldn't think of any reason this wouldn't be true, so he stayed the course with his assistant to the Secretary of Defense guise.

Not only that, they would pull the same ruse to get him into Fort Meade that they had used at Red River. A standard meet and greet with some high-ranking brass. Granted, there was a lot more brass on board Fort Meade than there had been at Red River, so his title wouldn't be quite as dazzling, but it would still get the job done.

Scarn had called ahead that Jack was coming, so it would be easy enough to get in. Not only that, they could use the actual reason he was there; checking into some shipments that had gone missing from Red River.

Jack sat in the rented car and tapped his fingers on the steering wheel as he watched the front gate. The soldiers on duty were checking people in, car after car full of soldiers and government contractors reporting for duty.

Then it started. The ringing. It was easy for him to miss it at first, but then it started getting louder. That high-pitched ringing in his left ear. Even once it got going, it was easy enough to ignore, but Jack also knew that it would herald other problems like the tremoring in his hands and eventually the headaches.

Jack pulled the copy of Wichita Lineman out of his inside jacket pocket and slid it into the tape deck. He went to turn the key and then stopped. He squeezed his eyes shut and then opened them again. His chest. There was a tightness in his chest.

"Shit," Jack whispered.

It was getting worse. He touched his sternum. He took a deep breath but couldn't. He was having a heart attack.

"You're not having a fucking heart attack," Jack said to himself.

Yes, you are, his brain said back. *People your age almost never die of a heart attack, but it has to happen to someone. Maybe you're the one.*

"I'm not fucking dying," Jack said.

He turned the key to the on position and hit play on the tape deck.

You're definitely dying. They're going to find you in this car. Angeline will never know what happened to you. The mission will fail, and all of those people will die because of you.

Jack started to hyperventilate, the tightness in his chest increasing as his breathing sped up. He looked at himself in the mirror, slowed his breathing down and rubbed his chest.

"You're fine. You're fucking fine. You're fine. You're fine."

This had only happened once before. It was after they served him the divorce papers from Angeline, the same ones he never signed. Now it was happening again. Was this some trend? Was this going to happen more often?

Jack stared at himself in the mirror, slowing his breathing down until finally the tightness in his chest reduced. A few more minutes and he felt mostly normal. He wiped some sweat from his brow.

"This is not the time to fall apart."

It seemed to stop. Jack still felt that his head was fuzzy, but the panic disappeared. He squeezed his eyes shut again and then opened them.

Shit, he thought to himself. *I'm hallucinating.*

The wave continued to subside, and then he realized that he wasn't hallucinating.

"It can't be."

It was McMasters, in the car at the gate being checked in. Jack looked at the line of vehicles and knew that he would lose him if he tried to drive in, so he jumped out of the vehicle and made his way across the road to the main gate beside the vehicle entrance. The soldier in the booth saw him coming and stepped out.

Jack watched as they passed McMasters through. The Russian spy hadn't seen Jack Bonafide coming, and that was a good thing. Jack didn't need to take him down, he needed to know where he was going and what he was after.

"Can I help you, sir?" The soldier asked.

Jack pulled out his credentials and flashed them to the guard, who waved him through. That explained how McMasters could get through the gate so easily. Security was not nearly as tight as it should be, particularly considering that this base housed the National Security Agency.

On the other side of the gate Jack saw a group of soldiers clustered around a Jeep and observed that one of them was wearing captain's bars.

"Captain!" Jack called out, getting the man's attention. He held up his DOD credentials. "You're on me. Let's go. We're taking that Jeep."

The Captain had initially tried to ask some questions, but Jack shut him down and instead gave clear instruction to follow the Crown Victoria sedan that had just pulled through the gate. It was clearly making a beeline for Savage Road, where the NSA buildings were located.

Is this guy's cover really good enough to get him in the building? Jack thought to himself. *Shit, I'm not sure mine is good enough for that.*

Jack thought back to all the surveillance and counter-surveillance skill development they had done during Operator Training Course for Delta. At the time, he hadn't really understood why they were doing so much of it, but he had trusted Colonel Beckwith and trusted that the old soldier had a plan.

Now it was paying off. Jack knew how far to hang back so he wouldn't tip off McMasters and how to take advantage of the Captain's knowledge of the base to use side roads to keep track of him.

After what had happened at Red River and what was now happening at what should have been one of the most secure installations in the country, Jack privately wondered if they needed a complete tear down and rebuilding of their security protocols for military installations? Who would he even bring that to? Tresham? Jack knew that Dick Marcinko had been making noises about doing something like that on Naval bases. Once again, the old SEAL was ahead of the curve.

As they neared the main NSA building, Jack watched McMasters pull up to the exterior checkpoint. He knew that this one would be more serious; he wouldn't be getting waved through with a wink and a nod. These were contract security officers. This didn't mean that they were better than the Army soldiers at the front gate, they were just different. They had different training and looked for different things.

"Pull into the parking lot," Jack said, pointing to a parking lot just outside of the perimeter fence.

The Captain complied and parked the Jeep, but kept the engine running.

"What are we doing, sir?"

Jack didn't answer as he watched McMasters talking to the security officer, while a second man walked around the vehicle with a mirror, scanning the undercarriage. The first security officer laughed. Apparently, McMasters was funny. He was a funny Russian spy.

"Kill the engine," Jack said. He knew that a vehicle sitting in the parking lot outside of the NSA building with its engine running was sure to draw attention. "Get on the net with the security force and tell them to stand up QRF."

"QRF?" the Captain asked. "Are we under attack?"

"Not yet, and I aim to see it stays that way."

Jack hopped out of the Jeep and walked to the security checkpoint. So much for this just being a recon mission.

The Terrace View Motel
Baltimore, Maryland
December 27, 1980

Carrie Davidson stepped out of the motel room and into the cool afternoon air. They had gotten lucky. Normally it would be freezing in Baltimore this time of year. It wouldn't just be freezing, it would chill a man or a woman to the bone. For whatever reason though, the temperature was fairly high.

Mac had opted to take a short nap on the floor of the motel room. Carrie offered him the bed, but he seemed more comfortable on the threadbare carpet. *To each his own,* she thought.

She walked across the parking lot and out to the sidewalk where she lit her cigarette. It was an old habit of hers, walking as far from any domicile as she could before lighting up. She took a deep inhale and then let it roll out through her nostrils. Carrie looked at the cigarette and shook her head.

It had been twelve weeks since her last one, and she had been going strong until Red River, until the Bonafide brothers showed up. Now it was like she never quit. Maybe killing a man did that to a person? Perhaps it was something about getting a little closer to death herself that helped reconcile what she had done.

He was a Russian spy, she told herself. *You just did unto him before he had a chance to do unto you.*

Carrie looked up from her cigarette and saw him. He was staring at her from down the street, from behind cold blue eyes. His jaw was clenched. He looked like the typical Baltimore gangbanger. Even if he wasn't, he was probably up to no good. Carrie had noticed the prostitutes in the parking lot down the street, and she suspected this man also had some crack rocks in the back of his mouth or in his pocket if he was bold.

She broke eye contact and walked back to the room.

Fort George G. Meade, Maryland
December 27, 1980

Jack approached the gate and pulled out his DOD credentials. The security officer on point held up an open palm, indicating that Jack should stop, or bad things may happen to him. Jack wisely complied.

"SECDEF?" The security officer asked doubtfully. It wasn't that he disbelieved Jack's credentials, but more that they were not expecting him or anyone from the Secretary of Defense's office. "They normally give us a heads up when you guys are coming, sir."

"I know, it's a bit of a mess," Jack said. "We're supposed to be touring every installation each quarter, and they sent me here. All I really need to do is walk around and press the flesh. You know the drill."

"Yes, sir. I'll just call in to the supervisor on shift and let him know you're coming."

Jack watched McMasters entering the building as the security officer called it in. Time was running short and Jack knew it, but he also knew that if he tried to rush this process, it would raise alarms.

The security officer hung up the phone and hit the trigger to open the gate. He waved Jack through.

Jack had always thought Fort Meade was a strange place with its mix of military, government workers and civilian contractors. The inside of the NSA building was a testament to that. The security officer at the front desk waved him over and Jack presented his identification to him.

"Let me get the officer on duty for you, sir," the security officer said as he picked up the phone. Jack held up a hand to stop him.

"Actually, I'd rather not make a fuss. Ideally, I'm in and out," Jack said with a wink. The security officer smiled his understanding and hung up the phone. "A man just came through here in a beige overcoat and thick black-framed glasses. I'm pretty sure he's a buddy of mine from my Eighty Second Airborne days. Can you tell me where he went?"

"He went to records room C, sir," the security officer responded and gestured down the hallway and to the left.

"Thank you," Jack said and headed through the checkpoint.

Jack thought for a moment about the fact that he was unarmed, but the truth was that he was never really unarmed. It was also highly unlikely that McMasters would be carrying a weapon. Getting into this building was quite a feat in itself, but getting in with a firearm? No way.

The records room corridor was fairly quiet, and relatively close to the entrance. This made sense as many people would come from other departments to request records, and it wouldn't do to have them running all over the building. At the end of the corridor Jack saw the signage for room C. He made his way to the door and then stopped. He looked around. There was no one in sight, but he also didn't know the composition of the room. From the spacing of the doors in the corridor he guessed it would be fairly large.

He reached out and slowly turned the doorknob. It clicked, and he opened the door. The room was indeed large, with long shelves that held rows of manila file folders. The way the shelves were set up made it impossible to get a clear read on the room. Jack stood beside the door doing a quick survey and guessed it was about twelve hundred square feet. Being as quiet as possible he closed the door, but the click of the lock catching sounded like thunder.

"What do you Americans call a man like you,

Jack?" a voice called out. "I believe the expression is a bad penny?"

It was McMasters. Jack hurried between two of the shelves, keeping his eye on the door.

"Been called worse than that."

McMasters laughed. He was moving. This guy wasn't some amateur. He wasn't going to let Jack pinpoint him by the sound of his voice.

"You know, I didn't think a whole lot of you or your nitwit brother after what happened in Texas," McMasters said. Jack knew that the Soviet was trying to get his goat. "But now, I have to say I'm impressed. Though your counter-surveillance skills could use some work. I saw you back on the road there, following me in the Jeep."

"Maybe I can take a correspondence course."

Jack tried to look through the open spaces between the file folders on the shelves, but he saw nothing. He looked back to the door and focused on it, trying to pinpoint McMasters with his hearing.

"Might be a little late in the game for that." He was moving again, but Jack could tell that he was somewhere to his right. "Seeing as we're in the fourth quarter. Did I use that analogy correctly? American sports always were my weak point."

Jack started moving. It wouldn't do to set himself up as an easy target. He walked around a corner and into another row of shelves, careful to still keep his eyes on the door. There was a good six-inch gap in each shelf between the top of the folders and the next shelf, but still he saw nothing.

"Depends on the sport, I reckon."

"I love it!" McMasters shouted. "American cowboy talk, right? I mean, I reckon?"

Holy shit this guy is out of his mind, Jack thought to himself.

"How about I give you an American cowboy ass whippin'? What do you think about that?"

"Did you know that Stalin was a big fan of American Westerns?" McMasters was moving again. "But not the ones with John Wayne."

"What the hell do you have against John Wayne?" Jack asked.

"Stalin thought his attitude was a direct threat to Communism," McMasters replied. "So, we tried to kill him."

Jack stopped.

"Bullshit."

"No, it's true," McMasters said. Jack thought he saw movement, but it was nothing. He turned again and walked. "In nineteen fifty-three."

Jack stopped. There was a logic to Jack's conversation. If he could keep McMasters talking, he could eventually pinpoint him.

"I think you're pullin' my leg."

No answer. Jack turned in time to see the movement. An object lashed out at him from the six-inch space at the top of the shelf, and he felt a searing pain in his right shoulder. Despite the assault Jack moved toward his attacker, reaching through folders where McMasters should have been, but he came up with nothing.

"Carbon fiber blade, Jack," McMasters called out, now in a different place. "Metal detectors don't pick them up."

Jack did a quick check of the shoulder wound. It was just a nick.

"Good on you," Jack said, and began moving toward the back of the room. "You sure seem to know a lot about me."

"Wondering about that, are you?" McMasters asked, his voice seeming to move through the shelves faster than Jack would have thought possible, almost like an echo. "Starting to think we might have a mole inside the CIA?"

"Thought crossed my mind," Jack replied.

"I'm sorry to inform you it's nothing as dramatic as that, there isn't just one mole feeding us information. It's just how the business goes. There are no secrets, Jack. Not like the ones you kept from Angeline about your work with Delta."

What the hell? Jack thought. How did McMasters know his wife's name?

The door clicked open and Jack turned his head to

the right, ready to pivot and go after McMasters. Instead of seeing McMasters heading out, he saw someone walking in. Just some staff member with his nose in a folder as he closed the door behind him.

"Get out of here!" Jack shouted. "Now!"

The man looked up, terror on his face, but it was too late. McMasters was on him in a second, the black blade of his carbon fiber knife to the man's throat.

"If you move, he dies," McMasters said calmly. He slid the tip of the blade an inch across the man's neck, drawing some blood, just to show his resolve. "You know I will."

Jack slowly held up both hands.

"What's your name, son?" McMasters asked.

"Jacob, Jacob Finley," he said, his voice stuttering.

"Well, Jacob. This is a big day for you. You've just met your first Russian spy. You know what that means, right, Jacob?"

"Yes."

"Good." McMasters turned his focus back to Jack. "It's decision time, Jack. You can save his life, or you can take me down. Just like in a western cowboy movie."

"There's no way you're getting out of this building."

"I disagree," McMasters replied curtly. "You see, that's why you're going to lose, Jack. That's why this whole country will lose. Do you know why that is?"

"Enlighten me, asshole."

"Because you lack resolve," McMasters reached down and nicked Jacob Finley's wrist with the blade and then put it to the man's eye. "That was Mister Finely's radial artery. He has about thirty seconds until he bleeds out and then he's dead. Now it's twenty-five."

Jack started to move, and McMasters nicked the flesh below Jacob's eye.

"I'll take it out. I'll take his eye out, Jack." Jack stopped. "So, like I said, it's decision time. Apply a tourniquet with your belt and save his life or take me down."

McMasters shoved Jacob into Jack, turned and calmly exited the room.

Jack caught Jacob and laid him down on the floor as he pulled off the man's belt and applied a hasty tourniquet. A voice in the back of his head kept telling him that this was the wrong move, that he should let this man die and apprehend McMasters, but he couldn't do it. The Delta operator in him kept telling him he could do both, that there would be enough time.

"You're going to be fine, but I have to go."

"Don't leave me," Jacob said weakly. The man was very, very pale. Jack wasn't sure if he had told Jacob the truth. His blood was everywhere.

Jack stood back up and reached for the door to pull it open, but it was jammed. McMasters had done something to it.

"Son of a bitch!"

Stepping back, Jack launched his size twelve into the space to the left of the handle and after three hard kicks finally stepped back, got a running start and threw his shoulder into it like he was back on the football field at Texas High School.

The door cracked open, and right away Jack could see why it had was jammed. McMasters had broken the doorknob off. Jack ran down the hallway toward the front door but didn't see the Soviet anywhere. Instead he caught the attention of the security officer at the front desk, who was already on his walkie and going for his weapon.

"DOD!" Jack shouted and held up both hands.

CHAPTER 4

The Terrace View Motel
Room 6
Baltimore, Maryland
December 27, 1980

Mac Bonafide stood at the window of the small motel room and pushed aside the curtain to see into the parking lot. It was the same show they had been watching all day. Drug dealers and pimps across the street, traffic driving by and not much of anything else.

"Where the hell is he?" Mac asked. "He was just supposed to run some recon, but that was hours ago."

"I'm sure he's fine," Carrie said, leaning back in her chair and rubbing her forehead.

She had been scanning the log books for hours gathering clues, but everything kept pointing back to the same answer. The Black Tsar was already in the country and probably had been for years. No shipments big enough to contain the weapon (even in pieces) had come through Red River from the suspected Soviet pipeline.

This made sense. If there was one thing the Soviets knew how to do, it was play the long game. The CIA may never know how the Soviets had smuggled most of the weapon into the country. Yet they had gone to great pains to smuggle in one last piece, and whatever it was it wasn't very big, which ruled out it being another Soviet agent in a body bag.

They knew that the tamper that would dramatically increase the yield of the weapon was removed in the USSR when the project was shelved. That had to be it. The item they were tracking had to be the tamper. This brought to mind a sobering thought. If they were going to such great lengths to get this tamper into the country, that must mean someone intended to use it.

"I don't like this," Mac said. He closed the curtain and turned back to Carrie.

There were three loud bangs on the door. Mac turned to look at it and then back to Carrie. She shook her head. Jack wouldn't be knocking on the door.

Mac looked out the peephole and then back to Carrie.

"Who is it?" She whispered.

"I think it's a pro," Mac answered.

"Please let me in!" A woman's voice shouted from outside. "He gonna kill me!"

"No!" Carrie insisted. "This is not why we're here."

"I can't just leave her out there," Mac protested. "What if she's in real trouble?"

"Then she should go to the police."

Mac stared hard at Carrie for a moment and then opened the door. A woman ran in. She was clearly one of the prostitutes they had seen working down the street. She flattened herself against the wall and looked at Mac.

"I saw you, before," she said. "Looking at Richie. You a cop or something?"

"I ain't a cop," Mac said. "But we'll help you call one."

"Shit," Carrie said as she looked through the open door.

The same man she had seen staring at her from down the street earlier was now walking toward them. He wasn't quite as tall as Mac, but he was at least a sturdy six foot two. He wore his long hair pulled back in a ponytail and Carrie would bet dollars to donuts he had a pistol shoved in his belt beneath the baggy pullover he wore.

"Close the door!" The woman shouted.

Mac saw him as well. He thought about closing the

door but figured there wasn't much point. So instead he stepped into the doorway.

The man stopped at the door and smiled.

"Good afternoon, sir," he said and then turned to Carrie. "Ma'am."

"Afternoon," Mac replied. His pistol was sitting on the table beside the window, out of sight but not out of reach.

"I seem to have misplaced my property. I think it may be in your room, if you would be so kind as to return it."

"There's just a woman in here, and I reckon she ain't your property."

The man maintained his smile.

"I'm sorry, where are my manners?" he said. "My name is Clarence. I work over there down the street. You folks aren't from around here, are you?"

"Not last I checked."

"Ah, I see. So you don't know where you are. See, you're just down the street from Lexington Terrace, and over at Lexington Terrace we have what some folks call a bit of gang problem. Though it's only really a problem if you don't live there, in my opinion."

"I got no problem with you," Mac said. "But you can't have her. So have yourself a little come to Jesus moment with that and then be on your way."

Clarence's smile faded.

"I'm trying to help you. Trying to help both of you,

but if you act in a disrespectful way toward me, I can't render said help."

"We don't have a problem here," Mac repeated. "Unless you make one."

Clarence stared at the tall Texan for a moment and then took a step back. Mac slowly reached to his right and wrapped his fingers around the grip of the Colt 1911. Carrie was ready to dive behind the bed if they started shooting.

Clarence smiled again.

"I'll see you soon, cowpoke," he said as he walked backward away from the room. "I'll see you real soon."

Mac closed the door and worked the deadbolt.

"Are you kidding me with this?" Carrie nearly shouted. "We're trying to— to do what we're doing and now we're in a fucking gang war?"

She had stopped herself from referencing the Black Tsar after remembering there was a prostitute in the room with them.

The girl remained silent. Carrie turned to her.

"What's your name, miss?"

"Charice," she mumbled.

"You want to call the police?"

"We can't call the police," Carrie said. "Even if we wanted to. They're going to ask too many questions."

"We can't leave either," Mac said. "Jack's coming back here, and even if we left a note or something there are no guarantees he'd find it."

"Then she has to go," Carrie said.

"Please don't send me back out there!" Charice pleaded. "He will kill me. He'll slit my throat and leave me on Lafayette Street. He will."

Carrie could be cold. It was a trait that had served her well in life and allowed her to make the decisions others didn't have the stomach for. This time though, this time was different. She could see it in the girl's eyes, she could see that she wasn't exaggerating. If they sent her back out there, that man Clarence would cut her throat.

"Fine," Carrie said. "But Jack better get back here soon, or this motel room will turn into the Alamo."

Mac pushed the curtain aside and looked out into the parking lot. He saw a short man in a bulky jacket walk to within fifty feet of their door and then just stand there.

"I agree."

Fort George G. Meade, Maryland
December 27, 1980

Jack Bonafide was embarrassed. He had screwed up, and he had screwed up big time. It wasn't a feeling he was used to. When he had started in Delta, Jack quickly acquired the nickname "Tex", which he didn't think was very original, but unfortunately it stuck. Then another guy showed up whose wife had actually stitched a miniature Texas flag to the back of his jean jacket, so naturally the nickname transferred to him.

After losing his nickname, Jack needed another one and became "Slick". They called Jack Bonafide "Slick" because he always did everything right the first time. He knew that he had probably inherited this ability from the same place his cousin Roarke had. Roarke also served with the Army but was quite a bit older than Jack and had fought in Africa during the Second World War. Roarke was known for being able to pick up any weapon from any country, disassemble and assemble it and fire it accurately with no training.

Jack had the same talent for weapons and tactics. He always set the perfect breaching charge, got his rounds on target and could run the most complex close quarters battle drills just like he was ringing a bell.

Not this time, though. First McMasters fooled him back in Texas and now he'd been on the ground in Maryland not twenty-four hours and had already blown his cover. None of the security staff or NSA people milling around him knew that. They all thought he was a legitimate assistant to the Secretary of Defense, but Jack knew. He knew he had screwed the pooch big time.

"What part of 'ghost operative' was unclear, Jack?"

Mike Tresham asked, repeating the words he had spoken back in the motel room outside of Fort Bragg. "I've got a pizza that's been in my refrigerator longer than you've been working for the CIA and you've already almost outed yourself in the middle of the freaking NSA building!"

"I'm sorry, sir," Jack said. "It won't happen again."

There was silence on the line.

"Look, Jack," Mike said. "I'm not nearly as concerned about this slip as I am that you're having trouble recovering from it. No bullshit. Tell me right now if you can't hack it. There's no shame in stepping down if you know you're out of your depth."

Mike Tresham's word choice was no accident. He knew exactly what to do to send Jack Bonafide on the warpath.

"I'm fine, sir."

"Are you sure?"

"I'm fine," Jack said again, more insistently this time.

"Good," Mike said. "You did the right thing, sounding the alarm like you did. We almost had that son of a bitch, and if we can grab him that will be quite a coup. What do we know so far?"

"The NSA staffers are going through the files to figure out what he took, and they told me they have duplicates of everything in a sub-basement. Once they grab those, I'll head back to the hotel and rendezvous with my team."

"That was a smart move, by the way. Bringing Mac along like you did."

"Thank you, sir. I thought he could be useful."

"I agree, but you do understand he'll have to go home once this is over."

"I do." Jack paused for a moment and then changed the subject. "Sir, McMasters said something strange when we were in the records room."

"What's that?"

"Did the KGB really try to kill John Wayne?"

"That they did."

"Then they are definitely going down."

"Mister Bonafide?"

Jack looked up to see one of the NSA staffers holding out a folder to him.

"I have to go," Jack said. "I'll keep you updated."

Jack hung up the phone and took the folder.

"What did he take?" Jack asked as he opened the folder.

"It was a shipping manifest for some items that came through here two weeks ago. We already cross-referenced the addresses with our database and identified them all except for one."

"You don't know where it is?"

"We know the location, but not what it is. All the others were government facilities and we're checking in one-by-one to confirm receipt, but the one we can't confirm is just a P.O. Box in Bethesda."

"Bethesda?"

"Yes, sir. There doesn't seem to be anything special about it. It's very strange."

Jack looked back to the folder and saw the post office address and box number circled in red.

"Thank you," Jack said as he stood up. "That man who was hurt, I think his name was Jacob? Is he okay?"

"We just heard from the hospital. He'll make it. Just barely but he'll be okay."

The Terrace View Motel
Room 6
Baltimore, Maryland
December 27, 1980

Mac Bonafide looked out the window again and saw that the short man with the bulky jacket remained in the parking lot about fifty feet from the door. It was very clear why Clarence had put the man in that position. He was there to make sure they didn't get away. Mac was also fairly certain that this man had either a sawed-off shotgun or a machine pistol under his coat, and if they tried to make a break for it that little guy would be ready to spray and pray.

Normally in a situation like this, Mac would look for an alternate route of escape, but they hadn't come up with much of anything. There was no back door and the window in the bathroom was too small to fit a human through.

"How bad is it?" Carrie asked. She looked to where Charice was sitting on the bed watching television as if nothing were happening.

"It's not good," Mac replied, closing the curtain. "They posted a lookout, and it's a safe bet they're going for reinforcements."

"I can't believe this. I've got the full power of the CIA and the United States government at my disposal, and I'm about to be murdered by drug dealers in a cheap motel in a shitty part of Baltimore."

"Look on the bright side, at least you won't die alone."

"You're right, I feel so much better." Carrie thought for a moment. "I know we don't want to risk losing contact with Jack, but we may not have a choice here."

"You're right, we don't have a choice. We're staying put."

"Think for a minute. If these guys come at us hard, we won't last five minutes," Carrie said insistently.

"Speak for yourself. If a whole platoon of NVA

regulars couldn't take me down, these shit heads won't be the ones to do it."

"Send her out!" A voice shouted from outside.

Mac looked back out the window and saw that Clarence was back, and the lookout had multiplied. There were now half a dozen men in the parking lot. None of them were hiding their weapons under bulky jackets. They were carrying them out in the open.

"I take it back," Mac said as he looked out the window. "I think we're fucked."

"We have to call the police," Carrie said.

"We have a case full of weapons and comms gear," Mac replied. "We can't explain that."

"We can't explain shit if we're dead!"

"I knew he'd come back," Charice said lazily as she sat on the bed. "He always does."

"I really don't like her," Carrie said.

"Three!" Clarence called out.

Carrie's eyes grew wide.

"Two!"

Mac ran across the room to the weapons case and pulled out the only thing they had that was even close to a heavy weapon, a CAR-15. He slammed a magazine into the magazine well and let the bolt slide forward, chambering the first round.

"One!"

It was dead quiet.

The first round slammed through the door and

missed Carrie's head by a quarter of an inch. She tackled Charice off the bed and took the girl to the floor as the next volley of fire erupted in the room. Right away Mac could tell that the men outside were firing a lot of nine-millimeter rounds, because the number of bullets impacting in the room was significantly less than the number of gunshots he was hearing. Most of the nine mil rounds weren't making it through the walls.

Mac had already taken up a firing position behind the bed. If the small arms fire wasn't stopped by the bed it would at the very least be slowed down. He had not started firing yet as he knew his 5.56 NATO rounds would punch a hole through anything they encountered, including innocent bystanders across the street. Firing blind in a situation like this was not an option. He would have to wait for them to try and make entry.

Carrie had taken cover behind the closet wall across the bathroom with Charice.

"Get her in the bathtub!" Mac whispered, pointing to the bathroom.

At first this order confused Carrie, but then she understood. The bathtub would withstand a lot more fire than the closet wall would.

"Do it, get in the bathtub!" Carrie said to Charice. The fire resumed, and a round cracked the mirror over the sink. "Now! Now! Go now!"

Despite being terrified, Charice complied, crawling

across the floor and into the small bathroom where she closed the door behind her.

"Are you armed?" Mac shouted as rounds snapped around them.

Carrie shook her head.

"Here," Mac replied as he dipped into the weapons case and pulled out a Beretta pistol and magazine which he then tossed to her. "Arm yourself. It's about to get hot in here."

Carrie tried to catch the pistol but fumbled it with her shaking hands. It wasn't like in the movies, where the calm and collected hero did everything right. Except that was exactly what Mac Bonafide was doing. He seemed perfectly content to sit behind the bed with his carbine waiting out the storm.

Carrie picked up the pistol from the floor and loaded it. She racked a round into the chamber and tightened her grip on the weapon.

She heard a loud crack near the door and then realized it was the door itself. They had just kicked it in, and a man was standing in it holding a shotgun. Carrie couldn't see his face because he was back-lit. He looked just like one of the silhouette targets they had practiced on at The Farm.

Everything slowed down. Even the sound of the gunfire died down, almost like something muffled it, like it was all happening underwater and to someone else. Carrie let out a breath, leaned out from the cover of the closet wall, got her sight picture and squeezed the trigger.

The silhouette man stumbled back and he fell to the ground.

"Holy shit!" Mac shouted with a smile. "That was some good god damn shooting!"

Carrie wasn't finished yet. She stood up and moved quickly to the door. She saw another silhouette man just a dozen feet beyond it, and she fired two rounds in rapid succession as she exited the motel room. One bullet found its mark in the man's chest and the other in his head.

Her face felt cold, and she could feel the cold sweat slick across her body.

It was too late to try to stop her, Mac knew that, so he leapt to his feet and moved forward.

Carrie caught movement to her left out of the corner of her eye. She flattened to the wall, turned and fired twice into the man who was almost on top of her. Both rounds hit him in the face, close enough to leave muzzle burns on his flesh and to splatter her own face with his blood.

She felt a zip as a round passed dangerously close to her head, and she saw a man running toward her with his pistol in hand. He was shooting at her.

This is it, she thought to herself. *You're about to die.*

Beside her she heard the window to the motel room (the same one Mac had been looking out of all afternoon) shatter, and then 5.56 rounds stitched the man who had been running at her. It was Mac, he was firing through the window with his carbine.

As her tunnel vision decreased and her field of vision opened back up, she saw that the remaining men in the parking lot were turning tail and running. They'd had enough of Carrie Davidson and Mac Bonafide for that afternoon. Probably for a lifetime.

Carrie felt her legs give out, and she dropped to a knee. Then her stomach emptied onto the ground. Despite this, she still kept a vice-like grip on her pistol.

She felt a hand on her back and turned to get her gun up, but Mac Bonafide snatched it away from her.

"Breathe!" Mac shouted. "Fucking breathe!"

Carrie realized she wasn't breathing and tried to pull in a breath but couldn't.

Mac slapped her hard across the face and that caused her to pull in a breath. She started to cry. The big Texan pulled her into his arms and held her for a moment.

"You're okay. You're okay. This is normal. Just breathe. You're okay. You did great."

Mac heard tires squealing in the parking lot and turned to look for the source. It was Jack.

Jack Bonafide pulled the car to a stop and leapt out of the driver's seat, pistol drawn.

"What in the hell happened here?" Jack shouted as he ran to the two of them.

"Couldn't be helped," Mac said as he pulled Carrie to her feet and walked her to the car. "Get in the car. I'll grab the gear."

Jack scowled as he loaded Carrie into the back seat, but he gave his brother the benefit of the doubt. Yes, he had thought it was possible Mac might get into a little scuffle with a drug dealer, but this looked like they had been in an all-out war.

Mac headed back into the room. He looked around and saw the number of bullet holes in the wall. It was amazing that neither of them had been hit. There were easily a hundred of the holes. He knelt down, closed the weapons case and locked it. They didn't really have anything else with them aside from the comms bag and Carrie's log books. He grabbed everything and was about to head for the door when he stopped and walked back to the bathroom.

He pushed the door open with his boot and found Charice lying in the bathtub. Her eyes were locked open and there were three bullet holes in her chest.

"Shit."

The sun was setting as Jack drove the sedan down West Lafayette, already heading for I-95 South which would take them to Bethesda.

Mac turned back in the passenger seat and handed

Carrie a wet towel he had taken from the bathroom. She looked at it like she didn't know what it was.

"For your face," Mac said. "You've got blood on you."

Carrie looked at her reflection in the rearview mirror. He was right. She was covered in blood. She began to scrub at it with the washcloth, but it wasn't coming off easily.

"What in the hell happened back there?" Jack asked.

"Pro came knocking on the door asking for help. Long story short, we let her in, and her pimp came looking for her. We declined to turn her over, and he came back with the cavalry."

"How did she know to come knocking on your door?"

"Hell if I know. I guess I'm just one unlucky son of a bitch."

"Or she saw you when you were eye balling her boss."

"Now ain't the time, brother," Mac said, steel in his voice. "Yeah, I fucked up. We all did. Bitchin' about it ain't gonna change that."

Jack tightened his grip on the steering wheel. He wanted to keep putting the screws to his brother, but he couldn't ignore the fact that he had also messed up big time. Arguably even more than the two of them had.

"You're right," Jack said. "We're all learning as we go here."

"Did you find anything out?" Carrie asked quietly from the backseat.

"You were right. Whatever we're after went through Fort Meade. It was logged in the NSA building."

"You went in?" Carrie asked in surprise.

"I didn't plan on it, but... I saw McMasters."

"Seriously?" Mac gasped and turned to his brother. "I hope you gave that son of a bitch what for!"

"I didn't get the chance. He got away, but not before I found out what he was after." Jack reached into his coat pocket and handed the folded-up sheet of paper back to Carrie. "It's a P.O. Box in Bethesda where the shipment went."

Carrie studied the manifest for a moment and then furrowed her brow.

"What is it?" Mac asked, seeing her expression in the rearview mirror.

"It's the weight. It's not heavy enough to be a component piece, so our original theory that the Black Tsar has already been in the country for a long time was probably correct."

"So what is it?" Jack asked. "What did they smuggle in?"

"The tamper device," Carrie replied. "It has to be."

"That's like the trigger?" Mac asked.

"Kind of. It has a separate detonator. The tamper is more like a supercharger on a muscle car."

"You know about cars?" Mac asked intrigued.

"I know a thing or two about a thing or two," Carrie said with a smile. "Let's just say my father's idea of bonding with me was wrenching on his GTO on the weekends."

"The tamper?" Jack asked in an effort to get them back on task.

"The tamper is what makes the weapon truly dangerous. Without it, the Black Tsar could still take down a small city, but with it? It could destroy a sizable chunk of the East Coast. Maybe not outright, but it would knock out the power grid, cause mass panic. Civilization would cease to exist."

"It's not that simple," Jack said, shaking his head. "They wouldn't blow their wad just to take out a few cities. It's more strategic than that. They want to balance the chessboard."

"Who's the biggest threat to the USSR?" Carrie asked.

"Apparently it's John Wayne," Jack quipped.

"What?" Mac asked with a raised eyebrow.

"Never mind. Think about it. They shipped it to Bethesda. They have someone there who's going to grab it from that P.O. Box, probably one of their sleepers. It's possible, but unlikely that they would then travel across the country with it. Too much risk."

"So, the target is on the East Coast," Mac surmised.

"And probably within an easy drive of Maryland."

"Shit," Carrie sighed.

"What?" Jack asked.

"Think about it. Maryland? Washington D.C.? Who's the greatest threat to communism?"

"Right," Mac nodded. "President Reagan. After all, which is the better bet if you want to assassinate an American President? A bullet or a hydrogen bomb? Damn hard to miss your target."

The Terrace View Motel
Room 7
Baltimore, Maryland
December 27, 1980

McMasters walked across the parking lot of the Terrace View Motel, being very careful not to draw unnecessary attention to himself. The place looked like a war zone. There were bodies everywhere, and nearly a dozen police cars and other emergency service vehicles.

He had been playing this game for a very long time, and all over the world. This time, though, this time was different. This Jack Bonafide was rough around the edges, but he had somehow tracked him down to the gate at Fort Meade, and then almost facilitated his capture at the NSA building. It was a damn good thing that Bonafide hadn't been working for the CIA very long, because with a little more experience under his belt he would be quite the formidable adversary.

"Excuse me, sir?" A police officer called out.

McMasters thought about the pistol secured in a skeleton holster in the small of his back. Shooting his way out of this was not an option. There were too many of them, and he didn't have enough back up. He would need every ounce of his KGB training and experience to get out of this one.

"Yes, officer. How may I be of assistance?"

The Baltimore Police Officer pushed his cover back on his head and looked McMasters over. He seemed harmless enough. Five foot eight, a little on the schlubby side with thinning blonde hair and glasses with thick black frames. The officer thought the glasses reminded him of the ones he had been issued in Marine Corps boot camp.

"This your room?" The officer asked, motioning to the door McMasters had been headed for.

"Yes, it is. What happened out here, if I may ask?"

"Gang shit," the officer said. "Looks like they went up against more than they could handle."

"It would appear so."

"You weren't curious?" The officer asked. "About what happened?"

"Of course I was curious."

"But you didn't stop and ask questions. You just walked on by."

"To be completely forthright with you, officer, I didn't really want to get involved. I figured I would read about it in the morning paper."

"It just seems to me that an act like this, I'd want to know what happened."

McMasters raised an eyebrow.

"Am I somehow a suspect?"

The officer looked hard at him for a moment, the flashing red and blue lights illuminating his face. He relented.

"Of course not. Whoever did this was a hell of a lot more dangerous than you," the officer said with a wink.

McMasters laughed.

"You never can tell!" He said with a smile. "May I go?"

"Sure," the officer replied, and then turned and walked back to where the rest of the police were gathered.

McMasters worked his key in the lock of room seven, opened the door and walked inside. He shut the door behind him, and the light came on.

"What in the hell happened out there?" He asked.

Miron and Vladimir both stood in the room with their weapons at the ready.

"We don't know," Miron said. "Everything was

quiet and then we heard shouting next door. Then it was quiet again and then shooting started. They had heavy artillery."

McMasters shook his head.

"It doesn't matter. We're leaving."

"Where are we going?" Miron asked. Vladimir (as was often the case) remained silent.

"Bethesda. It's not too far away, and we can't leave soon enough. This Baltimore place seems extraordinarily dangerous."

CHAPTER 5

Bethesda, Maryland
December 28, 1980

J
ack Bonafide sat on the bus stop bench and
watched the target P.O. box through the post
office window. It was possible that the Soviet
agent had already retrieved the tamper device
from the box, but protocols for these enemy agents
weren't really that much different from the ones for
their American counterparts. The P.O. box would still
be checked regularly, even once the device was
retrieved. The obvious question was, how regularly?

Jack had already used his DOD credentials to find
out that no one had emptied the box in a week. He
tried to press the issue to find out what was inside of it,

but the postmaster resisted, as he rightfully should have. Jack's supposed DOD status did not mean he deserved any special favors from the postal service, and the postmaster reminded him of this. Just letting Jack know that the box had not been emptied was a professional courtesy, but there was no way in hell the post master would get any more specific than that.

Jack understood and thanked the postmaster for his time. Now it was just a waiting game.

The tamper had to be in that P.O. box. It just had to be. It had come out of Red River less than a week ago, and the box had not been checked since then. Yes, they could request a court order and secure the tamper that was almost certainly in that box, but then it would be impossible to expose the greater plot.

It was also likely that there were several tampers out there. If this was the case, then it was even more imperative that they find the weapon itself and the KGB network behind it.

"Coffee?" Carrie asked as she approached the bench and held out a paper cup.

Jack took it and nodded his thanks.

Carrie sat down beside him. They had been changing locations all morning, careful not to linger in one place for too long.

"No luck, I assume?" She asked.

"Nope," Jack replied.

The two sat in silence for a moment.

"You know, your brother really stepped up back there," Carrie said. "Stepped up to the plate, I mean. I would have been in real trouble if it weren't for him. I just say that because I know I was resistant to bringing him along."

"Seems that way," Jack replied. "That he stepped up, I mean."

"He's quite a— quite a guy, isn't he?" Carrie asked. "He knows how to handle himself."

Jack looked at Carrie for a moment and then shook his head.

"What?" Carrie asked.

"Girls have been falling for that bad boy since he could walk and carry a tune—"

"Please!" Carrie said. "I am not falling for your brother." She paused. "He sings?"

"You wouldn't know it from looking at him, but yes, he does." Jack smiled slyly. "I do believe you're sweet on him."

"Eyes on the P.O. box, Bonafide."

Steven Waller adjusted his glasses in the rearview mirror and smoothed his hair back with his fingers. He smiled at himself to see how it looked, but as always, the smile made him look awkward. Steven was good at many things but acting normal was not one of them.

Steven noted the time on the dashboard clock and

thought about his cats. He didn't normally leave them alone for this long on a weekend as he spent most his time at home. He wondered if they even noticed?

He looked down at the stack of comic books in the passenger seat of the Dodge Dart and smiled again, but this time it was genuine. The copy of Uncanny X-Men number twenty-three was in mint condition and packaged in a way that he had been reassured would guarantee it stayed that way.

Steven had a lukewarm relationship with the X-Men series of comic books, and the only reason he had bought them was because of the frequent crossovers with The Avengers. Steven had begun a correspondence with another comic book fan in Delaware who suggested trading Steven's copy of X-Men twenty-three for a copy of X-Men number four. The latter was the first appearance of The Scarlet Witch, who would later appear in Avengers.

This trade was (to put it flatly) insane. Steven would get much more than he was giving. When he had bluntly asked Michael (the comic book fan he was corresponding with) why he would make such a trade, Michael had disclosed that he had three copies of number four but no twenty-three, and the latter was the only issue he was missing.

It made sense, and they had struck a gentleman's agreement to trade by post. It was done all the time, and Steven had no reason to believe Michael wouldn't come through. If Michael tried to rip Steven off, he would get much more than he had bargained for.

Steven smiled at that thought. How silly would that be? A KGB sleeper agent hunting down an American over a stolen comic book?

"How long do we wait?" Carrie asked.

"As long as we have to," Jack replied and sipped his coffee. "This is the hard part. It's not all blood and bullets, Miss Davidson."

"You forget I was sitting in Red River for weeks reading what amounted to Japanese stereo instructions," she said. Jack seemed confused. "That means it was boring, Jack. You don't get out much, do you?"

"People keep saying that to me."

Jack looked back across the street and through the building window at the large P.O. Box. There were three different sizes available, and the one they were watching was the largest. It was big enough to fit a small television. According to what they knew about the tamper device, it would fit in there.

Carrie's question was a reasonable one, and Jack knew it. They could only sit on this for so long before they would have to call in to Tresham to get an agent to sit on it while they started over and tried to manifest a new lead. This location made the most sense, but it wasn't a sure thing.

. . .

Steven walked down the P.O. box-lined hallway and stopped at number two fifty-six. The postal worker had taken the perfectly packaged comic book and assured him it would reach its final destination unmolested. While neither party had given a specific timeline, Steven figured he would get his X-Men number four in a couple of weeks. He only hoped Michael had taken as much care in packing it as he had.

The lock clicked as Steven turned the key in the P.O. Box and pulled the door open. He glanced at it and then reflexively pushed the door shut, but then he froze. There was something in there. There hadn't been a single piece of mail or a package in there for years.

Steven slowly opened the door and took a knee. It was a box, a box that took up nearly the entire P.O. Box. What in the hell was this? Was it a mistake? Unlikely. They didn't make mistakes, especially not ones this big.

The post office was mostly empty and surveying the room Steven saw that the few people in the building weren't paying any attention to him. He needed to get a hold of himself. No one suspected him or that there was anything unusual in this package. Why would they? If one were hunting Soviet sleeper agents, he most definitely did not fit the bill. Hell, that was the whole point.

To tell the truth, it wasn't getting caught that had

Steven Waller so alarmed. It was losing the life he had built. He always suspected this sort of thing could happen to an undercover like himself, and now he was experiencing it first hand.

Steven did not lack the resolve that had burned in his soul as a young recruit. In that same soul he also still believed that communism was the light that could bring the world out of the darkness. The sad truth (to him) was that he just really, really loved comic books. In his mind, they reflected the very thing he was doing; They were heroes with special abilities fighting against all odds to save humanity. That was exactly what he was doing!

If this new mission (assuming there was one) put him directly into the fight or even ended with him returning to the USSR, Steven wasn't sure how he would handle that. He would follow orders, but the life he had become accustomed to over the past decade would be forever changed. Goodbye Burger King, hello breadlines. Goodbye comic books, hello drawing in the dirt with a stick. Well, it wasn't quite that bad, but not far off. The closest he would get to a comic book in the USSR was an illustrated magazine called "Murzilka" and to Steven's understanding it starred a talking cat and an elf. No, thank you.

Who would take care of his cats? There were five of them! Who would take care of Sprinkles, Comstock, Mr. Ash, Lumpy and Bandit?

Steven took another look around and then reached into the P.O. box and pulled out the package. He closed the small door and stood up. Whatever was in the package was fairly large and weighed a modest amount. No, this would not be something simple. Whatever this was, it was serious.

Jack stopped mid-sip, and then set the coffee down on the bench next to him as he kept his gaze locked on the very average looking man who had just pulled a package out of P.O. box two fifty-six. Jack pressed the trigger on the small device that ran down his sleeve and the earpiece in his right ear crackled to life.

"Bravo Two," Jack said quietly. "This is Bravo One. Prepare for pursuit. We have our rabbit. Stand by for vehicle make and model."

"Roger that," Mac replied. "And I would again like to lodge my protest. I should be Bravo One and you should be Bravo Two."

"Fix your radio discipline and we'll talk," Jack replied curtly.

Down the street he heard an engine start and knew that it would be Mac in the sedan getting ready to follow this man. Jack and Carrie would be in a follow car ready to act as a blocking force if needed. It was unlikely, as Jack doubted this man had any support. These sleeper agents were generally out on their own.

That was the way they had been deployed, so that if one cell was taken down, it wouldn't expose the others.

Steven Waller exited the post office and looked around again. He was pretty squirrely, Jack thought to himself. Whoever this guy was, he may have been in sleeper status waiting for this moment for several years. Hell, maybe even decades. This meant that while he had probably received the best training the Soviet Union had to offer, it may have been a very long time ago, with little chance to practice his tradecraft since then. This guy was probably so rusty he could give you tetanus just by looking at you.

Steven crossed the street (just a dozen feet from Jack and Carrie) and unbelievably looked around again.

"Are you kidding me?" Jack asked and then triggered his radio. "Bravo Two, the vehicle is an orange Dodge Dart."

"Roger that," Mac came back. "This is Bravo One, out."

Jack rolled his eyes.

Steven fired up his Dodge Dart and pulled onto the street. Not thirty seconds later Mac Bonafide passed Jack and Carrie, directly behind Steven Waller.

"Let's go."

Steven had been careful, very careful. He thought about this as he drove down Moorland Lane and into the neighborhood known as Whitehall Manor. It was a very nice neighborhood, the perfect place to raise a family. Steven thought about that. Part of his cover should have been that he was a family man. That had always been the plan. He would meet some well-to-do woman, get married and start a family.

No, it wasn't the "plan". Those were his orders, but like so many other things in his life, he had come up short. He had gone to great lengths to explain this during that last communique with Moscow three years earlier, and after that there had been nothing. They had gone dark on him.

Had they given up, he wondered? It happened. He knew it did. They were referred to as "dead agents". Operatives who were determined to no longer be useful but had not done anything bad enough to require being recalled to the Soviet Union for punishment or retraining.

Secretly, Steven Waller had always hoped he would become one of these dead agents. Again, it wasn't that he didn't believe in the Soviet agenda or want to help his people. He just really enjoyed his American life. He enjoyed working for the defense department; He liked Burger King and yes; He liked comic books.

Steven pulled into the driveway of his modest two-bedroom house. It was one of the last left in the neighborhood, as the old houses from the forties and fifties were being torn down to make way for new, much larger family homes. That was something the Americans were very good at. They always moved forward.

Jack pulled the car to a stop and shut off the engine.

"We walk from here. We'll meet Mac."

Carrie nodded in the affirmative and the two stepped out of the car. No sooner had Jack closed the door than he saw his brother Mac heading toward them, walking a dog on a leash.

"Where did he get a dog?" Carrie asked.

"Let me guess, you love guys that like dogs?" Jack asked.

"Knock it off, Bonafide. You know, I'm sensing some jealousy."

"Yeah, I don't think so," Jack said.

Mac waved at the two of them as he closed in.

"He's down the street behind me," Mac said. "Address is one thirty-two. White house with a yellow fence."

Jack looked down at the dog.

"Where did you get a dog?"

"Someone's back yard."

"You stole a dog?" Carrie asked.

"People can't really own animals, Carrie," Mac said and then paused. "But yes, I stole a dog."

"Jesus," Carrie sighed.

"I'll put him back!" Mac assured her. "I just figured I wouldn't stand out as much walking a dog."

"A stolen dog," Jack corrected him. "You didn't think you would stand out as much walking a stolen dog."

"That's about the size of it."

Steven locked the front door behind him and made a bee-line for the kitchen. He sat the package down on the kitchen table and then went to the ironing board that folded into the wall. He pulled it out and unlatched a hidden compartment behind it. He reached in and pulled out a small pistol which he then tucked into the small of his back. He also pulled out five thousand dollars in cash and a passport. That would be all he needed.

Really, the whole thing was like something out of a comic book. Steven smiled at this thought. Perhaps he was about to become a comic book hero.

Steven walked back to the table and unwrapped the package. It was just a plain box. Being careful not to jostle it around too much, he cut the tape that was holding it together and took it apart.

"What are you?" Steven asked himself.

It was a piece of metal that looked a lot like a circuit board of some sort. It was about the size of a once folded newspaper. There was a sheet of paper with it.

The writing was Cyrillic. It made sense, in a strange way, to just write in the Russian style. If someone got a hold of this there wouldn't be much doubt as to where it had come from.

Steven read the three phrases on the slip of paper.

The chair is against the wall.

The roof is falling.

The coffee is hot.

"Oh no," Steven whispered to himself.

Jack, Carrie and Mac separated once they were within a few hundred feet of the target house, and Jack stood beside the fence that would take him into the house's backyard.

"Is everyone set?" Jack asked as he keyed his radio.

"Set," Mac's voice came back.

"Set," Carrie replied.

"Roger that. I'm going to make entry. Mac, you're in after two mikes and Carrie you stand watch."

Both Mac and Carrie sent their confirmation.

Jack felt a wave of calm wash over him. He was home. This was the part that he was good at, the part that made sense to him. He would make entry, take down a target and hopefully draw a clean and straight line right to this Black Tsar.

Jack slowly opened the gate. No creaks. This guy kept his maintenance up. Just one more vote for him being a Soviet. Americans never oiled the hinges on their outside gates. That was a real Commie thing to do.

The backyard was in good order, and Jack took note that there were no children's toys, no sign that anyone lived there other than a single man. That was a dream scenario. The last thing they wanted to have to do was wrangle a family who may or may not know what their patriarch was doing behind their backs. That would add a whole other level of confusion to an already chaotic situation.

Inside the house Jack saw movement, but it was not aggressive. He walked out into the middle of the back-yard and saw the same man from the post office standing in the kitchen looking at something on a table. It was the tamper; it had to be.

Jack moved slowly up the back steps, and drew his weapon, keeping it trained on the back of this man's head. Shooting him was the very last thing that Jack Bonafide wanted to do, but he also knew that the threat of being shot may be enough to make things go his way.

Jack stopped at the door. He was only about five feet from this man. He also took note of the pistol stuffed into the small of the man's back.

Fuck it, he thought to himself. It was violence of action time.

Jack moved forward and drove his foot hard into the door, breaking the lock. The man tried to turn but Jack was already on top of him. He pulled the pistol from the man's belt and tossed it behind him out the door and then gave the man a hard shove, sending him into the wall.

"Do not move!" Jack shouted, his weapon raised and trained on his target.

Steven Waller froze.

"Hands in the air. Slowly," Jack ordered.

Steven complied, raising his hands in a manner he thought appropriate. Was he really the world's worst spy? He had only had his mission for about three minutes, and it was already over. Should he try to resist? Fight back? No, whoever this man was that had just broken into his house, he was way outside of Steven's pay grade.

"Turn around," Jack said, and then keyed his mic. "Target secure. Make a soft entry around the back."

"Are you... FBI?" Steven asked.

Jack didn't answer. Mac and Carrie came in through the back door.

"Mac, secure him to the chair," Jack said as he looked at the tamper and the letter on the table. "Cyrillic," he said, more to himself than anyone else. "What does it say?"

Steven knew that the question was directed at him, but he declined to answer. He may very well have been the worst spy in the world, but he still had some dignity left. They would have to try a little harder than that to get information out of him.

"What does it say?" Jack growled and lunged forward as Mac was securing Steven to the chair with flex ties.

Carrie placed a hand on Jack's chest, stopping him mid-stride.

"May I have a word with you?" She asked.

Jack looked confused and slightly annoyed but Carrie had been pulling her weight so far. She had even surprised him with her skill level a few times. She deserved to be heard.

Carrie led Jack into the living room and spoke in a lowered voice.

"He won't respond to that kind of interrogation tactic," she said.

"How do you know?"

"We have no idea how long he's been asleep. It

could be years, it could be decades. He's probably forgotten most of his training for resisting interrogation, but if you go all Steve McQueen on him, the trauma reflex may bring it back."

"What do you want to do? Bake him a cake?"

Carrie sighed.

"No, Jack. I want to talk to him. Just let me try a different way. Have you looked around this room?" Carrie asked, gesturing around the living room. There were comic books stacked on the coffee table and framed superhero posters on the wall. Two cats sat quietly on the couch, and they seemed bored with the whole situation. "This is not some hardened KGB mastermind. He's like a child. He's probably been sitting in this house for the past ten years just hoping that no one would ever come calling. He wants to be caught, he wants to cut a deal. But if you go at him with both guns blazing, and his training kicks in, we may lose him forever."

Jack thought about it for a moment and then nodded.

Bethesda Post Office
December 28, 1980

McMasters looked at his watch. If was five on the dot. The Post Office would be closing. Vladimir went in first, pretending to peruse some stamps. Miron waited down the street, acting as a lookout.

This was not the ideal way to do something like this. Normally he would have set surveillance and waited for the sleeper agent to come to the PO Box, but they didn't have that kind of time. Due to the crime scene at the motel, they'd had to wait until morning to check out, as quickly leaving after a mass shooting would have drawn too much attention. Yes, one could make a case that they were fleeing out of fear, but there would still be questions asked. There was also the matter of Vladimir and Miron. When the police officer had questioned him, McMasters had said that he was staying there alone.

So, they had been delayed, but it wasn't the end of the world. Where the delicate scalpel did not work, the blunt instrument would.

McMasters entered the Post Office and walked to the service desk where a tall, slender and very pale man with a receding hairline was doing some paperwork. A shorter man with a much more fortunate hairline was at the kiosk beside him, also immersed in what must have been daily paperwork.

The tall, pale man looked up. McMasters saw that his name tag read "Phil".

"How can I help you?" Phil asked.

"I need some information," McMasters said slowly.

"Of course," Phil replied.

Vladimir drew a silenced pistol from beneath his jacket, turned and shot Phil's co-worker in the head. The man collapsed to the floor, but his blood and grey matter stayed on the wall behind him.

"Do not scream," McMasters said. "If you want to get out of this alive, I need you to maintain your composure. Do you understand?"

Phil nodded.

"What you do right now, Phil, will determine if you live or die." McMasters paused. "I need the name and address of the owner of box two fifty-six."

"I—"

McMasters held up a hand to silence him.

"Whatever you're about to say, Phil. Think it over. If you're about to tell me why you can't do it, those will be the last words you ever say. Please believe me." McMasters stared through him from behind cold eyes. "We didn't build this world, Phil. We're just living in it. Please don't make me do this."

The Home Of Steven Waller
Bethesda, Maryland
December 28, 1980

Jack looked at the clock on the wall. It was a little after five. They needed to speed this whole process up. Jack could assume that McMasters had the same clue he did, but probably didn't have this address. That didn't mean he would never figure it out. While the Soviet may have been playing for the other side, he seemed to really know his stuff. The cut on Jack's shoulder reminded him of that.

They still didn't know much about this man, the supposed Soviet sleeper agent. What they knew was that his name was Steven Waller, and he worked for the Department of Defense in data processing.

How in the hell does something like this happen? Jack thought to himself. It was one thing for these guys to live in the country masquerading as Americans, but this one was working for the DOD!

Steven hadn't said a word since Mac secured him to the chair.

Carrie waved the two brothers away, and Jack and Mac headed into the living room.

Carrie smiled and slid a chair across the linoleum, taking her seat opposite Steven.

"Hi Steven," she said. She waited for a moment, but there was no reply. "Look, you don't have to talk to me if you don't want to."

Steven said nothing. This was his chance to prove he wasn't a complete failure. All he had to do was not talk. He knew that the Americans were notoriously reticent to use physical force to get information out of detainees, so he considered his chances of holding out in this interrogation to be very good.

"It's just that... we're trying to stop something bad from happening. Something that would change your life here forever."

This seemed to get Steven's attention. He really didn't want much. In fact, he wanted nothing. He wanted everything to stay exactly the same.

"Do you know what that is?" Carrie asked, nodding to the tamper device that was sitting on the table. "I wouldn't expect you to, because it may have been a little before your time. Do you remember the Tsar Bomba?"

Steven looked to the device and then back to Carrie. He knew about the Tsar Bomba. It had been on a list of notable achievements by the USSR that they taught him about during training, but what did that have to do with anything? That whole weapons program had been scrapped after they saw firsthand what it would actually do if they unleashed it on the world.

"I assume you're too young to remember the test run at Sevemy Island?"

Steven did not respond.

"Because you look like you're in your mid-thirties, so, yes. Too young. That bomb had a fifty-megaton yield. Do you understand what that means, Steven?

What kind of damage that would do? It would erase New York City. Do you see that device on your table?" Carrie asked, nodding to the tamper. "That is a uranium-238 tamper. If they had applied that to the Tsar Bomba it would have doubled the strength of that yield. Can you imagine that?"

Steven lightly shook his head. He hadn't meant to, but he did anyway.

"I know. It's not something any of us wants to think about. You know, most people don't know this, but they didn't just make one Tsar Bomba. They made two." This got Steven's attention. "They were nicknamed the White Tsar and the Black Tsar. They detonated the White Tsar that day in nineteen sixty-one, but the Black Tsar went missing. They removed the tamper from it first, but then it vanished. It looks like we have found the tamper, but we have every reason to believe the Black Tsar is here."

"Here?" Steven asked. "In Maryland?"

"Yes, Steven. Even without the tamper it would make Hiroshima look like a sunny day at the beach. Is that what you want?"

"No."

"Full disclosure, Steven. I am an employee of the Central Intelligence Agency, but you probably already figured that out." Carrie paused. "But if they told me to detonate a weapon like that—"

"I wasn't going to detonate anything!" Steven said, cutting her off.

"Or play a part in that detonation?" Carrie continued. "I don't think that's something I would want on my head. Would you?"

"No," Steven said. "I wouldn't. But I want something."

Carrie cocked her head to the side.

"You want something?"

"Yes, I want a deal."

"So, you would let millions of people die if you don't get your deal?"

"I may not be the super spy I always hoped I would be," Steven said, becoming cold. "But I will not let myself be executed for treason or spend the rest of my life in prison."

"What do you want?"

"What do you think? Full immunity. A new identity, a house and a job. A good one, not this data processing bullshit. And I want my cats to come with me."

"Is that all?" Carrie asked.

"And I've got a comic book coming to that P.O. Box in a week or two. I want it."

"I don't think he's playing with a full deck of cards,"

Carrie said as she stood in the darkness of the living room with Jack and Mac.

"Do you think he knows anything?" Jack asked.

"I think he does. I just think being out here in isolation, cut off from his home country and waiting for a mission that he thought would never come made him a little nuts. He wants a comic book."

"What?" Mac asked in disbelief.

"Yeah, some comic book is supposed to be delivered to that P.O. Box in a week or two and he wants it. It's part of his deal."

"What else does he want?" Jack asked.

"The usual," Carrie said with a shrug. "New identity, place to live and a new job."

"And a comic book," Mac added.

"And a comic book," Carrie confirmed. "And his cats. The cats have to go with him. Apparently, they're vital to the future of the Soviet Union."

Jack rubbed his forehead.

"When I envisioned how this mission would go down," he said. "Comic books and cats weren't a part of it."

"We're going to have to break protocol," Carrie said. "We have to call Tresham. We have to get Steven's deal in place."

"We're really going to let this guy skate?" Mac asked.

"It's the biggest win in history, Mac," Carrie said.

"This guy isn't Julius Rosenberg. He's a second stringer who got left out in the cold. He isn't ready to fall on his hammer and sickle for Mother Russia. We're giving him next to nothing and potentially saving millions of lives.

Mac nodded his understanding.

"I'll make the call," Jack said. "All he ever wanted from me was enough actionable intelligence to make this thing official. I'd say we've got it."

Carrie sat at the kitchen table with Steven Waller and picked up the small sheet of paper with the Cyrillic writing on it.

"It seems strange, don't you think?" Carrie asked.

"What's that?" Steven replied.

"That they would write their codes in Russian? Seems a little obvious?"

Steven shrugged.

"They figure that if one of you got your hands on that the jig is probably up anyway."

"What does it say?" Carrie asked.

Steven smiled.

"I want my deal first."

Jack had been standing in the kitchen's corner speaking on the phone in hushed tones. As if on cue, he walked to Steven Waller and held the phone next to the man's ear.

"Hello?" Steven asked.

"Mister Waller, this is Mike Tresham. I am the assistant director of the Central Intelligence Agency. I understand that you have some information for us?"

"I do. I need written proof that my deal is in place."

"We're on a tight timeline here, Mister Waller. I can't get you that proof, but what I can do is give you my word. Despite what my ex-wife says, while I may be many things, a liar is not one of them."

"My comic book?"

"Yes, Mister Waller. You will get your comic book and your cats will be taken care of. I will see to it personally," Mike said. "But you need to understand that the information you are providing must lead to the apprehension of this Black Tsar."

"It will," Steven said. "The information they sent, there's no way it isn't real."

"Please give me back to Mister Bonafide," Mike Tresham said.

Jack took the phone and put it back to his ear.

"Don't trust him, Jack. Do you understand? I've played in the sandbox with these guys before. I do think he's what he appears to be, but you can never be sure. We're very close to this being actionable. As soon as you get something solid out of him call me back. Once we get that, Scarn will take over."

"Scarn?" Jack asked in disbelief. "Sir, I don't want

to question your judgement, but we've got the ball. Why not let us take it into the end zone?"

"It's not about what we want, Jack. We have protocols. Out there in the dark you can pull all the cowboy shit you want as long as you get the job done, but once you come into the light, things change. There are too many eyes on us as it is. We don't want to do something that might add more oversight to that equation."

Jack thought about this for a moment.

"What if I don't come back into the light?"

There was silence on the line.

"That's a dangerous game to play, Jack. If you're going to go that way, you better make sure you're holding all the cards that count." Mike paused. "And we never had this conversation."

The line went dead.

Jack looked at the phone for a moment and then dropped it back in the cradle.

CHAPTER 6

The Home Of Steven Waller
Bethesda, Maryland
December 28, 1980

Carrie held out the sheet of paper with the Cyrillic writing to Steven.

"What does it say?"

Steven looked at the writing and then back to Carrie.

"The chair is against the wall. The roof is falling. The coffee is hot."

"What does that mean?" Carrie continued to press him.

"The chair is against the wall means that we are now on a war footing."

"How so?" Jack cut in.

"It's not the first time it's happened. It just means that we have initiated a series of events that may lead to armed conflict."

"World War Three?" Mac asked.

"Not necessarily," Steven countered. "It could be an invasion of a neighboring country, or a skirmish to show our power and resolve."

"The roof is falling?" Carrie asked.

"Internal problems," Steven said. "There are several of those codes. That one is for the KGB."

Carrie looked up at Jack. This confirmed the rumors that had been flying around about some sort of split within Soviet intelligence. Those types of rumors were always going around, but this time it looked like they were for real.

"They send that out so we're on the lookout for rogue agents," Steven said.

"Do you know what's happening within the KGB?" Carrie asked.

Steven seemed to hesitate.

"It may be important to finding the Black Tsar," Carrie pressed him.

"It's the oldest story," Steven said. "The two princes warring for control of the empire. Not unlike the silent struggle between Cyclops and Wolverine for leadership of the X-Men."

"Wolver-What?" Jack asked.

"Never mind," Steven relented, realizing that his analogy had fallen flat. "I don't have any inside information, I just know what I've seen in the international news and what news comes out of the Soviet Union and my few communiques with Moscow."

"Such as?" Carrie asked.

"Yuri Andropov is the head of the KGB, but I assume you know this. What you may not know is that there have been rumors that his health is in decline. Because of this his two deputies are poised to step up and take control."

"But there is only room for one," Carrie concluded.

Steven nodded.

"So, you have a battle between the Deputy of Internal Security Makar Galkin and the Deputy of Foreign Affairs Konstantin Sokolov."

"And what does that have to do with the Tsar?" Carrie asked.

"I think that is what the rift is. I think each man is trying to find it and may have even deployed separate teams."

"So... they're in a race against each other," Jack said, silently wondering which side McMasters was working for.

"Probably. Keep in mind that this is all guesswork," Steven cautioned. "I could be wrong."

"Remember that airliner that went up in a mushroom cloud over the Atlantic Ocean last month?"

"Of course," Carrie said. It had been the only thing on the news for a week straight.

"The Israelis think that was Sokolov."

"Jesus," Mac gasped. "So if his people get the Black Tsar, he'll really detonate it."

"He's proven his resolve," Jack confirmed.

"The coffee is hot?" Carrie asked, moving on to the next code.

"It's a directional code. If we're delivered something like this, we take it to the location indicated by the code. There are hundreds of them."

"Where does this one lead you?" Jack asked.

Steven looked unsure.

"It's a good deal," Carrie said. "Mister Tresham will keep his word, but if you don't tell us what we need to know it turns into a trip to the electric chair."

"There's a house in Virginia. In Falls Church. Nineteen twenty-one Cherry Street. If I go there, someone will be waiting. If no one is there, and I have a package or a letter, I'm supposed to put it through the slot in the door."

Carrie looked to Jack. Jack nodded.

"Okay," Carrie said as she stood up. "You're going to have to take us there."

"That wasn't part of the deal," Steven blurted.

"If we don't find this thing, Steven, you don't have a deal," Carrie said. "Besides, if they're expecting you and one of us shows up instead? That's not going to work."

"I'm sorry, I'm not doing it," Steven said flatly. "Nothing you can say will make me stick my neck out like that. Not for you, not for anyone. So we will have to come up with a new deal."

Carrie sighed and turned to reach for the glass of water she had set on the counter. She felt something brush against her jacket, just below her ribs, and then a framed picture on the wall behind Steven shattered. It took a split second to process, then her eyes grew wide and she tackled Steven to the ground, chair and all.

"Shooter!" She shouted.

Mac reached out and flicked the light switch, darkening the room, and the two brothers hit the floor.

No one said a word.

The phone rang.

Jack moved quietly across the floor, pistol drawn, and reached up for the phone. It wasn't a coincidence that it was ringing at that exact moment and he knew it. He lifted the handset off the cradle and held it to his ear.

"She's fast," McMasters said. Jack didn't reply. "Right now, I have one of my men on a rooftop with a high-powered rifle. He missed that shot. He won't miss again."

"What do you want?" Jack asked.

"World peace."

"Sure."

"Come on, Jack. You know what I want. I know that you were in Israel with the Mossad last month, and I know that you know all about the Black Tsar. My boss—"

"Colonel Sokolov," Jack said, remembering the name of the KGB Colonel who had masterminded a terror attack on Israel in December. He intended for this name drop to throw McMasters off balance, and he could tell by the definable pause that it had done just that."

"Mister Bonafide, I'm impressed. Maybe you're not the simple cowboy I thought you were. But if you think I work for Colonel Sokolov, you're not that smart. Either way, that doesn't really matter. I want the device that is sitting on the kitchen table."

"Why?"

"Nothing as grand as you may be imagining. I'm not trying to vaporize the East Coast. I just need it put in a safe place."

"Does someone else want to detonate it? Sokolov's people?" Jack asked, realizing that McMasters must work for this Makar Galkin and not Sokolov.

"Let's just say that everyone within the KGB is not as forward thinking as Mister Galkin. They want to take us back to the 1950s." McMasters paused. "Maybe you're starting to see, Mister Bonafide, that I'm not your enemy."

"But you sure as hell ain't my friend, and there's no way you're taking this device."

"This is your last chance, Jack. All you have to do is walk out the front door. Go home to Angeline and live your life."

Jack reached up and dropped the phone back in the cradle.

"I've got an idea," Mac whispered. "Give me three minutes and then get him shooting."

"How the hell do I do that?" Jack asked.

"I think you know," Mac said with a smile, and then began low crawling backward out of the kitchen. "Improvise."

"Shit," Jack said with a groan.

"How are we getting out of this?" Carrie asked. Steven had been silent since she took him to the floor.

"We're working on it."

Jack reached to his belt and retrieved his folding knife, which he then used to cut Steven loose from the chair he had still been secured to.

"That man out there doesn't have a lot of interest in you living a long and happy life, you read me?" Jack asked. Steven nodded. "Play it cool, stay next to me and we'll get you out of this."

Jack looked to his watch. It had been about three minutes since the first shot was fired.

"Here we go."

Jack took a knee, grabbed an apple from a bowl on

the kitchen counter, and turned on the lights. He tossed the apple in the air. There was a loud crack, and the apple turned to apple sauce and splattered across the walls.

"Shit, he's good." Jack threw a phone book in the air and it was also perforated by the shooter.

Then he heard it, behind him in the living room. It was the sound of wood splitting and then fast footsteps. Someone (or several someone's) had just made entry through the front door. Jack spun around, bringing his pistol up but was quickly bulldozed through the kitchen table, breaking it into pieces.

He felt his gun fly out of his hand, breaking the kitchen window and landing somewhere in the backyard.

Carrie pushed Steven into a corner and put her body between him and the shooter on the rooftop. She knew that if Steven was killed during this exchange, nothing else they did would matter.

The lights were still on, and Jack could see his attacker kneeling over him. It was the passenger from the Ford Fairlane. The one Mac had assaulted with a beer bottle back in Victory, Texas. Jack unloaded on the man's right ribs, slamming his fist into them a half dozen times until the Soviet finally relented and stumbled back.

Jack leapt to his feet, picked the man up off of the ground and drove him not only into the wall, but directly through it. He stopped for a moment and heard the first round zip past his ear and through the wall. Then the shots started coming in rapid succession.

Jack's sparring partner (not wanting to miss an opportunity) took advantage of this distraction and hurled a table lamp at Jack's head, which sent him back into the kitchen. The Soviet came back through the wall and tied up with Jack in the middle of the kitchen, throwing several knees that Jack blocked with his forearms.

The Soviet paused for a split second but that was all Jack needed to turn the tide, throwing a series of upper cuts that sent the man stumbling back into the kitchen counter. Rifle rounds were still splitting the surrounding air, but miraculously none had found their mark.

For the first time since they had been in the kitchen and during this exchange, Jack noticed out of the corner of his eye the much larger than normal orange tabby cat sitting on the kitchen counter. It didn't move a muscle and seemed extremely bored.

The Soviet reached to the knife block on the counter and retrieved a butcher knife. He moved fast, lunging toward Jack. The former Delta operator went back to something those two brothers from Brazil had taught the unit members, redirecting his attacker's force. He turned as the man came at him and used his attacker's own momentum to spin him around and throw him through the rear slider window.

The home that sat on the other end of Steven Waller's backyard was empty, which made gaining entry and moving up to the second floor much easier for Mac Bonafide. He had hoped that the shooter would go rapid fire once Jack kicked the lights on and started moving around, and that wish was granted.

This lack of fire discipline made it easy to pinpoint the rooftop the shooter was using, though judging by the angle the rounds were coming from there were only three possibilities to choose from. This was all assuming he wasn't using a fifty caliber rifle from a mile away, which was unlikely. If that had been the case, the rounds would have been tearing the house apart, not just punching some holes in the walls.

Mac entered what looked like a child's bedroom and moved to the window. He stopped for a moment as the shooting started again. Yes, he was definitely in the right place. He reached out and slid the window open, being sure to stay as quiet as possible. With that rifle barking like that it was unlikely that the shooter would hear him, but there was no reason to be reckless.

The cool air hit his face as he crawled out the window and grabbed the edge of the rooftop. One properly executed palms away pull up brought his head up high enough to see the shooter, but not so high that if the man swung his rifle around and started taking shots at him that he would be caught in the open.

There he was. In the prone position behind what looked like a standard bolt action thirty ought-six. He had no idea Mac was behind him.

Mac held his position for a moment, and then quietly finished his pull-up, bringing himself fully up onto the rooftop. He moved slowly and quietly. He most likely could have just rushed the man and thrown him over the edge of the roof, but that was sloppy. There was no room for that right now. The stakes were too high.

As Mac got closer, he could make out the shooter's facial features in the shallow moon light. It was the same man from Victory City who had been driving the Ford Fairlane. The same one he had knocked out.

The shooting stopped, and the man turned to grab more rounds from his cargo pants pocket. Mac froze, but it was too late. The Soviet had seen him out of the corner of his eye. He froze as well.

"Hey there, Ivan," Mac said with a smile. "Got room for seconds?"

The Soviet moved fast, trying to swing the barrel of his rifle around, forgetting in the process he had been going for more ammunition because the rifle was empty. Not that it mattered much. Mac Bonafide was too fast for him. Mac grabbed the barrel of the rifle and yanked it out of the shooter's hands.

Mac tossed the rifle to the side and stood opposite the Soviet in the moonlight.

"Look, son. You don't have to die on this rooftop."

The Soviet stood motionless, eyes looked on Mac Bonafide like some kind of robot.

"Son, are you hearing me? Just come with me, all peaceful-like and we can put an end to this."

The Soviet smiled for a moment, how an adult might smile at a simple child. Then he clenched his jaw hard. His skin flushed, foam began to pour out of his mouth as his body spasmed. He stumbled backward until he fell from the rooftop.

"Jesus Christ," Mac said as he walked to the edge.

He looked down and saw the man's body on the lawn below, arms and legs at unnatural angles. He was dead.

"We're moving!" Jack shouted.

He badly wanted to follow the Soviet out the slider window and finish him off, but he knew that wasn't the right move. He needed to get Steven Waller to safety.

The shooting seemed to have stopped, at least for the moment. In the distance he could hear sirens. The police were finally responding to all the rifle fire. There was no way they could be there when the police arrived. They would have to answer way too many questions disclose that they were CIA, and then Jack would lose his chance to stay off-book and see this thing through.

Mike Tresham would then fire him from the agency.

Carrie responded to Jack's order, grabbing Steven Waller and pulling him to his feet. They moved out of the kitchen and into the living room. Jack didn't like exiting through the front door like this but going out the back wasn't an option.

He had also lost his weapon in the fight in the kitchen.

"Where's your firearm?" Jack asked as Carrie moved into the living room.

"In my purse," she said, gesturing to where it was sitting beside the front door. In all the confusion she hadn't been able to retrieve it.

Behind him Jack heard crunching glass.

He turned in the direction of the noise. It was the broken slider leading into the backyard. The Soviet was standing there, cut to shreds and covered in blood, but holding a pistol. It was Jack's. The Soviet had found it in the backyard.

The man raised the pistol, pointed it at Jack Bonafide and pulled the hammer back.

This was it. There was no play to make. There was no way this man was going to miss.

A shot rang out and the Soviet stumbled forward. He locked eyes with Jack and then fell to the floor.

Mac Bonafide entered the house, pistol at the ready. He had seen the man walk into the house holding a gun and made a reasonable assumption that he was up to no good.

"Brother," Mac said as he lowered his weapon. "I do believe you owe me a beer."

"I'll pay up when we get back to Texas."

Mac smiled and then his face changed. He turned back to the rear yard. Then Jack heard it too. It was a radio squawking. Mac brought his weapon back up and walked out the broken slider and into the yard. He saw it laying in the grass. It must have been kicked off the roof of the neighboring house when the shooter fell, and it landed on their side of the fence.

Mac crossed the yard and knelt down. He picked up the radio and held it to his ear.

"Miron? Report," the voice said. It was McMasters.

Mac pressed the call button.

"Miron ain't here. He decided he loves America and said to tell you he quits."

Mac released the button. There was no response. He looked over his shoulder to see Jack standing behind him. Jack nodded.

Mac keyed the radio.

"I heard you tried to kill John Wayne," Mac said, sounding genuinely upset. "Well, I tell you what,

McMasters or whatever the fuck your name is. You are one dead son of a bitch."

McMasters set the radio down and looked down the street to where Steven Waller's house was. He wanted to move in. Miron was dead, and there was a good chance Vladimir was as well. He shouldn't have gone through the front door the way he had, but the big Russian had always been successful in using brute force. At least, until he ran into someone equally skilled. Perhaps even more so.

McMasters thought about this for a moment. Had he let his ego run away with him? Such an American trait, that was. Perhaps he had been in this country too long, and it was starting to rub off on him. Just like it seemed to have with Steven Waller. The postal worker had told them that Steven was an avid comic book collector. How in the hell does that happen? A KGB Directorate S agent becoming a comic book collector? He had been asleep for too long.

The ego question, though, it was a good one. He had been treating these Bonafide brothers like a couple of country bumpkins that he was just going to run over. Except, that wasn't what was happening at all. By all accounts, they were beating him. The evidence was undeniable.

Miron and Vladimir were not a couple of second

stringers called up at the last minute. They had been hand-picked. They were the absolute best of the best. Now they were both dead. Not only that, but they had been dispatched easily.

Why had he been toying with Jack Bonafide? Why hadn't he just killed him, his brother and the girl back in Texas? Why hadn't he killed him in the NSA building? Why had he insisted on playing that ridiculous cat-and-mouse game with him?

There were only two possible reasons. Either it was his ego causing him to drag it out, or perhaps on some level he didn't want to go toe-to-toe with Jack. Was he afraid of the American? No, that was ridiculous. He wasn't afraid of Jack Bonafide. He was concerned, and there was a difference between the two.

McMasters tapped the steering wheel and stared at the house down the street. He could see them heading out the front door. Yes, he wanted to go after them. He wanted to attack. He wanted retribution for the deaths of his agents.

That was the ego again, and it wasn't the right move. He would follow them, set surveillance, and wait for another opportunity. It was time he really didn't have. Sokolov's people would come soon. It was not a matter of "if" but rather of "when". They had all the same information he did, most likely culled from his own reports to the KGB. This whole Sokolov versus

Galkin mess was making this situation far more complicated than it needed to be.

The damn tamper never should have even left the
USSR. Someone within Sokolov's circle had found it
and smuggled it out. So after finding out where it had
been sent, Makar Galkin ordered McMasters and his
men to follow it, and follow it they had. All the way to
Red River.

The idea had been to use stealth and surprise. To
fly below the radar and track the package to its final
destination. The operative who had smuggled it out
had chosen wisely; a sleeper agent who could be relied
upon to not be a fervent communist. One who would
blindly take it to its final destination.

Now, it was too late for that. Now, there would
have to be bloodshed, and a hell of a lot more of it than
McMasters had been banking on.

"Any of ya'll got quarters?" Jack asked as he drove the
sedan down the road, heading for the freeway.

"Now ain't the time for drinking games, Jack," Mac
replied.

Jack scowled at him and Mac could see that his
brother was serious.

"Pony up," Mac called out as he dug into his
pockets.

Carrie pulled some change out of her purse and then turned to Steven.

"Do you have any quarters, Steven?" Carrie asked.

"Are you gonna pay me back?" Steven asked.

"Are you fucking serious?" Mac asked. "Gimme your goddam quarters, son!"

"Geez," Steven sighed as he dug into his pockets. "Excuse me for living. I just don't make that much money."

Steven reached into the front seat and handed his quarters to Jack.

"What's on your mind, brother?" Mac asked.

"Something McMasters said," Jack replied as he pulled into a grocery store parking lot. "When we were on the phone. He said that I should go home to Angeline."

"So?" Mac asked.

"Why does he know about Angeline? I never told him about her. He brought her up back at the NSA building too."

Mac understood what his brother was implying.

Jack stepped out of the vehicle and walked to the payphone anchored to the outside of the grocery store. He dialed a number from memory and dropped in his quarters. He waited while it rang.

"You better be home, you son of a bitch."

The Home Of Corbett Bonafide
Texarkana, Texas
December 28, 1980

Corbett Bonafide sat on the edge of the folding chair that, along with a card table, served as the only piece of furniture in his living room. Lined up on the card table were six shot glasses, a bottle of Old Grandad, a Colt .44 peacemaker and six bullets.

The firearm was his brother's, and Corbett had inherited it after that Jap had killed him in Simeon, Texas, and then killed John's wife Carrie in her back-yard. Folks claimed John had lost his mind and gone on some kind of killing spree, but that never made much sense to Corbett. Why would a decorated Marine and Texas Ranger just suddenly snap and slaughter a half-dozen people?

He didn't have the answer to that question, and he figured no one ever would.

The Victrola in the corner played the only record Corbett Bonafide owned. Specifically, it was a copy of Hank Williams Ramblin' Man. Understand that this was Hank the first, not that jack ass Hank Williams Junior. Corbett wasn't quite sure what in the hell was wrong with that boy, but whatever it was, he wanted no part of it.

Before Corbett's wife had gone to be with her heavenly father, she had tried to get him to listen to other types of music, particularly church going music, but none of it ever took. Corbett knew what he liked, so why keep looking? It had been the same with her. He'd had his days alley catting around, but once he met Eleanor that had been it, and he never needed another.

Now she was gone. Perhaps it was for the best. The boys were also gone. They'd grown up all right but were a little too rambunctious for their own good. Eleanor had seen that in them and done her best to keep them on the right path.

Corbett knew Mac was back in town, but the boy hadn't stopped in to visit with him. That was also for the best. They'd never seen eye-to-eye, particularly after Mac up and moved out at sixteen. Mac had his reasons, but Corbett knew the truth of it. They had just butted heads once too often, and Mac couldn't accept his place in the pecking order.

Corbett picked up the bottle of whiskey and pulled the cork. He seamlessly filled each shot glass and then set the bottle back down and replaced the cork.

"Nobody's lonesome for me" played from the Victrola. Corbett smiled at that. It was true. Nobody was lonesome for him. Not the Marine Corps, not the Rangers and sure as hell not his sons. He cursed the Bonafide constitution. He would be seventy-four that May, but he could still walk all day with a pack on and whip anyone that crossed his path. Bonafide men took a long time dying, and he would not be any different.

That meant that there would be a lot more nights like this one ahead of him before he saw his Eleanor again.

Corbett picked up one of the shot glasses and downed the contents. He set it down and then picked up the colt and a single round. He slid the bullet into the wheel and then closed it and lay the pistol on the table. It was a ritual, one he had been performing for most of his life. It was something he always did before going to war. He had done it before War Two, before Korea and before Vietnam. He had done it most nights while he was on duty with the Rangers.

That all ended when they told him that his eyesight wasn't good enough to pass the medical qualifications. Corbett's declaration that he would whip any son of a bitch in the Ranger company in a head-to-head pistol shooting competition didn't seem to sway anyone in higher headquarters.

That was it. He was out. There would be no more wars for Corbett Bonafide. So now he performed his ritual in a quiet two-bedroom house, listening to Hank Williams and waiting for the clock to run out on him.

Corbett worked his way through the rest of the shot glasses and the rest of the bullets on the card table. He let out a sigh and looked back to the bottle of Old Grandad. Six shots were all he could handle anymore, and he damn well knew it. Any more than that and he would feel like hell the next day. It didn't use to be like that, but maybe age was catching up with him after all.

The phone in the kitchen rang. Corbett looked over his shoulder to where it was sitting on the counter. That was strange. No one ever called him. In fact, he didn't even know what his own phone number was, that was how little he cared for speaking to damn near anyone on the telephone.

He considered just letting it ring, but after the sixth ring it was becoming a bit annoying, so Corbett pulled his six foot four frame to standing and walked to the phone and picked it up. He just held it to his ear.

"Corbett?" Jack's voice came across the line.

"Jack?" Corbett asked. His eldest son was about the last person on the planet he had expected to hear from. Something was wrong. "What's going on?"

"I need you to do something for me, Corbett. I need you to go over to Ricky's place and stand watch on Angeline."

"Angeline? Why in the hell would I do that? That woman is a fucking nightmare."

"Look, me and Mac are involved in something. We're tangling with some dangerous folks and they might come after her to get at me."

"Well, I wish them good luck. They're gonna damn well need it," Corbett said, the tone of annoyance clear in his voice. "What in the hell did you two get into now?"

"Now you listen here, you mean old cuss!" Jack snapped. "I ain't got time for your shit! I've never asked you for a damn thing, but I'm asking now. If you've still got some fight left in you I need you to head over there and be ready for one."

Corbett thought about it for a moment. His reflex was to just keep pushing back, but something was wrong, and he knew it. It was true, Jack had never asked him for a thing. If he was asking now, it must be serious.

"Okay, I'll do it. But I'm still gonna crack you one good the next time I see you for raising your voice to me."

"Fair enough."

"What's the composition of the enemy?"

"I'm not sure, but it may be some kind of Soviet special forces."

Corbett raised an eyebrow.

"You shittin' me?"

"I shit you not, old man. You better be ready."

Corbett smiled.

"Ready? I've been waitin' on this my whole life."

Jack hung up the phone and stared at it for a moment,

then walked back to the car where Mac, Carrie and Steven were waiting.

"You think they'll really go after her?" Carrie asked.

"It's the right move," Jack said. "It's the only thing that would stop me."

"Who did you call?" Carrie asked.

Mac laughed and Jack shot him a dirty look.

"Our father."

"Don't you think you should call the authorities?" Carrie asked.

"No, I don't believe I should," Jack replied. "I can count on one hand the number of people I trust, and he's one of them. We may not get along very well, but he's the one I'd want on my side in a fight."

"Look, Jack, I'm sure your dad is tough—"

Mac laughed at this.

"Tough?" Mac asked, sounding almost indignant. "Darlin', Corbett Bonafide has killed more people than cancer. Tough don't even enter into the equation. If a bunch of Soviet assassins are actually going to go after Angeline, and he's standing in the way? Shit. I wouldn't give a bucket of piss for their future."

Corbett Bonafide set the phone back down in the cradle and walked back to the card table. He considered taking a few more belts of bourbon, but then decided against it. He needed to be at his best if what his boy had just told him was real.

It was a fact that he and Jack had never really gotten along, but Corbett knew the truth of it. He had been hard on both of the boys because he knew that they were something special. He also knew that they thought he didn't care about them, but that was not the truth of it. Neither one of them knew how many nights he had sat in the chair in the corner of their room watching them sleep, thinking about how he was going to do right what his own father had not.

Perhaps that was and always has been the way of fathers; having the best of intentions, but never quite sure if you really did things right, or just thought you did.

Even if things hadn't worked out the way Corbett hoped they would, this was something he could do for his son.

He picked up the Colt and walked through the kitchen, then out the back door and into the yard. At the end of the grass, just before the fence line sat a shed. It was older than both of his boys, and Corbett had built it right after he came back from the second war. He had put his things in there and only retrieved them when called upon to do so.

Now he had been called upon once again.

Corbett pulled the small key from his pocket and unlocked the door.

Inside, the shed was squared away. Everything was where it belonged, and it was immaculate. On one long shelf a tarp was draped across some tools, but they weren't the type of tools most men kept in sheds. Corbett pulled the tarp back. Beneath it was a Colt .45 pistol, a trench knife, a sawed-off shotgun and several boxes of ammunition.

Corbett smiled. It was a smile that would chill a man's blood, because it meant that things were about to get downright biblical.

CHAPTER 7

Jay's Highway Motel
Falls Church, VA
December 29, 1980

McMasters sat in his car fighting back the sleep that was aggressively trying to overtake his consciousness. It had been a fairly short drive from Bethesda to Falls Church, maybe only forty-five minutes, but he stayed awake through the night to make sure they didn't move.

He looked at his watch and saw that it was midnight.

The Bonafide brothers, the woman Carrie and the turncoat spy had stopped at this small motel in this backwater town to get a night's sleep before continuing.

It was that last part McMasters needed to know. Was the relay in this town, or would they move again?

McMasters felt that crazy thought drifting through his head again but suppressed it. It was too crazy, even for him.

It was the idea of teaming up with Jack Bonafide. Would the American even do it? They both wanted the same thing, to stop the Black Tsar from being detonated. Did McMasters really think Sokolov would detonate it?

He had worked with the old Colonel frequently in the past and looked into the man's shark's eyes. If called upon to give an honest accounting of what he saw in those eyes, what would he say?

Yes, Sokolov will detonate that weapon. He would detonate one hundred of them.

Honestly, McMasters didn't really care if the Black Tsar destroyed an American city, but he cared about what that event would do to his homeland. He knew they couldn't beat the Americans. It was a hard thing to admit (even to himself) but he had run the numbers frequently and played out the war games on his own. They just couldn't beat the Americans. At least, not yet.

So a strike like that on American soil would mean the end of the Soviet Union.

McMasters shook it off. Now was not the time for theories and politics. He had a job to do, and he would do it. If Sokolov's people materialized, he would handle them.

The phone rang, and he picked it up. He said nothing.

"Is this you?" A voice asked. There was a long pause, and then it continued. "Comrade Vitka?"

This man knew his real name. It had to be KGB. No one else would have the number.

"Yes," he replied. "Who is this?"

"There is a storage unit on the edge of town, on South Washington and Woodland Avenue. Meet me there in thirty minutes."

The line went dead. It was them. They were here.

Mac Bonafide cracked the window to let some cold night air in. With the four of them in the small motel room it was getting hot fast, and the windows were fogging up.

"So what's the play?" Mac asked.

Jack looked to Steven.

"You'll take us to this house?"

Steven was obviously uncomfortable with the idea, but he nodded. He knew that the only way out of this was through it.

"Good," Jack said. "Then it's you and me. We'll leave in ten."

"Wait, what?" Carrie asked. "You're leaving us here?"

"You're QRF," Jack said. "If we get popped in the first five minutes, you'll still be around to take another swing at it."

Steven appeared alarmed, but Jack looked at him and shook his head.

"I don't like it," Mac said. "We should go in hot, full force."

"No," Steven cut in. "He's right. The guy we'll be meeting, he won't be like me. As much as I hate to admit it, I'm bad at this. But someone who the KGB gave this much responsibility to, he'll be good."

"I still don't like it," Mac repeated.

"You don't have to like it," Jack said, putting his foot down. "But that's how it's going to be."

Mac clearly wanted to lodge another protest, but instead he nodded his understanding.

"I'm going to walk the perimeter," Jack said as he moved to the door. "Help Mister Waller get ready."

Jack walked in the cold night air and scanned the surrounding parking lot and streets of Falls Church. This place was a real dead-end town, not quite the stage he had expected for the kickoff of world war three. That was a sobering thought. None of it quite seemed real, not how his missions with Delta had.

Iran, Central America and Iraq had all been deadly serious jobs, jobs where he lost men and where he almost lost his own life, but not one was like this. It made matters all the stranger that this mission was taking place in his own country. That wasn't how things were supposed to go. The reason they had gone to those other countries was to take the fight to the enemy and make sure it never hit their own shores.

Except that was exactly what had happened, and now it was Jack Bonafide's job to nip it in the bud.

Jack pulled his collar up against the cold and rubbed his hands together as he walked around the back of the motel. That was when he noticed it. His hands were tremoring again.

"Shit," Jack said as the ringing in his ears started.

This time it was different. It got progressively louder, louder than it ever had before. Then the pressure in his chest. He felt his left arm going numb.

"No, no, no," he whispered as he fumbled for the Walkman in his jacket pocket.

Jack slipped on the headphones with the orange foam covering on the earpieces and tried to hit play on the cassette deck, but his hands were shaking so badly that he dropped it, yanking the headphone cord from the audio jack as it hit the ground.

A white-hot pain shot up his spine, and he followed the cassette deck to the ground, dropping to one knee.

His vision blurred, and the ringing got louder. He reconnected the headphones and hit the play button.

The music started playing, and just as it always did, the moment it hit Jack's ears he felt the symptoms beginning to subside. Jack looked around the parking lot. Every light was out. No one was around. No one had seen it.

He let out a breath. This was bad. Until now the symptoms were more of an annoyance than anything else, just some trembling hands and the ringing in his ears. Then he'd had that episode outside of Fort Meade, and now this. It was getting worse. Was it time to pass the ball? Did he need to bring someone else in to take over?

"No," Jack said and stood back up.

There was a reason Charlie Beckwith had chosen him to be a founding member of Delta Force. There was a reason Colonel Cain Ernst had asked him to lead the assault force on that raid into Iraq. There was a reason Mike Tresham had asked him to chase down the Black Tsar and god dammit he was going to finish the job even if it killed him.

McMasters pulled his car to a stop at the gate of the storage unit and scanned his surroundings. He had driven the last half mile with his headlights out. It was a tricky maneuver but there was enough moonlight that he could find his path and not give himself away.

For the briefest of moments, he had thought about not coming to the meet. He did not know who he was meeting there, only that they were KGB. He didn't know if they were Galkin's people or Sokolov's. Either way, if he didn't show up it would red flag him with the intelligence group.

If that happened, he would be declared an ineffective agent to be "decommissioned" as they often put it. This was code for that ineffective agent being killed. The Soviet Union (as far as McMasters knew) did not have a retirement home for KGB agents. Particularly not for ineffective ones.

McMasters thought about that for a moment. An ineffective agent. That was what he had become. He didn't like the sound of that.

Then he saw them. The first man emerged from the tree line. He was wearing overalls, some type of night vision and he carried a cut down assault rifle with a silencer fixed to the end of it. The gear this man had, McMasters had never seen before. It just confirmed that they were indeed Alpha Group, a special unit within Soviet special forces often attached to the KGB for missions like these; a group that Colonel Konstantin Sokolov had control over.

It was more than just the advanced gear that made

these men special, or even that they belonged to the ultra-elite Alpha Group. They all knew that this would probably be a one-way trip. Once activated, they would be engaging American law enforcement or military on American soil. There was no coming back from that. Their task would be to inflict as much damage as possible to support the mission and to not be caught alive.

Five more men emerged from the tree line behind the first and then fanned out to set security. They did not seem overly concerned about being seen, and there was no reason they should have been. There was no one around for miles.

McMasters stepped out of the car. As the men drew closer, he recognized that they were carrying American weapons. The short rifles were CAR-15s and one man was carrying a light machine gun of some sort. What in the hell were they going to do with that, he wondered? What did they think they were about to do?

McMasters held up his open hand. The first man stopped and flipped up his night vision.

He said nothing.

"The dishes are dirty." McMasters called out, offering the standard challenge for KGB officers abroad.

"Then break them," the man replied. "I am Arkady. I am now the commander in the field."

"What are you talking about? I received no such order."

"You just did. From me. Do we have a problem here, Comrade?"

McMasters wanted to protest further, but deep down he knew that he was at a disadvantage. He had worked with Makar Galkin for many years, and trusted the man, but it was clear that the power struggle was over and Colonel Sokolov had won, at least in Falls Church, Virginia. There was no reason for McMasters to die over it.

"No," McMasters said.

"Excellent," Arkady replied.

"They're in a motel at the center of town. If we hit them—"

"No," Arkady said, cutting him off. "We need to know where their connection is. I also find it highly unlikely that we would take men like this alive. I assume you have installed a tracking device?"

"You know about them? The Bonafide brothers?" McMasters asked, the surprise in his voice clear.

"Yes. We have access to the same intelligence you do," Arkady replied, the irritation in his voice clear. "The tracking device?"

"Yes," McMasters said.

Arkady held out his hand.

"It might be best for me to retain control of the tracker," McMasters said.

"Why would that be best?"

"I'm familiar with the technology."

Arkady made a "give it here" gesture with his hand.

McMasters relented and after retrieving the device from the car handed it to Arkady. Down the road he heard a V8 engine coming toward them.

"Who is that?" McMasters asked.

"The rest of the team," Arkady replied.

"How many are you?"

"Twelve."

"Twelve?" McMasters asked in astonishment.

"Your time here has made you soft," Arkady said. It sounded like a statement of fact versus a question or even just an observation.

"How dare you speak to me like that!" McMasters snapped.

Arkady raised his silenced carbine and pointed the barrel at McMasters.

McMasters froze.

"I'm not sure if I want to kill you or not," Arkady said conversationally. "An extra set of hands is always useful, but not if they are attached to a mouth like yours. Should I?" Arkady asked. "Kill you, I mean?"

"No," McMasters said without hesitation. "I can be useful."

Arkady stared at the man for a moment from behind cold blue eyes. He lowered the carbine.

"We shall see. You will sit up front with the driver.

Take us to this motel. We will follow them from there at a safe distance."

The Alpha Group members loaded into the Ford Econoline van and McMasters slid into the passenger seat and slammed the door shut. He looked over his shoulder to see the soldiers sitting quietly in full gear. Then McMasters saw something that astonished him. One of them was securing a mortar tube in place.

What in the hell are they going to do with a mortar? McMasters thought to himself.

Just keep putting one foot in front of the other, that was what Jack knew he needed to do. Don't overthink it. Just get the job done. This process kept cycling through his head as he walked through the parking lot and back to the room.

Jack stopped at the doorway and listened. He could hear them talking inside, helping Steven get ready. Jack knew that they were depending on him. He could do this.

Then Jack noticed something on the wall outside of the door. It looked like a chalk mark, or maybe a scratch someone had made with a rock. It almost looked like a mark for a dead drop or a target. Was he being paranoid? Who could have done that? Jack turned and scanned the parking lot and the streets beyond again but saw nothing. Even if someone had figured out where they were and marked their exact room, it wouldn't change anything. They would proceed as planned.

Jack reached out, turned the knob and walked into the room.

Mac looked up from the floor when Jack walked in. He had the gear bags open and was doing an inventory, getting prepped in case McMasters came at them. Mac could tell that something was wrong, and Jack knew it, but the younger brother said nothing.

"Everything wired tight?" Jack asked as he closed the door behind him.

"He's good to go," Mac replied and stood up with a carbine in his hand. "We'll hold fast here and wait to hear from you."

Jack nodded.

"I'll get in touch the moment we make contact." Jack looked to Carrie. "How about you? You good?"

"I'm good," Carrie said with a smile. "We should only be ten minutes out if you need us."

"Hopefully it won't come to that."

Jack walked out of the motel room and into the night and could see that Carrie had followed him. He turned to her.

"Can I talk with you?" Carrie asked and then looked to Steven. "Privately?"

Steven took the hint and walked to where the parked car.

"What is it?" Jack asked.

"You had a team, right? When you were with Delta?"

"I had an assault team, yeah."

"I just want to make sure that you know you still have one."

"What do you mean?" Jack asked, his voice a mix of annoyance and confusion.

"You're acting like you're the only one on this job. You keep leaving us behind to play the lone wolf."

"I'm not playing," Jack shot back. "I just need to get to this thing before McMasters does."

Carrie held up her hands in a placating gesture.

"I understand, I do, but you could utilize us more than you are."

Jack locked eyes with her for a moment and then relented.

"Okay, I get it. You're right. Even when I was with Delta, I was probably more lone wolf than I should have been. Maybe that's why Tresham's whole ghost operative idea was so attractive to me. It implied that I would be on my own."

"But you're not."

"Like, I said, I get it. So, don't worry, the moment we know something actionable you'll be getting a call. Be ready."

. . .

Arkady sat quietly in the front seat of the cargo van, watching the motel across the street through his night optics. He saw the shorter of the two men exit the motel room with another man that he knew to be the rogue Directorate S agent, Steven Waller. What a mess that was. If only the vetting process had been more stringent, and the KGB had not taken this sleeper business so seriously, none of this would be necessary.

Arkady understood that it would be a challenge to check in on these men and women that had been left behind in America at the service of their country. However, this laxity led to a man like Steven Waller now working for the Americans.

"Are you going to take him?" McMasters asked, leaning forward out of the back seat.

Arkady gave him a stern sideways looks.

"Comrade, if we attempt to capture him now, how will we know where they are going? This man and I are in the same predicament. We need to find the Black Tsar. He will lead us to the only person who may know where it is."

"I understand if it's classified, but once we find it, what are we to do with it?" McMasters asked, deciding to go on a bit of a fishing expedition.

Arkady turned fully around in his seat.

"You said you could be useful," Arkady said.

"I can," McMasters replied.

"Then perhaps you should be like one of Lenin's useful idiots and keep your questions to yourself."

McMasters nodded, unsure how to respond to that. He knew what he wanted to say, but he also understood that it would not be met with the response he might hope for.

A crunching of gravel signaled a second van which parked beside the passenger side of the vehicle Arkady and McMasters were in. Arkady turned to the driver of his van.

"No survivors," Arkady said.

The driver was a big man, with scars crisscrossing his face that marked him as a veteran of the war in Afghanistan and who knew where else. This man nodded.

Arkady reached out and shook his hand.

"The Motherland thanks you for your service, Comrade," Arkady said. "You will not be forgotten."

Without another word, Arkady slid out of the van and walked around to the passenger side of the second vehicle. He opened his door and got inside, and without further ceremony they drove away.

The men in the first van began opening doors and getting out, checking their weapons and McMasters watched as one even set up the mortar. He noticed a few of them slipping something into their mouths.

The driver pressed a rifle into McMasters' hands

and then pressed a small item into his palm. McMasters opened his hand and looked at it. It was a suicide pill.

No survivors.

We're not supposed to get out of this, McMasters thought. *And if we're not supposed to get out of this, Arkady is going to set off the Black Tsar.*

The Home Of Ricky Michaels
Texarkana, Texas
December 28, 1980

Corbett Bonafide pulled his truck to a stop in front of the Michaels house and cut the engine. He sat quietly for a moment and listened to the night. Angeline Michaels lived in what anyone worth their salt in East Texas would consider to be quite a respectable double-wide trailer in the park behind the Piggly Wiggly, but Corbett had heard through the grapevine that she was staying with her father at the moment.

Corbett couldn't pretend to understand all the ins and outs of his son's personal affairs, but he figured this change in location for Angeline had something to do with Jack's sudden reappearance and just as quick disappearance on Christmas Eve.

Things seemed quiet. Soviet Special Forces descending on Texarkana to get leverage on Jack Bonafide was a crazy idea, but it wasn't insane. That thought kept circulating in Corbett's head. Jack had told him about Delta Force, told him about what they were doing and what it meant. Corbett and Mac were probably the only people on the planet who knew the truth about this.

Corbett remembered sitting on the back porch with Jack sipping whiskey while his son told him about the special unit and about Colonel Beckwith. This was when Jack had told him they might go after the hostages in Iran.

"Seems like you're the sort," Corbett had said, and never looked away from the cornfield behind the house.

I'm proud as hell of you, and I hope you get the job done and come back safe.

That was what he should have said, but he didn't. Instead, he did the same thing his father did. He left everything unsaid for another day. Now his oldest son was taking on some Soviet Special Forces, and while Corbett knew that Jack Bonafide was as tough as they came, he also understood that everyone has their limit. It's just a matter of how long you take to meet it.

A light came on in the house. Corbett had been waiting on that. He knew it wouldn't take Ricky Michaels long to have heard the engine and investigate. Corbett quietly got out of the truck and walked up the steps. He reached the door just in time to see Ricky open it and face him, back-lit by the light from inside the house.

"Corbett?" Ricky asked in disbelief.

"Daddy, what in the hell is going on out there?" A voice called out from behind him, and Corbett knew it to be Angeline's.

Corbett pushed the door open and walked into the living room. Angeline saw him and froze. The two had never liked each other. Neither had ever come right out and said it, but there was always a palpable tension between them.

"Corbett," Ricky said. "It's after midnight. What's going on?"

Corbett turned to Ricky.

"Jack called me. Trouble's coming. I need—" Corbett stopped. He stopped, and he listened. Then he reached out and flipped the light switch off with his left hand while his right found the Colt pistol beneath his jacket. "I need you two in the basement. Now."

Ricky didn't like it. He wasn't some damn coward and he didn't think it was the right thing for him to be hiding in the basement. Even if he didn't like it (and didn't particularly care for Corbett Bonafide) he trusted the old Ranger. Ricky knew that if Corbett Bonafide shows up at your door at midnight and tells you to get in the basement, he's got a damn good reason for it.

Now, Corbett stood in the living room alone. He stood and he listened. He could hear them. He wasn't sure exactly where they were; it was almost like some heightened sense he had always had. They were out there. He knew it.

He moved quietly through the house and into the kitchen where he unlatched the back door and quiet as a ghost moved out onto the back porch. He latched the door behind him and walked out into the yard and then into the cornfield behind the house where he disappeared.

Marat and Nestor stood in the darkness and watched the house. Nestor had finally stopped complaining about not being attached to the main assault element that was going to Virginia, and for this Marat was grateful. The younger man (Nestor) seemed to not understand that any role they played in this operation was one they should be proud of.

Was Marat happy that they had been dispatched to East Texas to kidnap a woman and hold her hostage as a contingency plan? Of course not. The older and much more experienced Alpha Group operative (much like Nestor) would have preferred to be in Virginia. However, he understood the importance of their job. It was unlikely that the main force would fail, but if they did and they could not stop this American agent, they would be the ones to stop him.

In all fairness, Marat understood that Nestor had not enjoyed the opportunities his senior brothers had. Marat had already covered himself in glory in the mountains of Afghanistan, while Nestor seemed constantly sidelined with one bizarre injury after another. Now, though, now would be his time.

The last communication Marat received from command had been a warning: *These people are not to be taken lightly.* Until that point Marat had taken this mission seriously, but not as seriously as he would have taken the Virginia job. Now things had changed. If he was honest about it, the warning had spooked him. Command never gave out warnings like this.

The two men stood in the darkness down the road from the house, each carrying a CAR-15 and a Colt pistol. If they were compromised there would be nothing native to identify them as agents of the Soviet government. Even the night optics they carried would not be traced back to the USSR. They had been purchased from an American company called Fluid Dynamics.

"Who was that?" Nestor asked quietly.

"I don't know," Marat replied.

He looked back down the road and then to the

house again. Was there anyone else coming? Had someone found them out?

"Should we still go?" Nestor asked.

"Of course we should still go. It's a woman and her father." Marat thought about it for a moment and then nodded his further confirmation. "Yes, we are going."

Marat took a step forward and then stopped as he heard a hammer being cocked behind him. He froze.

"Throw 'em away," A gravely voice called out from the night behind him.

Nestor looked to Marat, as he had also frozen in place.

"Don't look at him," the voice said. "He ain't the one holding a gun to your head."

Marat nodded as he threw his carbine in the dirt, and Nestor followed suit.

"Pistolas too."

Both Marat and Nestor complied, removing their sidearms from the drop holsters secured to their legs and throwing them beside the carbines.

"Turn around. Real slow like."

The two Russians turned around and came face to face with the tallest American they had ever seen. He was a much older man but stood at least six foot four and did not look like someone to be trifled with.

"I do believe I'm the rascal you're lookin' for," Corbett Bonafide said.

. . .

Ricky Michaels held the old trench gun in his hands and watched the door to the cellar. If it opened and he saw anyone other than Corbett Bonafide, he was ready to shoulder the weapon and give them the good news.

Angeline sat in the corner holding a lantern turned as low as it would go without plunging them into darkness. Ricky knew that she was scared, but she damn sure wasn't going to show it.

Upstairs he heard footsteps again. They were heavy, like they belonged to someone about the size of a small bear. Corbett fit that bill, but a man couldn't rely on sound alone.

"Open up," Corbett's voice called from outside.

Ricky walked up the steps, still keeping the shotgun at the ready and reached out and unlatched the door. He opened it and found Corbett standing alone outside. His face and shirt were covered in blood.

"Go to the washroom and wipe yourself off before Angeline sees that," Ricky instructed.

"Hm," Corbett grunted. "When did we all get so sensitive around these parts?"

Despite his protest, Corbett complied with the request. There was no reason to scare the girl any more than she probably already was.

"We'll be back. You latch the door behind me and stay put," Ricky said over his shoulder as he exited the cellar.

Angeline walked up behind him and did as instructed.

Ricky walked to the washroom where Corbett was toweling off. The older man looked at Ricky in the mirror behind him.

"I didn't hear gunshots," Ricky said.

"Gunshots?" Corbett asked incredulously. "I ain't some fuckin' amateur. I start shootin' those boys full of holes and I'll have every type of law within ten miles out here before you can skin a beaver. I did it quiet like, up close and personal," Corbett stood up to his full height and turned to Ricky. "Don't worry, I gave 'em a fair fight."

"What's a fair fight with you look like?" Ricky asked.

"Well, shit, I don't know," Corbett spat. "Ain't my fault if they're a couple of pencil necks that can't handle getting stabbed a few times without falling over."

"Who were they?" Ricky asked as he followed Corbett back outside.

"Some sort of Soviet spies."

"Soviet spies?" Ricky asked in disbelief. "In Texarkana?"

"Near as I can figure it, they were probably tryin' to get to Angeline. Planned on using her as leverage against Jack."

"Guess they didn't get the memo that those two are split."

"Guess not," Corbett replied as he led Ricky out the door and to the edge of the field.

Corbett parted some stalks and Ricky could see two bodies lying in the dirt. By the look of them they'd been cut up pretty good.

"Jesus Christ," Ricky gasped.

"Jesus never used a Bowie knife like that," Corbett smiled as he kneeled down beside the bodies.

"Should I call the Sheriff?"

"Nah. Sheriff's still pissed about what Jack and Mac did to him over in Victory on Christmas Eve." Corbett said, referencing the events following Mac's apprehension of the two Soviets who had escaped from Red River Army Depot. "I doubt he'll be much for lending a helping hand."

"So, what do we do with them?"

"Same thing Texans have been doing with trespassers for as far back as I can recollect. Bury 'em in the yard."

CHAPTER 8

The Target House
Falls Church, VA
December 29, 1980

J ack had said little to Steven Waller since they had left the motel. In fact, he hadn't said a single word. The skill of asset development hadn't quite taken root in the consciousness of Jack Bonafide, and he still saw the Russian as just another tool he needed to employ to get a step closer to the Black Tsar.

Steven reached out and turned on the radio. A late-night DJ was on, threatening to play the entire last album from The Monkees if no one called in.

"Turn that off," Jack said.

"I like The Monkees," Steven said.

"If you like not getting shot in the head more, turn it off."

Steven let out a sigh and clicked the knob back into the off position.

"Are we close?" Jack asked.

"Almost," Steven replied, leaning back in his seat.

The neighborhood was quiet, and Jack stopped himself from invoking the old cliché that it seemed too quiet. Steven leaned forward in his seat, squinted his eyes and then pointed at a house on the corner.

"That's it. That's the address."

Jack pulled the car to the curb and shut off the engine. The structure was a modest single-family home, not unlike the one they had tracked Steven himself to.

"You're sure you don't know him?" Jack asked.

"I don't. I was only given the address."

Jack turned back to the house.

"I have an idea, if you want to hear it," Steven said.

Jack could sense the trepidation in Steven's voice. Hell, maybe Carrie was right. Was he being too closed off to what everyone else had to say? This man was taking a big risk by helping them, even if he was getting a fair deal from it.

"Okay," Jack said, relaxing his tone a bit. "Let's hear it."

"If I'm right, and this man is waiting for someone to come and shut this thing down, he'll be happy to see us.

Regardless of what American propaganda might say, we aren't just one big death cult. What is your American intelligence telling you about the KGB right now?"

Jack tapped his fingers on the steering wheel for a moment. Divulging classified information to a known Soviet sleeper agent seemed like a bad idea, but who was he going to tell?

"Just like your code said, that there's a split. Two factions going at it, each with very different goals. One is being run by a guy named Makar Galkin and the other is being run by a Colonel Sokolov."

"Sokolov?" Steven asked, his eyes wide. "Is a Colonel now?"

"And the head of Foreign Affairs for the KGB. Next in line to replace Andropov. If he can get Galkin out of the way."

"He was my training officer," Steven said, and sat back in his seat. Jack could see that the man was obviously rattled.

"You've met him?" Jack asked.

"Oh, yes," Steven replied quietly. "He used to... he used to make me... he made me strangle cats."

"Jesus," Jack said.

"That was his training method. He believed that if I killed these cats, I would never have a problem killing a human. It was always in this brick room in the building, where I would have to meet him in the mornings, before breakfast. He had some theory about fear hormones and an empty stomach. He would meet me there and bring a cat out of the cage."

"You don't have to talk about this," Jack said. He could sense that Steven was close to crying.

"No, it's okay. Maybe I need to. He would make me pet the cat and talk to it. Make me be friendly to him, and then he would give the order. If I refused, they beat me. I only refused a few times until I learned."

"How old were you?"

"I was ten. It changed me."

"That's why you had so many cats," Jack said, understanding.

Steven turned to Jack, a wetness in his eyes.

"I believe you, you know. When you say that you will uphold the deal they gave me. But perhaps now you understand why my cats need to be cared for. They can't die. They can't ever die."

Jack nodded his understanding.

"I get it now. I didn't before, but I do now," Jack said.

Steven smiled, and it was a smile that signaled his belief that they would take care of his cats.

"So, what's the plan?" Jack asked.

"We knock on the front door, tell him who we are and hope for the best."

"That's your plan?" Jack asked in disbelief.

"Do you have a better one?"

Jack thought about it for a moment. He didn't.

"Not at this exact point in time."

"Mister Bonafide, if Colonel Sokolov's goal is really to set off the Black Tsar in the United States... you wouldn't be able to find enough people to fill a phone booth who would support him on that. Even the KGB agents deployed to support his goal probably don't truly understand what they're doing. Only a true maniac would want something like that, and despite American opinion to the contrary, we don't have that many of those."

"So, we're just relying on this guy being a good Samaritan?"

"No, Mister Bonafide. We only have to rely on him not being insane."

Jay's Highway Motel
Falls Church, VA
December 29, 1980

"What did you say to him out there?" Mac asked as he finished his inventory of the gear bags. "Try to talk some sense into him?"

"How did you know?" Carrie asked with a smile.

"Because I've been trying to talk some sense into that man for damn near my whole life. Does no good.

He always finds his own way, and things mostly turn out okay."

"Mostly?" Carrie asked, sitting on the bed across from Mac.

Mac shrugged.

"You know how it is. Not every mission can be a success."

Carrie thought about this for a moment.

"I know I'm not supposed to ask," she said.

"Then don't."

"But the mission at Desert One. He was on it, wasn't he?"

"Maybe. Can't say," Mac replied with a wink.

"That must have been hard."

"Like I said, not every mission can be a success. We all know that. You have to go into this kind of thing ready for some push back. If you always go in thinking you'll win, well, that's a recipe for disaster."

Carrie looked at Mac Bonafide. He was rougher looking than this brother, with a few scars peppering his face and a little grayer in his hair. He was also a lot bigger and seemed like his movements were graceful when he wanted them to be, but clumsy when he wasn't paying as much attention to them.

She reached out across the bed and put her hand on his.

Mac held her gaze and smiled.

He was across the bed before she could even think

to react or protest (not that she would) and picked Carrie up and pushed her against the wall.

"Should we be doing this?" Carrie asked, her breathing labored.

"Stop talking, darling," Mac whispered, and kissed her as his hands began working the buttons on her blouse.

Carrie moved her hands to his belt buckle and let him push her against the wall.

Then he stopped. He heard it first.

"It can't be," he said.

Then he realized it could. It was a long, slow whistle high overhead. The same sound he'd heard so many times in Vietnam.

"What is it?" Carrie asked.

"Down!" Mac shouted, and threw her to the floor, covering her with his own body a split second before the mortar round tore the room apart.

Carrie opened her eyes and saw that Mac was still on top of her, but his eyes were closed. She had been out, but she did not know for how long.

"Wake up," she whispered, lifting her head up to reach his ear.

His eyes opened and looked into hers, but he didn't move.

They both heard it; footsteps closing in on them

and the sound of voices speaking, but they weren't speaking English. They were speaking Russian. Carrie could feel a wetness on her, and an electric shock raced up her spine as she realized it was blood. She just didn't know if it was hers or Mac's.

"Run," he whispered. "You have to run, and don't you look back."

"I'm not leaving you!" She hissed.

"You will!" Mac snarled. "If I don't make it out of this, it can't be for nothing. You have to get to Jack. Tell him what happened."

"I'm not leaving you."

Then she was light, light as a feather. She realized what had happened. He was gone. Mac had stumbled to his feet and snatched up the carbine lying on the floor beside him.

There was no talking, no shouting or cursing. No swearing of oaths and no angry battle cry. There was only cold professionalism.

Mac Bonafide put the stock of the carbine to his shoulder, got his sight picture and began engaging targets of opportunity. Unfortunately, these weren't Baltimore gangbangers with poorly calibrated automatic weapons.

Mac felt the first round hit him in the ribs like a baseball, but he knew it hadn't just hit him. It had gone through him. Why in the hell hadn't he been wearing a vest? Probably because he hadn't expected someone to mortar Jay's Highway Motel.

Carrie scrambled behind the tattered remains of the bed and began sorting through the shattered weapons that had been in the gear bag, until she finally found a pistol in working condition. She chambered a round and made the weapon unsafe.

"Get in the bathroom!" Mac shouted as he moved backward away from the advancing Russian soldiers.

Mac dropped to a knee and grabbed something from the floor, then stuffed it in his pocket and started his retreat again.

None of the Alpha Group men seemed in much of a hurry and were taking their shots selectively. They knew that there was nowhere for the Americans to run, so there was no reason to pursue them with much vigor and unnecessarily expose themselves.

Carrie had made it past the closet and into the bathroom, and Mac grabbed her, lifted her off her feet and dropped her into the bathtub. He turned and grabbed the door, ripping it off its hinges.

"We're going to die," Carrie said. Tears were streaming from her eyes as she lay in the bathtub. She looked at Mac and could count a half dozen bullet holes in the man. She didn't understand how he was still alive and moving.

"We ain't fucking dying today," Mac said, and

pulled the object he had retrieved from the floor out of his pocket. It was a detonator. "Get low, lay flat."

"What are you going to do?"

"Never you mind, darlin," Mac said. His voice was shaky and there was a wetness in his eyes. "You just tell him... you tell him I didn't quit."

"No!" Carrie shouted as Mac picked up the door.

"You get to him! You tell him what happened!"

Mac slammed the door down on top of the bathtub, sealing Carrie in.

He stood back up and turned to what was left of the motel room. He could see the men advancing, about a half dozen of them by the looks of things. There was no time for any other move, no place for a smart-ass remark and not a second left on the clock. Mac looked down at the detonator in his hand and back to the advancing Russians.

He was going to buy his brother some time.

Mac thumbed the detonator.

From within the bathtub Carrie felt the thump of the explosion more than she heard it. She had wanted to push the door off of the bathtub and jump out, but something told her she would be wasting the chance that Mac had just given her; the chance to make it out of this thing alive. It was best to hold fast and wait.

She lay silently and gripped the nine-millimeter

Beretta in her right hand. She heard footsteps, but it was more than one person. Carrie drew back the hammer on the pistol.

The door scraped against the tub. Light began to creep in. Someone was taking the door off.

Carrie sat up in the bathtub as fast as she could and raised the pistol, but just as quickly it was snatched out of her hand. She threw a wild punch but felt a strong pair of hands grab her, pick her up and slam her into a wall.

Her eyes had finally adjusted back to the ambient light, and she saw the face staring at her. It wasn't Mac. It was one of the Russians. The man's face was covered in blood and his teeth were broken, but he was still alive. He was still alive, and he was strangling her. He was strangling her, and she was dying.

Panicking wouldn't do any good, she knew this. Even as she could feel herself entering the very beginning stages of losing consciousness, Carrie raised her right leg and reached to her calf, where she had strapped a small dagger. She slipped it from the sheathe with her right hand. This man was so intent on strangling her and watching the light in her eyes go out that he didn't notice the movement.

Carrie could see the darkness swimming inward from the edges of her peripheral vision and she squeezed the knife handle and drove it upward, into the soft underside of this man's jaw. His eyes locked on hers, obvious surprise in them before he collapsed to the floor, releasing her.

Carrie hit the ground clumsily and felt something crack in her shoulder as she did. Throbbing pain instantly radiated from her arm to her neck. Then the blows started coming, kicks to her ribs and her head, accompanied by shouts in Russian. They were angry because Mac had blown them up and she had just stabbed their friend in the head. They were angry, and she would be the one to pay.

More kicks, more punches and another sick crack that came from somewhere deep in her back. Carrie drew a quick breath, mostly to not scream, but even that seemed pointless. There were too many of them, they were too strong and she was alone. This was really it. This was how she would end. She would be beaten to death.

She felt the blood on her face. Then she heard the quiet pop of the suppressed weapon. Wait, no, that was backwards. The pop had come first. What was happening? There was no time to think, no time to put together the pieces. Carrie knew she had to act.

Out of the corner of her eye she saw a pistol laying on the floor. She rolled on her side, grabbed it and brought it up in time to put two rounds into the man moving toward her. He collapsed to the ground, and she saw another shadowy figure, but this one was firing on another of the Russians.

Carrie stumbled to her feet and kept her weapon up as the mystery figure turned toward her.

"Don't shoot!" He shouted.

Carrie kept her weapon up as he stepped into what little light there was.

"You son of a bitch!" Carrie shouted.

It was McMasters.

"Be that as it may," McMasters said sharply in his perfect American accent. "Your man there might still make it if we get him to a hospital right now!"

Carrie turned to where McMasters indicated and saw Mac's body crumpled against the wall. It looked wrong, broken and smashed.

"Mac!" She shouted reflexively and darted to where he lay.

McMasters followed her and began tearing open a first aid kit. Carrie glared at him.

"We don't have time for this," McMasters said calmly. "If you want him to live, we have to go right now."

"Why are you doing this?" Carrie asked as she grabbed some gauze and bandages and began packing Mac's wounds to keep him stable for the trip to the hospital.

"I'm a patriot, not a mass murderer. The men behind this don't intend to use The Black Tsar as a bargaining chip. They intend to detonate it."

The Target House
Falls Church, VA
December 29, 1980

Jack scanned the street as they walked to the front door of the house. Every fiber of his being was screaming at him that this was a bad idea, but there was no way around it. Waller knew more about this than he did. Any plan that Jack came up with would be pure guesswork.

They approached the front door and Steven stopped, then looked over his shoulder at Jack. Jack nodded and indexed his weapon. Hopefully, he wouldn't need the pistol, but if things went south, he would be ready.

Steven reached out and knocked on the door. They waited for a moment. There was no answer. Jack scanned the street again. It was dead quiet, but it was also one in the morning; there was no reason there should be a lot of noise in a residential neighborhood. Further down the street he noticed a parked Ford Econoline van. That seemed strange for this street, but not unusual enough to set off alarm bells.

Steven knocked again. They waited again. Still no answer. Steven looked over his shoulder at Jack and shrugged.

"Maybe he's not home?" Steven asked quietly.

Jack waved him off the steps and back toward him. He then began walking in a wide loop around the house, heading for the side entrance gate he had noticed, assuming it would lead him to the backyard. He drew his Colt 1911.

"What am I supposed to do?" Steven asked.

"Get back to the car!" Jack hissed. "I'll come get you when it's clear."

Steven wasn't sure about this, but complied with Jack's order, and headed back to the car.

As Jack rounded the corner of the house everything was still quiet, and he could see the gate in front of him. There was no visible lock, so he reached up and thumbed the latch and it swung open with a small creak. Jack froze where he stood and waited. He waited for the sound of someone stirring in the house. Intellectually he knew the squeak wasn't loud enough to give them away, but he had been wrong about that before.

Nothing.

He stepped forward into the yard and could feel the frozen grass crunching beneath his feet. No way around that, so he moved as silently as he could around the back to the rear porch. He looked at the steps. They were old. They would creak.

He stepped onto the first plank. No sound, no creak. Second plank, nothing. One to go. Jack stepped up and felt the slight give of the wood under his foot. He froze again.

Creak.

He could see through the window of the back door. He was in full view. If someone wanted to take a shot at him, he would be a sitting duck, but there was no movement from inside. He slowly dropped to a knee and pulled the small lock picking kit from his jacket and went to work.

When Colonel Beckwith had first brought an actual convicted felon in to teach Delta operators how to pick a lock, Jack had thought it seemed a little out there. They had spent literally thousands of hours breaching doors and assaulting with violence of action. How often were they really going to need to pick a lock? The answer was all the freaking time. Now he was so practiced at it he could pick most locks in his sleep, and this one was no different.

That seemed a little strange. If this house was a KGB way station, why was it such a soft target? He could tell just by the feel of the door that there wasn't even a deadbolt. It was just the lock in the doorknob. It might make sense that the location wasn't hardened because too many advanced security measures might give it away, but still.

Jack felt the last tumbler fall into place and stowed his lock picking kit. He picked his pistol back up from where he had set it on the porch and reached up with his free hand to turn the doorknob. The door opened, and he moved into the house, staying in a low crouch.

It was quiet inside. He knew it sounded like a cliché from a bad movie, but it was too quiet. Jack moved in a low crouch through what appeared to be a laundry room. At the other end of it he could see a living room area and moved toward that, clearing the house.

The lights came on. Jack popped up in a ready firing position and acquired his first target.

"Don't do it!" Steven shouted.

Jack stopped. There were at least six of them. They were all geared up and heavily armed, carrying carbines. One man had a light machine gun. Steven Waller stood in the corner beside the front door. He had a plaintiff look on his face. Even without knowing it for sure, Jack knew he had somehow betrayed him. Then he remembered the chalk mark he had seen on the outside of the motel room. Dammit, that had been it. It had been a signal.

"Listen to your friend," a man who appeared to be the leader said with what was clearly a Russian accent. "You don't have a chance. No one here doubts your courage, but don't be a fool."

Jack maintained his grip on the Colt and looked this man in the eyes. They were shark's eyes. He had known plenty of men like this. The rest of the men in the room were the same. If he thought he had even a sliver of a chance he would gladly go down swinging, but he knew he didn't even have that. It would be pure suicide to take them on.

Jack moved slowly and raised his hands. One of the men stepped forward and snatched the pistol out of his hand. Another began frisking him and pulled out his lock pick kit and the dagger in his boot, then threw both in the corner.

Jack turned to Steven.

"It was you. You marked the motel room. When you went out to smoke."

There was something about Steven's face. He was ashamed.

"You don't understand. I had to."

The leader held up his hand to silence Steven and stepped forward.

"My name is Arkady. I think you know who we are."

"You're with McMasters," Jack replied.

Arkady laughed.

"McMasters is a fool. A polite tool of the softer members of the Politburo who like to play spy games. We are a different type of tool." Arkady paused for a moment and looked Jack over. "Jack Bonafide, correct?"

Jack nodded.

"We know about you, Jack. We were ready for you. You did your job well, do you understand?" Arkady asked. "You were just outmatched."

Jack said nothing. Arkady smiled.

"The stoic American soldier. I like you Jack. Will it help you to know how close you were?"

"What do you mean?" Jack asked.

"The Black Tsar, Jack. You almost beat us to it."

"Where is it?" Jack asked.

"You're standing on it."

Jack looked down at the floor and then back to Arkady. The big Russian was smiling.

"There's no fucking way you're getting a hydrogen bomb out of Falls Church, Virginia with no one knowing about it. You must realize that."

"We got it in here," Arkady replied curtly. "Why wouldn't we be able to move it to its final destination?"

"Then what?" Jack asked. "You set it off?"

"That is for me to know," Arkady said and then turned to two of his men and nodded.

The men stepped forward, and each grabbed one of Jack's arms, leading him back toward the rear entrance.

"Jack!" Arkady called out.

The men stopped pushing, and Jack Bonafide looked over his shoulder at Arkady.

"We launched a coordinated attack on the motel. Your brother and your lady friend are dead, but they died as warriors. You should know that."

Jack's eyes grew cold. He didn't know if this man was telling the truth or not, but the chill that set into his bones told him that this Arkady was not a liar.

"Have a nice day," Jack whispered.

"What?" Arkady asked, confused.

Jack locked eyes with him.

"Because the rest are fucking numbered."

McMasters pulled the car into the emergency entrance at the Falls Church hospital doing about sixty miles per hour and slammed on the brakes, fishtailing the car across the parking lot until it squealed to a stop in front of the big double doors.

The man jumped out and helped Carrie lift Mac out of the back seat and onto the gurney that was already being rushed to them. You didn't have to be a doctor to see that Mac Bonafide was in bad shape.

No sooner had Mac hit the gurney than McMasters turned and began heading back to the car.

"Where in the hell are you going?" Carrie shouted.

"You must have known I would not stay."

Without another word, Carrie pulled out the Beretta she had shoved into her waistband back at the hotel and held it on the Russian spy.

"You're not going anywhere."

McMasters didn't even break his stride as he opened the driver's side door and looked at her.

"Shoot me if you like, but every second you waste here brings him a step closer to death."

Carrie added a pound of pull to the trigger before

she relented. Killing this man wouldn't yield any kind of measurable result, and she could not ignore the fact that he had saved her life and possibly Mac's. She lowered the pistol.

McMasters nodded as he started the car back up and pulled out of the parking lot.

Carrie turned back to the emergency room doors and ran in after Mac. Everything hurt, and she could feel her ribs grinding together where the soldiers had been kicking her. At least one was definitely broken. She knew this because now that the adrenaline dump was wearing off; she was acutely aware of how much it hurt to take a single breath.

The gurney hadn't even made it into the main ER room but instead stopped in the lobby. Doctors and nurses quickly surrounded Mac. One doctor was on the gurney straddling him, performing compressions while a nurse inserted an IV. The rest of the medical team stood by.

"Come on!" The doctor started shouting.

A nurse reached up and touched him on the shoulder. She shook her head. Carrie felt her heart sink into her stomach. Mac looked like he had been dropped into a blender. Deep down, she had already known that no one could survive what he had been through.

The doctor stepped off the gurney and turned to the nurse. He looked defeated.

"Call it," he said.

"Time of death, one thirty-two AM," she replied.

Then Carrie saw Mac's hand twitch.

"He's still alive!" She pleaded.

The Doctor turned to her.

"Miss, I'm sorry but he's not. He's gone."

"No! I saw him move! Keep working!"

"Miss, he's gone."

Carrie raised the Beretta and pulled back the hammer.

"He's dead when I say he's dead!" She ordered. "You get back in there and you bring him back! Now!"

The doctor didn't move. He slowly raised his hands.

"Come feel his pulse," the doctor said. "Look for it."

Carrie's hand was shaking, but she kept the pistol up as she walked to Mac and placed the fingers of her left hand on his carotid artery.

There was nothing. Nothing at all. It was as silent as a church on Tuesday.

Her hands went numb, and the pistol clattered to the floor. She followed it, the world spinning and deep rolling sobs spilling out of her.

Jack walked into the backyard with the two men behind him. Again, he felt the frozen grass crunching beneath his feet. It brought back a strange memory of early morning football training late in the season, when the cold would set in. He remembered feeling that same crunch beneath his feet on the field.

It was still quiet. It was peaceful.

One man said something to the other in Russian. Jack keyed in on this. They were just behind him. They were within striking distance.

Jack Bonafide was fast; he was fast because he had to be. He pulled out the small razor blade he kept stashed inside of his belt and threw a wild swing with it. This wasn't a matter of precision, but equal parts estimation and luck. He knew how tall the men were and how close to him they were. Based on this he found his mark and slashed the first man's throat with the razor, sending a spray of blood into the night. The man fell to his knees, fruitlessly grasping at his throat where Jack had opened what looked to be a three-inch gash.

The second soldier was also fast like Jack was, but not fast enough. Jack stepped forward and grabbed the man's carbine, trying to wrestle it away from him. Then the man did exactly what Jack would have done. He released the carbine, transitioned to his pistol and fired two rounds. Both found their mark.

Jack felt the first round hit him in the left lower abdomen, and the second tracked up and hit him square in the chest. It was like getting hit with a base-ball bat being swung by Babe Ruth. Jack fell to the ground and stared at the sky above him.

He heard shouts from inside the house, still in

Russian. Then footsteps. More shouting. Then nothing. It was quiet again.

Jack felt a numbness and a heat, but his heart was still beating. The bullet hadn't hit his heart. He was holding his breath. Not holding, exactly. There was nothing in his lungs. He needed to breathe soon. He needed to blink. That was a weird thing to think about. He had kept his eyes locked open so that they would think he was dead. The need to blink seemed to be stronger than his need to breathe.

There was no pain yet. He knew that would come later. He took his first breath, but it didn't come. His left lung had collapsed.

Jack moved slowly, his hand tracking down to his right cargo pocket. He worked the buttons and opened it. From inside he retrieved the emergency first aid kit he had made himself. The Russians missed it when they frisked him. It was small, barely worth noticing. All it contained was a cravat, a tourniquet, a syrette of morphine and a decompression needle.

He could feel that he was bleeding from the gunshot in his abdomen, but that was low on the priority list. He needed air. He could feel the darkness starting to creep in around the corners. He would pass out soon.

Jack felt along his ribs with his left hand and found the insertion point for the needle. With his right hand he pressed it in, and the first breath came in like a burst of life. His eyes became wide. It wasn't over. Jack reached down and grabbed the cravat as he slid his belt off. He then palmed a handful of dirt and packed it into the wound.

Now the pain came. It hurt, a deep searing ache that he could not escape. He badly wanted to use the syrette of morphine, but he knew he needed a clear head.

After packing the wound, Jack laid the cravat over it and looped his belt around his abdomen, cinching it tight. He sat up and looked around. There was still movement in the house. There were no available weapons, so he clutched the syrette of morphine in his hand and stumbled to his feet.

The bodies were gone. The man who shot him must have carried his friend away.

Jack's ears were ringing, and his vision came in and out of focus. It was hard to say if it was the concussion symptoms or the effect of being shot twice.

He paused for a moment to take a few breaths and steady his nerves, and then he moved in the only direction he knew how: forward.

There was no time for tactics, no time for planning. It was all or nothing.

The lights were on inside the house, and this time Jack could see one soldier in the laundry room doing something, but his back was to the window. Jack moved up the steps quickly, just in time for the soldier to turn and see him.

Too late.

Jack slammed his foot into the door, kicking it open and right into the soldier's face. The man fell to the floor and Jack landed on him, swinging the syrette of morphine overhand and into the soldier's neck. It had the intended effect and the man's eyes glazed over almost immediately.

The attack had been pure adrenaline, and Jack knew it would wear off soon, probably at the least convenient moment. Considering this, he moved fast and pulled the soldier's pistol out of the man's drop holster, did a brass check and barreled forward into the living room.

There were two more men in there. They had realized something was happening, but again it was too late. The former Delta operator used his intuitive shooting skills and hammered each man right between the eyes, not even breaking his stride as he headed for the front door.

As he moved through the living room, he noticed the large hole in the floor. It was about six foot by six foot, and they had removed several planks to make it. The Russian commander hadn't been lying. Jack had been standing right on top of the Black Tsar. He had been so close.

There was no time to stop and think about this as

Jack ran out the front door and into the street. He heard the engine to his left and turned to see two pairs of tail lights a few hundred feet away.

He patted his pocket and could feel that the car keys were still there. He was going after these sons of bitches. Jack started for the car and then stopped. His head was spinning. He looked down and saw that his pants were covered in blood. The cravat had not held during all the action. He was bleeding out. His ears were ringing, and his breathing was labored.

Everything went black.

CHAPTER 9

Bethesda Naval Hospital
Bethesda, Maryland
January 2, 1981

J ack opened his eyes and focused his vision. He could see that he was in a hospital room, this much was obvious. His ears were ringing, but it was a low intensity. He took a breath and could feel that it was full. His lungs were both working again, at least they seemed to be.

He slowly ran his hands across his body and could feel the stitches in his abdomen and chest, but nothing else. He seemed to be whole. Then he remembered where he was, and what had happened. He remembered coming in and out of consciousness and being told that he was going into surgery before he went back out again.

He was alive. Then he remembered something else. The Russians and The Black Tsar. More importantly, he remembered that both had gotten away from him. He slowly started to press himself up to a seated position and could feel that everything hurt. It wasn't the first time he had felt this kind of physical pain, but it was nothing compared to the psychological pain induced by his complete and absolute failure.

"Relax, Jack," a voice to his left said.

Jack turned his head to see Assistant Director of the CIA Mike Tresham sitting across from him in a chair. There was a cup of coffee and a newspaper on the table beside him and it looked like the man had been there for a while.

"Mister Tresham," Jack said weakly.

"Seriously, Jack," Mike said as he stood up. "You're not all healed up yet. Take it easy."

Jack nodded and allowed himself to lay back against the pillow. Then he remembered, he remembered what the Russian commander had said.

"Mac and Carrie?"

Mike looked at him sternly.

"Ms. Davidson is fine. A couple of broken ribs and some bumps and bruises, but she's already been released."

Jack didn't want to ask, but he knew he had to.

"Mac?"

"Mac... shit," Mike said. "I'm sorry as hell, Jack. She got him to the hospital but he didn't make it."

Jack looked away from Mike and stared at the ceiling. He couldn't remember a time in his life when he had ever wanted to cry, but this was one. His brother was dead. Mac Bonafide was dead and it was Jack's fault. It was his fault and he knew it. He had gotten his brother killed. He had almost gotten Carrie killed.

"What happened?" Jack asked.

"Soviet operatives launched a full scale assault on the hotel in Falls Church, mortars and everything. They were after that weapon and they were going to do anything they had to to get it. Your brother held off an entire assault team nearly single-handed. Killed all of them, too, but he'd already been shot a dozen times and blown up. Honestly, I don't know how in the hell he stayed breathing as long as he did."

"That sounds about right," Jack said with a smile. He knew that he had not even begun to process his brother's death.

"We found you in the street in front of the target house after Carrie called it in. Also found the three dead operatives inside the house and the hole in the floor. I'm guessing that's where the weapon was?"

"I fucked up," Jack said. "I was standing right on top of it."

"There were too many of them Jack. We knew we

were looking for this bomb, but never in a million years did we think there would be Soviet special operations units on American soil. That was a fight you weren't going to win."

"I thought we were just going up against McMasters," Jack said, then thought about it for a moment. "It's a funny thing, though. I have this weird feeling that him and this team aren't connected."

"Agreed," Mike replied. "We know about the split within the KGB, and it sounds like each side deployed their own people to get to the weapon first. We just don't know who owns who."

"I can get to the bottom of it," Jack said quickly.

"No, you can't," Mike said. "You're off of this, Jack. Scarn's running point now."

"Scarn?" Jack asked incredulously. "That's the wrong move, sir!"

Mike stared hard at Jack for a moment.

"You're not just off the mission, Jack. You're out of the agency."

Jack felt the wind come out of him.

"Sir, I know I screwed up but-"

Mike held up a hand.

"It's not your fault Jack, and it's not my decision. It's the Director. I'm the one who screwed up, not you. I thought that based on your track record in Delta and your performance on the Iraq job with the Israelis that this thing would work, and I was wrong. I thought that pulling in someone from the outside to shake things up would give us an edge. Shit, I'll be lucky to still have my job this time next year."

Jack said nothing. He felt like shit over what had happened with the mission, and now it sounded like it might cost Mike Tresham his position as assistant director. Jack knew had to find a way to make this right, even if he wasn't quite sure how he would do that.

"What about Carrie? Is she going to be working with Scarn now?"

Maybe if she was, Jack could get her to keep him up to date.

"No, Jack. She's out too."

"Out of the mission?"

"No, out of the agency."

"Jesus Christ! What in the hell is going on?"

"She pulled a gun on an ER doctor," Mike said flatly. "I get why she did it, but we can't take it back and we can't overlook it. She's already been debriefed and released from service."

"Where is she now?"

"Back home in Knoxville, Tennessee."

Jack filed that away.

"Look, Jack," Mike said, his voice becoming more commanding. "I know you probably haven't had the time to process what happened to your brother. It'll take a while for it to sink in, and you'll be going through a lot of different emotions. Anger will be one of them.

It's important that you understand you can't go off half-cocked trying to find his killers."

"I understand," Jack said.

"You agreed to that a little too fast for my tastes," Mike said. "Whether you believe it yourself or not, if you interfere with a federal investigation you will be arrested and you will be prosecuted."

Jack thought about that for a moment. It wasn't that he needed to think about it, but that he could sense he needed to give the appearance that he was.

"Sir, I've been working for the United States government my entire adult life. I know what our investigative branch is capable of and I know the violence our forces can bring to bear. I fully expect that you will find Mac's killers and that you will bring the wrath of God down on them when you do."

Mike smiled.

"You know we will, Jack."

Jack nodded.

But not if I find them first, he thought to himself.

Physical Therapy Department
Bethesda Naval Hospital
January 12, 1981

Jack stared hard at the device in front of him and blew into the tube again. He watched the floater drift up along the marked lines, but it didn't quite hit the goal. He was still only running at sixty percent lung capacity.

The surgeon had repaired the left one, but it was barely functioning. They told him he would have to work to get it going again, but once he checked into respiratory therapy, he started to think there was something else going on. Something more than just rebuilding his lung capacity.

All the breathing exercises that they assigned him were hard. Not only that, they were incredibly hard. He found he had a naturally fast breathing pace, three times faster than it should be, and that was not an effect of the wound or the surgery. Jack Bonafide was thinking it had always been that way, and he just had never noticed.

There was another problem too. He routinely stopped breathing for extended periods of time. The respiratory therapist at one point clocked him doing a two minute accidental breath hold. She pointed out that he sighed a lot or suddenly pulled in a big breath of air. These were both signs of something called apnea, at least that was what she said.

"How do you feel when you run?" Angela Merril asked him.

She was a fairly put together woman in her mid-thirties. A former yoga teacher who had gone back to school for physical therapy and then attained a specialization in respiratory therapy.

"What do you mean?"

"Do you like it?" She asked.

"Like it?" Jack asked, confused by the question. "I don't really think about it like that, I just do it."

"I see," she said, and wrote something down in her notebook.

Angela thought that Jack Bonafide had been harboring respiratory problems most of his life, but had always been able to tough his way through it. So, she began teaching him breathing exercises, some from physical therapy and some from yoga. Jack didn't much care for these, but she had promised that it would make him a better runner, which was good enough for Jack.

Some exercises were slow and almost meditative, while others were fast and even got his heart rate up and had him breaking a sweat.

Jack still had a job to finish and a score to settle, so he was willing to do whatever he had to in order to get better and get the hell out of the hospital. If Mike Tresham thought Jack Bonafide was just going to roll over on finding his brother's killer the assistant director had another thing coming.

Jack hadn't really heard anything from Carrie, but that wasn't a surprise. She couldn't be taking her release from the agency very well.

"He's not giving you any trouble, is he?" A voice asked from behind Jack as he sat at the table blowing into the device.

Jack looked over his shoulder and saw Captain Mary Pritchard, the surgeon who had repaired his lung standing in the doorway.

"He's a hard worker," Angela said quickly. "Getting better all the time."

Mary looked at Jack for a moment, and then a sly smile crept across her face.

"Yes, he is. Mission oriented, right Jack?" Mary asked. "You work hard when you have something you need to do?"

"That's about the size of it," Jack said with a nod.

"I talked to Mister Tresham on his way out last week. He told me a story about a young man who was told to stand down and step aside."

"I heard that story, too," Jack replied.

"Maybe that story doesn't yet have an ending?" Mary asked.

"Hard to say, Ma'am."

Physical Therapy Department
Bethesda Naval Hospital
January 22, 1981

Jack sat at the formica-topped table in the physical therapy unit and blew into the device. This time the floater not only hit the mark he was aiming for, but drifted well above it.

"Wow!" Angela exclaimed. "Captain Pritchard was right about you. You've come a long way, Jack!"

Jack smiled and sat back in the chair.

"Thanks."

"It would be one thing if you were just trying to rehab a collapsed lung, but I think we stumbled on some other problems going way back."

Jack looked around the unit at the other men and women going through their physical therapy. He felt good. He noticed a difference in his ability to fill his lungs, even at rest. There had been something else, too. Something he didn't expect.

The ringing in his ears was gone. He first noticed it a few days earlier, when he woke up and the all too familiar noise wasn't there. Then he noticed that other symptoms were also gone or greatly reduced. No more tremors in his hands, no more night sweats. Nothing.

Could it have been the breathing, he wondered? Something about it calming his brain down? Whatever it was, Jack Bonafide didn't much care. He felt like a new man, better than he was before.

Now it was time to go to work.

Frank's Place
Knoxville, Tennessee
February 1, 1981

Carrie Davidson sat at the bar with her third glass of whiskey in front of her, three fingers worth. Lately she had found that was enough to hold the demons down. Three fingers down her throat and she could forget.

The bar was the first one she had ever been to when she was eighteen. True, the drinking age was twenty-one, but her fake ID was good enough (and she was pretty enough) that she could get past the doorman and get a taste. That hadn't lasted long, because she liked it a little too much, just like her father had. He'd met his end in an alleyway with a liver large enough to suit a full-grown horse and a bottle of Southern Comfort in his hand. She was twenty when that happened, and she never touched the stuff again.

At least, she never touched it until they let her go from the Central Intelligence Agency for mis-conduct, and that was something that would be stamped on every job application she ever put in. So, for the moment she was living off of her savings, Top Ramen and whiskey. The only thing she did was drink, sleep and go to the range.

Every day Carrie Davidson arrived at Topper's

Range on Holston Hills Road and practiced her combat firing. She fired until her hands were raw and her ears were ringing. She drank to forget, but she fired her weapon to be ready. They were still out there. The men who had killed Mac were in the ground, to be sure, but the rest of that team were out there somewhere with The Black Tsar.

Intellectually Carrie knew she would never be part of the team assigned to recover it. Hell, she couldn't even get in the front door at Langley if she was driving a tank, but she still had to be ready. She knew what that bomb could do, and if it ever went off, it would change America forever.

The men who had shot Jack and taken the weapon had gone dark. While Carrie didn't have many friends left in the agency, she had enough that she knew they were getting nowhere fast.

So, there she sat at the bar at Frank's Place, three fingers of whiskey in front of her, bruises on her knuckles and hate in her heart.

Frank Callahan slid an ashtray across the bar toward her. Carrie looked up at him.

"Just in case," he said with a smile.

Frank was an old Korean War vet, a former Army infantry soldier who had taken a liking to Carrie when he found out she planned on working for the CIA. It wasn't something that she'd had to keep a secret, but she still kept the circle of those in the know small.

Somehow Frank had slipped in there, and he'd been a friendly ear to complain to ever since.

Carrie took him up on the suggestion and fished a packet of Camels out of her pocket. She lit one and took a drag before knocking back the rest of the whiskey in the glass. She slid the glass across the bar to him, an even exchange (as far as she was concerned) for the ashtray.

"Fill 'er up, chief," she said with a smile.

Aside from being someone who she could talk to about what was really going on (most of it) Frank also protected her from herself. On more than one occasion he had cut her off when she probably needed to be. In the moment, she was never happy about it, but when the sunlight hit her face the next day she always understood why he'd done it.

Carrie knew that Frank had lost nearly his entire platoon in the thick of the fighting at the Chosin Reservoir. He understood loss in a way that most could not.

Frank refilled Carrie's glass and slid it back across the bar to Carrie. He held out his hand.

"That's four glasses," he said dryly. "You know the rule. You got to pay the tax."

Carrie looked at him for a moment and then shrugged.

"Fine," she said, and reaching to her waistband pulled out the Beretta 1951 that rarely left her side and handed it across the bar to him.

Frank normally didn't let anyone carry in the bar, but after hearing Carrie's story, he'd made an exception. She was a real American hero, and like most heroes she'd gotten a raw deal. If carrying that iron around made her feel better, she had earned the right.

Carrie looked at the glass and tapped her finger on the bar.

"You got quarters?" She asked.

Frank hit the lever on the cash register, dipped in and returned with a stack of quarters that he then dropped into her palm.

"Gracias," she replied, and sliding her stool back stood up and walked back to the hallway that led to the single restroom.

She stopped at the payphone on the wall, picked up the handset and began feeding quarters into the slot. She dialed a number from memory. It rang three times on the other end before someone picked up.

"It's me," she said, keeping her voice low. "Any news?"

"No," the man on the other end replied.

"Shit," she spat. "I thought you said you had a lead?"

"I did," he said. "It just didn't work out."

"Just thought I'd check. Don't forget about me. I'm ready."

"I know you are." He paused. "How are you doing?"

"Not good. I need resolution."

"I know," he replied. "Soon. I'll have something soon."

"Fine," Carrie replied, and then thought for a moment before continuing. "Stay safe."

She hung up the phone and turned back to the bar. It briefly crossed her mind that if anyone found out what she was doing, the best-case scenario would involve spending the rest of her life in prison. The worst case would be her execution as a traitor to her country.

Arlington National Cemetery
Arlington, VA
February 1, 1981

Jack Bonafide stepped out of the sedan and drew a deep breath. It felt good. It was getting easier to do that, easier to breathe deeply and he'd even been able to run a few miles outside of the Naval Hospital. Granted, it was a hell of a lot more challenging than it had been before he took a bullet in his lung, but he could do it. That was the important thing.

This wasn't the first time Jack had been to Arlington, and he knew it most likely wouldn't be the last.

The long rows of headstones stood as a stark reminder of where he had come from, those he had lost and those that would still be lost if he didn't get back on track.

There had been no news about The Black Tsar, or the Soviet special ops team he had gone up against. While Jack was not privy to the details of the investigation, he still had friends in the Agency from his days with Delta and could find out at least that much. He knew that Scarn was hitting a brick wall and it showed no signs of yielding to his efforts.

Jack walked through the rows of headstones and stopped at a specific one.

He had missed the funeral. It was through no fault of his own; he had still been in recovery and was expressly forbidden from leaving the hospital because of his high risk of infection. They had buried his brother in section thirty-eight of the cemetery.

Jack looked down at the headstone and smiled. There was a small Texas flag stuck in the ground, and beside that was a half empty bottle of whiskey. Some of Mac's friends from the SEAL teams had been there. Jack had heard that they afforded him a funeral with full military honors, and that despite his expulsion from the unit all of his teammates had shown up and pounded their tridents into the coffin, just like they would have for any brother lost in battle.

The truth was that no one actually knew what had happened, but word had passed thorough the special operations grapevine that Mac was killed in action. This piqued the curiosity of the other unit members, because they knew he had died in Virginia. How in the held had he been KIA in the United States?

Jack knew. As he looked at his brother's headstone he thought for a moment about tracking down Carrie. It seemed strange that the woman hadn't already gotten in touch with him. Damn strange. She was the only person alive who really knew what had happened at the motel in Church Falls. Jack had seen the photos and it was obvious that they had launched a full-blown attack. There had even been a mortar deployed. Those Soviets (whoever they were) hadn't been taking any chances. That attack was the definition of overkill.

The CIA along with local and state authorities had spun quite a tale about a gas explosion, but that was already falling apart. There were too many veterans living in the area who knew what weapons fire sounded like, and it didn't sound a damn thing like a gas main going off.

"I'm sorry as hell, brother," Jack whispered as he looked down at the headstone. Then he thought about it. "Actually, no I ain't. You went out just the way you would have wanted to. Like you were in a fucking action movie, stackin' bodies and fuckin' skulls."

Jack leaned over and picked up the bottle of whiskey. He uncorked it and took a swig. He sure hoped some peacenik hadn't spiked it with anti-freeze.

"Thought I might find you here," a voice called out from behind him.

Jack turned to see Agent Michael Scarn standing a dozen feet behind him.

"You snuck up on me," Jack said before turning back to the headstone.

"I may not be much good at tracking down hydrogen bombs," Scarn said as he walked to the headstone. "But I'm still pretty good at sneaking up on people."

"Won't happen again," Jack cautioned him.

"No, I doubt it will." Scarn looked at the headstone. "I know we didn't get off on the right foot, but I was sorry to hear about what happened to your brother."

"He knew what he was getting into," Jack replied.

Scarn nodded his understanding. That was the way of these men.

"You probably know I didn't just come for a social call. I went to the hospital first, but obviously you weren't there. Your doc was pretty unhappy when she found out. Especially since it seems you took her car."

"She'll get over it."

"I know you're still in the loop, Jack. So you probably know that the only place we're getting with this investigation is nowhere, and we're getting there at lightning speed."

"Figured as much. Didn't really need someone to tell me," Jack said, and then immediately felt poorly for the tone of his response. Even though he and Scarn didn't see eye to eye, there was no reason to rub salt in the wound.

"You got closer than anyone," Scarn said, ignoring the obvious slight. "In fact, you were standing right on top of it."

"Still lost it," Jack said. "And the team. And my brother."

"But you still got close. I'm hoping there's something you might know that can help me."

Jack turned to Scarn.

"They took my after-action report at the hospital. Six ways to Sunday. Not sure there's anything left."

Scarn turned to the headstone and then back to Jack.

"I want to make sure he didn't die for nothing," Scarn said. "That's what this is about. So if you know anything-"

"Walk away," Jack said.

"What's that?" Scarn asked sharply.

"Walk away, Scarn. You're trying to leverage my brother's death to get information from me? Open your mouth again. Do it. I fucking dare you."

Scarn stared hard at Jack Bonafide for a moment, but did not say a word.

Bethesda Naval Hospital

Bethesda, Maryland
February 1, 1981

Jack had made the thirty-minute drive back to the hospital and returned to his room with no one being the wiser. At least, that was what he thought. As he closed the door of the room behind him the light clicked on, and he turned to see his surgeon sitting in a chair across from him.

"You know, Jack," Captain Mary Pritchard said coldly. "I have to wonder if you would have pulled this shit if I were a man?"

Jack smiled sheepishly. He liked the woman. In a strange way she reminded him of his mother. She had a hard face and had seen action in the Korean War as a young ensign. She didn't take any crap, but she also didn't dish any out.

"Sorry, Ma'am," Jack replied.

Captain Pritchard held out a hand.

"Keys, Jack."

Jack pulled the car keys out of his pocket and tossed them across the room and into her hand. She shook her head as she stuffed them into her pocket.

"None of us are sure who you are, Jack. You're not military and you also don't seem to be employed by the government, but you could take my car keys during a conversation in the hallway without me knowing. What's a private citizen doing in our fine military hospital?"

"Flights to Hawaii were overbooked," Jack replied as he walked across the room and pulled his duffel bag out of the wall locker.

"Going somewhere?" She asked.

"I feel better, Doc. No reason to take up a bed that someone else might need."

"You're not healed yet, Jack. Not fully. You try to leave now and you risk a respiratory infection."

"Life's a risk," Jack replied. "We all gotta die sometime."

Captain Mary Pritchard stared hard at this mystery man she had pulled two bullets out of and shook her head.

"You fixed for traveling money?" She asked.

"Yes, Ma'am," Jack replied.

"And you understand that you're leaving against doctor's orders?"

"Yes, Ma'am."

Captain Pritchard held out her hand, and Jack shook it.

"Watch your six, Bonafide. I don't want to see you on my operating table again."

The Home Of Corbett Bonafide

Texarkana, Texas
February 3, 1981

Jack knew he should make his way to Knoxville, Tennessee to track down Carrie Davidson and find out if she knew anything that could be helpful in his hunt for The Black Tsar and this Russian spec ops team. Even knowing that, he understood that it wouldn't be right if he didn't at least make a stopover to let his father know what had happened.

True enough, by now Corbett must have known that his younger son had died, but most likely he wouldn't know how or why. Jack and his father had never had much to say to each other (which isn't the same as not getting along) and there was no reason that the passage of time would have changed that, but in this one instance something needed to be said. Jack's father needed to know how his boy had died.

Jack pulled the rental car up the short driveway to the Bonafide residence, put it in park and cut the engine. He looked at the rusted mailbox in front of the house and then to the old porch with the single rocking chair and the small stool that sat beside it. Jack thought back to many evenings sitting on that stool while his father took his position in the rocking chair, smoked his cigarettes and stared into the night.

Every Bonafide man was a world heavyweight champion of sitting in silence, and Jack and his father had been no different. Even after Mac left home it had been that way. Neither knew of any other kind of life, and so they flat out didn't think of a thing of it.

The front door opened in the darkness. No light had come on inside, because Corbett Bonafide would never give away his position like that. Old habits die hard, particularly when they're owned by old men.

"Reckon you should come in," Corbett said with a wave. "I'm fixin' to empty a bottle of bourbon."

Corbett sat quietly while Jack told the story of what had happened. For the first time he told the whole story, every last detail. If his father couldn't be trusted to keep that secret, then it was a sure bet not a soul in the world could be.

Corbett didn't say a word as he worked his way through the bottle of Kentucky bourbon, at the most offering a silent nod to some key points of the story. Once Jack had finished, Corbett looked at the table for a moment and then back to his son.

"So, what are they doin' to track down these sons of bitches?"

"Not much," Jack said with a shrug. "They've got nothin' to go on."

"And you?"

"I've got some irons in the fire." Jack stopped for a moment and then realized something. "Shit, I almost forgot. Sorry about the wild goose chase."

"What do you mean?" Corbett asked.

"When I called you that night and told you to keep an eye on Angeline."

"Wasn't no wild goose chase. I caught those sons of bitches creepin' through Ricky's yard. Fixed their wagon good."

"What?" Jack nearly shouted. "Why in the hell wasn't that the very first thing you said when I came up the steps?"

Corbett reached out and cracked his son across the side of his head with an open hand.

"What in the hell?" Jack snapped.

"Told you I'd crack you one good if you ever raised your voice to me again," Corbett said dryly. "Consider yourself cracked."

"You call the police?"

"Yeah," Corbett laughed. "And then I had Santa Claus and the Easter Bunny come over for poker and whiskey. No, I didn't call the fucking police."

"What did you do with them?"

"Buried them in the yard," Corbett said as he refilled his bourbon glass. "Well, specifically my yard. Cut 'em up something good at Ricky's place, but didn't want it blowing back on him if they were ever found, so

I threw their carcasses in the back of the truck and then planted them in the back."

"I want to see the bodies," Jack said.

Corbett cocked his head to the side for a moment, and then he smiled as he realized what his son was getting at.

It was well after one in the morning by the time Jack and his father finished digging up the two Russian operatives that Corbett had buried in the backyard. The two operatives were barely recognizable. It was clear they'd put up a fight, but they'd gotten more than they bargained for.

Jack got down in the hole and lifted each body up to his father, who laid them out in the dirt. Jack leaned back against the side of the hole to catch his breath.

"Winded?" Corbett asked. "That ain't like you. That was more Mac's style, what with his smoking and all."

"Got shot in the lung," Jack replied.

"Slow you down much, did it?"

"Nah," Jack said as he hopped out of the whole. "I had a backup."

"Good lord gave us two of damn near everything for a reason."

Jack looked over the bodies and then began going

through he pockets. He noticed that the men were still wearing their tactical vests.

"They had some good gear on them," Jack said wonderingly. "You didn't take any of it?"

"Took a few grenades and some ammo for a special occasion if one should come up, but nothin' else I needed."

Jack moved down to the pants cargo pockets of one man and pulled a sheath of papers and a map out. The items were wrapped in plastic and secured with a rubber band. He started taking it apart and then motioned for the flashlight.

"Goddam," Jack whispered.

"Watch your mouth," Corbett chastised his son. "Don't blaspheme."

"Sorry, sir."

"What you got there?"

Jack paused for a moment, double checking what he was seeing.

"Well, unless this is the most elaborate trap in the history of the world, I think I know where those bastards went."

"Don't it seem strange?" Corbett asked. "The map, I mean? Seems almost like they gift wrapped their location and handed it off to you."

Jack stood up and pocketed the map.

"Like I said, this would be the most elaborate trap in the history of the world. Truth to tell, these two probably never imagined something like this would happen. They most likely thought they'd gotten the short end of the stick and been left with the boring job of kidnapping a woman to use as leverage. They didn't reckon on a nasty as a bag of feral cats Texas Ranger stepping in."

"Former Ranger," Corbett corrected him.

"Ain't nothin' former about it," Jack said, and then waved to the bodies. "You can ask their opinion if you like."

Corbett smiled a little.

"Shit, they got off easy. Can you imagine what would have happened if they'd found Angeline and she was within arm's reach of a shotgun?"

Jack shook his head. He wondered what she was doing right then. Missing him definitely wouldn't be on the list.

"You're going after them," Corbett said.

"That I am," Jack replied. "You in?"

Corbett looked at his son for a moment and then shook his head.

"I want to, you know I do, but putting my ego aside I know it's not a good idea. I like to pretend I haven't lost a step, but the truth is I'm not the man I was. Going up against these two in the dark on my home turf, yeah that wasn't much of a challenge. What you're walking into? I have to be honest, I'm more likely to get you killed."

"I understand."

"You got some backup? Someone you can call on?"

"I just might."

Jack checked his watch and saw that it was nearly two in the morning. He hadn't slept in quite a while, but figured he'd start the ten-hour drive to Knoxville to at least get some of it out of the way. When he got tired enough, he could always pull into the woods and catch some shuteye.

His father had offered to let him take his truck and Jack accepted. The two men began to load up the bed with supplies. Mostly weapons and ammo but some food and camping gear as well. Jack wasn't sure what he'd need all of this stuff for, but he sensed that it made the old man feel better to help him.

Jack slammed the tailgate shut and turned to his father.

"I have to head out. Better to get some road behind me before the sun comes up."

Corbett nodded.

Jack walked around to the driver's side door and could see his father watching him in the side mirror.

"Jack," Corbett called out. "I want you to know... I want you to know that..." his voice trailed off.

Jack looked over his shoulder at him.

"I know."

An Undisclosed Location
North Bath, New York
February 3, 1981

The house was quiet. It was a quiet and unassuming house that sat on a well-trafficked corner of the small North Bath neighborhood. Two unassuming cars were parked out front, a new station wagon and a much older Honda Civic. It was a perfectly crafted illusion, a perfectly crafted lie.

Arkady sat his notebook down on the kitchen table and watched the man walking toward the house. He wore a turtleneck sweater to guard against the chill February air and wire-rimmed glasses. Despite this man's best efforts to look like just another American taking an afternoon stroll, the trained eye would know that he was anything but average.

He had hardened features, his shoulders broad and his gait purposeful. He took the steps one-by one and used his key to enter the house. Arkady watched him walk into the kitchen, and smiled.

"Illya," he said by way of greeting. "You are the last to arrive."

"And by an effect of that," the Alpha Group senior NCO responded. "The most cautious."

"Perhaps," Arkady replied.

"Nestor and Marat? Did they return from Texas?"

Arkady shook his head.

"Neither man checked in by the designated time. We can only assume that we have lost them."

Illya seemed confused.

"How? All they had to do was kidnap a single woman?"

"It matters not. We only needed her to stop Bonafide, and he has been stopped, regardless."

"The rest? I know that we lost four men at the house."

Arkady shook his head.

"We are six now."

"Six?" Illya asked in disbelief.

"Not counting Waller."

"The assault force at the motel?"

"All dead."

Illya pulled out a chair at the table and sat down deflated. They had entered the country fourteen strong and were now down to six.

"I assume that we still have the weapon?"

"We do."

"And we go forward as planned?"

"Is there any other direction but forward, Comrade Sergeant Major?"

Illya smiled. He had always respected Arkady, even when they were simple Spetsnaz operatives, long before selection for Alpha Group. He thought about the situation for a moment.

"What about Waller? He must have undergone combat training with Directorate S. Is it possible to re-purpose him? Press him into service?"

Arkady shook his head.

"That was twenty years ago. He has grown quite soft, and while his technical skills remain I would not want to put a gun in his hand unless there were no other option."

"So he at least remembers how to work the device?"

"Yes. We have been performing rehearsals. Because of its age, the tamper will begin degrading once attached to the main housing and activated. Our esti-mates say we will only have twenty-four hours before it becomes useless."

"So, we must keep Waller alive to attach and acti-vate it when the time comes?"

"Yes."

"And he cannot train us to do it?"

"Not unless you want to go to engineering school for four years," Arkady said with a smile. "We knew this would be the case, and we are prepared for it."

"I am curious," Illya said as he leaned forward at the table. "What does Waller think will happen once he activates the device?"

"I have told him that once the device is active, we

will make our escape to a location outside of the blast radius and take him with us."

Illya chuckled.

"The Americans have made him both soft and gullible." Illya looked at the black and white photos on the table and examined them. "We have begun the next phase?"

"I would have waited," Arkady said, "But with our forces so diminished, time is of the essence."

"I understand," Illya acknowledged. "Is it possible... do you think we should chance a communication with Colonel Sokolov?"

"Have we failed?" Arkady asked, his voice sharpening slightly, but enough that Illya picked up on it.

"No, Comrade Colonel."

"Then we stay in the dark. We do what must be done."

Steven Waller sat in the small bedroom that had been converted into his office and surveyed the city plans they had provided him. He looked to the calendar on the wall. There was little time left.

He kept telling himself that he was in an impossible situation back at the motel and the target house. He had received a dead drop three months prior. He didn't get them often anymore, but on occasion they came and he never took them seriously. Why? Nothing ever came of it. Until this time.

This particular message said that American agents may contact him and if this were to happen, he should chalk mark any location they took him to. After receiving this message, Steven Waller just went on about his life. Until he received the tamper at the PO Box, and then Jack Bonafide showed up at his door. Then he knew that this time was different. This time was real.

He wondered if Jack had taken care of his cats, like he had promised he would? It was such a silly thing to be concerned about at a time like this, but regardless of that he still couldn't push it out of his mind. He also could not ignore the fact that if this team was success-ful, none of it would matter. There would be no more America for his cats to live in, or anyone else for that matter.

Steven knew that there was no way these men were operating at the behest of the Kremlin. This was some rogue faction. They spoke often of fighting for Mother Russia, but Steven knew this wasn't the truth. What they were planning would not create a stronger Soviet Union. It would just push them back to the dark ages of Joseph Stalin. No, worse than that. This new world order would be the equivalent of Tsarist rule.

Steven realized that he had been tapping the surface of the desk relentlessly with the small screwdriver in his hand and sat it down. He turned and looked over his shoulder to where The Black Tsar sat on two sawhorses in the room's corner. It didn't look like much. It didn't look like something that could topple an empire that had stood for over two hundred years.

CHAPTER 10

The Rite Spot Trailer Park
Texarkana, Texas
February 4, 1981

J ack knew he needed to get on the road, but he also understood that there was something else that needed doing. Specifically, he knew that he needed to sort things out with Angeline. Maybe that wasn't even the right way to think about it. Things weren't ever going to be "sorted out" between the two of them, but he didn't like the way he'd left things.

It wasn't even a question of if they wanted to go through with the divorce. Jack knew that Angeline already had her mind set on it. She was done with him, even if he hadn't quite reconciled with that fact.

Maybe it was because they had dated through most of high school, and she had followed him around like a lovesick puppy dog when he joined the army and finally asked her to marry him when he made E-5.

This had been what Jack considered a "tactical decision". Trying to support a family on anything less than a non-commissioned officer's pay just seemed like bad planning, and so he had made her wait. When he finally picked up sergeant, he'd popped the question. She immediately said yes, and she acted like being made to wait hadn't bothered her any, but that wasn't the truth.

She always held it against him. Angeline Michaels privately thought that making a woman wait like that was a real low-down thing to do, but she had already constructed her future life in her head, and she would follow through with that plan no matter what.

Then Delta happened. Her husband vanished. It had been bad enough waiting on him all through Vietnam, but now this? This wasn't like Jack's deployments to Southeast Asia. No, this was worse. Even when he was at home, he wasn't really at home. He was always training or running missions with the boys. Then when he was physically with her, he still wasn't.

Finally, she left. It was when he disappeared to Israel for seemingly no goddam good reason. She left and she didn't look back. She packed her things and hopped the first Greyhound to Texarkana.

Then the divorce papers came. They came, and they sat but Jack never signed them. He wanted an explanation first.

So, there he stood in the Rite Spot trailer park behind the Piggly Wiggly. This was apparently where Angeline was laying her head in a respectable double wide. He looked at the door for a moment. The lights were on. She was clearly inside.

Jack stepped forward and rapped twice on the door.

There was a moment of silence.

"I shoot first," a voice called out. "Ask questions after the fact."

Jack hesitated for a moment.

"It's me," he said.

There was another moment of silence, and then the door unlatched. Angeline stood in the portal, a sawed-off shotgun at her side.

"We'll I'll be a son of a bitch. Jack fucking Bonafide."

"Can we be civil?" Jack asked.

Angeline reached for something beside the door and came back with a stack of papers.

"Sign these and I'll be whatever you want," Angeline said. "Just not your wife."

"What happened?" Jack asked. "I thought we would work things out?"

"And then you went to Israel!" Angeline countered in her Arkansas twang. "How is that working things out?"

"It's my job, Angeline. I can't just say no!"

"But you can say no to me, right?" She asked.

"It's not like that."

"What's it like, Jack?" Angeline said. "Because it sure seems like for things that get your attention I'm at the back of the line."

Jack didn't know how to respond to the accusation.

"I left Delta," he said.

"Good for you."

"Don't you see?" He asked plaintively. "I'll have more time for us now."

"Really?" She asked.

"Yes!"

"Then stay the night."

Jack's mouth opened part way, but no words came out.

Angeline nodded with a smirk.

"That's what I thought." She thrust the papers out at him. "Sign!"

Jack took a step back.

"I'm going to show you," he said. "I just have to do this one last thing."

"Isn't that always the way?" Angeline asked. "Just

one more job. Just one more mission. Just one more thing that's more important than me."

"I-I'm telling you. It's not like that."

"Sign!" She shouted.

"No," Jack said quietly, and walked backward away from the trailer. "I'm going to show you."

Frank's Place
Knoxville, Tennessee
February 5, 1981

Carrie Davidson walked into the bar with a slight limp. She had spent the morning doing room clearing drills at the range, and run straight into a wall, making (in her opinion) a royal ass out of herself in the process.

She wasn't injured but her pride had taken a few bumps and bruises.

"Been walking long?" Frank asked with a smile.

"Ha ha," Carrie said and held up three fingers.

Frank looked at the clock on the wall.

"It's not even eleven."

"Well, hell Frank, if you're not serving why are you even open?"

Frank shook his head and fished a bottle and glass from beneath the counter.

"You'll get old before your time if you keep this up, Carrie." Frank filled the glass and held it for a moment. "I'm not telling you not to drink. I did my fair share when I came back from Korea."

"Then don't."

Frank sighed and pushed the glass across the bar to her.

"If you weren't such a goddamn hero, I would have cut you off a long ago."

"That's me," Carrie said and then downed the glass. "Big time hero."

She turned and looked at the payphone in the hallway.

"I've never asked," Frank said.

"And I've never told."

"Well, it's just... it seems like the only person you can really talk to is on the other end of that phone."

Carrie shrugged.

"Maybe that's why I can talk to him. I don't have to look him in the eye while I confess my sins."

The front door opened, letting the cruel light of day in. A man entered who Carrie didn't recognize, but Frank did. He was a good six foot four, rough as shoe leather and with a limp of his own to match Carrie's. He walked to the jukebox without a word and began loading nickels into it.

Hank Williams started playing, and Carrie tapped out the beat on the bar as she reached for an ashtray

"Girl as pretty as you shouldn't be smoking," the man said from behind her.

Carrie didn't respond.

"You must not be from around here," he continued. "Polite thing to do when a man speaks to you is to respond."

"I'm not polite," Carrie said.

"Maybe I like that," he continued.

"Take a walk, Marcus," Frank said sharply.

Marcus glared at Frank. The biker had been running guns at a low level in northern Tennessee and in Kentucky ever since coming back from Vietnam, and because of this he thought he was a much bigger deal than he was. Frank knew for a fact that Marcus had tried to get in with the Hell's Angels and they had impolitely told him to go pound sand. Ever since then, Marcus had been trying to hold together a very loosely organized band of misfits headquartered in Knoxville.

"I ain't doing nothing wrong, Frank. You got no call to be treating me like that. I'm just trying to conversate with the lady," Marcus said, and placed a hand on Carrie's shoulder.

Carrie turned and threw a hand into Marcus's throat, dropping the big man to the floor like a pile of bricks. She stood up, lit her cigarette and took a drag as he floundered on the floor, choking for air.

"Never touch me again," she said coldly.

Frank and Carrie both saw Marcus' right hand

going for his pistol, but Frank was faster on the draw, pulling his double barrel sawed-off shotgun from behind the bar and leveling it at the man on the floor.

"Walk," Frank snapped. "Now. You're fucking banned."

Marcus froze, but did not seem to be ready to give in quite yet, so Carrie gave him a push. She drew her Beretta 1951 and held it casually by her side.

"And before you go asking," she said. "Yes, I know how to use it."

Jack drove into Knoxville around noon on a Thursday. He'd been playing his Glenn Campbell tape at the beginning of the drive but then shut it off pretty quickly. It got him thinking about his brother a little too much, and at that exact moment in time it wasn't a good thing. It was a distraction from the task at hand. There would be plenty of time for mourning later.

The drive hadn't been too bad, a fairly straight shot. Jack pulled over somewhere in Arkansas (he wasn't sure where) and grabbed forty winks, just enough to get him alert again and ready for the rest of the haul.

The radio signal faded in and out as he passed through the more rural areas, but mostly it was country music, farm reports and fire and brimstone preachers. That was how he knew he was back in the south again, and that was the way he liked it.

Driving into Knoxville the signal came back clear again, and he heard a news story about someone setting a paper airplane flight record out in Washington. Something about that made him smile. True, Jack Bonafide didn't have any use for paper airplanes, and wasn't sure he'd ever even made one, not even as a kid. For some reason though, that story reminded him of why he was doing what he was. Perhaps in a strange way that story was America in a nutshell. You could bet dollars to donuts that no one in the Soviet Union or East Germany was having a paper plane flying contest.

Once he had arrived in Knoxville, Jack ran into another problem. He didn't know where in the hell Carrie Davidson would be, assuming she was even still in town. Jack wondered if he might try to go it alone and not waste his time with this, but then he remembered what she had said to him back at the motel.

He needed a team. Even if he thought he was better off as the proverbial lone wolf, that didn't mean it was true. Yes, it would take a little time to track her down, but she was one of the few people in the world he knew he could trust. Plus, she had already gone up against these people and lived to tell the tale. Hell, from the sound of it, her and Mac had been in a damn war.

Then Jack had a thought. It was a silly idea, but it just might work. He pulled the truck over at a gas station and put it in park. He walked to the phone booth, pulled out the phone book and began thumbing through the D section until he hit Davidson. There were more than a few of them, but sure enough he found a Davidson, Carrie listed. Jack smiled as he tore the sheet out.

Knoxville didn't seem like much to Jack, but he figured folks from Knoxville would probably say the same thing about Texarkana. Southern towns were like that; they only seemed to mean something to the folks that had grown up there.

The map he'd bought at the gas station told him Carrie's place was on a road on the outskirts of town, but it was a crapshoot if she still lived there. The phonebook was a few years old, old enough that she could have moved out when she went on duty. Either way, he figured he might find something. He'd at least give it twenty-four hours to try to track her down before he gave up and headed for the location on the map he'd taken off those Russians.

Jack watched the rows of little stores, gas stations and bars as he passed. He thought a cold beer wouldn't be the worst thing that ever happened to him as he drove by one of the run-down bars. The door to the place opened and a tall older man with a ready smile walked out with a much younger woman. She wore what one could only describe as a sour expression on her face. Jack thought to himself that despite her scowl she wasn't hard to look at, a split second before he slammed on his brakes and skidded off to the side of the road.

He sat there for a moment watching them in the rearview mirror as the engine of the old Ford idled.

"Well, I'll be a son of a bitch."

"I wanted to call you," Carrie said, the guilt in her voice obvious as she sat at the bar with Jack. Frank had put some distance between himself and the two, sensing that this was private. "I really did."

"I know," Jack said. "It isn't easy, dealing with something like this."

"I cared about your brother," Carrie said.

"He was a good man," Jack replied.

"No, I... I cared about him," Carrie said, staring into Jack's eyes.

Jack understood what she meant.

"Oh," he said. "I see."

"It just kind of happened. Nothing ever really came of it, but it was there. It was real and I haven't been able to come back from it."

"What in the hell happened out there?" Jack asked, partially because he wanted to change the subject.

Carrie replayed the story of the attack on the motel and the subsequent rush to get Mac to the hospital. She left out the part about McMasters showing up. She wasn't sure what Jack would think of that.

"Shit!" Jack spat. "We never even had a chance."

"We just didn't know what we were going up against," Carrie said. "No one did."

"Well, we do now," Jack replied.

"There's something else," Carrie said. "Something Mac said before he..." her voice trailed off.

"What is it?" Jack asked.

There were tears in Carrie's eyes, but she did her best not to let them turn into a flood.

"He said to tell you he didn't quit."

Jack Bonafide was not a man given to displays of emotion, but even for him this was nearly too much. In his brother's final moments, the man had been most concerned that his big brother might think he had laid down without a fight. Jack turned and took another drink from his beer and steeled himself.

He reached down into his pocket, retrieved the plastic-wrapped map and slapped it down on the bar.

"They're going to pay for what they did," Jack said coldly as he slid the map across the weathered wood surface to Carrie. "They're going to pay and we're going to secure that bomb."

Carrie slid the map out of its plastic sheath and unfolded it. Her eyes grew wide as she realized what she was looking at.

"This can't be real," she said, shaking her head. Her eyes met Jack's. "It's a trap. It has to be."

"Everyone makes mistakes, darlin'. Even the best in the world slip up now and again. I don't think it's a trap. I think that there is just our luck turning."

"Doesn't it seem strange that they would carry that around on them?"

"These were two highly trained special operations soldiers outfitted with weapons and gear who thought they were going up against a single woman."

Carrie thought about it. He was right. It made sense.

"Tresham won't let me back on this mission," Carrie said, shaking her head.

"Yeah... that may not be much of a problem," Jack said with a smile.

"You too?" She asked.

Jack nodded.

"So, we have no support of any kind?"

Jack shrugged.

"Honestly, it's not much different from the situation we were in before." Jack paused for a moment. "Though Mister Tresham might have said something about arresting me if I interfered with the investigation."

"Fantastic," Carrie said sarcastically.

"If you've got a better idea, I'm all ears."

Carrie thought about this for a moment.

"You won't like it," she said.

"What is it?" Jack asked.

Carrie held up a finger, stood up and walked back to the hallway. She dug some change out of her pocket and dialed a number. Jack watched her talking on the payphone for a moment, then she hung it up and walked back to the bar.

"What was that about?" Jack asked.

Carrie looked at him for a moment, as if mentally calculating how she would say something that was difficult.

"I know someone who can help us. Who can help us understand what we're up against. Maybe give us an edge."

"Who?" Jack asked.

"I can't tell you," Carrie held up a hand to silence the protest that she knew was coming. "Trust me, Jack. If I tell you who it is, you won't meet with him."

Jack let out a frustrated sigh. There wasn't time to be going back and forth like this. He was just going to have to take her at her word.

"Fine, you can keep your secret. Where do we meet him?"

"Well, I assume we're heading for the point on that map?"

"We are."

"New York City," she said. "The bar in a hotel called The Wyndham New Yorker."

"Fine," Jack said as he stood up. "I'm trusting you."

"I won't let you down, Jack," Carrie said. "We owe it to Mac to finish this."

Jack pushed the door open, so he was the first to see them lined up alongside the road. To their left were six motorcycles, one for each man, neatly aligned. The biggest of the six men took a step forward.

"I got no quarrel with you," he called out, indicating Jack. "Step aside and we'll get this over with."

"Get what over with?" Jack asked, more than slightly annoyed by this interruption.

"That bitch you're with owes me," Marcus snarled.

Jack turned to Carrie.

"What in the hell did you do?" Jack asked.

"Something that needed doing," Carrie replied.

"Shit."

"Just, you know... take them down," Carrie said, waving at the group.

Jack raised an eyebrow.

"You've been watching too many movies. There's six of them. Who in the hell do you think I am, Bruce Lee?"

Carrie turned back to the group. She pushed aside her jacket and rested the heel of her palm on the butt of the Beretta pistol.

"You all are living in a fucking fantasy land if you

think you're laying hands on me," Carrie said. "But if you want to step out of fantasy land and get real, I'll be more than happy to oblige."

Jack couldn't help but smile at this. He was getting the sense that Carrie Davidson had put a lot of effort into dropping her country roots and her Tennessee twang when she went off to college and then joined the CIA, but it was now coming back full force. He could also tell that the gun fights at the motel in Baltimore and then again in Church Falls had changed her. Mostly in a good way, but she also seemed to be getting a might short on fear, which wasn't always a positive.

The door opened behind Carrie and Jack, and Frank Callahan stepped out. In his right hand he held a battered and scarred baseball bat. He glared at Marcus.

"Marcus, what in the hell are you playing at?" Frank asked. "You've got two fucking warrants out for you and you're messing around here trying to beat up a woman?"

"Listen here old—" Marcus started, but Frank pointed the bat at him and shut him down.

"Not a fucking word." Frank turned his attention to the man beside Marcus. "And what about you, Wade? I called your mom. She's on her way over here right now to whoop your ass for fucking around with these nitwits when you should be at the lumberyard." The man beside Wade snickered, and Frank directed his wrath at him. "And as for you, Tim, you've got an outstanding note with Eddie Carls and he's on his way over here to fucking collect. So, way I see it you all should make yourselves scarce!"

A few of the men (Wade and Tim included) began heading for their bikes, and Marcus could read the writing on the wall.

"This ain't over," Marcus said.

"Yes, it is," Frank insisted. He reached into the small of his back and pulled out a .38 pistol. He turned to Carrie and Jack. "You two get out of here. I imagine you've got better things to do with your time."

The Home Of Corbett Bonafide
Texarkana, Texas
February 5, 1981

Supervisory Special Agent Michael Scarn stepped out of the black sedan and looked around what to him appeared to be a barren landscape. It was also the land owned by a former Texas Ranger by the name of Corbett Bonafide.

Corbett's personnel file made sense to Michael Scarn, because it looked a lot like Jack Bonafide's. The man was a former Marine with service in World War Two, Korea and even a short stint in Vietnam as an advisor with MACVSOG. The man had three silver stars and eighteen purple hearts. Scarn had needed to read that last part twice, but it was true. A track record like that meant Corbett Bonafide either had the best luck in the world or the worst.

Agent Adam Hunt stood beside Scarn surveying the land and the small house on it. Hunt did not care for Scarn (as many seemed not to) and was not terribly pleased with how the mission had been going.

"Don't you think this is kind of grasping at straws?" Hunt asked as they approached the house.

"I don't believe I asked your opinion," Scarn replied, then thought better of it. If it was possible, he had an even lower opinion of Hunt than the more junior man had of him. Scarn had come into the CIA straight out of Cornell, while Hunt had ascended from his position with Marine Force Recon in Vietnam. They could not have been more different if it was planned. "Look, we have nothing right now. We will not say that to Tresham, but we both know it's the truth. Bonafide made a beeline for this place after he left the hospital, and I wonder if there was a reason for that?"

"Homesick?" Hunt asked with a smirk.

Scarn did not appreciate the humor.

"A man like Jack Bonafide does nothing by accident. His whole life is planned. It's... it's precise. Like a watch. It would be one thing if he just kind of made his way here, but he came here like it was his job. You see what I'm saying?"

Hunt thought about it.

"Okay, I get what you're saying."

Adam Hunt also knew that Michael Scarn was right about something else: They were getting nowhere fast. There was a hydrogen bomb out there that could destroy a big chunk of the East Coast and they had about as much idea where it was as they did of where Jimmy Hoffa was buried.

Scarn made his way around the side of the house and came to a small plot of land. Then something on the edge of it by some corn stalks caught his eye. He walked across the yard with Hunt following him and stopped.

"What does that look like to you?" Scarn asked, motioning to the ground.

"Dirt," Hunt replied, and then looked closer. "Freshly turned dirt."

Scarn looked back and forth between the two rectangles of freshly turned dirt.

"Maybe about the size of a grave?"

"Evening," a voice called out from behind them.

Scarn looked over his shoulder and saw Corbett Bonafide.

That is one scary son of a bitch, Scarn thought to himself.

"Mister Bonafide," Scarn said, walking forward and holding out his hand.

Corbett's hand dropped to the grip of his Colt .44 revolver. Scarn froze in his tracks. Adam Hunt didn't move but was ready to push aside his jacket and go for his pistol if the occasion called for it.

"Unless the county assessor snuck in when I wasn't looking and moved my property line, I do believe you're trespassing."

"Mister Bonafide, we meant no disrespect. We're conducting a federal investigation—"

"You FBI?" Corbett asked.

"No," Scarn replied slowly.

"ATF?"

"No."

"Well, shit, son. That don't leave much. I know you ain't CIA, because I'm pretty sure that would make what you're doing here illegal."

"It's complicated, Mister Bonafide."

"No, I don't believe it is," Corbett said coolly. "Now get off my property."

"What's that?" Scarn asked, motioning to the two graves.

"Dirt."

"In the dirt?" Scarn asked insistently.

"Worms."

"Hm," Scarn grunted and nodded his head. "Fine, we'll be back with a warrant."

. . .

Scarn closed the door of the sedan and sat silently with Hunt in the back seat. Scarn looked at him in the rearview mirror.

"I thought I asked you to stop sitting in the back seat. It makes me feel like I'm your driver."

"I'm six-two," Hunt said as he pulled out his file folder. "You're five-ten. I need room to stretch out."

"That makes no sense."

"So are you really going to do it?" Hunt asked. "Get a warrant, I mean?"

Scarn thought about it for a moment.

"No," Scarn replied. "We need to find another way to get to Jack Bonafide."

Cameron, North Carolina
February 6, 1981

Jack turned off of Highway Twenty-Seven and onto Parker Street, a small road just outside of the main town, and about thirty minutes northwest of Fort Bragg. It had been a six-hour drive to get there, and neither Jack nor Carrie had said much.

The truth of it was that neither really knew how to

start the conversation that they both knew needed to be had. The sun was setting as Jack drove between the trees and turned down a long driveway.

"Where are we going?" Carrie asked.

She had noticed that they drifted off course a ways back, but decided to let it play out.

"To visit a friend," Jack said. "Someone that may be able to help."

The Home Of Charles Alvin Beckwith
Cameron, North Carolina
February 6, 1981

Jack stood in front of the door to the unassuming family home while Carrie waited a safe distance behind. Jack wasn't sure what kind of reception he would get knocking on the door of Charging Charlie Beckwith, founder of Delta Force, at this time of night, but best to play it safe.

Jack rapped on the door three times and then started to stand at attention and stopped himself. Inside he heard footsteps and then the unmistakable sound of the hammer being pulled back on a Colt 1911 pistol.

"Here we go," Jack muttered.

The door opened, and Jack came face to face with

his former commanding officer. At first, Charlie Beckwith looked at Jack with his usual stern countenance, then slowly he broke into a broad smile. Jack watched him make his weapon safe and stuff it back into the skeleton holster in his back.

"Jack Bonafide!" Charlie exclaimed and reached out and shook the Jack's hand. "What in the hell are you doing out here?" Charlie looked over Jack's shoulder to see Carrie standing at the bottom of the steps. "Hell, son, it's February in North Carolina out there. Get inside."

Jack and Carrie sat at the kitchen table while Charlie Beckwith made tea for them. Jack knew that the Colonel had put in his retirement papers, which accounted for some of his behavior change, but it was still a little jarring. As long as Jack had known Charlie, he had always been the tough as nails commander who brokered no quarter and asked for none in return. Now he was making them tea.

"Where are Katherine and the girls?" Jack asked as he looked around.

"Visiting her mother in Atlanta," Charlie replied as he set down the tea mugs and took a chair.

"I didn't know you were one for tea, sir," Jack said as he took a sip.

"Picked it up from the Brits while I was with 22

SAS," Charlie replied. "I don't make a habit out of it, but I can't handle coffee after nightfall anymore. Keeps me up. And can the "sir" stuff. Neither of us are on duty anymore."

"How's that going?" Jack asked with a raised eyebrow.

Charlie seemed to think about it for a moment and then shrugged.

"It's not what I wanted. We both know that. Katherine knows it too. Think she figured I could use some time to sort things out." He turned to Carrie. "I don't believe we've met."

"Carrie Davidson, si- I mean, Charlie," she replied and shook his hand. "I'm CIA." She stopped herself. "I mean, I was CIA."

Charlie looked to Jack.

"I heard a rumor," Charlie said. "That you'd thrown in with the spook shop."

"I wanted to tell you," Jack said, but Charlie held up a hand.

"We both know how this works, Jack. I get it. But the obvious question is, what are you doing here?"

"We're not with the CIA anymore," Jack said.

"Right, you're a NOC."

"No, not like that," Jack shook his head. "They let us go because we screwed the pooch."

"It wasn't our fault," Carrie shot back. "No one understood what we were going up against."

"But we do now," Jack countered.

"So I ask again, what can a washed up old Army Ranger do to help young Jack Bonafide?"

"Tactical support," Jack replied. "Mainly weapons and communications. I'm not asking you to get into the unit locker or anything, but I thought you might have some connections."

"What do you have now?" Charlie asked.

"Not much. A couple carbines and a pistol."

Charlie looked at Jack for a moment and then to his back door.

"I might be able to help you out."

Jack had never seen a work shed so well defended.

The building didn't look like much, maybe twenty feet by twenty feet, and it was pretty clear that Charlie had built it himself. While the former special operations commander was a world class warrior with few peers, those skills did not seem to have transferred to carpentry. Jack had seen nothing like it. He was pretty sure the strange building had five corners, and a roof that sloped at least ten degrees.

"A fine building," Jack said as Charlie worked on one of the three locks on the main door.

"It was my first attempt!" Charlie snapped.

The last lock came off and the door swung open.

The three walked inside and Charlie reached out and hit the light switch.

Nothing happened.

"Did you do the electrical too?"

"No one knows you're here," Charlie scowled. "You can disappear."

Charlie walked to the breaker box and began fiddling with the wires.

Carrie leaned in and whispered to Jack.

"Jack, we need serious hardware to go toe-to-toe with these guys. I don't know if what he's got lying around his shed will cut it."

"Here we go!" Charlie declared as sparks flew from the box and the lights came on.

After Carrie's eyes adjusted to the light, she looked around the large room.

"Holy shit," she whispered.

The room was outfitted like an armory. There were at least two dozen rifles and carbines, dozens of pistols, crates of ammunition, explosives, three light machine guns and what looked like a rocket launcher.

"Why do you have all of this?" Jack couldn't help but ask.

"Just call it being ready for a rainy day," Charlie said with a smile. "And this doesn't include what I've got buried in the yard."

. . .

Jack slid the last of the gear bags into the bed of the truck and slammed the gate shut. Even he had to admit that this seemed like overkill, but like Carrie had said, they had no idea what they were going up against. Better to have a couple light machine guns and not need them, than to need them and not have them.

Jack could tell that Charlie seemed uncomfortable after they loaded everything out, like he wanted to ask a question but already knew the answer.

"We can't take you with us," Jack said flatly. "Believe me, si— Charlie. If I could, I would, but this is probably a one-way trip. And if we do survive, the first-place prize will be a life sentence in Leavenworth."

Jack could tell that Charlie didn't like this, but aside from being a world class ass kicker, Colonel Charlie Beckwith was also a husband and father. It was one thing to touch down on foreign soil with a rifle in his hand when his country called upon him to do so, but this would be different.

Charlie nodded.

"Where are you going?" He asked.

"New York," Carrie volunteered, and then looked at Jack and shrugged.

"I'm not that far away," Charlie replied. "And I'll be ready if you need me."

Jack reached out and shook his former commander's hand, then he and Carrie got into the truck and pulled down the long dirt driveway. Jack looked in the mirror and saw Charlie Beckwith in the distance, looking every inch the old warrior that he was. It reminded Jack of what another old Colonel had once told him.

"At the end of this ride all you're left with are some ribbons and a handful of ashes. Waiting for another battle that will never come."

At least Charlie Beckwith had a family. Jack didn't even have that.

CHAPTER 11

An Undisclosed Location
North Bath, New York
February 7, 1981

S teven Waller stood up from his desk and looked at the cloned tamper device he had created. It was a perfect match for the one they had gone through so much trouble to smuggle into the United States. The Alpha Group commander had requested that Steven make this clone in case the original was damaged.

Was it possible Jack Bonafide was still out there? Was it possible that the opposing faction within the KGB was closing in? There were so many possibilities that might end with this house being raided and

Arkady and his team being taken down, but those scenarios also ended with Steven Waller spending the rest of his life in a cage. Or worse.

That was the image that kept Steven up at night; being led down a long, dark hallway in some American prison. Then the heavy steel door would open, and he would see the electric chair. Never mind that Steven didn't even know if they used the electric chair in the state of New York, that was still the image that haunted his sleep.

He had heard stories about executions in the electric chair not working properly, about heads catching fire but the condemned man still not dying. It was a horrible thought, being restrained in that chair with your head on fire, screaming and knowing that your only reprieve would be death.

Steven turned and looked to the Black Tsar again.

There was another way.

They had left him with everything he needed to detonate the device himself. Yes, the death toll would be catastrophic, even in this small town, but most likely it would be less than whatever they had planned. Or would it be worse? What if they intended to set it off in the ocean or somewhere like that, like the Israeli plane that had detonated over the Atlantic Ocean a few months prior? Then Steven would be unnecessarily sentencing millions to their deaths.

The door to the bedroom opened, and Steven

turned to see Arkady standing in the entrance. At least it wasn't Illya. Arkady treated Steven fairly well, but the other man acted as if he could shoot Steven Waller in the head without a second thought.

"How goes your work?" Arkady asked as he pulled out a chair and sat down across from Steven.

"Well," Steven replied with a nod of his head. "It's going well."

Arkady leaned forward and picked up the cloned tamper device from the desk and looked it over. Steven knew that the Alpha Group commander had no idea what he was looking at and was just putting on a show.

Arkady met Steven's eyes, as if he had heard what the man was just thinking, and the look on Steven's face gave his thoughts away.

Arkady smiled.

"You have doubts," Arkady said. It was a statement, not a question.

Steven said nothing. He was unsure what the correct answer would be.

"Tell me what's on your mind," Arkady pressed.

"It's just... it's just that I don't want to hurt anyone."

"Neither do I," Arkady said. He surveyed Steven for a moment and then continued. "Empires have been built and destroyed by men who didn't want to hurt anyone, Steven."

Arkady paused, obviously expecting a response.

"I suppose," Steven replied. "But what we are doing here, what other outcome could there be but death?"

"Why are you here, Steven?" Arkady asked. The question obviously confused Steven. "Speak your mind, tell the truth."

"I am... I am a prisoner."

Arkady raised an eyebrow.

"Are you really?"

"What else would you call it?"

Arkady shrugged.

"Have we ever told you that you couldn't leave? Put a gun to your head? Harmed you in any way?"

Steven thought about this for a moment. It was true. In fact, he had summoned them himself with the chalk mark on the wall back at the motel.

"I suppose not," Steven mumbled.

"Why would we? We are your countrymen," Arkady said. "More than that, we are brothers within the Soviet intelligence apparatus. Did you retire when no one was looking? I thought you were just doing your job here as instructed."

"I was out there for so long," Steven protested. "You don't know what that's like!"

"It's true," Arkady agreed. "I don't. Yet now we are in the same boat, so to speak. I guess the question is, will you help me row it or not?"

"Where is it going?" Steven asked, deciding to press his luck a bit.

Arkady leaned back in his chair and became more serious.

"You want to know what the plan is."

"I think I deserve to know. If it's true that I am not a prisoner, and that we are all working for the common good."

"We will detonate the Black Tsar in the New York subway system at a location where it will incur limited casualties, but will bring America's financial epicenter to its knees. At the same time, we will conduct a coordinated strike on one of the wealthiest men in New York."

"What?" Steven asked, surprised by this revelation. "I had assumed perhaps a politician, or even the president."

"The president?" Arkady said and then laughed out loud. "Who cares about the president? Comrade, presidents come and go. This man that we will kill, this man has done something far worse than any president could ever do."

"What has he done?"

"I cannot say," Arkady replied. "But believe me when I tell you it is what some might call a capital crime."

"I just don't want to hurt anyone."

"Twenty-seven million dead."

"What?" Steven asked.

"That is how many people we lost in the Patriotic War. Twenty-seven million Soviets, because we allowed the balance of world power to tip too far in one direction. Now we see it happening again. America is too powerful. We don't seek to destroy this country, only to hobble it."

Steven looked to the Black Tsar and then back to Arkady.

"I am with you, Comrade."

Illya looked up from the floor where he was cleaning a carbine as Arkady walked in. Two men sat beside him, reassembling already cleaned weapons. Arkady watched as one man performed a function check on a carbine.

"Did he buy it?" Illya asked.

"Yes, because I told him the truth."

Illya cocked his head to the side.

"What do you mean, the truth?"

"Exactly that," Arkady replied. "I told him we will detonate the weapon below street level as a diversion and assassinate Mister Feldman."

"You did what?" Illya demanded and stood up quickly.

Arkady stood his ground.

"What would you have me do?" Arkady asked.

"We need him to attach the tamper to the weapon and properly activate it. He was getting scared. I sang the Soviet national anthem to him, reminded him of his patriotic duty and he remembered his place."

Illya nodded his approval and then looked to one man seated on the floor beside him.

"We are ready to deploy to the Washington Heights station," Illya said.

"You understand your task?" Arkady asked.

"Yes, Comrade Colonel," Illya replied. "We've performed our reconnaissance on the deep access tunnel and the location is perfect. All we need to do now is return and load the weapon into it."

Illya closed the door behind him as he stepped out into the hallway with Arkady.

"Is there any word on the men the CIA has looking for us?"

Arkady smiled.

"They're a joke. They're in Texas."

"Texas?" Illya asked confused. "Do you think they are the reason Nestor and Marat went dark?"

"Unlikely. Nestor and Marat both missed their check-in long before this Agent Scarn arrived there. No, I would guess the only reason he is in Texas is because that's where Bonafide is from and he's grasping at straws."

Illya seemed to think about this for a moment.

"And Bonafide?"

"He's no threat. He barely survived last time, and our sources within the agency tell us they have fired him and directly ordered him not to follow up."

"Did he strike you as the kind of man who follows orders?"

Arkady shrugged.

"I will not worry about a factor I have no control over," Arkady said. "Scarn, on the other hand, we have control over. Unlike Bonafide, he follows the rules."

The Wyndham New Yorker
New York City, New York
February 7, 1981

Jack Bonafide finished his second loop around the block and met Carrie across the street from the entrance to the bar at the Wyndham New Yorker Hotel. Carrie had also performed her own hasty reconnaissance, and everything seemed normal. No strange vans with piles of cigarette butts outside of them, no Soviet assault teams and no CIA.

No one knew what Carrie Davidson knew. Specifically, that her confidant was holed up at the luxury hotel waiting to make his next move.

"Look," Jack said. "I understand the need for secrecy, but I don't like walking into a meet like this with no idea who I'm meeting."

"If I told you, you wouldn't go," Carrie said.

"Well, that doesn't make me feel better."

"Do you have another play?" Carrie asked.

Jack stared at her hard for a moment and then shook his head.

"All I've got is a map with a location marked on it that doesn't make any damn sense."

"He can help with that," Carrie said. "I'm sure of it."

"Okay," Jack replied.

"There's one more thing," Carrie said hesitantly.

"Which is?" Jack asked.

'You're not going to like it."

"What?"

"I need your weapon."

Jack laughed and looked down the street and back to Carrie.

"Wait, you're serious?"

Carrie held out her hand.

"I ain't giving you my weapon, Carrie."

"It's a bar in a luxury hotel, Jack. What's going to happen?"

"I might have asked the same thing about staying at a motel in Church Falls and look how that turned out."

"We don't go in there with a gun on your hip," Carrie said. "Full stop."

Jack stared hard at her for a moment and then let out a sigh. He scanned the street for a moment to make sure no one was watching, then pulled his Colt 1911 out of its holster and passed it to her.

"I'm trusting you," Jack said. "That means something."

"I get it," Carrie said as she stashed the weapon in her purse. "I won't let you down."

Jack caught the implication in her last statement. Carrie Davidson thought she had let Mac Bonafide down.

Jack sat down at the table the host had pointed them to and looked around. This most definitely was not the environment he was used to.

Carrie surveyed the dining room and it was clear she was expecting someone. She turned to Jack.

"Maybe you should sit on your hands," she said, obviously becoming nervous.

"Sit on my hands? Who in the hell are we meeting?" Jack asked insistently. Then as if on cue a man entered the room and he got his answer. "Son of a bitch."

McMasters walked across the dining room toward them. Despite having grown a heavy beard, the Russian had not changed his appearance much. He was hiding in plain sight.

Jack moved for Carrie's purse, and she gripped his wrist with a surprising amount of strength and locked eyes with him.

"If you do this, if you do this here, he died for nothing. Is that what you want?"

Jack clenched his jaw. Carrie could feel his pulse pounding through his wrist beneath her fingers. He was ready to assassinate the Russian right then and there.

"Fine," Jack hissed, and withdrew his hand.

"Did I come at a bad time?" McMasters asked with a warm smile.

"No, Anatoly," Carrie responded. "Please, have a seat."

"Anatoly?" Jack asked.

"It's his name," Carrie said with a shrug. "You didn't really think his name was McMasters, did you?"

Jack turned to Anatoly, the former Delta operative's rage clearly seething beneath the surface.

"I feel we're getting off on the wrong foot," Anatoly said. "As you Americans say. First, I did not kill your brother. I tried to save him."

Jack felt his world drop out from beneath him, and he turned to Carrie.

"Is this true?"

Carrie nodded her affirmation.

"Why didn't you tell me?"

"How do you think that would have gone over, Jack?"

"I fought in the Patriotic War, you know," Anatoly said conversationally. "You call it World War Two, but for us it was no World War. We were defending our homeland."

"Well, tie a yellow fucking ribbon around the old oak tree for Ivan and his Patriotic War," Jack said.

"Jack," Carrie sighed.

Jack had a few more choice words chambered but relented.

"I fought in Stalingrad," Anatoly continued as if he had not heard the interruption. "Six months of fighting. You've seen nothing like it, and you wouldn't want to. That single battle became the reason that I do what I do, for my service to my country. To ensure that nothing like that ever happens again." Anatoly paused for a moment and took a sip from his glass of water. "Are we that different, you and I, Jack? If you're being honest with yourself, are we really?"

"Yes," Jack said flatly. "I never would have tried to kill John Wayne."

For a moment Anatoly thought his American counterpart was joking and then realized Jack was serious.

"We are from two different worlds, Mister Bonafide. I don't expect you to understand mine any more than I understand yours."

"Show him the map," Carrie said.

Jack looked at her for a moment and then sighed. Turning to a KGB agent for help was the last thing he wanted to be doing. Regardless of his feelings on the matter, Jack also knew that they didn't have any choice. Begrudgingly he reached into his jacket pocket, retrieved the map and handed it to Anatoly.

"I could have you executed for this," Anatoly said with a smile. "High treason, working with an agent of a foreign power." He sensed that Jack did not appreciate his humor. "Sorry, spy humor."

"How long have you been talking to him?" Jack asked quietly as Anatoly studied the map.

"He called me first, at that same bar."

"How long?"

"About a month," Carrie replied

"Jesus. You want to talk about high treason?"

"I didn't have anyone else to talk to!" Carrie said. "You were nowhere to be found and-"

"It's the subway system," Anatoly said, cutting them off. He laid the map out on the table.

Jack looked at the lines drawn over the street map and understood.

"I'll be goddamned. He's right. It's the New York City Subway system."

"A subway car," Carrie said. "If they get it on a subway car, they can send it anywhere in the Five Burroughs."

"But why?" Jack asked. "Just to blow up New

York?"

"That will blow up more than New York," Anatoly assured them.

Jack looked back to the map, and the one point marked in red.

"I still don't understand why they would carry this map," Jack said.

"Didn't you carry maps in Iran?" Anatoly asked.

Jack looked up with obvious surprise on his face.

"Yes, Jack," Anatoly said with a smile. "We knew that you were in Iran with Delta. We Soviets like to pretend that arrogance is purely an American trait, but we can be guilty of it as well. Those men you took the map from never imagined they would be captured or killed on their mission. So they didn't plan for it."

Jack stared at Anatoly for a moment.

"Doesn't it bother you?" Jack asked.

"Does what bother me?" Anatoly asked.

"That your men died? It would bother me. I'd want my pound of flesh."

Anatoly smiled.

"That's another difference between us, Jack. It's not just about killing John Wayne. You weep for every fallen soldier, for every agent that dies in the line of duty. You decorate your walls with stars and your lawns with flags. For us? It's just Tuesday." Anatoly paused, warming to his subject. "You stand for the rights of the individual, but we stand for the destiny of the collective. Together, working as one, we can build a better tomorrow."

"You're just forgetting one thing," Jack said as he slid his chair back from the table and stood up.

"What's that?"

"We're Americans. We're kind of assholes and we like it that way, and ain't nobody gonna tell us it has to be another."

Carrie watched as Jack walked out of the bar with the map in his hand. He was obviously upset, but even he wouldn't be able to deny that this meeting had yielded fruit.

"He will turn you in, you know," Anatoly said. "For talking to me."

"I know," Carrie said. "That's what makes him who he is."

"I'm leaving New York," Anatoly said.

"Are you going back?"

"No," Anatoly said. "And probably not for quite some time. The two KGB deputies, Sokolov and Galkin, are at war with one another over who will replace Andropov, and the rest of us are caught in the middle. I worked for Galkin. I'm certain the team that hit you at the motel worked for Sokolov."

"So, Sokolov wants to set off the Black Tsar?"

Anatoly nodded.

"To what end, I don't know. I was just supposed to get the tamper back after we had tracked it from its origin station."

"Was he right?" Carrie asked.

"Was who right about what?"

"About your men. Was Jack right? Do you really not care?"

"It's complicated," Anatoly replied.

"No, it's not," Carrie pressed. "Maybe that's the real difference between you and us. How you feel about the people you lose is simple. And just in case you were planning on thinking on it any further, you didn't lose those men because of Jack or his brother. You lost them because two people that you work for sent their own teams against each other."

There was something in Anatoly's eyes, a shift that let Carrie know he cared and that he didn't disagree with what she was saying.

"It's a dangerous world," Anatoly said, and then looked out the window to where Jack Bonafide was standing on the sidewalk. "Your man is waiting for you."

"Are you staying? We could use a hand."

Anatoly laughed out loud.

"That's unlikely. Jack was right, you and I are both committing high treason just by having this conversation. We're not about to become Batman and Robin."

"If we were, I'd be Batman."

Anatoly looked her over and then smiled.

"I do believe you would." He reached into his pocket and handed her a card with an address scrawled on the back. "It's for a safe house in Brooklyn, if you need it."

"One of yours?" Carrie asked, turning the card over in her hand.

Anatoly nodded.

"Unmanned," he said.

"If we walked into it and looked down the barrel of a few KGB agents, that would be a convenient way to tie up loose ends."

"That it would."

Carrie stepped out the door and saw Jack turn to her.

"I'm not sure how I feel about what happened in there," Jack said.

Carrie stopped and spun on her heel.

"What was your play, Jack? If I didn't pull a rogue KGB agent out of my back pocket, how were you ever going to make the connection that those lines represented the New York subway system? Have you ever even been to New York, Jack?"

"A couple times."

"It is what it is, I did what I did," Carrie said, and then began walking again. "I don't want to keep going in circles over it. If you think you need to turn me in, do it. Otherwise, we need to hit that location point on the map and see what we find."

"What in the hell is he on about?" Jack asked, looking past Carrie and back into the bar.

Carrie turned and saw Anatoly waving wildly at them, a look of surprise on his face. No, it wasn't surprise. It was shock.

Jack and Carrie moved quickly back into the hotel and found Anatoly standing at the bar watching a news story unfolding on the television.

KGB headquarters bombed in Moscow! Twenty-three dead!

"What in the hell?" Jack asked, turning to Anatoly.

"They're saying that both deputies of the KGB are dead," Anatoly said. He was as white as a sheet. Right away, Jack knew he was as surprised by this as they were. "Makar Galkin and Konstantin Sokolov are dead. Andropov is in the hospital."

"Jesus Christ!" Carrie gasped. "What does this mean?"

Jack looked at Anatoly.

"Will the attack stop?" Jack asked.

"No," Anatoly replied. "It will speed up the sched-ule. It would be one thing if only one deputy were dead. They would assume it was a power grab. But Andropov and both of his deputies hit at the same time?"

Carrie understood.

"They will think it was us," she said.

"Yes."

Dick's Roadhouse
Texarkana, Texas
February 7, 1981

Supervisory Special Agent Michael Scarn stirred what passed for coffee at Dick's Roadhouse and watched the patrons come and go. As Texas roadhouses went, it wasn't bad, but it also wasn't what he was accustomed to. Growing up in New England and attending Cornell he was used to a certain lifestyle, and those tastes, once developed, were hard to forget. The concoction the waitress had served him did not quite measure up to the standards for coffee set in the Scarn household.

He looked to the clock on the wall and saw that it was nearly four in the afternoon. Scarn knew that Angeline Bonafide worked the swing shift, and that there was no rear entrance for employees, so she would have to come in the same front entrance everyone else did.

"What if there's nothing here?" Hunt asked as he sipped his beer.

Scarn's disapproving look when Hunt had ordered his beer (he was still on duty) had not gone unnoticed, but at this point, the former Recon Marine didn't really care. He was beginning to get the distinct feeling that they were on a wild goose chase, and it was one he didn't much care for. Too much was hanging in the balance.

The bell on the door jingled and Hunt turned to see a woman walk in. She looked to be about five foot ten, with long dark brown hair and a figure that could only be described as otherworldly.

"Holy shit," Hunt whispered.

Scarn turned to look at the woman as she walked across the room.

"That's her," Scarn said. "Keep it in your pants."

"That's a fucking ten," Hunt said. "Just in case you ever need a reference point. What the hell is that woman doing working at a roadhouse in Texarkana?"

"Mrs. Bonafide!" Scarn called out.

Angeline Bonafide stopped and spun around, a scowl on her face.

"You pissed her off," Hunt said.

"Who in the fuck are you?" Angeline demanded.

The way she had snapped at Scarn was jarring and took him aback momentarily. He was used to being in altercations both verbal and physical, but not with someone who looked like she could have just walked off of a runway in Paris. However, now he understood why she was working in a roadhouse in Texarkana, and why she was being divorced from one Jack Bonafide.

"Mrs Bonafide—"

"Michaels!" Angeline shouted. "You call me Bonafide again and you'll be lookin' for your balls on the side of the road."

Hunt snickered.

"What are you laughing at pretty boy?" Angeline said, turning her wrath on Adam Hunt.

"Nothin' Ma'am."

"Mrs. Michaels," Scarn said. "We're federal agents."

"Ask me if I give two fucks."

What on earth is wrong with this woman? Scarn thought to himself. *If Bonafide actually put a ring on her finger, he's crazier than I thought.*

"We're here on a matter concerning Jack Bonafide," Scarn pressed on. This woman had every intention of steam rolling him, and he decided to stop giving her opportunities. "He's in violation of a federal order to stand down from an investigation—"

"You're barking up the wrong tree, law dog, so why don't you fuck off and—"

Adam Hunt stood up from his seat and looked down at Angeline Michaels.

"Look lady, can the horseshit," Hunt ordered.

"You're pissed, I get it. I've met Bonafide. He's a dick and if I see him again, I'll rap him one good for you. In the meantime, we're trying to stop a lot of innocent people from getting hurt and your ex-husband plays a part in that. Maybe you're used to men falling all over themselves around you but I ain't that breed. So, the next thing that comes out of that pretty mouth of yours better be 'yes, sir, how can I help?' or as God is my witness you're going in the fucking trunk of my car. Am I understood?"

Angeline's face changed.

"Yes, sir. How can I help?"

"So, he went to New York," Scarn said thoughtfully as they exited the roadhouse. "That doesn't give us much to go on."

"It's something," Hunt said, and turning around looked back at the building.

"What is it?" Scarn asked.

"I think I'm in love," Hunt replied with a smile.

"Agent, that woman is the definition of a walking red flag."

"Looks green to me," Adam Hunt said with a smile.

As if on cue, Angeline Michaels exited the road-house and made a beeline for a small yellow Honda Civic in the parking lot. She opened up the rear hatch.

"What in the hell is she doing?" Hunt asked.

"Probably getting a rocket launcher," Scarn replied, only half joking.

Angeline pulled a small duffel bag out of the Civic, slammed the hatch shut and walked to the two of them.

"What's that?" Scarn asked.

"Traveling bag," Angeline replied. She opened up the trunk of the car they were standing next to and tossed it in.

"Where in the hell do you think you're going?" Hunt asked.

Without missing a beat, Angeline reared back and slammed her fist into Hunt's jaw, knocking him to the ground.

"God damn!" She howled, grabbing her right hand with her left. "You got a jaw like fucking granite!"

Hunt jumped back to his feet and Scarn grabbed him by the arm.

"You two knock it off!" Scarn said.

"What in the hell was that for?" Hunt shouted.

"I gave you that one back in the diner on account of what you said about innocent people getting hurt. You talk to me like I'm some fucking street whore again and I'll give you a fucking Texarkana smile!"

"What in the hell is a Texarkana smile?" Hunt asked, astounded by how this woman was talking to him.

Angeline held up her thumb and pulled it vertically across her throat.

"You can't threaten to kill a federal agent!" Scarn said.

"I can threaten to do whatever the fuck I want!" Angeline shot back and then seemed to drop to a lower gear. "Besides, you two need me."

"Like hell we do!" Hunt replied.

"I know him," Angeline said. "You don't. I know how his mind works. It may seem like he's just some wrecking ball smashing his way through life, but there's something like a program that's always running in the back of his head, putting bits and pieces together."

"I find that a little hard to believe," Scarn scoffed.

"You're a federale, right?" Angeline asked in a mocking tone.

"Yes, I am," Scarn responded.

"That's strange," Angeline said as she looked around the parking lot. "So, you have the full power of the United States government at your beck and call, but here you are in a Texarkana roadhouse parking lot trying to get help from a soon to be divorced waitress?"

Scarn said nothing.

"I'll tell you what he's doing right now," Angeline pressed on. "He's probably gone to someone he trusts for help, which for Jack Bonafide looks like a truck full of guns. Then he picked up someone else he trusts to help him load said guns and made a beeline for New York. Once he gets there and finds who he's looking for, he'll see a half dozen ways to sneak up on the problem, but instead he'll come at it the only way a Bonafide knows how."

"Which is?" Scarn asked.

"Straight fuckin' through."

Scarn said nothing for a moment and then nodded his head.

Hunt leaned in and spoke into Scarn's ear.

"I bet she fit right in, in that family."

"I heard that," Angeline said as she opened the rear door of the sedan and got in.

"That was my seat," Hunt said as he got into the front passenger's side.

"Well, she fixed that problem," Scarn replied as he got in and started the engine.

Hunt tilted the rearview mirror to look back at Angeline.

"Just answer me one question. What is it you're getting out of all of this?"

Angeline reached into her bag and pulled out a sheathe of papers.

"A fucking divorce."

Washington Heights
Manhattan, New York
February 7, 1981

Jack Bonafide pulled the truck up to the curb in front of the 191st Street train line and looked back at the folded map in his hand.

"This is it," he said as he looked around. "And now it makes sense."

"What do you mean?" Carrie asked.

Jack gestured to a vendor selling trinkets down the street and the handwritten sign he had taped to his table.

New York's Deepest Subway Station

"Why so far down?" Carrie asked.

"I can't say, but it's special, so there's a reason they'd want to set it off here. Maybe something about how it networks with the other tunnels."

"Jesus Christ," Carrie gasped. "Could it bring the city down?"

"How would it do that?"

"Well, I minored in city planning. No good reason, I've just always found it interesting. I studied this city for a while, mainly because there's an amazing network of tunnels beneath the streets dating all the way back to the Mount Prospect Tunnel in eighteen thirty-seven. In theory, if you set off a hydrogen bomb in the right place... the whole network would come apart and the city would collapse."

Jack looked back to the tunnel.

"We'll head in, run some recon and see what we find."

"Wait," Carrie said, placing her hand on his arm.

"What?"

"You're parked in a red zone."

"I don't think that's our biggest concern right now."

"You're a wanted fugitive driving a truck full of guns and a rocket launcher."

Jack thought about it for a moment.

"Yeah, I guess you're right," he said. "We'll move."

The tunnel that ran from the street entrance to the train platform was long, quite a bit longer than Jack had expected it to be. He hadn't been in any kind of tunnel since Vietnam and back then they had been a lot smaller than this one. So why did this entrance tunnel feel like it was getting smaller? He'd never had claustrophobia before, perhaps this was something new?

Jack had had little in the way of concussion symptoms since going through the respiratory rehabilitation at Bethesda Naval Hospital that had fixed his breathing. With each passing day he could feel his lungs getting stronger. If a little claustrophobia was all that remained, he could live with that.

They emerged onto the train platform and found it to be mostly empty.

"Okay, I'll say it," Carrie said. "This place is creepy as hell."

Jack laughed.

"After everything you've been through over the past month, this bothers you?"

"I don't like caves."

Jack looked around but saw nothing unusual, then walked to the edge of the platform and peered down the track and into the darkness. He knew that there were access tunnels along the tracks, and it made sense that one of them could lead to some little-used room or another tunnel that might be a good place to hide a hydrogen bomb.

He narrowed his eyes and leaned a little further into the darkness.

"Careful!" Carrie said, reaching out for him.

"I ain't gonna fall," Jack said, sounding almost annoyed, and then pointed into the darkness. "Do you see that?"

Carrie leaned out on the platform and peered into the dark tunnel.

"See what?"

"That," Jack said pointing into the darkness. "There's a chem light down there. It's almost out but it's there."

Carrie tried her best, but for the life of her could not see what he was pointing at.

"I don't see it, Jack."

"It's there," Jack said as he hopped off the platform and onto the tracks.

"Are you nuts?" Carrie shouted.

"The schedule on the wall says we have ten minutes until the next train comes through," Jack said, pointing to the sheet under glass on the wall. "So we'd better get a move on."

Carrie hopped off the platform and landed on the tracks, to see Jack already jogging into the darkness. She reached into her pocket and retrieved a penlight, and then almost as an afterthought drew her Beretta. As if on cue, Jack also drew his Colt 1911. It was unlikely they would magically run into the bad guys in a subway tunnel, but stranger things had happened.

Were it not for the small penlight, the darkness of the tunnel would have immediately swallowed them. Then she saw it. In the distance, barely visible but it was there; a green chem light laying on the ground to the left of the tracks. How in the hell had he seen that all the way from the platform?

Jack picked up his pace and Carrie followed suit. She watched him raise his weapon to the ready position as they closed in on the chem light and she brought hers up as well. What did he see? Were they about to get in a fight? She could feel her heart rate increasing, but she kept her nerves steady. All of those hours out at Topper's Range were about to pay off. At least, she hoped they would.

Jack slowed to a walk and then stopped. He held up an open hand. Carrie knew that in the military this was the sign to stop. A fist would have meant to freeze in place. Carrie wanted to say something, ask what he was seeing, but she knew that she would break noise discipline. She needed to follow his lead.

He looked to the left and then turned to face something.

"It's an access door." Jack ran his hands along the edges of the door. "It's marked up like someone pried it open."

Carrie walked to the door and saw that there was also a padlock on it.

"It's a new lock," she said, touching the cold steel. "This was just put on."

Jack dipped into his jacket pocket and retrieved his lock pick kit. He took a knee and began working on the lock. Within a minute it opened. It surprised him they would go to all of this trouble and then use such an easily defeated lock.

He pulled the door open and stepped inside. There was no reason to be overly cautious, as whoever had done this was unlikely to have locked themselves inside.

In the glow of Carrie's pen light Jack saw a steep slope ahead of them, and far below he could see what looked like old train tracks. He knew there were old freight lines running beneath much of the city, but he'd never seen one before.

"At what point do we call this in?" Carrie asked.

"Depends on how fast you want to go to prison,"

Jack replied, looking over his shoulder at her. "Even if we show up at Langley with the bomb in the back of my truck and the Soviet agents hogtied beside it, we probably still go to prison. It's just a question of how long we go down for."

"Fantastic."

It only took a few minutes to negotiate the slope, but once they hit the bottom, they found themselves in another long tunnel, this one much older than the subway tunnel above. It was covered in ancient linoleum. On the wall Line 38 was stamped.

"Look at this," Carrie said, shining her light on the wall. A series of lines with similar number stamps were engraved on the concrete. She studied it for a moment. "It's an overlay of the city. It's some old freight line that goes all over Manhattan."

"I think you were right," Jack said. "If it went off down here it might collapse parts of the city."

Carrie stood in silence for a moment, and Jack could see that she was thinking about something.

"What is it?" he asked.

"The rivers," she said. "There's a huge network of rivers and lakes running beneath Manhattan. In theory, if you set off a strong enough hydrogen bomb at this depth and used those tunnels to channel the blast..."

"You could flood the city."

CHAPTER 12

An Undisclosed Location
North Bath, New York
February 7, 1981

T hey were coming and going more frequently now. Steven had noticed this. The tempo was building; something would happen soon.

He didn't think Arkady was lying to him about what he had said, but he thought the Alpha Group commander was holding something back. There was still one piece of the puzzle that Steven Waller didn't have, and that was the piece he needed.

Arkady was smart, no question about it. He was smart and he was shrewd, but Steven didn't think that he was onto him. Steven Waller would continue playing possum, collecting the information he needed while simultaneously trying to not get his head blown off.

He had noticed that sometimes the house was nearly empty. On one occasion the house actually was empty, for about thirty minutes. Steven had been alone. He briefly considered making a run for it, but he knew that he was still missing that essential piece to the puzzle. Without it, he might not be able to stop what they were trying to do.

Yes, Steven Waller had decided he needed to stop this. He didn't know what that would mean for him, but his innate moral compass was telling him it was the right thing to do. He believed what Arkady had implied about his patriotism, but at what cost?

The phone was in the kitchen, and it was the only one in the house. To make a phone call he would have to leave his room, enter the kitchen, make the call and then get back to his room with no one noticing.

The problem with this plan was that the men seemed to like to congregate in the kitchen. Why in the hell couldn't they spend their time in the living room like normal people? Because these men were not normal people, that was why. Besides this, Steven had noticed that the Alpha Group men really seemed to enjoy eating. He had never met people who ate so much and so often.

Steven sat quietly and listened to the two men talking. A moment later he heard the door open and shut. Then it was silent. He waited another minute. Still nothing. This was it; he was alone. He stood up slowly from his chair and paused again. Still no noise.

These men were not quiet, so unless they were deliberately setting him up, Steven Waller knew that he was almost certainly alone in the house.

Steven turned and walked to the hallway. Every step echoed like thunder. He couldn't get the single repeating thought out of his head: Why would they leave him alone like this? These men were professionals, the absolute top tier of Soviet Special Forces. How could they make such a simple mistake?

The hallway was empty. Steven looked down to the right where it led into the kitchen. There was nothing, no one. He walked in silence but was legitimately concerned that the pounding of his heart would give him away. What in the hell was he thinking? This wasn't his responsibility. The CIA must have other men like that John Bonafide working on this problem. Why was it left to him to save the day?

Finally, Steven emerged into the kitchen. Then, he had his answer. He understood why they had left him alone in the house. Through the window blinds he could see two of the men standing in the backyard smoking. It was Illya and another man.

This meant that he only had whatever amount of

time it took them to finish a cigarette to make his phone call. For once, Steven cursed the fact that he had never smoked. He had never taken up the habit because he thought it would shorten his life. Now it seemed it could have quite the opposite effect, as he had no idea how long it took to smoke a cigarette. Because of that lack of knowledge he did not know how much time he had to make the phone call.

As if being urged on by some other power, Steven walked to the phone and snatched it off the receiver fixed to the wall. He dialed a number from memory and waited while it rang. Steven had memorized most of the phone numbers for different American governmental agencies. While he was in engineering school, he had realized he had a strange skill for memorizing long strings of numbers, and now it was truly paying off.

"Central Intelligence Agency switchboard, how may I direct your call?"

"Pass a message to the team working on the Black Tsar. The Russians are located at 1021 Farm Street in North Bath, New York."

"I'm sorry, what—"

Steven quietly hung up the phone. His hands were shaking as he watched Illya and the other man stamp out their cigarettes and turn back to the house.

. . .

Illya opened the kitchen door and stepped in from the cold. The chill of upstate New York was nothing compared to Moscow or Siberia, but it was still unpleasant and he had no desire to stay in it longer than he had to.

He stopped and looked around. Something was wrong. He could feel it in the little hairs on the back of his neck.

"What is it?" The other man asked.

Illya held up a hand to silence him and began walking down the hallway. Steven Waller was the only one in the house, at least as far as he knew. Illya stopped at the doorway to Steven Waller's room. He stepped inside.

Steven looked up from his worktable.

Illya looked around the room and then back to Steven.

"Have you been in here the whole time?" Illya asked.

"I thought I was not supposed to leave?" Steven asked innocently.

Illya surveyed the room again and then nodded his agreement.

"Fix the tamper to the weapon," Illya said curtly.

Illya walked back down the hallway and into one

bedroom where his two best men were standing with their gear ready to go. He looked each man in the eyes.

"You understand what I am asking of you?" Illya asked.

Both men nodded.

Illya waved to them both to follow him and led them back down the hallway to Steven Waller's room.

Steven looked up from the Black Tsar, where he had finished screwing in the tamper and connecting the wires.

"Is it activated?" Illya asked.

"Yes," Steven replied.

"Show me."

Steven picked up a testing device from his workbench and connected it to the detonator. After a moment there was a small beep and he held up the device to show three green lights.

"Good," Illya said as he raised his silenced pistol and put it to Steven's head.

"But I still have some modifications to make!"

"No," Illya said. "You don't."

Illya pulled the trigger and a puff of pink mist escaped Steven Waller's head. His body collapsed to the floor. Illya turned to where the Black Tsar was sitting on the two sawhorses.

"It's time."

The Upper West Side
New York City, New York
February 7, 1981

Arkady dialed the number from memory as he sat in the back of the Econoline van. By now the mission would be underway. Illya would have executed Steven Waller and they would be loading the Black Tsar into the second van for its trip to Washington Heights.

When he had learned of the attack on KGB headquarters and the apparent death of Colonel Sokolov, he had to admit that it had given him pause. The man who set them on this path to begin with was dead.

Most people assumed the Americans were somehow involved with this, and it would clearly look as if what his team was about to do in New York was retribution for that attack. It could set into motion a series of events that would engulf the entire world in the fires of war.

This thought gave Arkady pause, but nothing more than that.

La Guardia Airport
New York City, New York

February 7, 1981

Scarn took the steps two at a time as he debarked the private jet that had taken them from the airfield in Texarkana to New York. He did this not to move faster toward a destination, but to get away from Angeline Bonafide/Michaels.

The woman was completely out of her mind and had spent the entire flight marveling at the fact that she was in a private jet while she drank from a flask that she had stashed in her travel bag.

It was a quick walk across the tarmac to the nearest payphone, where Scarn dropped in a quarter and put in a call to the Langley switchboard.

"This is Scarn. Access number bravo two four five zero." He waited a moment. "Yes, we just touched down at La Guardia. We have an asset in tow." He waited again. "I'm not sure how useful she is, but we decided it was worth a shot."

"We've received some intelligence that the Russians who hit Bonafide may be in Upstate New York, in North Bath," a woman's voice said.

"What's the source?"

"Unconfirmed, but he referenced the Black Tsar."

"Okay, sounds actionable. Are you dispatching a team?" Scarn asked.

"Consider yourself dispatched."

"That's ridiculous. North Bath is nearly five hours away from here. We'll be driving all night."

"You have your orders. Would you like me to give you the address?"

They had lost faith in him. That was the only explanation for this. Sending him all the way to upstate New York on what sounded like a wild goose chase? Yes, the caller had referenced the weapon by name, but that could easily be Bonafide trying to throw them off the trail while he made his own move, or even the Russians themselves trying to derail the investigation!

Hunt stood beside Angeline at the terminal entrance. He could tell by the look on Scarn's face that something was wrong.

"What is it?" Hunt asked.

"We're going to Bath, in upstate."

"Why in the hell are we going there?"

"Because we have orders!" Scarn said firmly, and then immediately felt poorly for it. He was taking his anger out on Hunt. "Look, it's not my first choice but there's a tip that's worth following up on, and we're the only ones close enough."

"I'm game for a road trip," Angeline said with a smile, and then took another shot from her flask.

Washington Heights
Manhattan, New York
February 7, 1981

Jack's feet hurt. He hadn't stood guard duty in quite a while, and he forgot how much a man's feet could ache just standing in one place. He had opted to stand post on the platform while Carrie set up an observation post on the street.

Since the Russians had locked the door to the access tunnel from the outside, it was a safe bet that they would return the same way. When they did, Jack and Carrie would find out just what they were up to.

Jack reached into his shirtsleeve and clicked the button that attached to the earpiece in his left ear.

"Anything?" He asked. Since there were only two of them on the net, they had dispensed with strict radio protocol.

"Negative," Carrie's voice came back. "I assume you're still coming up empty?"

"Affirmative."

Jack stopped and watched two men coming down the stairs, but he knew they weren't the ones he was looking for. There was something about them, something that told him they weren't Soviet spies.

"We can't do this twenty-four seven, Jack," Carrie said. "We have to either call it in or start taking shifts."

"We can't call it in before we have eyes on the weapon. If we do, we lose everything." Jack thought about it for a moment. "Okay, we'll take shifts. I'll go until midnight and then you can take over."

"Roger that," Carrie agreed, and then the line went dead.

Jack stood in the relative silence of the subway station. If it would happen, if the Russians would show up toting a monster hydrogen bomb along with them, it would happen soon. It had to. He knew this because it would be too risky to leave a hide site like the one they had found unattended for too long. Too much risk of discovery.

Jack also understood that if nothing happened by morning, they would have to call it in to Mike Tresham, and then explain why two former operatives who had been directly and lawfully ordered to stand down were still active on this mission. The next obvious question was how that would go down. Would he just quietly let them put the handcuffs on him (and probably get shipped off to Leavenworth) or would he run.

Jack Bonafide wasn't designed to live in a cage. Because he knew this he also knew the answer to that question.

Jack looked back down the dark tunnel. He had thought he heard something but then shook his head.

Then he heard it again. It could be anything; rats, the homeless. There were stories of whole groups of underground dwellers in these tunnels.

What if he was wrong about them coming in through this entrance? What if they would get back into the subterranean tunnel from another access point? He thought about this for a moment. It wouldn't hurt to re-check that door. If they came in through the main entrance while he was down there, he wouldn't miss them. Quite the contrary, they would run right into each other.

After thinking about it for another moment Jack checked to make sure no one was watching him and hopped off the platform and onto the tracks.

North Bath, New York
February 8, 1981

Supervisory Special Agent Michael Scarn was right. The drive had taken just over five hours, and they arrived in North Bath well after midnight. Scarn had slept a little on the plane and during the first hour of the drive, so he offered to handle the rest of the trip.

Angeline Bonafide proved to be no less of a handful

on the drive to North Bath than she had on the flight from Texarkana to La Guardia.

They had needed to pull over twice to survey the map they'd picked up at a gas station to find Farm Street. Scarn couldn't get over the feeling that he was in a bad comedy sketch; two bumbling inspectors being sent on a wild goose chase all over the countryside while someone else was doing the real work.

The town of North Bath was exactly what Scarn expected it to be. A big, giant, nothing. Not exactly the type of place where a group of Soviet super spies would stage their attack on America. Or maybe that was what made it the perfect place?

Scarn laughed at this thought. It was absurd. They would most likely have to drive five hours just to get to the target site. Not exactly the model of Soviet efficiency.

No, this whole scenario was exactly what it seemed. They would check off this box to keep the brass at Langley happy and then get back to business. Scarn kept reminding himself that he didn't need to actually find and defuse this Black Tsar, he just needed to locate some actionable intelligence so that they could then put together a mission profile for Delta or ST6.

The three drove up Farm Street at half past midnight. The sound of the snow crunching beneath the sedan's tires sounded like thunder.

"You should kill the lights," Hunt whispered.

"Really?" Scarn asked, and then immediately felt foolish for the question.

Of course they should kill the lights. He wasn't taking this seriously enough. Yes, it was a big nothing in the middle of nowhere, but there was no reason to be taking unnecessary risks. He shut off the lights and slowed the car to a stop a few houses down from the target house.

Scarn checked his notebook and then turned to Hunt.

"Utility records showed the call came from the target house," Scarn said.

"So, a Soviet agent just decides to dime his own team out?" Hunt asked.

"I know, I know," Scarn said. "It's someone trying to have some fun with us. If it is, they're getting cuffed and taken to the police station."

"They have a police station in this town?" Angeline asked mockingly.

"Oh, and what?" Hunt replied. "Texarkana is the Paris of the south?"

"Fuck you."

"Did you ever stop to think your mouth might be making your life a lot harder than it has to be?"

"Fuck you twice," Angeline said as she unscrewed the cap of her flask and put it to her lips.

Her head whipped back as it exploded with the rear window, painting the inside of the car red. Hunt went for his weapon at the exact moment that three more rounds ripped into his chest in quick succession.

Scarn was processing everything in reverse. He realized the windshield had shattered and he heard the loud cracks of unsuppressed rifle fire.

The engine is still running; he thought to himself and quickly threw the car into reverse and slammed his foot against the accelerator. For a brief moment Scarn felt relief that whoever had just fired on them seemed to have stopped shooting. Then he realized to his horror that not only had they not stopped firing, they were laying down a heavy volume of fire. He had thought they stopped because all the windows in the car were shattered, but he could still hear the 'ping' of rounds hitting the body of the car and an occasional zip as one passed his head.

Then things went from bad to worse, he felt the car glide as it hit a patch of ice and then fishtail, slamming into two parked vehicles. His head cracked against the side of the door and everything went black.

Bogden lowered his carbine, looked to Egor and began walking back to the house.

"Where are you going?" Egor asked. "We need to go check that car."

Bogden stopped, looking moderately annoyed.

"No one could have survived that," Bogden replied.

"We still need to check."

"They'll be coming soon," Bogden insisted. "We have a job to do."

"And this is it!" Egor said. "We have our orders. Anyone approaching the house after midnight was to be annihilated."

"Look at that car!" Bogden nearly shouted. "We emptied two magazines into it."

"In the time that you have been arguing with me, we could have investigated this and been back in the house."

Bogden sighed and began walking toward the car.

Scarn opened his eyes. Following the cacophony of the rifle fire the night was eerily silent, save for one noise. He could hear only the sound of boots crunching on snow, a sound that was gradually growing closer to the car.

He kept his eyes closed and slowly moved his hand to where he had stashed his pistol in the side pocket of the door. He would have to shoot left-handed, which was less than ideal. Taking his weapon out of its holster during long drives was a bad habit, one for which he may be about to pay dearly.

They were speaking in whispers, but they were very clearly speaking Russian. They weren't even trying to hide it.

Scarn knew that he would only have seconds to make this work, and if he guessed incorrectly where they were, he would be dead.

The footsteps stopped. Scarn stopped breathing. He tried to keep his heart rate slow. His pistol sat on his left thigh, his finger on the trigger. Then he heard the voice. It was right next to his ear. Scarn spoke Russian.

"Look, they're all dead."

If Scarn had practiced the move ten thousand times it couldn't have been smoother, despite the adrenaline surging through his bloodstream. He avoided the urge to move quickly and remembered what the instructor had kept saying during his last combat shooting course.

Slow is smooth, smooth is fast.

Scarn turned to his left as he leaned back across the console and into the passenger seat, raised his pistol and fired two rounds, one into the head of each man standing only feet from him. He felt his ear drums go and a loud ringing, but he had hit both of them.

He thumbed the seatbelt release and opened the door of the car. After pulling off such a perfectly timed pair of gunshots he tumbled out of the car ass over teakettle. He hadn't counted on how much firing his weapon in the car would disrupt his inner ear balance.

The world was spinning, but he kept his weapon up and on the two men who lay (clearly dead) on the ground. Scarn stumbled to his feet and brushed some glass and blood away from his eyes.

"Fuck!" He shouted as he looked at the target house just up the street.

Scarn knew there may be intelligence inside, and if he hesitated and there was anyone left, they would be in the process of destroying it while he was trying to get his shit together. There was no time to think or plan.

He holstered his pistol and snatched a carbine and two magazines from one of the dead men. He performed a brass check and began running full tilt toward the house.

This is stupid, he thought to himself. *You will be dead before you even hit the front door.*

Michael Scarn did his best to silence the internal monologue as he ran up the front steps, weapon raised. His next move was a calculated risk, but as it was unlikely that there was anyone in the house that didn't need killing, it seemed like the right move.

Scarn put a controlled pair through the door and then slammed his shoulder into it, breaking it open. He stumbled again as he entered the living room, but quickly got back on target and cleared his corners.

Nothing.

He turned his barrel on the hallway and moved down it, clearing each room as he went.

Nothing. The place seemed empty. He entered the last room and realized who had called the tip in. It was Steven Waller, slumped back in his chair in front of a worktable. He had a clean hole between his eyes.

Scarn moved back into the hallway and through the kitchen, exiting into the backyard. Then he saw it. A barrel full of burned paper.

"Shit!" Scarn whispered.

He lowered his weapon and dug into the ashes.

They were still warm. The two men who had fired on him had been burning anything of intelligence value. Scarn pulled something out that wasn't quite burned and looked at it, trying to read it through the scorch marks.

"Richard Feldman?" Scarn read the name out loud.

It sounded familiar, like a name he had heard before. Then he remembered where he had heard it. Feldman was a hedge fund owner in New York who was under investigation by the FBI. He was also one of the president's largest campaign contributors, which may have been part of the reason a charge would never stick to him.

Scarn moved back into the house and found the kitchen phone. He dialed a number.

"This is Scarn, access number bravo two four five zero. Put me through to Tresham. Yes, I'll hold." There was a long pause before the connection went through and the line picked up.

"What is it, Scarn?" Tresham answered. It was clear by the tone of his voice that he knew this call must be important.

"Sir, we got to the house in North Bath, the one the tip came in on."

"And?"

"It was real. I've got two dead Russians and some actionable intel."

"What is it?"

"You know that Richard Feldman? The hedge fund owner?"

"What about him?"

"His name was in a burn barrel with some other papers they were getting rid of. I don't know why, but they want him."

"Okay," Tresham said. Scarn could hear that the assistant director was getting out of bed. "We're on it. You stay put. State Police are en route."

The line went dead. Scarn looked at the phone for a moment like he didn't know what it was, and then placed the handset back in the receiver. He looked around the house. It was quiet.

Back at the car Michael Scarn found the two Russians still dead in the street. By now some neighbors were awake and milling about, but still keeping their distance from the carnage. Scarn pulled out his badge and flashed it to the gawkers. It was best if they knew that some form of law enforcement was on the scene. In the distance he could hear sirens wailing in the night.

Scarn looked down and realized he was still holding the carbine. He dropped it. It wouldn't do at all for the State Police to arrive at the scene and shoot him.

As the police came down the street, the red and blue flashing lights illuminated everything. Scarn turned and looked at his car. There must have been fifty holes in it. The windows were shattered. In the backseat sat Angeline and Adam.

Most of Angeline's head was gone. Her one remaining eye stared straight forward, no spark left in it. It was whole, but it looked dead. Adam Hunt's eyes were closed, and he easily had a dozen bullet holes in him.

How in the hell had Scarn not been shot? Then he felt it, like a bee sting in his right shoulder. He looked down at his right hand and saw that it was covered in blood. He followed the path up to the bullet hole in his right shoulder.

Then he promptly passed out.

The Home of Mike Tresham
Langley, Virginia
February 8, 1981

"No, sir!" Mike Tresham said insistently into the phone as he paced back and forth in his living room, which had been set up as a hasty command center. "We can't do it that way. If the intel is right and the Soviets are on their way to hit Feldman, we'll only have one shot at this. I've already got Delta on standby down at Fort Bragg, I just need you to give clearance for those men to get airborne." Tresham paused for a moment and listened. "No, sir, we do not have time to wait for the president to suspend habeas corpus."

Tresham began pacing faster, and as he wiped his forehead with the back of his hand, he realized he was sweating. Something bad was about to happen, he could feel it. Should he put in a call to Marin Sutcliffe? See if her Strike Team could step in? That would be a dangerous road to head down. That woman had already established them as a private military once before in Israel, and while Mike had given her permission to operate in New York unencumbered, calling on her was likely to embolden her further and open a Pandora's Box that would be hard to close.

Mike listened as the Director of the CIA hemmed and hawed, not wanting to take a decisive stance.

"Look, I take full responsibility!" Mike finally said. "If anyone asks, I made the call."

There was silence on the line.

"No," the director said. "You're right. We have to move now."

Stratford Arms
New York City, New York
February 8, 1981

Arkady slowed the van to a stop alongside Central Park and looked up at the looming apartment building. Intelligence had told them that this was where he was, in apartment twenty-two. These were like no apartments Arkady had ever seen in Moscow, aside from perhaps those occupied by members of the Politburo. No, these were more like houses masquerading as apartments.

Petr began securing his gear and checking his weapons.

"Everything goes as planned," Arkady said.

Even as he said the words, he could hardly believe that they were finally at this point. Even more unbelievable was the idea that he and Petr may actually walk away from this mission in one piece. Arkady had worked from the very beginning under the assumption that he was already dead. There was no way to accomplish the task they had given him and finish it with a beating heart.

Yet, there they were. There was no sign of resistance. This man would have some kind of security force, but they would be no match for the Alpha Group commander and his top assaulter. No more than the Afghan guards had been years before.

"I am ready," Petr said.

"Good. This man Richard Feldman is about to learn that he cannot just discard his past without consequence."

CHAPTER 13

Washington Heights
Manhattan, New York
February 8, 1981

J ack finished his walk down the track and arrived at the same access point they had found earlier that day. It was still locked. He tested the padlock and found it to be secure. It was exactly as they had left it, no question. Should he actually go inside to be thorough?

No, at that point it would be too easy to miss them. Jack gave the lock another pull, then turned to head back down the track.

Then he saw it. A flashlight coming toward him. It was still far away, probably all the way to the platform but definitely heading toward him. He moved slowly and flattened himself against the wall, drawing his pistol with one hand and triggering his radio with the other.

"Carrie, rise and shine. They're here."

There was a brief pause, and then Carrie's voice came on the line.

"Shit, I was asleep."

"I know, but now it's time to move. I want you to go to the entrance and hold fast in case they try to rabbit."

"Roger that."

Jack raised his pistol and began moving toward the light, careful to stay against the wall so they wouldn't see him. Eventually they would notice him coming toward them and either fire on him or run, but he wanted to close as much of the gap as possible before that happened.

This time he had brought a Maglite with him instead of relying on Carrie's underpowered pen light. Once he clicked it on, whoever was coming toward him would be blinded. If it was possible, he wanted to take at least one of them alive, but he wasn't willing to risk Armageddon in Manhattan to do it.

As they grew closer Jack could feel himself getting warm, and his heart rate increase. These were the highest stakes he had ever played for, no question about it. Back in Delta they had often said that failure was not an option, but this time it was truer than it ever had been.

Jack held position against the wall, weapon raised, with the Maglite positioned beneath the pistol.

Finally, he saw the outline of the first man. They were only twenty meters away. Amazingly they still had not seen him.

Click.

Jack's flashlight illuminated the tunnel and was followed by two shots from his Colt 1911.

Everything happened fast. The first man went down hard, Jack had hit him. The other dropped whatever they had been carrying and began sprinting back the way they had come. Jack advanced and got back on target to take down the runner when he felt his legs sweep out from beneath him and he hit the ground with a hard slam.

Illya jumped back to his feet and turned to see his weapon laying on the ground. He was wearing body armor, which had absorbed the gunshot. The pistol was too far away, so he retrieved the long knife from his boot and went for Jack Bonafide.

Jack rolled to the side, avoiding the knife strike that came down hard exactly where he had just been lying. He rose up to a half-kneeling position and threw a fast hammer strike to the back of Illya's hand, causing it to reflexively open and the knife to clatter to the ground.

Jack finished his ascent from the ground and stood

opposite the Russian. Then he recognized him.

Illya looked at Jack for a moment and then smiled.

"I remember you," Illya said. "You're the brother."

"I remember you too," Jack replied. He looked quickly to the crate and then back to Illya. "Is that it?"

"It doesn't matter," Illya said. "The die is cast, and you will not be the one to stop it. You will not be the hero in this story, Mister Bonafide. You're just going to be another casualty of war."

"Then we might as well get on with it," Jack spat and stepping forward threw a hard kick to Illya's shin, followed by an equally hard elbow to the head.

Illya stumbled a bit but shook it off and counter attacked, coming at Jack like a freight train. He picked the smaller American up and slammed him into the ground. Jack quickly found himself mounted and then realized they had landed next to Illya's knife.

The Russian rolled to his right, reached for the blade and snatched it up off the ground.

Carrie had heard the gunshots as she jogged down the steps to the platform. Her heart was pounding, and she knew that she was over gripping the Beretta 1951 pistol in her hand. She relaxed her grip. Not too much, but just enough.

She rounded the corner into the long tunnel and felt something slam into her. It felt like she'd just taken a hit from an NFL linebacker, and right away she knew she had also hit her head on the cement when she went down.

Carrie sprang back to her feet like she was made of rubber and realized her weapon was still in her hand. She hadn't dropped it. She raised it but the man who had hit her was already heading away and rounding the corner.

"Shit!"

There was no other option, so she began sprinting up the stairs after him.

Illya lunged forward and Jack sidestepped what was (in his opinion) a very clumsy attack. Then he realized why. If this man was who Jack thought he was, he'd probably never gone up against another skilled commando. He was a bully who was used to toying with amateurs. He was counting on an easy win, but he would not get it, not this time.

This realization caused Jack to relax his posture a bit and get lighter on his feet. Illya came at him again, and Jack sidestepped this attack as well, grabbed his wrist and twisted it back hard enough to drop the man to his knees. This caused Illya to release his knife for the second time. Jack delivered a hard kick to Illya's ribs that collapsed him to the ground.

"We can do this as long as you want," Jack said as

he scooped up the dropped knife and threw it away. He then walked to where his pistol lay and picked it up. "But I think we both know how this is ending."

"You're half right," Illya hissed as he pulled something from his pocket.

It was a detonator.

"You're bluffing," Jack said firmly. "There's no way you'd be detonating a bomb that size with that Radio Shack piece of shit."

"No, you're right," Illya said as he shook his head. "I could never set off the Black Tsar with a detonator like this." He looked at Jack coldly. "But I can set off the C4 attached to it."

There was no hesitation, no room for thought. Jack raised his pistol and fired two quick rounds. Illya's head snapped back, throwing up pink mist in the shallow glow of Jack's dropped Maglite. The Russian crumpled to the ground in an awkward position, his open hand still on the detonator.

Jack let out a breath.

Carrie had not run this fast and this hard since high school track. Even back then, when she was arguably in her athletic prime, she had never been that fast and now she was trying to keep up with a man who was a highly trained Soviet assassin. This was a race she would lose, and she knew it.

She couldn't stop to take a shot at him because he was just barely out of range, and the seconds it would cost her to stop and take aim would be enough for him to be well out of firing range of the nine-millimeter pistol she was carrying

Shit, I'm going to lose him, she thought to herself.

"Hey buddy, slow down!"

Carrie watched in horror as a police officer walked around the corner, right into the path of the fleeing man. Without even breaking his stride, the Russian fired twice into the foot patrolman and the officer hit the ground.

He turned the corner and she followed, both of them emerging into some kind of public square. He grabbed a woman and pulled her close to him, putting his pistol to her head. He stopped and looked at Carrie grimly.

He said nothing.

Carrie raised her weapon.

"It's over!" Carrie shouted. "Killing her won't help anything."

He smiled, and there was a look on his face as if he were entertaining a dim-witted child. The woman wasn't struggling. She was frozen with fear.

Carrie kept her weapon steady, eyes fixed on the link between her front sight and her target. Then she realized something: this man had come all this way to kill Americans.

He would kill the girl.

Carrie let out a breath and pulled her trigger.

Jack dropped the heavy case he had been dragging and took a step back. The Russian was dead, and the bomb was cleared from the train tracks.

The second man had taken off, but Carrie should have been at the entrance ready to sweep him up. Jack triggered his radio.

"Carrie, what's your status?"

Nothing.

Jack emerged into the main tunnel. It was only as he leapt back onto the platform that he realized it was a minor miracle a train hadn't come through while he and the Soviet were fighting on the tracks. He had completely lost sight of that at the moment and now realized it could have easily cost him his life.

He triggered the radio again.

"Carrie, report!"

Nothing.

Jack saw a payphone on the platform and weighed his options. He had no idea what Carrie was up against with the runner, but he also knew that seconds counted. He was assuming it was the Black Tsar in that crate, but he couldn't be certain, and popping it open to check inside seemed like a bad idea.

He thought back to how much of a climb it was to reach the street, and if she would even be there.

"Shit!" Jack hissed and walked to the payphone.

The Home of Mike Tresham
Langley, Virginia
February 8, 1981

Mike Tresham looked at his hands, held them out in front of him and observed the slight trembling. It wasn't nerves. No, it was something far more sinister that was causing this. It was the coffee. He had been going through it like water ever since this thing had begun.

Just ten minutes earlier they had received a call back from Fort Bragg that the Blackhawks that should have been taking Delta Force's Alpha Squadron to New York had experienced a malfunction, followed by an additional malfunction in the backup. They were ferrying a new helo in from across the base, but it had delayed the launch time by thirty minutes.

Mike knew that those were thirty minutes they may not have.

There were a half dozen intelligence analysts and two field agents camped out in Mike's home, with more equipment and personnel on the way. It wasn't enough, and Mike knew it. He was not being given the resources he needed because unbelievably the director had still not completely bought into the theory of the Black Tsar and the Soviet agents.

The bombing of KGB headquarters and the attack on Andropov (head of the KGB) hadn't improved things. The director was having a hard time believing that a Soviet spy apparatus that had just lost its headquarters and top three commanders was behind a grand conspiracy to detonate a hydrogen bomb in the United States.

The phone rang again, and an analyst snatched it up.

"Yes," the analyst said. "What's your access number?" The analyst paused. "You're what?"

"What is it?" Mike asked.

The analyst looked up at him.

"It's someone named Jack Bonafide. He claims that he works for you?"

"Well, I'll be a son of a bitch," Mike said, unable to hold back a smile. "Give him to me." Mike took the phone. "What's happening, Jack?"

"The Tsar is here," Jack said, still recovering his breath. "At the Washington Heights station in New York, in the tunnel."

"Are you sure it's the weapon?"

"I can't say I'm one hundred percent, sir, but the

Russian I just killed in the tunnel seemed pretty damn convinced."

Mike started snapping his fingers and gesturing to one of the action boards that had been set up to collect leads. Specifically, it was the one on Richard Feldman.

"It's not over, Jack. They had two jobs, setting off the Black Tsar was just one of them."

"What's the second?" Jack asked.

"We think they're going to hit a finance guy, a close friend of the President."

"Why in the hell would they do that?"

"We don't have that information yet, but the attacks were probably coordinated, which means it's about to go down. I need you to get over there and stop it."

"Me?" Jack asked in disbelief.

"Yes, you! Delta should have launched already but they're having transpo problems."

"Sir, I don't know where Carrie is!"

"I don't give a fuck where Carrie is!" Mike said. "Are you doing this or not?"

"Fine, I'm on it. Just give me the address," Jack replied. "But I need you to link up with NYPD and find Carrie."

Stratford Arms
New York City, New York
February 8, 1981

Arkady knocked quietly on the door then stood in silence as he waited. Both he and Petr wore loose fitting electrician's overalls and carried work bags with them. They secreted their suppressed pistols beneath the overalls, and within the work bags were the broken-down carbines.

Arkady looked at his watch. It was late. They were exactly on schedule, but it was possible that the residents of this apartment would not answer the door at this time of night. This would not be the end of the world as there was always a Plan B, but it would be less than ideal to do things that way.

Arkady pulled a reverse door scope from his pocket and held it up to the peephole in the door. This device allowed him to look inside of the apartment. There was nothing, only darkness.

Finally, he heard footsteps from inside, and a light switched on. A young man who looked to be in his mid-thirties was walking to the door, rubbing the sleep from his eyes. Arkady reached inside of his overalls and retrieved his silenced nine-millimeter. He removed his reverse scope from the door so that the man inside could see them. If he could not see outside, it may raise an alarm.

"Can I help you?" He asked.

"Yes, sir. So sorry to bother you this late, but there's

been a small electrical fire in the basement. We're checking outlets for any sign of damage," Petr said in perfectly accented English.

"A fire?" The man asked.

"Yes, sir. If it overloaded the circuits, it may cause other fires. It will only take a minute."

There was a pause.

"Okay," he said, and Arkady could hear the click of the door being unlocked.

The door opened, and Arkady raised his pistol and shot the man dead.

Petr closed the door and locked it as Arkady carried the work bags to the east-facing wall of the main room and began unloading them. Petr retrieved a stethoscope from one bag and put it to the wall. He listened while Arkady began running det cord along the same wall in a giant square.

"Anything?" Arkady asked after Petr had been listening for a minute.

Petr looked to Arkady and shook his head.

"No, they must be asleep aside from the guard on duty." Petr seemed to think for a moment. "What do we do after this?"

"What do you mean?" Arkady asked as he stood up and began assembling his carbine.

"I never thought we would survive this mission,"

Petr explained. "And it looks as if the KGB is crippled. The man who sent us on this mission is now dead. What will we do? Where will we go?"

"That, my friend is a worry for another day. For now, we must stay on task."

Petr nodded his understanding and turned back to the wall.

The Apartment of Richard Feldman
Stratford Arms
New York City, New York
February 8, 1981

Richard Feldman opened his eyes and stared at the ceiling. He couldn't sleep. The bombing of KGB headquarters had shaken him. What in the hell did it all mean? Did it somehow involve him?

His friends in high places had assured him that the American government had nothing to do with the attack. So far, it seemed like an act of homegrown terror. That was hard to swallow considering the Soviet Union's track record with terrorists, but that didn't mean it was impossible.

Richard threw off his covers and sat up in bed, sliding his feet into the slippers that sat on the floor.

Perhaps a cup of tea would do the trick. He clicked on the light beside the bed and immediately heard a stirring from the kitchen.

He smiled. They were good.

A head popped in through his door.

"Sorry for the disturbance, sir," Walters said. "Is everything okay?"

"Everything's fine," Richard replied. "Just can't sleep. Thought I'd make some tea."

"I can handle that for you, sir," Walters said.

"No, no thank you," Richard said as he stood up and crossed the room. "I can do it myself."

Walters was a good man; former secret service like Richard's entire guard force. There were four on duty that night, one in the lobby and three in the apartment. Before it had only been Walters on the detail with another man available for traveling, but ever since someone celebrated the fourth of July in KGB headquarters, Richard felt that he needed to turn up the volume on his own protective detail.

If anyone knew the truth about his past, they would probably want to quadruple it. Either that or have him executed.

Richard walked across the living room to the kitchen and began rifling through the cabinets for his favorite tea.

. . .

Richard Feldman opened his eyes and brushed some debris away from his face. He sat up. He did not know how long he had been out, but there was a hole in his living room wall, and he could see Walters on his knees with his hands behind his head. A quick survey of the carnage showed that the other two guards were dead.

"Richard Feldman?" Arkady asked as he advanced on the man sitting on the floor of the kitchen.

"What in the hell is this?" Richard shouted, rising to his feet. "Who are you?"

"My name is Arkady Radovich," Arkady said. "But let's not get off on the wrong foot. Perhaps, instead of calling you Richard Feldman, I should call you Tolya Rodin?"

The old Ford fishtailed as Jack ran yet another red light on his way to the Stratford Arms. This was a bad plan, and he knew it. Not only that, it wasn't even really a plan at all. The only thing he knew was that the Russians may try to hit a financier named Richard Feldman.

The likelihood was that this scenario would only break down one of two ways. Either he would show up and find absolutely nothing, or he would go toe to toe with an elite team of Soviet assassins. To be honest, he wasn't sure which option he preferred.

He had been less than impressed with the man he

fought in the tunnel. If the rest of them were like that, this would be an easy day at the office.

He couldn't stop thinking about Carrie, and he couldn't shake the feeling that he had abandoned her. Yes, he believed that Mike Tresham would connect with NYPD and track her down, but the simple fact was that he had left her behind. Right or wrong, that was the truth of it.

Jack looked up at the street signs and saw that he was at the target site. He pulled the truck to a stop behind an Econoline van along the park entrance and killed the engine. There was the faintest ringing in his ears. Was it coming back? Was the breathing theory wrong? Then he realized what was happening. It wasn't that the breathing theory was wrong; he was just pushing himself harder than he had in a long time.

It wasn't over yet.

"I don't know what you're talking about," Richard Feldman said.

"You know who we are, Tolya, don't you?" Arkady asked.

"I've never seen you before in my life."

Arkady turned and put the barrel of his pistol to Walters' head.

"Are you sure?" Arkady asked.

Richard let out a sigh.

"What do you want me to say?"

"I want you to stop lying, Tolya. Wouldn't it feel good to tell the truth? Just this once?"

"They sent you, didn't they?" Richard asked.

"In Russian, please," Arkady said with a smile, speaking the mother tongue.

"Directorate S?" Richard Feldman spoke in Russian.

"After a fashion," Arkady said. "You must have known this couldn't last forever."

"I had my hopes," Richard replied. "After all, it has been so long."

"But you must know we never forget. And as for forgiveness, well... you know how that one goes too."

"So what do you think will happen?" Richard asked. "I assume you are here to kill me?"

Arkady nodded.

"To what purpose?" Richard pressed on. "Most of the KGB command structure is dead. Andropov still has not regained consciousness. So, the people who sent you here are gone. You know better than anyone how the Politburo rewards loyalty. Lined up against a wall in the square with a blindfold on and a cigarette in your mouth?"

"You're a clever one, Tolya," Arkady said. "But you will not fool me."

"They have the names of every Directorate S agent in the country," Richard blurted.

This got Arkady's attention.

"What do you mean by that?" Arkady asked. "Who does?"

"The Americans. Just today they struck a deal that will soon net them a set of logbooks with this information in it."

Arkady studied him for a moment.

"You lie."

"It's not a lie," Richard said. "It's the truth. The KGB as you know it is about to be completely destroyed. So, yes, you can kill me. If you really feel that you need to. Or you can work for me."

Jack slipped in the front door as quietly as possible. He thought it would be best not to have to explain to a doorman what he was doing in the building without permission at two in the morning. As it turned out, this would not be a problem.

Inside the lobby he found the doorman and another man who must have been a security guard lying on the floor behind the front desk. Both were dead, executed at point blank range cleanly and quietly. Jack thought about using the phone to call this in to Tresham, but he knew there may not be time.

The directory confirmed Jack's main concern, which was that the apartment was on the twenty-second floor. Normally he would never take an elevator on a job like this, but the prospect of running up twenty floors with his concussion symptoms already starting to come back was a non-starter.

Arkady could not deny the truth of what Richard Feldman was saying. He had known it the moment he saw the front of the Lubyanka Building (KGB head-quarters) laid open like a smashed pumpkin. You didn't have to be a member of the Politburo to know which way the wind was blowing.

"You are friends with the American president?" Arkady asked.

"I am," Richard replied.

"So, you are a man who can get things done."

"What are you doing?" Petr asked quickly.

Arkady held up a hand to silence his subordinate.

"I am such a man," Richard replied.

"Do you know what we have done here?" Arkady asked.

"If you work for me," Richard said. "It will not matter. I can have the attorney general of the United States on the phone in three minutes, and an unconditional pardon in five."

"Sir!" Walters shouted. "You can't do this!"

Arkady raised his pistol and fired a round into the security guard's head, and the man collapsed to the floor.

"And that?" Arkady asked. "You can pardon that?"

"I can pardon anything." Richard said. "You know I'm telling the truth. Killing me nets you nothing. Accepting my offer wins you the world."

"You are not seriously considering this?" Petr nearly shouted.

Arkady turned and fired two rounds into Petr's chest, dropping the man where he stood. He turned back to Richard Feldman, his weapon still raised.

"Pick up the phone."

Jack sat in a low crouch on top of the elevator as it made its slow crawl up to the twenty-second floor. While he knew he couldn't run up the stairs, he had no intention of standing in the elevator and presenting himself as the proverbial fish in the barrel.

He watched the sweat that was dripping off of his brow splash against the metal beneath him. He could feel that he was hitting a fatigue point, but he knew he just had to hold on a little while longer. The ringing in his ears was getting louder, and his heart rate was out of control, but he knew he had at least five more minutes left in him.

The floor markings were rolling by and finally he saw that the elevator car had hit twenty, and he cracked the hatch back open, ready to drop into the car when he heard the ding of the door opening.

Ding.

Jack opened the hatch fully, waited a few beats and then dropped into the elevator car with his Colt at the ready, but there was nothing, no one. Not only that, it was quiet. It was way too quiet for a team of Russian assassins to be hitting an American financier.

He moved out of the elevator and into the hallway. Apartment twenty was in plain view and turning to the left Jack saw number twenty-two. It should be the target. What in the hell was he supposed to do now? Kick in the door at two in the morning and hope the resident didn't have a heart attack? Worse yet, what if the man had a guard force and Jack ended up in a gunfight with a friendly unit?

Jack walked the twenty feet to the doorway of apartment twenty-two. He raised his weapon and slowly reached out and knocked on the door. A moment later it swung open, and a very surprised looking Richard Feldman came face to face with Jack Bonafide.

"Can I help you?" Richard asked.

It was wrong. He was wrong. He was too calm. Jack looked past the man and saw the Russian commander from the house in Falls Church standing in the room behind him. It was the man who had told Jack that his brother was dead and who had tried to kill him.

Jack was past Richard and knocking Arkady to the ground before Richard could even process what was happening. Jack pushed Arkady's head against the floor and placed the muzzle of his pistol to the Russian's head.

"You're fucking done."

"Stop!" Richard shouted. "That man is my employee!"

Jack froze, but kept his weapon pressed into Arkady's face, deforming the flesh of his cheek. He realized that the big man wasn't resisting in the slightest. Something was wrong.

Jack turned to Richard Feldman.

"This man is an operative of the Soviet government!"

"Prove it!" Richard responded.

Jack looked back to Arkady, who remained motionless on the floor. Why wasn't he trying to fight back? Plus, Richard was right. Jack had no proof that this man was a Soviet operative. Something had happened here. The room was destroyed. There was a giant hole in the wall and there were bodies everywhere.

Jack carefully stood up, keeping his weapon on Arkady.

"I have been pursuing this man for months, all the way from Virginia. Sir, I assure you he is who I am saying he is."

"And I am telling you that this man just saved my life!" Richard exclaimed and then pointed to Petr's body on the floor. "That man was trying to kill me-killed my entire guard force and Arkady here arrived at the last moment and killed him."

Jack looked to Arkady and then back to Richard.

"What in the hell is happening here?" Jack asked.

"Exactly what I said," Richard replied coldly. "And according to the United States Attorney General this man is absolved of any past crimes and he is now a citizen of the United States."

"I don't think so," Jack said. He brought his weapon back up, sighted in on Arkady and pulled the hammer back.

"Are you really about to murder my private security chief?" Richard asked. "In my home? Unprovoked?"

Jack couldn't believe this was happening. This was the man who had been responsible for his brother's death, who had tried to unleash a hydrogen bomb on New York City and now this Richard Feldman had apparently bought him a pass?

Richard walked to the phone and picked it up, which Jack responded to by turning his gun on the man.

"I'm just calling someone who can straighten this all out," Richard said, holding the phone.

Jack nodded.

CHAPTER 14

The Home of Mike Tresham
Langley, Virginia
February 8, 1981

"What in the hell are you talking about 'stand down'?" Mike Tresham nearly shouted into the phone. "I just had NYPD pull a fucking hydrogen bomb out of the Washington Heights subway tunnels and we've linked this guy to it!"

"Mister Tresham, I understand this is an emotionally charged subject," Attorney General David Kelvin said calmly. "But I need you to get yourself under control. Am I understood?"

Mike paused for a moment and then let out a breath.

"Sir, we believe this man is involved not only in smuggling this weapon into New York but also in the death of Jack Bonafide's brother, and based on our most recent reports, his wife as well."

"Mister Tresham, I'm looking at your agency reports right now and I'm not seeing any Jack Bonafide listed on your personnel manifest. Who exactly is this?"

"He's a former Delta operative, sir. We brought him into the NOC program."

"And he's current?" Kelvin asked.

"It's... complicated, sir."

"No, Assistant Director Tresham, it's not. The truth is never complicated. Are we dealing with some kind of rogue agent here?"

"If it weren't for Jack Bonafide, New York would most likely be a graveyard right now!"

"Be that as it may," Kelvin pressed on. "If he was operating without sanction and you knew it, we're about to have a whole other problem. Or you can start being more cooperative."

"What are you saying?"

"Look, Mister Tresham. We both know that none of this is above board, and that applies to both of us. The bottom line is that this Arkady Radovich as of fifteen minutes ago is now a United States citizen with full immunity and in the legal employ of Richard Feldman."

"This is fucking nuts. That guy is a Soviet operative!"

"Under the command of who, exactly? Makar Galkin and Konstantin Sokolov are both dead, Andropov may as well be, and the KGB is in a full-on tailspin. If this man was working directly for any of them and will talk, I don't give a good goddamn who he used to work for." Kelvin paused for a moment. "And need I remind you that Richard Feldman has the ear of the President of the United States?"

Mike Tresham gripped the phone so hard that he momentarily thought he might break it.

"No, sir."

"This is a win, Mister Tresham. Even if you can't see it that way right now. We potentially have an asset with very fresh intelligence on what the Soviets are doing, and you won't be seeing the inside of a jail cell by sunrise."

The Apartment of Richard Feldman
Stratford Arms
New York City, New York
February 8, 1981

Jack Bonafide couldn't remember ten minutes ever lasting this long. Richard Feldman had been waiting on hold after placing a call to the Attorney General of the United States. Arkady was sitting in a chair, but Jack had the uneasy feeling that the Russian knew he was about to win.

"Yes, sir," Richard Feldman said as someone came back on the line. "Yes, he's here."

Richard turned and held out the phone to Jack.

"It's for you."

Jack walked to where Richard Feldman stood and took the handset, all the while monitoring Arkady Radovich.

"This is Bonafide."

"Jack, this is Mike Tresham."

"Mister Tresham, are you updated on the situation?"

"Yes, Jack. We just hauled that fucking hydrogen bomb out of the Washington Heights tunnel. You did good, really good."

"Thank you, sir."

"But I need you to do one more thing for me," Mike said. "And you will not want to hear it."

"What is it?"

"I need you to leave that apartment and head to Langley."

"With the Russian?"

"No, Jack. Alone."

"I don't understand," Jack said, turning away from the other two men in the room.

"This is an evolving situation, Jack, and we don't fully understand what happened or what will happen. I assume you heard the news about KGB headquarters getting hit earlier today?"

"Yes, sir."

"We need to know what in the hell happened over there, and Mister Feldman has reason to believe that this man, this Arkady Radovich, may know something."

"He was responsible for Mac's death."

"I know," Mike said, holding back the additional detail of Angeline's murder just hours earlier. "And I understand what I'm asking of you."

"I can't just walk away from this," Jack said.

"Shit, Jack. Look, as of twenty minutes ago, Arkady Radovich is an American citizen and has been granted full immunity for past crimes by the President of the United States via the Attorney General."

"Bullshit."

"It's true. If you kill that man you will execute an American citizen who has no criminal record, in front of a witness who is close personal friends with the President. You'll go down for murder one." Mike paused for a moment. "Look, this fucking sucks. I get it, but it's the way it is. We don't get the world we want, Jack."

Jack turned and glared at Arkady, his pistol still

raised. His hand tightened on the grip of the Colt. He could feel his heart beating behind his eyes.

Then, he released the hammer and holstered the weapon.

"Fine. I'm on my way to Langley." Jack said, the defeat in his voice impossible to hide. "But I need to find Carrie first. I lost her in Washington Heights."

"No, just come straight to Langley," Mike countered. "I already know where she is."

"You do?"

"I'll explain it to you when I see you."

The line went dead. Jack looked at the handset for a moment and then placed it back in the cradle.

This wasn't how it was supposed to go. Mac was dead, Carrie was who in the hell knew where and this Arkady Radovich character just gets to walk? It wasn't right.

Jack began walking to the door.

"Jack," Arkady called after him. Jack turned. "What happened before, it was never personal."

Jack stopped. He wanted to say something. He wanted to swear an oath against the Russian, say something, anything that would get across his deep intention to kill this man. Instead, he just walked away. He walked away without a word, because he knew that Arkady Radovich, formerly of Alpha Group, was telling the truth.

CIA Headquarters
Langley, Virginia
February 8, 1981

Jack could barely keep his eyes open, and because of this he readily accepted the cup of coffee offered to him by the liaison at the door. Mike Tresham had guessed (correctly) that Jack had not slept in nearly forty-eight hours.

Jack Bonafide was a man of great endurance and, yes, this extended to staying awake, but every man has his limits.

They issued Jack a badge that said 'Visitor' with nothing to show that he worked for the agency in any capacity. This was probably because he did not. This also begged the question of what was about to happen to him. Was he a hero, or a fugitive?

Jack followed the liaison down the winding corridors until he stopped at a set of double doors with a secretary positioned outside of them. Jack noticed that she made a point of finishing her typing before she looked up at the two of them, and without a word buzzed them in.

Jack entered the room then stopped when he realized where he was. Behind the large oak desk sat Bill Casey, the director of central intelligence. Beside him stood Mike Tresham. Jack didn't know much about Bill Casey other than he had served in the OSS during World War Two and been brought on board right before Tresham.

"So, this is the guy?" Bill asked, turning to Mike Tresham.

"Yes, sir."

Casey turned back to Jack.

"Well, I'm not sure if I should pin a medal on you or throw you in a cell."

Jack wasn't sure how to respond to that, so he didn't.

"I never liked Mike's whole 'ghost operative' idea," Casey went on. "You're living proof that I was right."

"There's a hydrogen bomb at Fort Meade right now that says otherwise," Tresham countered.

Casey shot the man a dirty look and then returned to his subject.

"So you're now on full duty," Casey said. "You're not a fucking ghost operative, whatever the hell that was, and you're not a NOC. You're a goddamn field agent, the kind we can keep track of. What do you think about that?"

"If it keeps me out of a jail cell, I think it sounds pretty good," Jack replied.

"Hmph," Casey grunted. "Not quite the recitation of the Star-Spangled Banner I was hoping for, but I guess I'll take what I can get. Have they briefed you on the rest of the operation?"

"Rest of the operation?" Jack asked.

"We haven't," Tresham offered. "I'll do it."

"I'll give you the room," Casey said, standing up. He walked to Jack and offered his hand. Jack took it. "You know I have to give you some shit for the way you did things, but you're a goddamn hero, Bonafide. But now you're a hero who needs to play by the rules."

"Yes, sir," Jack said with a nod.

Casey exited the room and Jack turned back to Tresham.

"The rest of the operation?" Jack asked and then realized what it must mean. "He's talking about Carrie?"

"Partially," Mike said and then continued. "That's a good place to start. She's being held at the thirty-third precinct in Washington Heights."

"Being held?" Jack asked. "What in the hell are you talking about?"

"She shot a woman, Jack."

"Who?"

"It was an impossible situation. The Russian that ran after you surprised them in the tunnel and gave Carrie quite a chase, then he took a woman hostage. Carrie made a judgment call and went for a headshot. She missed. She still shot him dead, but at a terrible cost."

"Jesus!" Jack gasped. "Are we picking her up?"

Tresham stared at Jack for a moment and then shook his head.

"What in the hell are you talking about?" Jack nearly shouted. "We can't just abandon her!"

"She's a rogue agent, Jack! She wasn't on duty and to the New York district attorney she just looks like a woman with a gun who was chasing a man and then shot him and a woman."

At least she got him, Jack thought to himself. That was something.

"She was trying to stop the fucking bomb, just like I was!"

"And if you two had switched places, you would be in a jail cell right now instead of her."

"If you don't get her out, I walk."

"Look, Jack, you'll have to have your own 'come to Jesus' moment over this, because it's just not happening. I'll do what I can to cushion the blow, but she's going down for murder one." Tresham paused. "If you think you need to walk away over that, I won't stop you."

"Shit," Jack spat and looked at the floor. He took a long and very uncomfortable pause. "I ain't walking, but I'm also not just going to let it go."

"Whatever you feel you can do within the boundaries of the law, that's just fine," Tresham said. "But pay close attention to that 'boundaries of the law' part."

The door opened a crack, and the secretary stuck her head in.

"He's here," she whispered. "Should I let him in?"

"Yes," Tresham replied with a nod.

Jack turned to see Agent Scarn walk in. Something about the man looked different. He looked almost... shaken.

Tresham exited without another word and closed the door. Jack knew something was wrong. He could feel it.

"Hi, Jack," Scarn said.

"What's this about?" Jack asked curtly.

"We hit a house in upstate New York," Scarn said. "That was where the Russians were operating out of. Waller called the tip in."

"Waller?" Jack asked in surprise. "I thought he was working with them?"

Scarn shrugged.

"Odds are he was just going with the flow, trying not to get his head blown off. Then maybe as he learned more about what they were planning he had a change of heart."

"That sounds right," Jack confirmed. "He didn't strike me as a true believer. I was surprised as hell when he turned on us."

"There's more," Scarn said slowly. "We were in Texas, me and Agent Hunt. We visited your father."

Jack laughed.

"How'd that go over?"

"About as you'd expect," Scarn replied with a weak smile. "Your father is quite a character. He didn't give us anything worth using. So we followed up the only other lead we had."

"Which was?"

"Angeline," Scarn said.

"I'm betting she was less help than the old man."

"Quite the opposite, actually. She had this theory that she knew how you thought, that she could get in your head and help us."

"Angeline wanted to help you?" Jack asked in disbelief. "Bullshit."

"Well, she didn't exactly wrap herself in the American flag. She wanted her divorce papers signed."

Jack shook his head and grimaced. He knew he needed to just suck it up and get it over with.

"Fine, I'll sign her damn papers."

"She was with us when we went to the house."

Jack cocked his head to the side.

"Why was she with you on a hit?"

"We thought it was bullshit. We- we didn't think it was real. There was no reason to think it was real."

Jack felt his hands go cold.

"Where is she?" Jack asked.

"I'm sorry as hell, Jack. You have to believe me. If I could trade places with her, I would."

"Where is she?" Jack repeated, raising his voice.

"They hit our car before we even got to the house. If it means anything, she never saw it coming."

Jack felt the coldness spread from his hands to the rest of his body. He knew that something about his demeanor had changed based on the way Scarn was looking at him.

"Do you need to sit down?" Scarn asked.

Jack glared at the man.

"No, I don't need to fucking sit down!" Jack replied.

"I don't know what to say."

"Are they dead?" Jack asked pointedly.

"Who?"

Scarn was confused. Was Jack talking about Angeline and Hunt?

"The sons of bitches who killed her," Jack clarified.

Scarn nodded in the affirmative.

"Did you do it?" Jack asked.

"Kill them?" Scarn asked.

"Did you kill the men who killed my wife, Agent Scarn?"

"I did," Scarn replied.

"Then I'm not raw about it," Jack said. "And I figure we're about as even Steven as two men can get."

There was something more, something behind Jack's eyes that Scarn couldn't decode. The man was putting up a brave front, that much was obvious, but would he break down? Would he allow himself that bit of vulnerability? He sure as hell wouldn't do it in front of Scarn, but perhaps when he was alone?

Scarn also couldn't help but notice that Jack had referred to Angeline as his "wife". It was becoming clear that he may never have let her go. What had been going on there? Why had she felt the need to chase him all the way to New York to get him to sign the divorce papers? Scarn had noticed that the date on them was nineteen-eighty.

Thirty-Third Precinct
Washington Heights
New York City, New York
February 8, 1981

Anatoly Vitka took off his hat and smoothed his thinning blonde hair back as he waited for the desk sergeant to finish looking over his credentials and run his request up the chain. Anatoly knew that the cover identifying him as Robert McMasters, administrative officer for the Department of Defense, had been burned after what happened at Fort Meade. He also knew that it was unlikely a New York police precinct would have enough pull (or desire) to check in with the DOD to find that out.

His credentials looked good, and he had his business cards and other identification that matched up with it. It would be enough to get him into the holding cells. Once he was in there, it would not be nearly as challenging to get out, even if he had to leave a few bodies in his wake.

He was being foolish. He knew this, but despite that knowledge he would still move forward. Why was this? There was nothing special about her. He had been with women far more attractive than Carrie Davidson and her personality certainly left something to be desired.

All the same, there was something there, something hard to define. Even if Anatoly didn't know what this thing was, it was enough to cause him to not want to see her go to prison for the rest of her life.

"DOD, eh?" The desk sergeant asked and eyed Anatoly warily. "What do you want with the skirt? She's a real hard case you know. Never seen anything like it."

"We have reason to believe the man she was chasing may have been a foreign agent."

"What? Like a spy?" The desk sergeant asked.

"Something like that. We need to know why she was chasing him."

"Well, upstairs said it's the desk sergeant's discretion, and seeing as he is me, I don't see any harm in it," the desk sergeant said as he handed Anatoly back his fake DOD credentials. "Officer Roberts here will escort you to her cell."

Anatoly thought the holding cells in precinct thirty-three would have done any Moscovite worth his salt proud. They were quite a dreary affair, and the lights could not seem to decide if they wanted to stay on or off. It was quickly getting to the point where the intermittent flashing from overhead was hurting his eyes.

"That's her," Officer Roberts said, gesturing to the end of the cages where Carrie Davidson sat alone on a bench. "Hey, do you remember how to get out of here?"

Anatoly raised an eyebrow. He wasn't sure what the point of the question was.

"I imagine I do."

"Good," Officer Roberts smiled. "It's just that I haven't had a solid meal in eight hours, and if it's all the same to you, I'll just leave you here."

"No problem."

"Just check in with the desk sergeant on your way out," Officer Roberts said as he turned and began heading back to the exit.

Anatoly looked back to the cell. At least that would be one less person he would have to go through to get back out. He noticed another exit at the end of the hall, just past Carrie's cage, and wondered if he might be fortunate enough to have it lead him back outside the building with her in tow.

He walked to the end of the hallway. Carrie looked up and saw him, then quickly looked around to see if anyone else was watching. She rose to her feet.

"What in the hell are you doing here?" Carrie whispered.

"I know what happened. I'm here to get you out."

"Get me out?" Carrie asked.

"To Brooklyn," Anatoly said with a smile, referencing the safe house he had mentioned earlier.

"How did you even get in here?"

"How did I get into Fort Meade?" Anatoly replied with a shrug. "It's what I do. It's the getting out that is the hard part.

"I'm locked in a cage."

"I have a lock pick. It won't be hard. I've done something like this before, but that was in Afghanistan. Much hotter and more beheadings there. This should be easy by comparison."

"I can't."

"What are you talking about?" Anatoly asked, his confusion obvious. Why would she not jump at the chance to be free?

"I shot that woman. This is where I belong."

"Ridiculous," Anatoly scoffed. "You were trying to save her."

"I was arrogant," Carrie said. "I was arrogant, and I was stupid, and she paid for it with her life."

"This is war," Anatoly said pointedly. "And in war people die."

"Not here," Carrie said. "Not here they don't. That's the point. That's why the CIA isn't supposed to operate on American soil. And I wasn't even working for the CIA. I was a rogue agent. A rogue agent who shot an innocent woman."

Anatoly stared at her for a moment.

"I'm not going anywhere," he said. "I'm... marooned, as you say. No one knows I'm here. So, I'm thinking I'll stick around for a while. Take a holiday."

"KGB agents get to take holidays?" Carrie asked with a weak smile.

"Everyone needs a holiday, Carrie Davidson. Even KGB agents." Anatoly paused. "There's nothing I can do to change your mind?"

Carrie shook her head.

"I will get what I deserve. Mercy isn't it."

Anatoly nodded his understanding, even if he didn't truly understand.

"Like I said, I'll be around. In case you change your mind."

CIA Headquarters
Langley, Virginia

February 8, 1981

The elevator was eerily silent as Jack Bonafide, Michael Scarn and Mike Tresham descended into the subbasement that housed the forensic autopsy department. Langley didn't have a morgue in the traditional sense, so the forensic autopsy department was used to house bodies if the need ever arose.

Tresham had needed to pull some serious strings to get the bodies removed from the crime scene so quickly and then ferried to Langley in record time. The reason was simple: he wanted to get Jack off the hook as soon as possible. The sooner he made the I.D. and then made peace with what had happened, the better. It looked like something serious was about to come down the pipe, and he needed young Jack Bonafide in top form.

The elevator ground to a halt, and the doors rolled open to reveal the forensic autopsy department. Right away, Jack noticed that they were working on cadavers, dissecting them to find clues about what had happened to them.

Jack turned to Tresham.

"They're not—"

"No," Tresham cut him off. "This is just where she's resting."

Scarn thought that was a strange way to put it, for Tresham to say that Angeline was "resting". Then he thought better of this reaction. He was becoming aware that he had a cold personality, and in many scenarios it was unbecoming.

Jack followed the two men across the large room and into a second room, where a body lay on a table with a sheet covering it. It was her. He knew it right away. Scarn shut the door with a soft click.

"You know, Jack," Tresham said. "This can wait if you need it to."

"No," Jack said as he shook his head. "This has to happen now. I need to know if it's real."

Tresham understood. He reached out and pulled the sheet back. They had done something with some sheets of gauze to cover the part of her head where the Russians had shot her, but that same lone eye stared out into the abyss.

"It's her," Jack said. "That's Angeline."

Tresham pulled the sheet back over her body.

The three stood in the hallway outside the main room. They had been delivered cups of coffee and were sharing a silent moment as they decompressed from what they had just seen and done.

Jack broke the tension.

"What the hell happened in Moscow?" Jack asked. "Was that us?"

"No," Tresham said with a hint of a smile. "That wasn't us."

"So what happened?" Scarn asked.

"Jericho Black happened," Tresham replied.

"Jericho Black?" Scarn asked, his confusion obvious.

"This kid we met in Israel," Jack offered. "Name of Will Hessler. He was working for the Mossad."

"What kind of Jewish name is 'Hessler'?" Scarn asked.

"He's not Jewish," Tresham replied. "He's American. He was involved in a bunch of shit in San Francisco a few years ago, then suddenly became an Israeli citizen and left the country. Then he resurfaces as this lunatic Mossad operative with a photographic memory."

"I'd love to hear how in the hell he pulled that off," Jack marveled.

"He's socked in at the Moscow Embassy right now," Tresham said.

"Our embassy?" Jack asked in disbelief.

"No one knows that!" Tresham said sharply, pointing his long finger at Jack. "It stays between us."

"Of course."

"Look," Tresham said. "This thing with the Israelis isn't over yet, and if what I'm hearing from Moscow

Station is correct, we'll see more bodies drop before the day is over." Tresham stopped and turned to Scarn. "Agent Scarn, I'm sorry, but you don't have clearance for what I'm about to say."

"Understood," Scarn said curtly, and turned and walked away.

He had wanted to push back, wanted to be indignant and insist that he be involved. Then he recognized it again, that aspect of his personality that only pushed others away and made him look like a fool.

"That was strange," Tresham said as he watched Scarn walk away.

"What's that?" Jack asked.

"I don't know," Tresham shrugged. "He's usually kind of a princess about that sort of thing. But he took it like a man."

"So, what's going on?"

"We're doing a deal with the Palestinians," Tresham said. "Right now."

Jack's eyes grew wide.

"What kind of deal?"

"They're saying they have a logbook they somehow lifted from the Russians, and it has the name of Directorate S agents hiding in the United States."

"How many?" Jack asked.

"We don't know," Tresham replied. "But even if it's just one, it's a big deal."

"How can I help?"

"Look, Jack, this will sound fucking crazy, but I need you to go manage the exchange."

"Sir, isn't there someone more qualified to handle something like this?"

"No one's ever done anything like this, Jack. So, no, there is no one more qualified. I need your adaptability to be on hand in what could become an evolving situation."

"Okay, I'll do it," Jack thought about this for a moment. "What about the Israelis?"

"What about them?"

"Well, what will they think about us handing a pile of cash over to their mortal enemies?"

"I guess we'll never know, since telling them about it isn't exactly on my list of things to do."

Jack understood. He didn't like it, but he knew that was how the game was played. He didn't trust many people, but on the short list of those he had confidence in, Mike Tresham's name stood out in bold relief. It wasn't that Jack thought Mike had his best interests at heart, but that if the assistant director planned on wearing out the tool that was Jack Bonafide, he would have a damn good reason for it.

"When do I leave?"

"Forty-eight hours," Tresham said. "In the meantime, get some sleep and some food, get yourself cleaned up and re-outfitted."

A door opened at the end of the hallway, the same

one Scarn had exited through, and a young man entered. Jack thought he looked like he was about eighteen.

"Oh, good, you're here," Tresham said, waving the young man over. "Jack, this is your analyst."

"My analyst?" Jack asked.

"Analyst/Concierge," Mike clarified. "He'll set you up with whatever you need and keep you up on current events. His name is Clark, Clark Finster."

"I'm a genius," Clark said, and then visibly winced and shook his head. "Sorry, I do that. It's like a tic, but I'm not insane. I went to Harvard. Shit. I did it again."

"Calm down, Clark," Tresham said, and put his hand on the young man's shoulder. "But he's not lying, Jack. He'll be a valuable resource for you. Believe me, I had to pull some serious strings to pry him away from the analyst's section."

"Pleased to meet you, Clark," Jack said, holding out his hand.

Clark stared at Jack's hand.

"Shake it, Clark," Tresham said.

"Oh," Clark said, and reached out and shook Jack's hand.

Clark flipped on the lights in the small room and gestured to the cot in the corner.

"It's not much; they're kind of crash rooms for

when people get too tired to work," Clark said. He pointed to the small dorm fridge with a microwave on top of it. "That's stocked with some Swanson's dinners. Again, not much, but it'll get something in your stomach. We'll probably be here until we head over to Bethesda for the trip to Jordan."

"Jordan?" Jack asked.

"That's where the exchange will happen. A Palestinian big shot named Ferran Koury is claiming to have a logbook with a list of Directorate S agents in it."

"Tresham mentioned that."

"Well, our intelligence says it may be real. If there's even a possibility it is, we have to take a swing at it."

"Where are we meeting him in Jordan?"

"Middle of nowhere," Clark replied. "He just gave us grid coordinates. We've got a Marine Force Recon team going in right now to do a site survey and make sure we can even land there. 15ᵗʰ MEU was already in the area, so they were able to launch on short notice."

"Why out in the middle of nowhere?"

"That's what makes us so sure this is for real. He's going to a lot of trouble to make sure he doesn't get caught."

Jack thought about it for a moment.

"He's probably more afraid of the Russians than he is of us."

"Makes sense."

"What's he getting?"

"Ten million in gold," Clark said. "That's why you're coming. To lift the gold. I haven't done a push up since grade school."

"Okay."

Clark stared at Jack for a moment.

"That was a joke," Clark said. Jack said nothing in return. "This is going to be a long few days."

Jack walked to the cot and sat down. He wanted to get something in his stomach, but his desire to close his eyes was rapidly overriding that instinct.

"I'll wake you up in about six hours. We should get the first reports in from the recon team by then." Clark paused at the door. "Is there anything else you need?"

Jack thought about it for a moment.

"Who do you report to?" Jack asked.

"Besides you?" Clark asked.

"Yes."

"Tresham, but that's it. For all intents and purposes, we're in an operational blackout."

"In that case, there is something you can do for me."

The lights came on, and it was shocking. Jack opened his eyes and sat up on the edge of the cot. Clark had already pulled open the refrigerator door and begun unwrapping one of the frozen dinners.

"Tresham wasn't joking about the concierge part,"

Clark said as he popped the dinner into the microwave. "I get it, you know? I get that you're important, that you're an asset."

Jack wasn't sure how to reply to that, so he remained silent. He saw that his duffel bag was sitting beside the cot. It was the same one he had left in the truck back in Washington Heights. He couldn't help but wonder what had happened to the rocket launcher. On a small table beside the cot he saw his Colt 1911, the same one that his father handed down to him. It had been disassembled and cleaned. He looked back to Clark.

"Did you do that?"

"I hope you don't mind," Clark said. "But I know it's best not to just let a weapon sit after it's been fired."

Jack picked up the pieces and put them back together, then did a quick function check on the weapon.

"You know how to use one of these?" He asked as he slipped the firearm back into its holster.

"I do."

"Seems out of character," Jack said. "If you know what I mean."

"I'm an apple that fell pretty far from the tree, Jack. Grew up in Arkansas, not too far from where you did."

"You don't have an accent."

"There's a reason for that," Clark said. "It shouldn't be this way, but people in the Ivy League don't take you seriously when you talk like- well, when you talk like we do."

Jack smiled.

Clark reached out and handed Jack a folder marked with the seal of the Central Intelligence Agency. Jack took it and opened it to the first page. It was Carrie's arrest report and mugshot.

"What are you planning on doing with that?" Clark asked.

"Nothing," Jack said as he thumbed through it. "Yet."

"Well, whatever it is it will have to wait. We've got a plane to catch."

Jack looked up at Clark.

"Marines gave the all clear?"

"They did. It's just a patch of hard-packed desert with nothing for a hundred miles in any direction."

"So we can't bring any unexpected guests or put a sniper on a hill," Jack said. "Which of course means they can't either."

"Everything's pointing at this guy just wanting to do a legitimate exchange."

"How will we know if the logbook is for real?" Jack asked. "And not just a book with a bunch of names in it?"

"We have a few Directorate S operatives under surveillance in cooperation with the FBI. They're not doing anything at the moment so we're just sitting on them, but they might be in there. Steven Waller may also be in there."

This made Jack think about Steven's cats, and the promise he had made to take care of them. After Steven seemingly betrayed them Jack had thought nothing of it, but after finding out the man died getting them the location of the Russian Alpha Group, he felt a renewed need to honor that promise.

"What happened to his cats?"

"What cats?" Clark asked.

"Waller's cats. He had five cats."

"How the hell do I know what happened to his cats? What kind of weird question is that?"

"I... kind of promised I would take care of them. Considering what he did for us."

"Let me just make sure I have this straight. You're this stone-cold Delta Force solider and CIA super-agent, and you want to adopt five cats?"

"It's the right thing to do."

"Have you ever had a single cat?"

"No," Jack replied.

"Tell you what, let's just wrap up this exchange and then I'll look into the cats for you. If they're still alive, I'll split them with you, because I don't think you understand what goes into taking care of five cats."

"You can't split five cats evenly."

"Depends on how sharp your knife is," Clark quipped, which earned him a dirty look. "All right, fine.

We'll give one to Tresham. We'll tell him it's a matter of national security."

This idea seemed to satisfy Jack.

"When do we leave?"

"We're wheels up at Bethesda in three hours. We'll hop to the Naval Station at Rota, Spain to refuel and then straight into the desert. We'll be landing five miles off of a specific mile marker on Al-Badiyah Highway."

"That is the middle of nowhere," Jack said, remembering the region from the overland escape and evasion plan he had filed before the mission into Iraq with the Israelis. It seemed so long ago, but it really wasn't. "It makes sense."

"How are you feeling?" Clark asked, seeming legitimately concerned.

"Fine, I guess," Jack said as he started shoveling the Swanson's dinner into his mouth. "Still tired, but I figure I'll catch some sleep on the flight over."

"I meant about that," Clark said, nodding to the dossier that Jack had laid on the cot.

"I'm fine," Jack said. "I can compartmentalize. Let's just get this done."

Brooklyn, New York
February 8, 1981

Anatoly walked down the moonlit street and stopped under a lamppost. He waited a moment as he surveyed the simple two-story brownstone on the other side of the street. The safe house was unmanned, just like he had told Carrie. So much had happened in the last twenty-four hours though, it was possible that may have changed.

Returning to his suite at the Wyndham-New Yorker was a non-starter. Not that he thought his cover there was in any way compromised, but the stakes were now significantly higher. Now that the KGB had been hit, there was no telling what information may have been compromised, right down to Sokolov's little doomsday device. That thought sent a shiver down Anatoly's spine.

If that logbook was indeed missing, and if it somehow made its way into the hands of the Americans? It would make the plot to set off the Black Tsar in New York look like child's play. That could not be allowed to happen.

Anatoly surveyed the windows but saw no motion. The lights were on, but he knew that was because of a timer switch. That way no one would think the building was abandoned and investigate. There was even a radio on a timer that would play news reports for two hours each evening and then shut itself off.

As he walked across the street, he thought again about Carrie Davidson sitting (willingly) in her cage at the thirty-third precinct. Should he give it another try some other time? See if after a few days of being locked up she was more amendable to him freeing her? It was a dodgy play. Sticking his neck out like that too many times would certainly result in him losing his head.

Anatoly took a knee beside the front stoop, pulled a brick loose from the facade and retrieved the hidden key. He ascended the steps and worked the lock but found to his surprise that it was open. His right hand went to the grip of his pistol, and with his left he pushed the door open.

Then he saw it. Scrawled on the wall just to the right of the open door.

The castle has fallen.

"Oh my God."

CHAPTER 15

Al-Badiyah Highway
Jordan
February 9, 1981

J ust as Jack was feeling recharged, they hit the ground in the middle of the desert. It was a surprisingly smooth landing, considering that the pilots were landing a C-130 on flat desert, with no runway. The Marines had set up a make-shift runway complete with lights that the pilots could trigger by remote once they were within range of the grid coordinates. Jack remembered that Delta had pulled the same stunt at Desert One. Hopefully, this mission would have a better outcome.

Jack had to admit he was impressed with this

Clark Finster kid. He had been handling everything that needed doing, and despite being about twenty pounds overweight and looking like he might die if you tried to make him run a mile, he hadn't shied away from flying into the desert with his assigned field operative. That meant something to Jack Bonafide.

Clark stood at the front of the plane coordinating with the pilots while Jack finished securing his gear and re-checking the cases with the gold in them. He was only carrying a carbine and his Colt pistol. Originally, this Ferran character had wanted no weapons present, but had finally settled for agreeing to not shoot each other.

Jack had put his foot down about that one. There was no way he was flying into the middle of the Jordanian desert unarmed. That would just be foolishness. There were way too many things out there that could kill a man.

The C-130 rolled to a slow stop, and before it had even fully ceased moving the gears kicked in to lower the rear ramp. The goal was to be on the ground for as short a time as possible. Ferran and his men would already be nearby, so it was unlikely that should prove a problem.

For the briefest of moments Jack felt thoughts of Angeline, Mac and then Carrie creeping into his head. He wondered what his father was doing right then, and if Ricky Michaels knew yet that his only child was dead.

He pushed them away, back into the darkness where they belonged.

Jack stood up and walked to the ramp. He pulled a flare from his jacket pocket, lit it and threw it into the darkness. It illuminated the desert around him and the plane as he stepped onto the hard-packed ground. It was cold. He kept forgetting about that, about how cold the desert could get during the winter months. He even felt the light crunch of snow beneath his boots. Not much, just a dusting, but enough that it mattered.

Then he heard it. The sound of small four-cylinder engines moving toward him. He gripped the carbine and turned toward the sound. He made sure not to make any movements that his visitors could perceive as threatening, but he also didn't plan on fumbling for his weapon like a jackass if things went south.

There were three Land Rovers, driving with their headlights out across the desert. They had been waiting for the flare, and when they saw it, that served as their homing beacon. The three vehicles stopped in a row, but the engines continued to idle.

"They have good taste in cars," Clark said as he walked down the ramp and stood beside Jack.

"You don't have to be out here," Jack said.

"Neither do you," Clark replied with a smile. "So I guess we're both in the habit of making bad decisions."

The doors of what appeared to be the lead vehicle opened, and men stepped out. Some were taller than others.

Jack narrowed his eyes.

"Is that a dwarf?"

"I think they want to be called 'little people'." Clark corrected him.

"I think he's a Jihadist dwarf."

"Jihadist little person," Clark pursued. "But, yeah... that's weird."

"Are you the representative?" Ferran called out.

"I am," Jack replied, still keeping his hands on the carbine.

The men beside Ferran stopped, but he continued to walk toward Jack.

"That's far enough!" Jack said sharply. "I want to see the logbook."

"Do you really think I would come all the way out here without it?" Ferran asked with a wry smile and looked beyond Jack to the open ramp of the C-130. "Did you really come here alone?"

"Is there some reason we shouldn't have?" Clark asked.

"I am in a business almost entirely populated by liars," Ferran said. "People who tell the truth and keep their promises are quite unusual. One could almost say that type of behavior is jarring."

"Let's just do this," Jack said, not interested in the

little man's soliloquy. "Someone will eventually notice a plane parked in the middle of the desert."

Ferran did not appreciate being interrupted, but he understood what was at stake in this trade and wasn't willing to put it at risk just to finish his speech.

Ferran reached into his jacket pocket and retrieved a worn yellow logbook. Jack nodded and walked back up the ramp of the C-130 to where they had stowed the gold. He reached around behind each of the four crates and carefully clipped the tripwire he had attached to them that ran from the crates to a thermite grenade. In the unlikely (or likely) event that Ferran and his gang had tried to storm the plane and grab the gold, they would be rewarded with a nasty surprise for their efforts.

Jack and the co-pilot each grabbed a handle and carried the moderately heavy box down the ramp and dropped it on the desert floor. After three more trips like that, the four heavy crates sat aligned on the ground.

"Before you go getting any ideas," Clark said. "There's a proximity detonator in each one. If it gets a mile from this plane without us deactivating it, well, you can guess how that story ends."

"You're not fools," Ferran said. "I would expect no less. May I?"

Clark nodded.

Ferran and his men opened the crates and began counting the gold bricks.

Jack leaned into Clark.

"Proximity detonators?"

"Sounds real, right?" Clark asked with a smile.

There was some back and forth between Ferran and his men, but after a very long ten minutes all the gold had been counted and they were satisfied with the tally.

"You kept your word," Ferran said, again sounding surprised by this result. "I will keep mine."

The little man handed the logbook to Jack, who then passed it to Clark.

"He will verify the contents," Jack said as Clark walked back up the ramp of the C-130 with the logbook. "So I'll need you to wait around for a few minutes."

"And then you disarm the proximity detonators?" Ferran asked.

"Yeah, sure."

Clark stopped near his gear inside the plane and clicked on a penlight. He began scanning the contents.

"Jesus Christ!" Clark gasped.

"Is he in there?" Jack called out as he walked up the ramp to where Clark sat. "Is Waller in there?"

"Yeah, I found him right away. Each entry has the cover name, the real name and the station address and even a skill ranking from one to five."

"So how many are in there?" Jack asked.

Clark continued flipping through the pages for another full minute and then looked up at Jack Bonafide in the half light.

"All of them."

Jack didn't have time to respond before he heard shouting in Arabic from outside. He turned to the ramp and saw the men running back to their vehicles. Off in the distance he could see headlights coming toward them. Jack ran down the ramp and called after Ferran.

"What in the hell is going on?"

"We're about to have company!" Ferran replied. "I trust you're satisfied with the authenticity of the logbook, so it's best if we part ways."

"Jordanian Army?" Jack asked.

"No, they know not to come out here. It's almost certainly the Muslim Brotherhood. When they arrive, it would be best if you are gone. Will you disarm the detonators?"

"What?" Jack asked in confusion and then remembered Clark's ruse. He made the sign of the cross in front of him. "There. Disarmed. Go with God. Or whatever."

Jack watched as the men finished loading the crates of gold and then piled back into the Land Rovers and sped away.

"Shit."

Jack ran back up the ramp to find Clark talking to

the pilots.

"We have to go. Now!" Jack shouted.

"What's going on?" The pilot asked as his co-pilot began running through the pre-flight checklist.

"Muslim Brotherhood coming in hot."

No sooner had the words left Jack's mouth than a loud 'ping' sounded in the plane, then another.

"No shit!" The pilot shouted and then turned to his co-pilot. "Get the fucking ramp up! Now!"

The gears whined as the ramp lifted from the desert floor and began to close up the rear of the big plane. The gunfire became louder and Jack could hear the engines of the trucks closing in on them as the vehicle headlights grew brighter. They were three big five tons, which meant that fully loaded they were probably about to go up against at least sixty fighters.

There was a loud 'clunk' as the ramp locked into place, and the 'pings' of the rounds hitting the skin of the plane became nearly constant. Jack felt a lurch as the plane began to move forward.

"Don't worry!" The pilot shouted. "This thing can take a lot of 7.62 before it becomes a problem."

Then there was a loud 'whoosh' and turning to his left the pilot watched an RPG pass within a foot of his window, just missing the plane.

"Belay my last!" The pilot shouted as he hit the lever to drop the ramp. "Light those motherfuckers up!"

Both Jack and Clark locked themselves into bolts

on the floor with safety straps that were then hooked to their belts. Jack walked to a large item bolted to the center of the floor with a tarp secured over it. He pulled the tarp free to reveal eighty-four pounds of Utah made wrath of God, otherwise known as an M2 Browning fifty-caliber machine gun.

Jack sat down behind the weapon, wedging his feet in against the legs of the tripod. As the ramp lowered, he could feel the first rounds coming into the plane. They had welded a steel plate over the fifty cal, but there was no way to be completely protected. He just needed another few seconds for the ramp to be open enough to fire through.

"Hey!" Clark shouted. "Don't you think it's kind of ironic that you're about to fire an anti-aircraft weapon from an aircraft?"

"Now's not the time, Clark," Jack replied as he worked the action and watched the ramp drop fully open. He saw the headlights of the trucks following the plane only a few hundred feet away and could even see a man in the back of a truck shouldering an RPG. "Say goodnight, Gracie."

Jack dropped his thumbs to the butterfly triggers and the fifty cal began pouring out a stream of fire, shredding the first truck and all of its occupants within a matter of moments. Clark had been unprepared for how the recoil of the big gun would shake the entire plane and he slipped, landing hard on his back.

The plane began to pick up speed as Jack eviscerated the advancing trucks, which, despite the onslaught of his fifty caliber rounds, continued to return fire, and even made a clumsy attempt at firing an RPG that went wild, streaking off into the night.

Then Jack felt it, that sudden feeling of lightness you get when a plane leaves the ground.

"We're airborne!" The pilot shouted.

Still having rounds left, Jack saw no reason to let up on his attack. The C-130 lifted into the night as Jack continued firing. The plane looked as if it were ascending to the heavens with a long and fiery tail in its wake.

Jack felt Clark slap him on the back just as he ran out of rounds and the bolt locked forward, the barrel of the machine gun glowing red in the darkness.

"Close the ramp!" Clark shouted. "We're going home."

Andrews Air Force Base, Maryland
February 10, 1981

It all happened fast. No sooner had Jack and Clark stepped off the plane than Agent Scarn met them.

"You two have to come with me," Scarn said firmly.

"We need to report in at Langley," Clark said, confused by the order.

"No," Scarn said. "You don't. Order of the assistant director."

"What in the hell is going on, Scarn?" Jack asked. "Do you know what we just went through?"

"I do," Scarn replied. "That's why I'm here. You don't have to like it, Jack, but I need you to trust me."

There was something in Scarn's eyes. Something about the man had changed. Jack nodded his understanding. He turned to look over his shoulder and saw both of the pilots being led away by heavily armed men.

"What's happening to them?" Jack asked.

"They'll be fine," Scarn replied. "They're going into protective custody, and by noon tomorrow those men with them will be the only ones who know where they are. The paper will run a story that they were both killed in a training accident."

Clark looked down at the logbook he was clutching in his hand and then back to Scarn.

"This is a big fucking deal, isn't it?" Clark asked.

"Yeah," Scarn replied. "It's a big fucking deal."

The Sleepy Time Inn
Langley, Virginia
February 14, 1981

Jack Bonafide looked Clark Finster directly in the eye. He knew the man by now. They had spent a great deal of time together and he had plumbed the depths of the CIA analyst's soul. He knew what it took to build him up but more importantly he also knew what it took to break him down.

Jack slammed the card down on the table.

"Go fish," he said.

"Son of a bitch," Clark replied as he leaned back in his chair. He looked around the squalid motel room. "I mean, seriously, how long have we even been here? I feel like time is standing still."

"As long as it takes," Jack said as he reached for his beer. He stopped for a moment and looked at Clark. He understood that the young man had never been submitted to this level of quarantine before. "Look, it happens. Before a mission with Delta they would quarantine us like this for at least a few days. It ensures that no one talk to you and you don't talk to them. Because, trust me, you wouldn't mean to, but you might say or do something that would put the mission at risk."

"But what in the hell is the mission? We can assume it has something to do with the logbook, but all Scarn did was drop us off here fifteen years ago and tell us to stay put."

"And that's what we'll do."

Clark threw his cards down and leaned back in the chair. He wasn't normally a drinking man, but the case of Lonestar beers in the room's corner was looking pretty good.

Then there was a click at the door. Jack's hand reflexively went for his pistol, but then he stopped. No one knew they were there.

The door opened, and the two men saw Scarn and Tresham standing at the entrance.

"Well, it's about fucking time," Clark said.

"Watch it!" Tresham snapped, pointing a finger at the young analyst. He walked into the room with Scarn and closed the door behind them. "We would have been here sooner, but things are really catching fire out there."

"What's going on?" Jack asked.

"The second you sent that message about the logbook I had to start plugging leaks and make sure that information didn't get out," Tresham said.

"About the logbook?" Clark asked.

"Did you ever think it would contain every single Directorate S agent deployed to the United States in it?" Tresham asked.

"Of course not," Clark said. "That would be insane."

"Except that's what actually happened," Tresham corrected him. "And information like that... you can't just let it get out."

Jack eyed Tresham warily.

"You're not saying..." Jack said.

"No," Tresham said. "We're taking those people down. One-by-one. That's why you two are here. This is where the planning begins. But you have to understand, if that information leaked out? The markets would crash. There would be mass panic. This country as we know it would cease to exist."

"You really think it would be that bad?" Jack asked.

"That bad?" Tresham asked incredulously. "That's the best-case scenario."

Jack understood. Fear was a powerful adversary, and fear was exactly what they were up against.

"What's the first move?" Clark asked.

"First, we—"

A knocking at the door cut Tresham off.

Scarn's head turned toward the sound.

"Who in the hell is that?" Scarn asked.

Tresham drew his pistol, and everyone knew what that meant. The Assistant Director of the Central Intelligence Agency had not pulled a gun on anyone or anything in nearly fifteen years.

"No one knows we're here," Tresham whispered. "For a goddam good reason."

Tresham stepped back as Scarn moved to the door. He wasn't foolish enough to put his eye to the peephole. Instead, he drew his Beretta and reached for the doorknob. He pulled it open quickly, keeping his weapon up.

"Did I come at a bad time?" Anatoly Vitka asked.

"Tell me why we shouldn't just shoot you and leave you in the parking lot." Jack said after the door had been closed.

Scarn still had his pistol on Anatoly, but it was immediately understood that the Russian had a card to play. He wasn't foolish enough to just show up at the location for no reason.

Anatoly looked to the logbook that sat on the table beside the deck of cards.

"Do you even understand what you have there?" Anatoly asked, a barely detectable tone of condescension in his voice.

"What do you know about it?" Jack asked.

"That it contains the identities of every Directorate S agent deployed in the United States," Anatoly replied. "And a few in Britain, if you hadn't figured that out yet. Also one in Australia, but no one cares about him."

"Jesus Christ," Tresham said, rubbing his forehead.

He had known right away who Anatoly was from the descriptions in Jack's after-action reports. Now this man had confirmed his fears. The logbook was a ticking time bomb, and other people knew about it.

"You thought you had scored the golden goose, didn't you?" Anatoly asked. "Instead, you just triggered Sokolov's dead man's switch."

"What are you talking about?" Clark asked.

"There is a protocol," Anatoly said. "It's a meltdown sequence that is initiated if the entire Directorate S operation were ever compromised. It was an impossible scenario, so the KGB allowed Sokolov to set it up. We assumed that if this ever happened all was lost. To be honest, we're not that far away from that very scenario after the bombing of the Lubyanka building and the deaths of Sokolov and Galkin."

"What happens?" Tresham asked.

Anatoly's face became grim, and it did not go unnoticed.

"A series of messages will be released. I received the first one when I checked in to our safe house in Brooklyn. That's why I started following him," Anatoly said, gesturing to Scarn. "I knew he was part of the team hunting the Black Tsar, and that he would eventually lead me to you, which is exactly what he did."

This revelation visibly pained Scarn. He had screwed up again.

"What was the message?" Clark asked.

"The Castle has fallen," Anatoly replied. "It means that the Directorate S program is compromised, and the Americans have destroyed the KGB."

"What are you supposed to do when you get that

message?" Clark asked. "Exfil?"

"No," Anatoly said. "Inflict mass casualties. Any way I can. Go out in the proverbial blaze of glory, just like an old west cowboy."

"How many?" Scarn asked, turning to Clark.

"What?" Clark asked.

"Directorate S agents in the United States that are about to go nuclear."

Clark was silent for a moment and then answered.

"Thirty-two."

"There are thirty-two ticking time bombs out there?" Tresham asked.

"Not including whatever networks they have built," Anatoly said. "They should be developing networks of assets, like-minded Americans who will turn against their own country. Depending on how well they have done their jobs, you could be looking at three times that many."

"But there are at least a few Steven Wallers, right?" Scarn asked hopefully.

"Maybe," Anatoly shrugged. "But is that really a gamble you want to take?"

"Understood," Scarn said.

"Why are you doing this?" Jack asked. "What's in it for you?"

"Sokolov only believed in two outcomes to his plan. Him running the KGB and eventually the entire Soviet Union and taking us back to the dark ages, or nuclear

Armageddon. If these sleeper agents start staging attacks and it is traced back to the Soviet Union? It will be the latter."

"I have a hard time with the idea of trusting you," Jack said coldly.

"As you should," Anatoly replied. "But understand one thing, Jack. I love my country. That is all that matters to me. If helping you stops a war that would turn the Soviet Union to ashes, that is what I need to do."

Jack held the Soviet's gaze for a moment and then nodded.

The motel room was starting to smell bad. The five men had been holed up for the past six hours while Anatoly did a data dump of everything he knew, and both Clark and Scarn wrote furiously trying to keep track of everything. This had also fully satisfied Jack's concern that Anatoly may still be playing both sides. Now he knew there was no way that was the case. What he was doing amounted to high treason.

"So," Clark said. "We have at least thirty-two agents about to go active and potentially another hundred and fifty attached to them."

"That seems right," Anatoly confirmed.

"We have locations and names on all of them?" Tresham asked.

"Confirmed," Clark nodded. "So it's time to call in the big guns, right?"

"Negative," Tresham said. "It can't happen that way. We launch some giant operation to take them down and we'll definitely have leaks. Then we go from these agents taking their time setting up their attacks to potentially a mad rush. Then we have panic in the streets."

"So what's the move?" Jack asked.

"It stays in this room. Tight-knit. We take them down one-by-one and hopefully no one gets wind of what's going on until we're done. Or at least close to it."

It made sense, at least on paper. Anatoly had projected it could be as long as six weeks before all the agents would be activated. It would take time for what he called "the messengers" to get word to all the individual sleepers.

Clark looked up at Tresham.

"Are you suggesting that the four of us try to take down over one hundred enemy agents?" He asked.

"Five," Anatoly offered.

"What?" Clark asked.

"Five," Anatoly repeated. "I have a stake in this too. You need the extra pair of hands."

"Whatever," Clark said, shaking his head. "Fine, five. It's still impossible."

Tresham clenched his jaw for a moment and then shook his head.

"You're right. We need more manpower."

"What exactly do we need?" Jack asked.

"A team of deployable agents," Tresham said. "Not affiliated with the CIA and able to work outside the box. Ideally trained in espionage as well as war fighting and able to operate secretly within the country."

"That's a pretty big wish list," Scarn said.

Jack was drumming his fingers on the tabletop when he stopped and looked up at Tresham.

"I think I might know where we can find them."

Anatoly raised his hand.

"You don't have to raise your hand," Tresham said.

"Well," Anatoly said. "I know where you can find at least one. She's sitting in a jail cell."

Tresham understood, but filed it away for the moment.

Jack stood up and walked to the phone in the room's corner.

"What are you doing?" Tresham asked.

Jack just held up a hand as he picked up the phone and dialed a number from memory.

He waited a moment as it rang.

"Colonel, it's Jack, Jack Bonafide. Yes, sir, we pulled it off." Jack paused for a moment. "Well, that's kind of why I'm calling you. You're still technically the commanding officer, right?" Another pause. "Well, sir, I have a favor to ask. How big? Well, how big a favor is borrowing a couple assault teams?"

CHAPTER 16

The Brooklyn Navy Yard
Brooklyn, New York
February 21, 1981

They had gotten lucky, snagging the old brick warehouse in the long-decommissioned Brooklyn Navy Yard. Technically, the CIA owned it, but Mike Tresham had quietly put in a request to render it inactive for renovations, and then didn't order the renovations. Instead, it was now the operating base for Jack Bonafide's team.

That was the easy part.

Sleeping spaces were hastily constructed, as well as a common area and planning room. Jack, Scarn, Clark and Anatoly had already been living there for several days and had begun the planning. Tresham returned to Langley, as his most important function was now to pretend as if nothing were happening and to keep the CIA out of Jack's way.

At first, Tresham hadn't been sure about putting the entire operation under Jack's control, but then after Clark related how the former Delta operator had handled himself in Jordan, that was enough for the assistant director. That on top of how he tracked down the Black Tsar made him the most qualified man in the intelligence apparatus for what they were about to go up against.

During the setup process Agent Michael Scarn had quietly taken Mike Tresham aside and insisted that he be released from the unit.

"What in the hell are you talking about?" Tresham asked incredulously. "We need every swinging dick we can get on this thing!"

"I... I don't have it," Scarn said. "Whatever it is that Jack has, and even Clark has, it's not in me. I'll get people killed."

"Like in New York?" Tresham asked pointedly.

Scarn nodded.

"Now you listen here, you son of a bitch. You did nothing wrong. In fact, you did everything right. If you hadn't pulled your shit together and hit that house when you did, we never would have known about the plan to hit Feldman. Now we're keeping tabs on him and that Russian Arkady because of what you did. Heroes aren't born, Scarn, they're fucking made. You're not going anywhere."

So, Michael Scarn remained on the team, whether or not he thought he should be there.

Anatoly was being kept on the definition of a short leash. No one trusted the former KGB agent, but they also couldn't ignore the fact that he was a bottomless well of information on the very people they were going up against. Not only that, he had trained many of them. His would be a face that they initially would trust until it was too late.

Jack's boots echoed as he walked across the concrete floor of the big warehouse, and then he stopped as he heard the lock on the main door catch as it creaked open. Michael Scarn walked in, guiding Carrie Davidson with his hand on her shoulder. She was handcuffed, wearing a blue jumpsuit and looked quite the worse for wear.

Carrie glanced around the building, looking like a scared animal who had been kept in the dark and was seeing the sun for the first time.

"This doesn't look like a federal prison," Carrie said.

She had already been suspicious when Scarn showed up to transport her and identified himself as Federal Marshall Kennedy, which he obviously was not.

Scarn turned her around and unlocked her cuffs. Carrie rubbed her wrists as she saw Jack heading across the room toward her. She couldn't help but smile.

"You're not free," Jack said, holding up a hand. "Even we couldn't pull that off. But you disappeared an hour ago with a fictitious United States Marshall named John Kennedy. You're now just a fugitive from justice."

"What is this?" Carrie asked, looking around the room.

"You'll want to sit down."

Jack laid it all out for her. He also made it clear that they couldn't make her charges go away. There would be no happy ending to this story for Carrie Davidson. They needed her because she was an experienced operative who had gone up against the Soviets on multiple occasions and gotten the better of them. Despite that, when all was said and done the most they could give her was a sack full of cash, a fake passport and a one-way ticket out of the country.

Carrie looked like she had just been slapped in the face. There was something different about her, different from how she had looked when he first saw her in the hallway at Red River. Her skin was more pale, it had lost some of the pinkness of youth. She looked hardened.

"Fine," she said. "I get it. It's not about me."

"It's also not about Mac," Jack said.

Carrie narrowed her eyes at him.

"What are you trying to say?" She asked.

"You know what I'm saying. Can you keep your personal feelings in check?"

"Can you?" Carrie fired back. "He was your goddamn brother."

"I know who the hell he was!" Jack snapped. "And yes, I can. This is about more than our need for vengeance. There are lives at stake."

Carrie wanted to stay on the offensive, but instead she sat back in her chair.

"I get it, Jack. I can keep it in check." She paused for a moment, holding his gaze. "I said I get it."

"Good," Jack said and stood up.

He wasn't sure how he felt about that exchange. On the surface it seemed like she would play ball, and there was no question that she would be an asset to this operation. Below the surface, though, there was something else. Something hard to define.

There was a knock at the door, and Jack gestured for Scarn to open it. The man at the door was easily six foot four and about two hundred and forty pounds. For the first time, Jack realized that Delta Force Master Sergeant Big Eddie Winfield looked a hell of a lot like Mac Bonafide.

Eddie scanned the room before stepping inside,

and when his eyes met Jack's a wide smile broke out on his face.

"I should have known you'd have something to do with this," Eddie said as he walked inside and crossed the room. Jack extended his hand and Eddie shook it. "I wasn't buying Colonel Beckwith's bullshit about an 'emergency training mission' for a second."

"Figured as much," Jack replied.

Eddie looked around the big warehouse.

"Jack, if I didn't know better, I'd think I was in an ops center."

The rest of the men filed in after Eddie, eight Delta assaulters in total, but these men were more than that. While they had been trained to an extraordinary degree in close quarters battle and all manner of war fighting, they were also schooled in surveillance and counterintelligence. It was almost as if Colonel Charlie Beckwith had seen this coming and planned for it in how he structured the training of Delta.

Jack said nothing as Eddie walked to the main planning board. It was covered with maps, copies of pages from the logbook, and dozens of copies of driver's licenses from different states.

"Is this real?" Eddie asked, turning to Jack with a look of disbelief on his face.

"Yes," Jack said. "It is."

Eddie turned back to the board.

"Jesus, Mary and Joseph," Eddie said. "Jack, if this was coming from anyone else, I wouldn't believe it."

"If I hadn't been through what I went through to get that information I wouldn't either," Jack said. "But it's all too real."

"This is them?" Eddie asked, motioning to the rows of driver's license photos.

"Yes. We were able to pull those from their cover identities."

"So we know who they are," Eddie nodded. "And where they live." He surveyed the board a moment longer and then cocked his head to the side. "Over half of them are in the Pacific Northwest. What do you think that's about?"

"There is a contingency plan for an overland invasion," Anatoly replied. "During the last ice age humans could walk from Russia to Alaska across the Bering Sea Land Bridge. It's broken now, but you can still traverse it with very little effort. In the event that we would stage a manned invasion of the United States, that was how we would have done it. Across the Bearing Straight, down through Canada and the state of Washington would be the beachhead."

Eddie thought about this for a moment and then made the connection.

"Wait a minute," he said. "What do you mean 'we'?"

"The Soviets," Anatoly replied with a smile. "That 'we'."

Eddie took a step forward and Jack held up a hand.

"He's on our side," Jack said. "For now."

Eddie looked around at the rest of the Delta assaulters who were all taking this in just like he was. He nodded his understanding.

"Are you saying this invasion plan is in play?" Eddie asked Anatoly.

"No, of course not," Anatoly said. "But we believe in overkill. When we first began developing a map for the strategic deployment of our agents, we still believed a war with the United States was inevitable."

Anatoly walked across the warehouse to where Carrie sat by herself in a chair. Despite having been given a bag full of fresh clothes, she remained in her blue jumpsuit. He could see there were bruises on her wrists from the handcuffs.

Back at the ops board Jack was briefing the Delta team on the plan they had developed so far.

Anatoly took a knee in front of Carrie.

"How are you?" He asked, real concern on his face.

"I guess I should be peachy keen," Carrie said sarcastically. "Considering I'm now a free woman. At least for the moment."

"Jack said they will get you a clean passport after this is over, help you make a fresh start somewhere."

"For what?" Carrie asked. "So I can see that poor woman dying in front of me every night when I close my eyes? So I can see her choking on her own blood and staring at me? I can do that just as well in prison. After this is over, I'm going back."

Anatoly clenched his jaw. He knew what she was feeling. He had been there himself. She was taking this very hard.

"Why would you do that?" He asked softly.

"Because only an animal would do something like that, would hurt someone who didn't deserve it the way that I did, and animals belong in cages." Carrie stared blankly for a moment, almost as if she were looking through him. "If I'm left on my own long enough, I'll put a gun in my mouth."

"You don't have to be on your own," Anatoly said.

"What do you mean?" Carrie asked.

Anatoly looked over his shoulder to see that no one was listening and then placed his hand on Carrie's.

"If they can make you a clean passport, it doesn't have to be American. It could be Soviet."

Carrie's eyes grew wide.

"I don't understand."

"I come from a small village in the Urals, in Western Siberia. After this is all over, the KGB will most likely be decommissioned and replaced with something else. No one will look for me. Kulikovo is such a small village, no one ever comes there. No one would ever come there looking for me." Anatoly met her eyes. "Or you."

There was a loud knock at the door, and everyone turned to the sound of it.

"I thought everyone was here?" Scarn asked.

"Mostly," Jack said with a smile.

"You called in someone else?" Scarn asked, restraining his reflex to push back. "It's just that I thought we were supposed to be updated on new additions."

"I didn't know if he'd come," Jack said with a shrug as he walked to the door and pulled it open.

The man standing at the door was six foot four (just like Big Eddie) but leaner and with a few thousand more miles on him. He had a Colt Peacemaker on his hip and a Marine Corps issue seabag hanging from his shoulder.

"I'm glad you came," Jack said.

"Well, it's not every day I get a call from you saying to pack every gun I have and drive until I hit the ocean," Corbett Bonafide said. "So, who needs killin'?"

Jack smiled and placed his hand on his father's shoulder.

"We'll get to that. For now, find yourself a locker

and check in with Agent Scarn to get a mission briefing. He's the one who looks like something crawled up his ass and died."

Corbett looked past Jack and nodded.

"We've met." Corbett paused for a moment and looked back over his shoulder and out the open door. "There's something else."

"What's that?"

"I had a passenger." Jack's face changed and Corbett read it all too easily. He held up his hands in a placating gesture. "I didn't have a choice, Jack. I just asked him to watch the house and within a few minutes he knew what was going on."

"He's in the truck?" Jack asked.

Corbett nodded.

Jack walked across the empty lot to find Corbett's truck with Ricky Michaels sitting in the passenger seat. Ricky looked up and his eyes met Jack's. The man looked tired, even more than he should have for his fifty-seven years.

"Ricky," Jack said by way of greeting.

"Jack," Ricky said.

"I figure you hitched a ride with Corbett for a good reason, and not just to visit the city?"

"They brought her home last week, Jack," Ricky said. "Brought her home so we could bury her."

There was silence for a moment.

"I'm sorry as hell, Ricky. You know I am."

As the words came out of Jack's mouth, he thought about the fact that he had not yet shed a tear over his dead wife, even if she had been hell bent on divorcing him. He would never know if they could have sorted things out and pulled it back from the brink at the last moment.

"I know that, Jack. I know." Ricky paused. "The ones you're going after, they're the ones that killed my daughter."

It wasn't a question. On some level Ricky already knew.

"I reckon they are," Jack replied slowly.

"I'm coming with you," Ricky said.

"No, Ricky," Jack said. "You're not."

"They wouldn't let me see her face, Jack. It was a closed casket. I asked if I could see her in the morgue, even if it was bad. The man at the funeral home, you know what he did? He begged me not to. Whatever those animals did it was bad enough that he said I wouldn't even recognize her."

"I get it Ricky, I-"

"No!" Ricky shouted. "You don't." He stopped for a moment and looked at the dashboard. "I'm sorry, Jack, but it's true. Until you have one of your own, and they bury her without letting you see her face one more time, you can't know what it's like."

"Ricky... it's just that this is a pretty serious operation and we-"

"Son, I was killing Japs on Guadalcanal before you were even a twinkle in your daddy's eye. I spent two years in a Jap POW camp and then killed more in the Philippines. I'll kill as many Russians as you need me to just like I'm ringing a fucking bell." Ricky paused for a moment and composed himself. "I get that I'm being emotional right now, but once I settle myself down, I can be useful. Just let me help."

Jack thought about it for a moment and realized that it was probably best to have Ricky somewhere he could keep an eye on him instead of roaming the streets looking for Russian spies to kill.

Jack walked back into the warehouse with Ricky Michaels in tow, and he could read the look on Scarn's face before the man even said anything.

"I know, I know," Jack said as he held up a hand. "This is the last addition, I swear."

"It's your show," Scarn replied.

Jack thought back to what Tresham had said about Scarn seeming different, and he had been right. Something was different about the man.

Jack looked at his watch.

"Okay, let's do a full mission briefing in five."

"Sounds good," Scarn said, and then stepped back

as a cat ran across his foot. "I've been meaning to ask you. Why are there so many cats in this warehouse?"

"Turn on the television!" Clark shouted as he ran into the main warehouse from one of the back offices.

"What is it?" Jack asked as Eddie turned on one of the television sets lined up against the wall. It was tuned to CNN. The crawler at the bottom of the screen said it all.

Mass shooting at a department store in Seattle.

"Is this what I think it is?" Eddie asked.

Jack turned to Anatoly.

"Yes," Anatoly said with a nod. "It's starting."

The story continues in:
Jack Bonafide Book 2: High Tension!

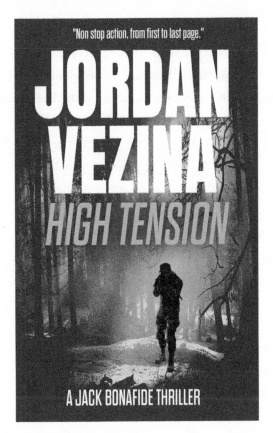

For Jack Bonafide, *it's kill or be killed...*

It's 1981 - and CIA spy-hunter Jack Bonafide and his ragtag team of volunteers have got their hands on the most explosive intel of the decade - the secret identity of every Soviet sleeper agent currently operating within the United States.

Now, it's a race against time to black-bag each and every one of them before Jack's prey even realize they're being hunted - because the moment they do, Bonafide's orders to 'capture or kill' could spark a nuclear apocalypse.

As if the stakes weren't high enough, the further Jack and his team descend into the shadows, the more unclear it becomes who the real enemy is - or what they'd be willing to do to get their own hands on that logbook.

"This one knocked my socks off, and I'm not even wearing any. There are more twists and turns than a rollercoaster and an ending that will leave you saying WTF! Anyone who likes Tom Clancy will love Jordan Vezina. He hits you right between the eyes and leaves you wanting more." -**David Bates**/ Amazon Review

"This was definitely an action packed thriller, with a very strong 80s action movie vibe, as is to be expected from this author. It does a great job of being a continuation of the first book, a self contained story, and setting up the next entry into the saga. If you like Russian

sleeper cells, threats of national calamity, and non stop thrills, you've come to the right place." -**Justin Birck-bichler/** Amazon Review

GET YOUR COPY OF HIGH TENSION!

"After the Black Tzar I was wondering how its sequel would stack up in comparison. The beginning of High Tension started out on an even note but quickly amped up significantly. It (High Tension) continued to spike from there so much so that it became that un-put-downable book that so many folks refer to. The tension is such that the hairs on the back of my neck will probably never lay down again. Thanks, Mr. Vezina, for another 5 star read!" -**Kindle Customer/** Amazon Review

Jordan Vezina is a fiction writer living in Northern California with his wife Emily where they run a business together. Jordan served in both the Marine Corps and Army Infantry, and worked as a bodyguard. This background provided much of the detail regarding weapons and tactics in the Jericho Black books.

The Jericho Black Universe contains the Jericho Black, Jacob Mitzak and Jack Bonafide series of books. In the future we will also introduce the Strike 13 and Ariel Sutcliffe series.

Make sure to subscribe and follow using the links below for updates on new releases

jordanvezina.com

me@jordanvezina.com